Sedro-Woolley Library
802 Ball Ave
Sedro-Woolley WA 98284

July 2009

die for you

Also by **Lisa Unger**

BLACK OUT
SLIVER OF TRUTH
BEAUTIFUL LIES

lisa unger

A Novel

Shaye Areheart Books
New York

This is a work of fiction. Names, characters, places, and incidents either are the product of the author's imagination or are used fictitiously. Any resemblance to actual persons, living or dead, events, or locales is entirely coincidental.

Copyright © 2009 by Lisa Unger

All rights reserved.
Published in the United States by Shaye Areheart Books, an imprint of the Crown Publishing Group, a division of Random House, Inc., New York.
www.crownpublishing.com

Shaye Areheart Books with colophon is a registered trademark of Random House, Inc.

Library of Congress Cataloging-in-Publication Data

Unger, Lisa, 1970–
Die for you / Lisa Unger.—1st ed.
p. cm.
1. Missing persons—Fiction. 2. Married people—Fiction.
3. New York (N.Y.)—Fiction. 4. Prague (Czech Republic)—Fiction.
I. Title.
PS3621.N486D54 2009
813'.6—dc22

2008039173

ISBN 978-0-307-39397-5

Printed in the United States of America

Design by Lynne Amft

2 4 6 8 10 9 7 5 3 1

First Edition

For Elaine Markson . . .

*My unflagging supporter, fearless champion,
and wonderful friend.*

die for you

Prologue

A light snow falls, slowly coating the deep-red rooftops of Prague. I look up into a chill gunmetal sky as the gray stones beneath me are already disappearing under a blanket of white. There's a frigid hush over the square. Shops are closed, chairs perched upside down on café tables. In the distance I hear church bells. A strong wind sighs and moans, picks up some stray papers and dances them past me. The morning would be beautiful in its blustery quiet if I weren't in so much pain—if I weren't so *cold.*

The side of my body that rests against the ground is stiff and numb. With difficulty, sore muscles protesting, I struggle to sit. I use the back of a park bench to pull myself to my feet. With the harsh wind pulling at my cuffs and collar, I wonder, How long have I been lying on the freezing stone, in the middle of this empty square? How did I get here? The last thing I remember clearly is a question I asked of a young girl with tattoos on her face. I remember her eyes—very young, damaged, afraid. I asked her:

"Kde?" *Where?* She looked at me, startled; I remember her darting eyes, how she shifted from foot to foot, anxious, desperate. "Prosim," I said. *Please.* "Kde je Kristof Ragan?" *Where is Kristof Ragan?*

Distantly, I remember her answer. But it's buried too deep in my aching head for me to retrieve. *Get moving,* a voice inside me says. *Get help.* I have the sense that there's an imminent threat, but I'm not sure what it is.

Still, I find myself rooted, leaning heavily against the bench, afraid of the tilting I perceive in my world, afraid of how hard that stone will feel if I hit it again. I am wearing jeans. My leather jacket is unbuttoned to reveal the lace of my bra through a tear in my sweater. My chest is raw and red from the cold. My right pant leg is ripped open, exposing a wound that has bled down my shin; I am having trouble putting weight onto this leg. My feet are so cold, they have gone completely numb.

The square is empty. It is just after dawn, the light gauzy and dim. A tall Christmas tree towers, its lights glowing electric blue. Smaller trees, also decorated, are clustered about, glinting and shimmering. The square is lined with wooden stalls erected for the Christmas market, the ornate black lampposts wrapped in glowing lights; wreathes adorn windows and doors. The fountain, dry for winter, is filling with snow. Old Town Square is a fairy tale. I think it must be Christmas Day. Any other day the tourists might already be strolling about, locals heading to work, bachelors stumbling home from a late night of partying. I used to love this place, feel as though I was welcome here, but not today. I am as alone as if the apocalypse has come. I've missed the action and been left behind.

I make my way slowly toward the road, holding on to the sides of buildings and benches, careful not to stumble. Tall spires reach into the sky; moaning saints look down upon me. I catch sight of myself in a shop window. My hair is a rat's nest; even in this state, vanity causes me to run my fingers through it, try to smooth it out a bit. There's a smear of mascara under each eye. I lick my finger and try to rub it away. My jacket is ripped at the shoulder. There's a bruise on my jaw. I am angry at the woman I see in this reflection. She's all ego, sick with her own hubris. I release a sharp breath in disgust with myself, creating a cloud that dissipates quickly into the air.

I move on, unable to bear my own reflection any longer. Up ahead I see a green-and-white police car. It is small and compact, barely a car at all—more like a tube of lipstick. I wish for the blue and white of a

Chevy Caprice with screaming sirens and two tough New York City cops. But this will have to do. I pick up my pace as best I can, lift a hand to wave.

"Hello!" I call. "Can you help me?"

A female officer emerges from the driver's side of the vehicle and moves toward me. As I approach her, I see she wears an unkind smirk. She is small for the bulky black uniform she wears. Her hair is dyed a brash, unflattering red but her skin is milky, her eyes an unearthly blue.

"Do you speak English?" I ask her when we are closer.

"A little," she says. *Uh leetle.* She narrows her eyes at me. Snowflakes fall and linger in her hair. *A hungover American stumbling through the streets,* her expression reads. Oh, she's seen it a hundred times before. *What a mess.*

"I need help," I tell her, lifting my chin at her disapproval. "I need to go to the U.S. Embassy." She's looking at me harder now, her expression going from some combination of disdain and amusement to outright suspicion.

"What is your name?" she asks me. I see how she slowly, casually rests her hand on her gun, a nasty-looking black affair that seems too big for her tiny white hand. I hesitate; for some reason I'm suddenly sorry I flagged her down. I don't want to tell her my name. I want to turn and run from her.

"Please show me your passport," she says more sternly. Now I see a little glimmer of fear in her blue eyes, and a little excitement, too. I realize I'm backing away from her. She doesn't like it, moves in closer.

"Stay still," she says to me sharply, pulling her shoulders back, standing up taller. I obey. There's more dead air between us as I struggle with what to do next.

"Tell me your name."

I turn and start to run, stumble really, and make my way slowly, gracelessly away. She starts barking at me in Czech and I don't need to understand the language to know I'm in deep trouble. Then I feel her hands on me and I'm on the ground again; this small woman is amazingly strong with her knee in my back. She's knocked the wind out of me and I'm struggling to get air again with her weight on top of me. I can hear my own desperate, rattling attempts to inhale. She's on her radio, yelling. She's pulling my hands behind me when I feel her whole body jerk as her weight seems to suddenly shift off of me. I hear her gun drop and clatter on the stones. I scurry away from her and turn around. She has fallen to the ground and is lying on her side, looking at me with those shocking blue eyes, wide now with terror and pain. I find myself moving toward her but I stop when her mouth opens and a river of blood flows onto the snow around her. I see a growing dark stain on her abdomen. She's trying to staunch the flow with her hand; blood seeps through her thin fingers.

Then I look up and see him. He is a black column against the white surrounding him. He has let the gun drop to his side, is standing still and silent, the wind tossing his hair. I get to my feet, never taking my eyes from him, and start to move away.

"Why are you doing this?" I ask him.

He comes closer, the muted sound of his footfalls bouncing off the buildings around us.

"Why?" I scream, voice echoing. But he is impervious, his face expressionless, as though I've never meant anything to him. And maybe I haven't. As I turn to get away from him, I see him lift his gun. Before he opens fire, I run for my life.

part one

parting

You shall be together when the white wings of death scatter your days.

—KAHLIL GIBRAN, *The Prophet*

1

The last time I saw my husband, he had a tiny teardrop of raspberry jam in the blond hairs of his goatee. We'd just shared cappuccinos he'd made in the ridiculously expensive machine I'd bought on a whim three weeks earlier, and croissants he'd picked up on his way in from his five-mile run, the irony lost on him. His lean, hard body was a machine, never gaining weight without his express design. Unlike me. The very aroma of baked goods and my thighs start to expand.

They were warm, the croissants. And as I tried to resist, he sliced them open and slathered them with butter, then jam on top of that, left one eviscerated and gooey, waiting on the white plate. I fought the internal battle and lost, finally reaching for it. It was perfect—flaky, melty, salty, sweet. And then—gone.

"You're not a very good influence," I said, licking butter from my fingertips. "It would take over an hour on the elliptical trainer to burn that off. And we both know *that's* not going to happen." He turned his blue eyes on me, all apology.

"I know," he said. "I'm sorry." Then the smile. Oh, the smile. It demanded a smile in return, no matter how angry, how frustrated, how *fed up* I was. "But it was so good, wasn't it? You'll remember it all day." Was he talking about the croissant or our predawn lovemaking?

"Yes," I said as he kissed me, a strong arm snaking around the small of my back pulling me in urgently, an invitation really, not the goodbye that it was. "I will."

That's when I saw the bit of jam. I motioned that he should wipe his face. He was dressed for an important meeting. *Crucial* was the word he used when he told me about it. He peered at his reflection in the glass door of the microwave and wiped the jam away.

"Thanks," he said, moving toward the door. He picked up his leather laptop case and draped it over his shoulder. It looked heavy; I was afraid he'd wrinkle his suit, a sharp, expensive black wool affair he'd bought recently, but I didn't say so. Too mothering.

"Thanks for what?" I asked. Already I'd forgotten that I'd spared him from the minor embarrassment of going to an important meeting with food on his face.

"For being the most beautiful thing I'll see all day." He was an opportunistic charmer. Had always been that.

I laughed, wrapped my arms around his neck, kissed him again. He knew what to say, knew how to make me feel good. I *would* think about our lovemaking, that croissant, his smile, that one sentence all day.

"Go get 'em," I said as I saw him out of the apartment door, watched him walk to the elevator at the end of the short hallway. He pressed the button and waited. The hallway had sold us on the apartment before we'd even walked through the door: the thick red carpet, the wainscoting, and the ten-foot ceilings—New York City prewar elegance. The elevator doors slid open. Maybe it was then, just before he started to move away, that I saw a shadow cross his face. Or maybe later I just imagined it, to give some meaning to those moments. But if it was there at all, that flicker of what—Sadness? Fear?—it passed over him quickly; was gone so fast it barely even registered with me then.

"You know I will," he said with the usual cool confidence. But I heard it, the lick of his native accent on his words, something that only surfaced when he was stressed or drunk. But I wasn't worried for him. I *never* doubted him. Whatever he had to pull off that day, something vague about investors for his company, there was no doubt in my mind that he'd do it. That was just him: What he wanted, he got. With a wave and a cheeky backward glance, he stepped into the elevator and the doors closed on him. And then—gone.

"I love you, Izzy!" I thought I heard him yell, clowning around, as the elevator dropped down the shaft, taking him and his voice away.

I smiled. After five years of marriage, a miscarriage, at least five knock-'em-down, drag-'em-outs that lasted into the wee hours of the morning, hot sex, dull sex, good days, hard days, all the little heartbreaks and disappointments (and not-so-little ones) inevitable in a relationship that doesn't crash and burn right away, after some dark moments when I thought we weren't going to make it, that I'd be better off without him, and all the breathless moments when I was sure I couldn't even *survive* without him—after all of that he didn't have to say it, but I was glad he still did.

I closed the door and the morning was under way. Within five minutes, I was chatting on the phone with Jack Mannes, my old friend and longtime agent.

"Any sign of that check?" The author's eternal question.

"I'll follow up." The agent's eternal reply. "How's the manuscript going?"

"It's . . . going."

Within twenty minutes, I was headed out for a run, the taste of Marc's buttery, raspberry-jam kiss still on my lips.

WHEN HE STEPPED onto the street, he was blasted by a cold, bitter wind that made him wish he'd worn a coat. He thought about turning around but it was too late for that. Instead he buttoned his suit jacket, slung the strap of his laptop bag across his chest, and dug his hands deep into his pockets. He moved fast on West Eighty-sixth Street toward Broadway. At the corner, he jogged down the yellow-tiled stairway into the subway station, was glad for the warmth of it even with the particularly pungent stench of urine that morning. He swiped his card and passed through the turnstile, waited for the downtown train.

It was past nine, so the crowd on the platform was thinner than it would have been an hour before. A young businessman kept alternately leaning over the tracks, trying to catch sight of the oncoming train lights, and glancing at his watch. In spite of the rich drape of his black wool coat, his expensive shoes, he looked harried, disheveled. Marcus Raine felt a wash of disdain for him, for his obvious tardiness, and for his even more obvious distress, though he couldn't have explained why.

Marcus leaned his back against the far wall, hands still in his pockets, and waited. It was the perpetual condition of the New Yorker to wait—for trains, buses, or taxis, in impossibly long lines for a cup of coffee, in crowds to see a film or visit a particular museum exhibit. The rest of the world saw New Yorkers as rude, impatient. But they had been conditioned to queue one behind the other with the resignation of the damned, perhaps moaning in discontent, but waiting nonetheless.

He'd been living in this city since he was eighteen years old, but he never quite saw himself as a New Yorker. He saw himself more as a spectator at a zoo, one who'd been allowed to wander around inside the cage of the beast. But then he'd always felt that way, even as a child, even in his native home. Always apart, watching. He accepted this as the natural condition of his life, without a trace of unhappiness about it or any self-pity. Isabel had always understood this about him; as a writer, she was in a similar position. *You can't really observe, unless you stand apart.*

It was one of the things that first drew him to her, this sentence. He'd read a novel she'd written, found it uncommonly deep and involving. Her picture on the back of the jacket intrigued him and he'd searched her out on the Internet, read some things about her that interested him—that she was the child of privilege but successful in her own right as the author of eight bestselling novels, that she'd traveled the world and written remarkably insightful essays about the places she visited. "Prague is a city of secrets," she'd written. "Fairy-tale rues taper off into dark alleys, a secret square hides behind a heavy oak and iron door, ornate facades shelter dark histories. Her face is exquisite, finely wrought and so lovely, but her eyes are cool. She'll smirk but never laugh. She knows, but she won't tell." This was true in a way that no outsider could ever really understand, but this American writer caught a glimpse of the real city and it moved him.

It was the river of ink-black curls, those dark eyes, jet in a landscape of snowy skin, the turn of her neck, the birdlike delicacy of her hands, that caused him to seek her out at one of her book signings. He knew right away that *she was the one,* as Americans were so fond of saying—as if their whole lives were nothing but the search to make themselves whole by finding another. He meant it in another way entirely, at first.

It seemed like such a long time ago, that initial thrill, that rush of desire. He often wished he could go back to the night they first met, relive their years together. He'd done so many wrong things—some she knew about, some she did not, could never, know. He remembered that there was something in her gaze when she first loved him that filled an empty place inside him. Even with all the things she didn't understand, she didn't look at him like that anymore. Her gaze seemed to drift past him. Even when she held his eyes, he believed she was seeing someone who wasn't there. And maybe that was his fault.

He heard the rumble of the train approaching, and pushed himself off the wall. He'd started moving toward the edge when he felt a hand on his arm. It was a firm, hard grip and Marcus, on instinct, rolled his arm and broke the grasp, bringing his fist up fast and taking a step back.

"Take it easy, Marcus," the other man said with a throaty laugh. "Relax." He lifted two beefy hands and pressed the air between them. "Why so tense?"

"Ivan," Marcus said coolly, though his heart was an adrenaline-fueled hammer. The moment took on an unreal cast, the tenor of a dark fantasy. Ivan was a ghost, someone so deeply buried in Marcus's memory that he might as well have been looking at a resurrected corpse. Once a tall, wiry young man, manic and strange, Ivan had gained a lot of weight. Not fat but muscle; he looked like a bulldozer, squat and powerful, ready to break concrete and the earth itself.

"What?" That deep laugh again, with less amusement in its tone. "No 'How are you'? No 'So good to see you'?"

Marcus watched Ivan's face. The wide smile beneath cheekbones like cliffs, the glittering dark eyes—they could all freeze like ice. Even jovial like this, there was something vacant about Ivan, something unsettling. It was so odd to see him in this context, in this life, that for a moment Marcus could almost believe that he was dreaming, that he was still in bed beside Isabel. That he'd wake from this as he had from any of the nightmares that plagued him.

Marcus still didn't say anything as his train came and went, leaving them alone on the platform. The woman in the fare booth read a paperback novel. Marcus could hear the rush of trains below, hear the hum and horns of the street above. Too much time passed. In the silence between them, Marcus watched Ivan's expression cool and harden.

Then Marcus let go of a loud laugh that echoed off the concrete and caused the clerk to look up briefly before she went back to her book.

"Ivan!" Marcus said, forcing a smile. "Why so tense?"

Ivan laughed uncertainly, then reached out and punched Marcus on the arm. Marcus pulled Ivan into an enthusiastic embrace and they patted each other vigorously on the back.

"Do you have some time for me?" Ivan asked, dropping an arm over Marcus's shoulder and moving him toward the exit. Ivan's gigantic arm felt like a side of beef, its weight impossible to move without machinery. Marcus pretended not to hear the threat behind the question.

"Of course, Ivan," Marcus said. "Of course I do."

Marcus heard a catch in his own voice, which he tried to cover with a cough. If Ivan noticed, he didn't let on. A current of foreboding cut a valley from his throat into his belly as they walked up the stairs, Ivan still holding on tight. He was talking, telling a joke about a hooker and a priest, but Marcus wasn't listening. He was thinking about Isabel. He was thinking about how she looked this morning, a little sleepy, pretty in her pajamas, her hair a cloud of untamed curls, smelling like honeysuckle and sex, tasting like butter and jam.

On the street, Ivan was laughing uproariously at his own joke and Marcus found himself laughing along, though he had no idea what the punch line had been. Ivan knew a lot of jokes, one more inane than the last. He'd learned a good deal of his English this way, reading joke books and watching stand-up comedians, insisted that one could not really understand a language without understanding its humor, without knowing what native speakers considered funny. Marcus wasn't sure this was true. But there was no arguing with Ivan. It wasn't healthy. The smallest things caused a switch to flip in the big man. He'd be laughing one minute and then the next he'd be beating you with those fists the size of hams. This had been true since they were children together, a lifetime ago.

Ivan approached a late-model Lincoln parked illegally on Eighty-sixth. With the remote in his hand he unlocked it, then reached to open the front passenger door. It was an expensive vehicle, one that Ivan would not have been able to afford given his circumstances of the last few years. Marcus knew what this meant, that he'd returned to the life that had gotten him into trouble in the first place.

Marcus could see the front entrance to his building, gleaming glass and polished wood, a wide circular drive. A large holiday wreath hung on the awning, reminding him that Christmas was right around the corner.

He watched as a young mother who lived there—was her name Janie?—left with her two small children. He found himself thinking suddenly, urgently, of the baby Isabel had wanted. He'd never wanted children, had been angry when Isabel got pregnant, even relieved when she miscarried. Somehow the sight of this woman with her little girls caused a sharp stab of regret. Marcus turned his face so that they wouldn't see him as they passed on the other side of the street.

"You've been living well," Ivan said, his eyes, too, on the building entrance. In the bright morning light, Marcus could see the blue smudges under Ivan's eyes, a deep scar on the side of his face that Marcus didn't remember. Ivan's clothes were cheap, dirty; his nails bitten to the quick. He didn't look well, had the look of someone without the money or the inclination to take care of himself, someone who'd spent too many years indoors. Ivan still wore a smile, but all the warmth was gone. It was stone cold.

"And you? Are you well?" Marcus asked, feeling a tightness in his chest.

Ivan gave a slow shrug, offered his palms. "Not as well."

Marcus let a beat pass. "What do you want, Ivan?"

"You didn't think you'd see me again."

"It has been a long time."

"Yes, Marcus," he said, leaning on the name with heavy sarcasm. "It has been."

Marcus felt himself moving toward the car; there was really no way around it. As he put his hand on the door, Marcus saw his wife leave the building, her hair back—the chaos of it barely tamed with a thin band—her workout clothes on, an old beat-up blue sweatshirt, well-worn sneakers. He thought of the breakfast they'd shared, how she'd worried about the calories. He ducked into the car and watched her pause, look about her. She had that steely expression on her face, the one she got when she was forcing herself to do something she didn't want to do. He could see it, even from a distance. Then she turned, quickly, suddenly, and ran away. Everything in him wanted to race after her but Ivan climbed into the driver's seat. The car bucked with the other man's weight, filled with his scent—cigarettes and body odor.

"Don't worry," Ivan said, issuing a throaty laugh. "I only want to talk. To come to a new arrangement."

"Do I look worried, Ivan?" Marcus said with a cool smile. Ivan didn't answer.

As they pulled into traffic, a line from the *The Prophet* came back to Marcus: "It is not a garment I cast off this day, but a skin that I tear with my own hands." Marcus could feel the life he'd been living shifting, fading. With every city block they passed, he left a gauzy sliver of himself behind. The strand that connected him to Isabel, he felt it pull taut and then snap. It caused him a pointed and intense physical pain in the center of his chest. But he took comfort in a strange thought: The man she would grieve and come to hate, the one she would not be able to forgive, had never existed in the first place.

2

"Rick," I said, fifteen hours after Marcus left for the day. It was going on ten P.M. Lasagna sagged in a glass baking dish, untouched on the counter. A salad wilted in the fridge. "It's Isabel."

"Hey, Iz!" he said brightly. I picked up on a strain to his voice, though, as if he was trying hard at that brightness. "What's up?"

"You guys working late tonight?" I struggled to keep my voice light, my tone easy. I had the television on, the volume too low to even hear. CNN news bites flashed quick fire on the screen—there was an insurgent bombing in Iraq, a celebrity had shaved her head and checked into rehab, a police officer in Chicago was shot. I could hear the water running though the pipes in our wall; our neighbor was taking a shower.

The hesitation on the other end caused my stomach to flip.

"Yeah," he said too late, drawing the word out, mock-forlorn. "You know how we do around here. No mercy." He gave a little laugh—a fake one, uncomfortable. He'd slipped immediately into cover mode.

"Can I talk to my husband?" I heard the edge creeping into my tone; I wondered if he did, too.

"Sure," he said. "Hold on a second." A flutter of relief then, my worry dissipating. *He's working late, forgot to call. Nothing he hasn't done before. You're being paranoid.* I waited.

"Iz," said Rick, back on the line. "I think he ran out to grab a bite. I'll tell him you called?"

"His cell is going straight to voice mail," I said, apropos of nothing.

"I think he said the battery was dead," he answered softly.

"Okay," I said. "Thanks." *You liar.*

I hung up. He'd put me on hold and tried Marc on his cell phone, didn't get him, came back and lied to me. It wasn't even just a suspicion; I knew it was true. I'd seen them cover for each other like that with clients; I knew Rick, my husband's business partner, had done it to me before for various reasons, some worse than others. I'd always found their dynamic a bit strange; they weren't friends. In fact, I sensed an antipathy between them, even though they worked well together. And one never failed to lie or cover for the other.

I poured myself another glass of wine, my second from the cheap bottle of Chardonnay we had in the fridge. As much as I loved my husband, nights like this reminded me about the hairline fissures in our marriage, the ones that creaked and groaned when pressure was applied, threatening to break us apart.

By midnight I was mildly drunk, zoning out on the television set, barely paying attention to what was on the screen. I was listening for the elevator, for the key in the door, for the ringing of the phone. My cell phone was warm in my hand; I'd been holding it for hours, pointlessly trying his number every few minutes. He'd been late before, MIA for half a day, but never like this, never without calling. He might ring drunk from a bar after a fight we'd had, or with some vague lie about work. But this was not like him. It was too . . . conspicuous. I took to watching the digital clock on the cable box.

12:22.

12:23.

12:24.
Where is he?

ONCE, NOT QUITE two years ago, Marc had been unfaithful with a woman he'd met while away on business in Philadelphia. The relationship lasted for two months, or so he told me later—long phone calls, a couple of last-minute trips out of town. Once she came here to New York while I was away at a writers' conference—though he swore she never set foot in our apartment. Not a *love* affair, exactly, but not a one-night stand, either.

I suspected something right away—on the first night he made love to me after returning home from Philadelphia after they'd met. It's the details that give people away, the things that writers notice that other people might miss. I don't mean the mundane things like lipstick on a collar, or the scent of sex. I'm talking about essence, the gossamer strands that connect us.

There was something absent about him, an emptiness to his gaze, that told me his thoughts were elsewhere. Our bodies didn't seem to fit together right. His kiss *tasted* different. I couldn't climax, couldn't cross the distance between us. This had never happened before; even our bad sex was good. We'd managed to make love well even when we were furious with each other, bone tired, or sick with the flu. We'd always been able to connect physically no matter what else was going on.

I wasn't as upset as one might imagine. There were no histrionics, no thrown dishes, or screaming assaults. I just waited for something tangible to prove or disprove my suspicions while the distance between us grew. I didn't blame myself, worry about what was wrong with me, where we had failed. It wasn't like that—*I* wasn't like that. He'd met someone, they hit if off and had sex. The sex was good and he wanted more. I knew this on an instinctive level. I knew him, how he admired beauty, how powerful were his appetites. She must have been something, though, for him to stray—that was less like him. I'd met people, too, over the years. I'd been tempted. In a way, I even understood. But it wasn't in my nature to be unfaithful or dishonest; I couldn't even lie about how much my Manolo Blahniks had cost. *But this is barely even a shoe! It's like a tongue depressor with some dental floss tied around it. You couldn't walk a city block in these, Isabel.*

The tangible proof turned out to be a text message on his cellular phone. He was in the shower; it was next to me on the bedside table. It was unusual for him to leave the phone out. Usually it was on his person, or tucked in his laptop case. I heard the buzz indicating that a message had been received. I couldn't stop myself from picking up the phone and opening the message.

A note from someone identified only as "S" read, *I can't stop thinking about you. I can still feel you inside me.*

Marcus emerged from the bathroom, a plume of steam following him into the bedroom carrying the scent of a sage-mint body wash we'd been using. I turned to face him. He saw the phone in my hand and, I suppose, the look on my face. We both froze, locked eyes. He seemed strange and unfamiliar to me, as though I was seeing him for the first time emerging half naked from our bathroom. There was an odd tightness from my throat into the muscles of my chest. The air around us was electric with tension.

"Are you in love with her?" I asked finally. I was surprised by the flat, unemotional quality to my tone. I suppose it was the last safe question, its answer determining everything else that followed.

"No," he said with a quick dismissive shake of his head. "Of course not."

"Then end it."

A pressing forward of the shoulders; a slight nod as if he was agreeing to meet me at a café somewhere. "Okay," he said easily.

"And go sleep somewhere else tonight. I don't want to be near you right now."

"Isabel," he said.

"I mean it," I said. "Go."

I was injured—my pride bruised, my heart cracked, if not broken. But mainly I was just disappointed. It was not that I had any illusions about him, about our marriage—hell, about marriage in general. I just thought he had more self-control; I thought he was a stronger man. To think of him lying, sneaking out of town, sleeping with a woman in a hotel somewhere—it cheapened him somehow, made him seem less to me.

We spent a few days apart, had some long phone conversations during which we agreed that there were problems in our marriage that needed to be addressed. There were tears, apologies made and accepted on both sides. He came home. We moved on. I don't know that I got over it, exactly. But the incident was slowly stitched into the fabric of our relationship; from that point on everything was a slightly different color, a different texture. Not necessarily bad, but not the same. We didn't seek therapy or hash over details or talk late into the night about why or when or could it happen again.

Those problems that we agreed existed—his workaholic nature, and mine, for that matter, his unavailability, my various neuroses and insecurities—were never actually addressed. I didn't struggle with newfound trust issues. I saw the incident as an aberration. And neither one of us ever brought any of it up again. At the time, I just thought we were being so intellectual, so sophisticated about it. But was it just denial? I never told anyone about it, not Linda, not Jack. I don't know. Maybe it was more like fear-induced laziness. You notice the lump under your arm but you can't bring yourself to have it examined, feel unable to face the diagnosis. You don't want anyone else to know; their concern would just make it real.

By three a.m. I was thinking of his affair, wondering about her, about all the things I hadn't wanted to know at the time—her name, what she looked like, her dress size, what she did for a living. Redhead, brunette, blonde? Stylish? Smart? I was wondering: Is he with her now? Or someone else? Has he left me?

Funny that I never imagined he'd been in an accident—pushed onto the subway tracks by a deranged homeless person, hit by a city bus, suffered a head injury from the crumbling facade of a postwar building, all those New York City–type accidents you hear about now and then. It just didn't seem possible that something like that could befall him. He was too, I don't know, *on his game.* He was a man in control of his world. He didn't believe in accidents.

By five A.M. I had run the gauntlet of emotions—starting with mild worry, moving through cold panic to rage. There was a brief period of nonchalance, then a return to fear, then on to hatred, through despondency ending with desperation. I was about to call my sister when the cell phone, still clutched in my hand, started to ring. The screen blinked blue: *Marc calling.*

"God, Marc. *Where are you?*" I answered, so angry, so relieved, so dying to hear that voice offering me a reason for this, something I could buy: *Come get me at the hospital, Isabel. I was mugged, hit over the head, just regained consciousness. Don't cry. I'm okay.*

But there was only a crackling on the line, the faint, distant moaning of some kind of horn or siren. Then voices, muffled, both male, tones angry, volume rising and falling, words impossible to understand.

"Marc!" I yelled.

Then there was screaming, a terrible keening. A horrible, primal wail that connected with every nerve ending in my body, causing me to cry out. *"Marc! Marcus!"*

But the screaming just went on, rocketing through my nervous system, until the line went suddenly dead.

3

What makes a great marriage? The kind you see on the diamond commercials—the shadowy walks and the glistening eyes, the held hands, the passionate kiss beneath stars, the surprise candlelight dinner. Does that even exist? Aren't those just moments, studded in the landscape of a life where you floss your teeth together, fight about money, burn the risotto, watch too much television? Did I have a great marriage or even a good one? I don't know. I don't know what that means. I loved him, couldn't imagine my life without him, showed him all the places inside me. In spite of all our individual flaws and the mistakes we made in our lives and in our marriage, we'd come together and stayed together for a while.

But those last moments in the kitchen when we'd shared croissants and kisses, when if there'd been more time we'd probably have wound up back in bed, making love again—they were just moments. If you'd tuned in on another day, you might have found us bickering over who was supposed to do the grocery shopping, or ignoring each other, him reading the paper, me staring out the window thinking about my current novel. You might find me crying over my miscarriage and how I hadn't been able to conceive since, him withdrawing, arms crossed. We'd been ambivalent about children in the first place. My pregnancy was an accident. You might hear him say so, as if that should make me feel the loss less profoundly. Each moment just a sliver of who we were; only he had the full picture.

* * *

By nine a.m. I was standing on the street outside Marc's office building. His software company leased the top floor of a small brownstone on Greenwich Avenue. There were other offices at that address, too—a lawyer, a literary agent, a mystery bookshop that occupied the storefront on the basement level. I'd tried the key I had to the street door but it didn't work. I remembered then, the break-in a month ago—someone used a key to get in and steal nearly a hundred thousand dollars in computer equipment. The locks had been changed after that, a new alarm system installed.

So I waited. I huddled near the stoop, trying to keep out of the brutal, cold wind. Across the street, the shops—a trendy boutique, a pharmacy, a sex shop—all had windows decorated in red and silver for the holidays. I watched people hustling along in their busy lives, coffee in one hand, cell in the other, big bags slung across their chests. They were thinking about work, about getting their shopping done, whether or not it was too late to send cards. Yesterday that was me—hustling, always one step ahead of myself, not present in the least. Twenty-four hours later I felt as though I'd been in a life wreck; my life was a crumbled mass of metal and I'd been hurled through the windshield. All the initial panic I'd felt when Marcus didn't come home, the shock and dread that gripped me after the horrifying phone call, had drained. At this point, I was stunned, bleeding out by the side of the road.

After the phone call, I'd dialed 911 for lack of any other action to take in my terror. The woman who answered told me a missing adult wasn't an emergency unless there was evidence of foul play or a history of mental illness. I told her about the screams, everything I'd heard. She said that maybe it was a television or something else—some kind of joke or prank; husbands did cruel things all the time. She told me the police couldn't even accept a missing-person report without evidence, a history, especially for someone over eighteen, especially for a man. The phone call didn't count as proof that something was wrong.

"Physical evidence, ma'am."

"Like what?"

"Like blood, or a sign of forced entry into the residence, a ransom demand—things like that."

She gave me a phone number to call, and an address where I could report in person, bringing photographs and dental records. *Dental records.*

"Most people just turn up within seventy-two hours."

"Most?"

"More than sixty-five percent."

"And the rest?"

"Accidents. More rarely, murders. And sometimes people just want to disappear."

Something about the tone of her voice made me feel foolish, ashamed. Like I was one of a hundred women she'd talked to that night whose husbands just hadn't come home. *Honey, he left you,* she wanted to say. *Wake up.*

The natural thing for me to do then would have been to call my sister and her husband, Erik, to tell them what was happening, to get their support. But I didn't do that. I couldn't bring myself to call Linda; I'd have to tell her about the affair then, wouldn't I, to give them the full picture? I couldn't face it. For all the same reasons, and a few others, I didn't call Jack, either. His antipathy toward Marcus was unexpressed but palpable just the same.

Jack and I had a complicated history. And beyond that, if Marc later learned that I'd called Jack in a moment of crisis, it would confirm all Marc's past accusations about our friendship. Marcus disliked our closeness, how often we spoke, claimed it was a shade beyond appropriate for a professional friendship. In fact, my relationship to Jack had come up in my worse arguments with Marc. He thought that I told him too much, that we saw each other too often, that the way he touched me was too familiar.

You don't understand our friendship.

An angry laugh. Then: *I understand your friendship perfectly. I think it's you who doesn't understand. You're too naive, too trusting.*

Please.

Of course, since *his* sleazy affair, Marcus had less to say about Jack. His commentary was reduced to annoyed glances.

But I wasn't thinking about any of that now. I was just hearing that horrible scream, my mind alive with dark imaginings. As I'd dressed and gathered photographs, I tried to calm myself by thinking of explanations for the phone call—maybe he'd lost his phone, or it had been stolen, and what I heard had nothing to do with him. Maybe he *had* left, was curled up in someone else's bed right now, had tossed his phone in a trash can on his way out of our life. Obsessively, I kept hitting *Send* on my phone, getting his voice mail over and over. Eventually, with the sun rising, I'd headed out to report him missing but I'd wound up at his office instead, standing outside, hoping for something to end this nightmare before it began.

Finally, I watched Rick strut up the street past the cute shops and trendy cafés, tapping on his BlackBerry, oblivious to my waiting by the staircase. He was tall, lanky with a mass of black curls, a thin, carefully maintained beard and sideburns. He wore a pair of faded denims, a T-shirt that read *Love Kills Slowly* beneath a thick leather jacket hanging open in spite of the cold. He walked right by me, took the stairs easily, light on his feet.

"Rick," I said.

He looked up startled from the slim black device in his hand. It took him a second to place me in this context. He didn't look well, pale and exhausted, harried.

"Isabel," he said, a frown sinking into his forehead. "What's wrong? What are you doing here?" He looked around, behind me, up and down the street.

"Marc didn't come home last night," I said. I watched his brows lift in surprise, his eyes glance quickly to the left, then come back to me—thinking of a lie, a way to stall. Before he could come up with one, I asked, "Was he really here when I called?"

Rick shoved the BlackBerry into his pocket and looked down at the concrete. I noticed the debut of coarse, wiry grays in his hair, of ever-so-faint crow's-feet around his eyes.

"No," he said simply. "He wasn't here. He never came back after his meeting yesterday. Never called." I felt the cold wash of disappointment, a deepening of my fear. "Come inside, Iz. It's cold."

I followed Rick up the stairs, thinking, trying to establish a time line. Marcus hadn't phoned me after his meeting as he'd promised to do. I'd starting calling around three in the afternoon to see how it went. At that point I wasn't even remotely concerned; he was so often absent-minded about our personal life, totally focused on business during the workday. It wasn't uncommon for him to forget promises to call. My calls to him went straight to voice mail—not uncommon, either. I wasn't even *that* concerned when he didn't come home for dinner. But as Rick and I neared the top of the creaky slim staircase, I had the ugly dawning that no one had heard from Marcus since early yesterday.

On the landing, I wrestled with the hope that we'd find him inside, having slept on the couch in his office, maybe hungover. *Izzy, I'm sorry. Things went badly at the meeting. I went to have a drink and had too much. Forgive me.* Even though nothing like that had ever happened before, I imagined it vividly as Rick punched in his security code, turned the key in the lock, and pushed open the heavy metal door. I imagined it so hard that for a moment it was almost true; I almost felt the flood of relief, the blast of fury.

But no. The office was silent, empty. Rows of desks, huge gleaming monitors, industrial-cool exposed vents and pipes in the ceiling. Marc's glass-walled office was dark, orderly. As we moved into the space, the electronic tone of a ringing phone sounded like a bird trapped inside a computer. Ricky dropped his bag and ran for it.

I watched him until he gave me a head shake to let me know it wasn't Marc or anything to do with him. I wandered into my husband's office, opened the light on the desk. I saw Rick glance at me through the glass, the phone still cradled between his ear and shoulder, as I sat in Marc's large leather chair, put my fingers on the cool metal of his desk. I stared at our wedding picture; we both looked so blissfully happy, it almost seemed staged. Behind us, a glorious sunset waxed orange, purple, pink. I sifted through a pile of papers and manila folders, glanced at sticky notes on the lamp and on the phone, looking for what I didn't know. Then I booted up his computer. Rick entered while I was doing this; he looked uncomfortable.

"He doesn't like anyone to be in here, Isabel."

"Fuck off, Rick," I said quietly, without heat.

He glanced down at his feet again, shoved his hands deep into his pockets, and hiked his shoulders up so high he looked like a vulture. I thought he was too old for the urban-chic look he was sporting. He needed a visit to Barneys, needed to maybe grow up a little. Marcus was the polished one in suit and tie, classic fashion with a trendy edge. Rick had fully cultivated his programmer-punk look and aura, down to the pasty white skin that seemed permanently bathed in the glow of a computer screen. I always thought it should be Marcus who interfaced with people, but he hated that part of the business. It was Rick and a team of account managers who pitched prospective clients, fielded inquiries, handled the ever-escalating needs of their customers. Marcus was the brains of the company, rarely seen but controlling everything. Rick was a little bit of a marionette. I wondered if he ever resented it.

"Do you know where he is?" I asked him. He opened his mouth to answer but I interrupted. "Do *not* lie."

He seemed to look at something far behind me. I examined his face. What did I see there? Concern—maybe even a little fear. He shook his head, curls bouncing. "No, I don't know where he is. I—I wish I did."

"When he didn't come back from his meeting, when he didn't call all day—you didn't think that was unusual? Cause for concern?"

He lifted his palms.

"What are you saying?" I asked, angry, incredulous. "That it *wasn't* unusual?"

No answer. No eye contact. I saw a sheen of perspiration on his brow. I let the silence hang between us, hoping he'd fill it, but he didn't. Finally, I told him about the phone call, trying to keep my voice even, to keep the sound of it out of my head. Rick sank into the seat across from Marcus's desk, rested his head in his hand while I spoke.

When he didn't say anything, I said, "I'm calling the police again." I reached to pick up the phone.

"Wait," he said, looking up, startled. No, not startled, stricken. "Just wait a second."

I let my hand rest on the receiver. "Rick, what is going on?"

Then there was thunder on the stairs outside the entrance to the office. The door exploded open and suddenly Ricky was up from his seat and I was up from mine, so quickly the chair on casters went careening, crashing against the wall behind me.

We were both frozen as a dozen people stormed through the door, weapons drawn, dressed in black from head to toe except for the white letters emblazed center mass: FBI.

Time seemed to slow and stretch. The men fanned out, moving behind desks and through the loft like rats in a maze. We were spotted by a tall, lanky woman with short-cropped blond hair as she headed in our direction; she started yelling at us. Her words were unintelligible to me; all I could see was the gun pointed in our direction. I watched Rick put his hands on top of his head, lower his chin to his chest, and close his eyes.

I thought, He's been waiting for this, expecting this moment. What have they done? I stood stunned, mute, my fingers touching the edge of Marc's desk, feeling like the bottom had dropped out of my life and I was free-falling through space.

When I met Marc, I had already resigned myself to the role of spinster aunt. And I was actually okay with that, maybe even relieved, after the parade of losers and weirdoes I'd had trekking through my life over the previous years. I had started to see myself as a dating oddball, as the kind of woman who couldn't manage to fit herself into a relationship. For me, the problem wasn't *meeting* men, a very common New York City complaint. I couldn't swing a dead cat without meeting a man—in the grocery store, in bookstores and cafés, on a subway platform. The problem was that no matter how auspicious the start, things just never lasted, never bloomed into anything permanent. I'd start to get that cool, apathetic feeling, begin to dread phone calls or zone out during dates. And if that didn't happen, he'd stop calling me, eventually disappear altogether. I rarely even got to the ugly breakup phase. Generally, there was just a slow fade to nothing.

"You know, Izzy," my sister, Linda (married, two gorgeous kids, outrageously successful photographer, older than me by five years, *thank God*, or I'd have to kill her), said one night over conciliatory Pinot Grigio, "have you considered that there's just no *give* to you? That you're looking for someone to fit into your life exactly the way it is now? You're not willing to bend or shift *anything*."

I bristled at this statement, thought it was patently untrue. "When it's right, I won't have to," I said defensively.

An ever-so-slight eye roll, a sip of wine.

"Right?"

She held my gaze for a moment, gave a quick shrug. "Well, in a sense. But more like when it's right you don't mind so much doing a little shifting and bending."

"Fight the good fight, Iz," called Erik, the perfect husband, from the kitchen. "Make *them* bend."

"Shh," said my sister as he walked into the room. "You'll wake them up." The kids: Emily and Trevor.

"Did *you* bend?" I asked Erik.

"Hell, *yes,* I bent. I'm still bending." He flopped his lean form onto the low suede chaise across from us, inviting himself into the sister talk session. He rolled his head back for maximum drama.

"Oh, please." My sister smiled at him, eyes glittering, reaching out with her bare foot to knock him on the knee. The way she looked at him embarrassed me sometimes—naked adoration. They adored each other. There was none of that insidious bickering or sarcasm, none of the whispered comments or veiled insults so common in my friends' marriages. Not that they never fought. Oh, they fought. But it was always so *aboveboard,* so earnest, and over quickly. Healthy; they were very healthy. Sometimes it made me sick.

I remember thinking that night, I'll never have this. It's just not going to happen. With this thought, instead of despair, my system flooded with a strange relief. I'd given up at twenty-eight years old. It felt good, a justified surrender.

"What about Jack?" She'd asked the question and I had answered it so many times that I just got up to refill my glass without comment.

AND THEN THERE was Marcus.

His first words to me: "I'm a big fan."

I smiled and thanked him for his kindness, took the book he held out to me. The first thing I noticed about him were his hands, how large and strong they were. I'd just finished a reading from my recent novel in a small bookstore to a small crowd who had, with the exception of this gentleman, all promptly left without buying a single copy. Outside, the wind pushed at the door, causing the little entry bell to jingle. Snow fell in fat, wet flakes that didn't bother to stick to the ground and make themselves pretty. I signed his book with a black Sharpie, thinking about my pajamas and down comforter, *Seinfeld* reruns. Out of the corner of my eye, I noticed the clerk at the counter issue a yawn. Other than the three of us, the store was empty; it was nearly nine o'clock.

I handed the book back to the stranger and then he just stood there for a moment, awkward. He was working up the nerve to say something. I expected him to start talking about the book *he* was writing, ask about getting an agent or publisher. But he didn't.

"Thanks again," I said. "I appreciate your coming out on such a terrible night."

"I wouldn't have missed it," he said.

I stood up then and took my coat off the back of my chair, barely registering the tinkling of the bell over the door. By the time I turned around, he was gone. I was so tired that night, so wanting to go home that, other than his hands, I hadn't really noticed much about him, wouldn't have been able to pick him out of a lineup. This was unusual for me. I absorbed details, energies, like a sponge, couldn't even stop it if I wanted to. The curse of the writer. But not that night. Fatigue, maybe, or just a single-minded focus on trying to get home? Or was it something about him, his energy, that allowed him to be overlooked, go unnoticed? Whatever the reason, I didn't think about him again as I said my farewells to the clerk and headed out onto the street.

He was waiting for me outside the door under a large black umbrella. I felt a little jolt of fear.

"I'm not a stalker," he said quickly, lifting a hand. He must have seen the alarm on my face, how I quickly turned back toward the shop door. He released an uncomfortable laugh, glanced up at the falling snow, maybe embarrassed that he'd frightened me.

"Is it crazy to ask you to have dinner with me?" he said after an uncomfortable beat.

"A little," I said, appraising him, looking into his eyes, assessing his body language. He was tall, powerful looking. His shoulders square, hand tense, gripping his umbrella. He didn't *look* like a nutcase, with his expensive leather laptop bag and good shoes. He wore a dark wool pea coat, with a gray cashmere scarf. His eyes were stunning in the lamplight, a wide, earnest light blue. An amused smile played at the corner of his mouth; his jaw looked as if it belonged on a mountain somewhere. I realized I was shivering, all exposed flesh starting to tingle.

"Well," he said, "go a little crazy with me, then. A public place, somewhere crowded." His smile broadened. I could see that he was laughing at himself inside, at the situation. I found myself smiling, too, at his boldness, at his allure.

"When's the last time you took a chance?" he asked, undaunted by my silence, by the way I must have been staring at him.

I might have just walked away, hopped a cab, and headed home. This is what I wanted to do, even started to move to the curb. But I had a rare moment of self-clarity: My sister was right about me. She'd said: *You're not willing to bend or shift anything to let someone into your life.* Or something like that. I suddenly, passionately, wanted to prove her wrong.

I looked at him with fresh eyes; he was still waiting, still smiling. Most men would have already walked away, embarrassed, angry. But not Marcus. What he wanted, he got. He'd wait, if that's what it took. Even then.

"Seriously," he started, and it was in that word that I first heard the lilt of his very slight accent. "If I wanted to kill you, I would have done it already."

I found myself laughing with him at that, and the next thing I knew, we were in a cab together, racing through the wet, cold night.

* * *

We wound up at Café Orlin, a dark and cozy spot, one of my favorite East Village haunts, and stayed there until the early hours, losing our sense of time and any self-consciousness either of us had, exploring the landscapes of each other's past, talking about books—mine, mostly (his interest and knowledge were *beyond* flattering)—and art, and travel. It was effortless, comfortable. When we finally left, workdays looming, the snow had stopped and the frigid night lay out before us slick and crystalline as he walked me home. He reached for my hand and I let him take it. His skin was smooth and dry, his grip so hard and strong it felt as though his bones were made from metal. Heat flooded my body as our fingers entwined.

At the door to my building, I turned to face him. *I'll call you,* I expected him to say. Or, *Thanks for a nice evening.* Something vague, something that left it all up in the air, something that later would have me wondering if the night had really been as special as I thought.

"Can I see you tonight?" he said. *What?* There were games to be played, protective walls to be erected, nonchalance to be feigned. He'd clearly misplaced his rulebook.

He must have registered my surprise. "Honestly, Isabel, I don't have time for games." Did he sound weary, in spite of his kind eyes, his gentle hand on my arm? "If you don't want to see me again, in your heart you already know that. So just say it now. No hard feelings. But if you do—just say yes."

I had to laugh. "Yes," I said. "I want to see you again. Tonight." I had plans—just dinner with Jack. I'd cancel them. I *would* bend and shift and let this man into my life. Why not?

"I'll pick you up at eight," he said, taking my hand and pressing it to his mouth. "I can't wait."

He left me swooning in the soft glow of street lamps as he walked quickly up my street and then turned the corner without looking back.

I halfway didn't expect to see him again. As I entered my building, I was already steeling myself for the disappointment that surely lay ahead.

RICK HAD BEEN taken into an inner office in handcuffs; he hadn't even turned to look at me. He hadn't even said one word, though I'd yelled after him, desperate, pathetic.

"Rick, *please* tell me what's going on!" I watched until he'd passed through the doorway with two agents and was gone.

"We have questions, Mrs. Raine," said the female agent. "So you will need ~~you~~ to wait here." She took me firmly by the arm and led me back to Marcus's desk.

I think it's fair to say I lost it a little. I ranted, demanded answers, raged about Marcus's disappearance. All the while, the tall blonde just looked at me like I was the most pitiable sight she'd ever seen. I eventually wound down, ran out of juice.

"Just have a seat, Mrs. Raine. There's a lot to talk about," she'd said, long on condescension, short on illumination. There was something strange about her. And she didn't seem quite official. She seemed more like a stripper with a cheap, dirty kind of beauty. I wouldn't have been surprised to see her drop into a deep, wide squat, start taking off her clothes. She held me in her gaze for longer than seemed appropriate, then she strode out, all legs and attitude. She'd closed the door behind her.

Exhausted, numb, I allowed myself to slump in the chair and watch through the glass as hard drives were removed, files confiscated, desk drawers emptied of their contents. It was all very rote, once the guns had been holstered. No one seemed overly hurried, everyone clearly with expertise in their assigned task. All the agents avoided looking at me. After a while, the whole situation took on a strange unreality, like something I was watching on television, something I'd turned on too late and didn't fully understand. I felt the bubbling urge to laugh at my predicament, followed by the urge to scream.

I noticed that none of the other employees arrived for work that morning. I imagined they were being turned away or taken into custody in the hallway downstairs. But I didn't know.

It occurred to me suddenly that I didn't have to just sit here and obey like a good little girl. What if Marcus was in FBI custody? I'd asked but hadn't received an answer. What if that's why he hadn't come home or been able to call? I felt a little lift of hope, a blast of adrenaline. Even if that wasn't exactly an ideal scenario, at least it would mean he was all right. That I could help him. I realized it was time to call in the troops—Linda and Erik, my mother and Fred, Jack. And I needed to get us a lawyer. Fast.

I caught sight of my own reflection in the glass wall of Marc's office. I looked slouched over, like an old woman, pale and harried. I wore a long black wool skirt and black leather ankle-high boots, a bulky sweater and wrap. My hair, long, past my shoulders, a black mass of unmanageable curls, was more chaotic than usual. I needed to pull myself together and take control of the situation.

I lifted the phone from the receiver and found the line dead. I looked up at the federal agents who were all still engaged in dissecting the office Marcus had worked so hard to build—months of renovation, hundreds of thousands of dollars in loans and our own money. I walked over to the door and found it locked from the outside. My mouth and throat went dry with the debut of panic in my chest as I tried the knob again. *They couldn't do that, could they? Hold me here like that without charge, arrest, without letting me call anyone?*

I started pounding on the door, moved over to the glass and started banging on that so that they could see me. But no one even looked up. I started to look at each of the people individually. One man had a deep red scar that ran from the corner of his right eye and disappeared into the collar of his black vest. He was stocky, had longish hair that hung, unwashed, to his collar. Another man had tattoos on his hands. There was a woman with a bright purple streak dyed into her white hair which she'd tried to hide under a stocking cap but which kept snaking out, dropping in front of her eyes.

I had a terrible moment of cold dawning, dread a lump in my abdomen, as I turned to see that the tall blond woman had entered the office. These people were not FBI agents. She had an ugly sneer on her face, held a large gun. It was more like a caricature of a gun, it was so dark and menacing, and yet it almost didn't register with me. I found myself moving closer to her.

"What's going on here?" I said, surprised at how steady my voice sounded.

"Marcus is wrong about you," she said. "You're going to be trouble, aren't you?" The words landed like a spit in the face. She wasn't even trying to hide her accent anymore. I recognized it right away.

"What did you say?" I asked. My voice came out in an incredulous whisper. "Who are you?" Though she was taller than me by about three inches, broader at the shoulders, stronger, I could see, at the legs and hips, I wasn't afraid of her. In fact, I was overcome by the urge to put my hands on her long, white throat—gun or no gun. She seemed to register this; I saw her eyes widen just slightly. Then she raised her hand quickly and brought the gun across hard on my temple. I didn't have time to ward off the blow, didn't even really feel it. I just heard a loud, private thud inside my head. A curtain of red fell before my eyes and the next thing I saw were her thick black boots as the floor rose up fast to greet me, then a blue light. Then black.

4

Someone yelling, "Help me! For the love of Christ, please help me!" There was the stench of urine, over that a heavy odor of antiseptic. And something else, something sweet and metallic. Blood. The soft sound of busy footfalls racing back and forth. A phone ringing. Harsh white light, too bright. That phone kept ringing, like a lance through my brain. I tried to move and felt bottle rockets of pain behind my brow and down my neck. When I finally adjusted to the light, I saw Linda's face. My sister. Her eyes were rimmed red, blue moons of fatigue beneath. Behind her, Trevor and Emily were huddled together, leaning against a white wall looking around them, with matching wide, green saucers for eyes. More curious than scared; they're like that.

"Are you out of your *freaking minds*? We've been here for *five* hours. She has a *head injury*." It was Erik's voice, I realized, loud and booming with anger.

I was lying on a gurney, parked in a busy, grimy hallway off an emergency room. I guessed it was St. Vincent's in the Village. How I'd gotten here, I had no idea.

There was a measured, deadpan response to Erik's ranting that I couldn't quite hear. Something about two strokes and a gunshot wound. "She's been unconscious for hours," he said loudly. "You can't tell me that's not serious. She's barely been looked at."

"Sir, you *will* get out of my face," responded a deep female voice, very stern and more loudly. "Sit down right now or you will be asked to leave."

Erik had a bad temper when it came to things like this. When he felt at the mercy of a bad system, he generally blew a gasket—no doubt he would have exploded into an embarrassing string of expletives had his children not been present. But if he said anything else, I didn't hear it.

Linda saw my eyes open and leaned in close. "Oh, Izzy, Izzy, Izzy," she said, putting her hand on my forehead. "Oh my God, *what* happened?"

Why was she whispering? Then I saw the cop, a uniformed officer sitting in a chair about five feet from Emily and Trevor.

"I don't know," I said, gripping her hand and trying to sit up but lying back down. I told her how Marcus didn't come home, how I went to the office, what happened there. The events of the night before and that morning came back in vivid snapshots; I was firing off frames of memory, my words coming out in a manic tumble. I wasn't sure how much sense I was making as my sister stared at me intently. She'd always looked at me that way, even when we were girls, even when I was telling her the most trivial things. She listened. I felt my face flush with the powerful brew in my chest—anger, fear, despair.

I saw all of those things on Linda's face, too. "Oh my God, Izzy. Why didn't you call me?"

"Linda, *where is he*?" I asked, a sob escaping me, tears coming in a hot, wet stream. "What's happening?"

She shook her head, looking as helpless as I was, gripped my hand. "We'll figure it out," she said bravely. "Everything's going to be okay."

She was always the optimist. Not me. The way I saw it, things could only get worse, but I didn't say so.

"Can I hold your gun?" Trevor had sidled over to the cop. Ten years old, blond as sunlight like Linda, and honey-sweet.

"Don't be an *idiot,* Trevor," said Emily, with an extravagant eye roll.

Thirteen, hair the same inky black as mine but straight as razors, same major attitude problem.

"Emily," said Linda. "Be nice to your brother. And Trevor, leave that officer *alone.*"

There was an unusually sharp, tense edge to her voice and both kids turned to stare at us. They were pampered children, treated tenderly at home and at school, rarely hearing an angry tone or unkind word. They both looked as if they'd been slapped. I'd never been sure how good it was for them to be treated so gently, worried that they'd be torn up when they stepped out of Montessori privilege and into the real world. Like right now.

The cop saw then that I was conscious, pulled a heavy black radio from his belt, turned away to talk. Something about the witness.

"Is that me? Am I 'the witness'?" I asked my sister.

"They've been waiting to talk to you," Linda said, nodding and rubbing her eyes.

"Who has?"

"The police," she whispered, leaning in close. "They found you in the office. Izzy, it's been destroyed, everything stolen or smashed, spray paint everywhere. Someone called nine-one-one. You were unconscious behind Marc's desk. They brought you here and called us. Detectives are supposed to come when you wake up."

"Those people—they weren't FBI agents," I said in an absurd statement of the obvious.

"No," she said, shaking her head. "They weren't."

"Why didn't they kill me?"

"Izzy!"

It wasn't a lamentation; it was a question of pure curiosity. They should have killed me. I saw them all, could easily identify any of them and would likely be doing so shortly. But they hadn't. Why not? To someone who constructed plot for a living, it seemed stupid, careless.

My sister put her head in her hand and I saw her shoulders start to shake a little. She always cried from stress or anger. Some people viewed it as weakness. But I knew it for what it was—her release valve. The kids crowded in around us, Trevor resting his head on his mother's shoulder, Emily taking my hand. Trevor's tangle of silky curls mingled with his mother's.

"What happened to you, Izzy?" Emily whispered in my ear. Her breath smelled like fruit punch. She'd never called me "aunt" for some reason, and I was glad for it. That title seemed too formal, too old-fashioned, put a distance between us that I hoped she'd never feel. I squeezed her hand, looked into her worried face. She was rail-thin, and all hard angles, a cool city girl with a poet's heart.

"I'm not sure," I said lamely. She turned away, glanced toward the cop, who had returned to his seat and opened a copy of the *Post.* He seemed impervious to our drama, just putting in his time.

"Where's Marcus?" Emily said, looking back at me. I tried not to cry again; one of us crying was enough. Children shouldn't have to comfort adults.

"I don't know, Em," I managed, squeezing her hand.

"What do you *mean*?"

Trevor had turned his eyes up to me and both he and his sister looked frightened now. Then Erik came up behind them, put a hand on each of their shoulders. Both kids turned to wrap their arms around his middle.

"Okay, everyone," he said, strong, light. He was not an especially tall man but there was a powerful, energetic force to him. Men liked him; women flirted with him. Everyone just felt better when he was around.

"Let's all try to pull it together. Everything's going to be fine."

He had four sets of uncertain eyes on him. I saw him muster his strength.

"It *is,*" he said brightly. "I promise."

* * *

It was hours more before I was treated—a deep gash at my temple cleaned, stitched, and bandaged. I had a severe concussion, according to the very young doctor who attended to me. He warned me to care for the wound, take my antibiotics and rest.

"Or pay the consequences. Head injuries are very tricky. Not to be taken lightly."

He was frighteningly pale, the skin on his hands nearly translucent, the veins beneath, thick blue ropes. He looked as if he lived day and night beneath the harsh fluorescent bulbs.

We were still in the emergency room, but in one of those curtained-off little areas no bigger than a shoe box, that same cop sitting outside. I could see his bulky shadow through the white gauzy barrier. The detectives who were supposed to come talk to me still hadn't arrived.

"A blow to the temple can be fatal," the doctor said gravely. "You're very lucky."

I didn't have the will to answer him. My sister sat beside me on a tiny, uncomfortable-looking stool, holding my hand. Erik had taken the kids to his mother's and afterward was planning to see what he could find out about Marcus, about the office break-in, if you could call it that. An odd calm had come over me; it was more like a brown-out, the result of a brain short-circuit. You can only handle so much pain, fear, grief before your head switches off for a while. That's how the psyche handles trauma. A clinical psychiatrist had told me this once during a research interview I was conducting for one of my novels; it made sense to me then. I understood it better now.

"Are you all right?" Linda asked when the doctor left. She'd repeated this question every fifteen minutes like a nervous tic since I'd regained consciousness.

"Can you just stop asking me that?"

"Sorry," she said, straightening out her back, then arching it into a stretch.

"You sound like Mom."

"Okay, okay," she said, raising her palms in the air a little and then letting them drop to her thighs. "I'm *sorry.* You don't have to get mean about it."

"Did Erik call?" I asked.

She took her phone from her pocket and checked the screen, though we both knew it hadn't rung. She shook her head. I opened my mouth but she interrupted me.

"I just tried Marc's cell and your apartment five minutes ago."

I closed my eyes. This wasn't happening. I saw her face again, the blonde. What had she said exactly? *Marcus is wrong about you. You're going to be trouble, aren't you?* Every time I heard her voice in my head, I felt sicker and more despairing. Another phrase that was still burned in my memory started echoing as well, as much as I'd tried to forget it: *I can still feel you inside me.*

"That woman," my sister said, reading my mind as usual. It has always been like this with us—calling each other simultaneously, finishing each other's sentences, buying each other the same gifts. "Are you sure that's what she said?"

"I'm sure."

She leaned forward, put her elbows on her knees. She got this careful, thoughtful look on her face that she gets when she's trying to be diplomatic. "I'm just saying—you *do* have a concussion."

"I know what I heard, Linda," I said. I felt bad immediately for my nasty tone but didn't apologize. Instead, I closed my eyes and turned away from her.

She was quiet for a second, but I heard her tapping her foot on the floor.

"Do you want me to call anyone?"

"Like who?"

"Like Jack?"

"No," I said. "No. Do you *ever* stop?"

I heard her stand up, issue a light sigh. "I'm going to find some food for us," she said.

"Good," I said blackly. "Take your time."

She rested a hand on my shoulder for a moment and then walked out. I heard her ask the cop if he wanted anything, which made me feel even worse for being such a bitch. Everyone always thought of Linda as the good girl, the sweet one. I was the black cloud. I was the bad sleeper, the finicky eater, the colicky baby, the one who gave our mother heartburn during her pregnancy. Even as adults, I was the one who forgot thank you notes, who was always late and didn't return phone calls. *She* never forgot a birthday, never failed to send flowers to the funeral of a distant relative, not only showed up everywhere on time but looking perfect and with an exquisite hostess gift. One of my top ten most dreaded sentences: *Your sister is such a treasure,* followed by a pregnant silence in which the subtext *So, what happened to you?* might easily be inferred. If they only knew. Not that she wasn't those things. Just that she wasn't *only* that.

I was glad for a few minutes of solitude to let some tears fall in private with no one fawning, telling me it was going to be okay. But I wasn't alone for long.

"Mrs. Raine?"

I turned at the male voice. "I'm Detective Grady Crowe."

Strictly by my estimate, the fiction writer notices approximately fifty percent more details than other people. These details get filed away for future use. This happens in a millisecond and I'm only barely conscious of it. In the case of Detective Crowe: I observed the clean, close shave, the tidy crease in his pants, the studied way his blue shirtsleeves peeked out of his black suede jacket. I noticed the careful cropping of his dark hair, the high arch of his brows, the polite smile that didn't manage to offset a hard glint in his eyes.

The fiction writer then uses these details to weave a narrative. I immediately assessed the man before me as a textbook overachiever, a person who paid close attention to fine points and appearances. Possibly in paying attention to these things, he occasionally lost sight of the big picture. Something about the straight line of his mouth made me imagine that he was relentless when it came to getting what he wanted, sometimes foolhardy, thoughtless, in his pursuit of it.

Often—usually—this narrative I create is very close to the truth but sometimes—only sometimes—it replaces the reality of a situation and keeps me from seeing things as they actually are. This is *not* a good thing.

Detective Crowe moved into the space without invitation from me and extended his hand. I sat up with difficulty and took it reluctantly. His grip was strong and warm, his nails perfectly manicured. He smelled like coffee. He lifted one of those carefully maintained fingers to his temple, raised his chin toward me.

"Someone got you pretty good." I thought I saw a smile play at the corners of his mouth and it infuriated me.

"Do you find what happened to me funny, Detective?" I asked, trying for a withering tone, but really just sounding sad.

Any trace of the smile, real or imagined, vanished.

"Uh, no. Of course not." His face took on an earnest expression as he removed a neat leather notebook and a stylish Mont Blanc from the lapel of his jacket. "I'm here to talk to you about your husband, Marcus Raine. About what happened at his office this morning." He flipped open a wallet and I saw his gold shield and identification card.

In my relief to talk to someone official about what had happened, I unspooled the string of events that had occurred. I noticed that he tried to interrupt me a couple of times by lifting his hand. I ignored him, kept going. I almost couldn't stop myself. I couldn't stop until he knew every horrible detail, as though getting it out, getting it on paper, would be the first step toward understanding, solving, fixing everything that had broken since Marcus didn't come home last night. He dutifully scribbled in his notebook as I ran through everything. I heard his phone vibrating in his pocket a couple of times but, to his credit, he didn't answer it. Occasionally, there were two of him, the real man and his doppelgänger, the shadowy double my brutalized brain was creating.

He asked a lot of questions: What led me to believe the people who stormed the office were there in an official capacity initially? The vests with FBI emblazoned in their centers. No, I didn't ask for identification. Could I describe any of them? Yes, and I did so to the best of my memory. Would I be able to identify any of them from photographs? I think so, yes. Did my husband have enemies? Any illegal dealings that I knew of? Anyone who would want to cause harm to him, me, or the business? No, no, no, no, and no.

"What do you think she meant by that?" the detective asked finally, when we reached a lull. He'd stopped writing at some point, stood now with his legs spread a bit, his arms crossed in front of him, like a beat cop on a corner.

"How should I know?" I said, annoyed. "I've never seen her before in my life."

"But she knew your husband?"

I wasn't sure how to answer; it was a loaded question. "Her statement seemed to imply that, yes," I said finally.

The detective appeared to want to pace, kept turning a bit at the shoulder, but there wasn't much room. He could only walk a step or two in each direction. I could hear his phone buzzing again.

"How was your marriage in general?" he said gently. "Sorry. I know it's personal."

"I don't understand." But I did.

"Were there problems?"

I saw a ring on his finger, a thick gold band. "Are there problems in *your* marriage?" I asked nastily.

"Yes, there are," he said, perching on the stool that my sister had been using. "Mainly, I'm the problem. Or so I'm told. Separated more than a year, legally divorced three months ago, can't bring myself to take off the ring. Stupid, right? She's already engaged to someone else. Getting married in a week."

I heard the hard edge of Brooklyn in his accent, Brooklyn in a prep-school cage. The gentleman cop with his nice clothes and fancy pen, but underneath he was a kid from the neighborhood, no doubt about it.

"Point is, I never saw it coming. I thought we were going to the Bahamas for our anniversary," he said. "She's going to the Bahamas on her honeymoon with another cop she met at the precinct Christmas party. How about that?"

I didn't know what I'd done to deserve so much unwanted candor. Maybe it was just his shtick.

"Our marriage was fine. Not perfect," I said with a shrug. "He had a brief affair a couple of years ago. It was long over. This is not about that."

He gave a careful nod, rubbed at his chin but didn't hold my gaze, seemed to look at some point above me. His eyes were so black that I couldn't discern the pupil from the iris. I wanted to lie back down, I was feeling so light-headed—but I couldn't stand the vulnerability of it. I stayed upright.

"And all that stolen computer equipment. Brand-new, right?" he said.

"Yes, that's right. Over a hundred thousand dollars' worth."

"There was another break-in, right? Last month?"

"Yes," I said slowly.

"Was there an insurance payout?"

I saw how things were adding up for Detective Crowe. "Where are you going with this?"

"Was there?"

"Yes," I said. "A check for about a hundred and fifty thousand arrived—" I couldn't bring myself to finish the sentence.

"This week sometime?"

"It came Monday."

"And where's that money now?"

"Probably in the business bank account. I don't have much to do with Marcus's company. I don't know."

"Software, right? Razor Technologies."

"That's right." An angry headache was starting, radiating out from the gash on my temple. The pain traveled down my neck and into my shoulders. The drugs they'd given me must have been wearing off.

"What kind of software?"

"Gaming software. They're freelance designers, creating games for a variety of systems, as well as for cell phones and personal computers."

"They do well?"

"It has been very lucrative. They sold a PC game to Sony last year called *The Spear of Destiny* and it was wildly popular, in fact. They have other clients, too. Smaller."

"Like who?"

I searched my memory for names of other companies Marcus might have mentioned but I couldn't remember. "I don't know," I said finally.

"You don't know?" He looked at me with a skeptical frown and a quick cock of the head.

"You know, I honestly don't have that much to do with Razor Tech. And Marcus is really the brains of the company, conceptualizing games, writing the code, and running the business. Rick Marino, his partner, does most of the client interface." Distantly, I remembered Rick Marino in handcuffs. But I hadn't asked myself what happened to him if the people who stormed the office were not FBI agents. The possibilities lurked in the periphery of my awareness, nagging but not acknowledged.

The detective scribbled something in his book.

"Look," I said, starting to feel a terrible constricting in my chest. "Something awful has happened to my husband. Are you going to *help* us?"

"Mrs. Raine," he said softly. "I *am* here to help you. But I need to know everything about this situation before I can determine what happened to your husband."

I nodded and finally decided it was time to lie back. He reached to help me but I held up a hand. I didn't want him to touch me.

"Is there family we can call, somewhere or someone he might have gone to without telling you?"

I shook my head. "Marcus doesn't have any family. His parents died when he was a boy. He was raised by his mother's sister in the Czech Republic. He came to the U.S. as soon as he was able to after communism fell in 1989, earned a scholarship to Columbia and worked various jobs as he went to school, got his master's in computer science." I found myself smiling a little. I had always been so proud of Marcus, of his intelligence, of his strength and fearlessness, of his machinelike drive toward getting what he wanted. Even when all these things had worked against us as a couple, I was still proud of him.

"Was he having any problems with anyone? Colleagues? Clients?"

"Not that he mentioned," I said. Then: "Well . . . the earlier break-in? Whoever it was had a key and knew the alarm code. That was strange."

"A disgruntled employee?"

I nodded. "There was an investigation. Still ongoing, I think. The police were looking at a programmer Marcus had fired a few weeks earlier. He'd made some threats. I don't remember his name."

"I'll look into it."

I was staring at the ceiling, willing myself to be strong, to be solid. But I kept seeing dark spots in front of my eyes, feeling that fuzzy, light feeling that comes right before you pass out. I tried to measure my breathing.

"You okay?" I heard the detective ask.

I opened my eyes and glanced toward the two of him—the solid one and the blurry, shadowy figure behind him. "Do I look okay to you?"

"No," he said, shaking his head. "Not really. I'm sorry." He put the cap on his pen, let his hand drop to his lap.

"If those people weren't FBI agents," I said when he didn't say anything else, "then what happened to Rick Marino? He was there with me; they took him away. I thought he was being arrested."

"Rick Marino is dead," he said simply. His delivery could have used a little work. I could tell he thought it was better not to soften the blow, that it was a policy he'd decided on long ago. He continued speaking into the stunned silence, where I was having trouble processing the information and forming an appropriate response.

"We found his body in the office along with the bodies of two other employees—Eileen Charlton and Ronald Falco."

I tried to visualize their faces, to think of the last time I'd seen them. The company party we'd had at our apartment last year. Eileen was a game designer and artist. She was petite, bookish with round wire-rimmed glasses. I remembered Ronald, a sound engineer, as lanky and shy with a mild stutter. Were either of them married? Did they have kids? I couldn't remember.

"I'm sorry," he added, an afterthought.

"What's happening?" I asked, my voice catching in my throat, coming out in a raspy whisper.

"We'll find out," he said, putting away his pad and pen. I could see he believed it but I already had the sense of a yawning black abyss opening in my life. I was about to tumble in and I really didn't think Detective Grady Crowe was going to be of much help. I could already see he was out of his depth. I just didn't realize yet that I was, too.

WHEN I TOLD my sister that Marcus and I were getting married, I didn't get the reaction I expected. She didn't know Marcus well yet, it was true. Our courtship had been short and intense. But I had fallen, hard and headlong. And he seemed to have, as well; he proposed just a few months after we'd met.

He took me to Prague and we stayed in the Four Seasons near Mala Strana. We'd rented a car and driven about an a hour to the small town where he'd been born and had lived until he left for good. There was no family for me to meet. His mother's sister, the aunt who'd raised him, had died a year earlier, he explained, after suffering from ovarian cancer.

But we wandered through the quaint cobblestone streets with the tourists, stopping in shops and having a local beer at the pub. He knew everything about the history of the town, Kutná Hora, once the second most important town in Bohemia because of its silver mines, now just a side trip tourists make while visiting Prague.

He spoke with the locals in Czech, explained to me how things had been during the communist era. How there were lines around this block for oranges that had come from Cuba, how this thriving store once was just a hollow space with empty shelves, how the communist propaganda had been taught in that tiny school.

On the way back to the city we stopped at a small Bohemian restaurant which, with its heavy oak tables, wood paneling, and thick ceiling beams, could have been plucked from the Middle Ages, if it weren't for the jukebox and the young thugs smoking cigarettes and drinking enormous glasses of beer at the bar. The waiter brought a giant cast-iron platter of meat and potatoes. We ate until we were stuffed.

He'd been quiet all day. Not sullen or morose; just contemplative, maybe a bit sad. I just assumed that it was hard for him to be back in the place where he grew up, where so much had been lost—his parents, his aunt. I didn't press him to talk.

"Isabel," he said when we were done with our meal and waiting for our dessert. His accent was heavier than I'd ever heard it, had been since we'd arrived in the Czech Republic, as if being home, speaking his native language, reconnected him to a part of himself he'd neglected, even tried to quash. "I never thought I'd bring anyone here. Never thought I'd want to."

"I'm glad you shared this with me," I said. "I feel so much closer to you." He was looking at me attentively; I felt heat rise to my cheeks. He wasn't handsome, not beautiful in the classic sense. But his intensity, the hard features of his face, had a kind of magnetic power that lit me up inside. He dropped his eyes to the table.

"I want to share *everything* with you," he said softly. He reached into his pocket and slid a blue velvet box across the table toward me. "Isabel. Maybe it's too fast. I don't care. I could have done this the night I met you."

I opened the box to see a gleaming, cushion-cut ruby in a platinum setting. It was breathtaking.

"Isabel," he whispered, grabbing both my hands. "This is my heart. I'm giving it to you. I'd die for you. Marry me."

I remember being stunned but nodding vigorously, tearing as he put the ring on my finger and came to kneel beside me and take me into his arms. People around us looked on; one woman, another American—I could tell by her Tommy Hilfiger sweater and khaki pants, but mainly by her sneakers—clapped her hands and released a happy little cry.

What had I expected to feel in that moment? I didn't know. You see it from the outside, stylized and engineered to sell in films and commercials. You hear the stories your sisters and girlfriends tell. But you only know how it's *meant* to feel. It's one of those moments in your life, in your relationship—the markers, the milestones, the important snapshots. But I could only experience the moment as I experience everything, observing, narrating. How Marcus was as close to emotional as I'd ever seen him. How the men at the bar turned to look at us, one of them sneering. How the lights were too dim for me to really see the ring. How a truck passed by and caused the bottles on the shelves behind the bar to rattle slightly. And I observed myself: happy, surprised, and, dare I admit it, a little relieved that my life wouldn't pass without this moment. From the outside, I supposed it looked very romantic. But that's where romance dwells, isn't it, in the observation? Inner life is far too complicated; one doesn't *feel* romance. You feel *love,* and even that isn't one note resounding above all others; it's one element in the symphony of your emotions.

"I DON'T UNDERSTAND," my sister said. "You barely know him."

Marcus and I had announced our engagement over dinner at my sister's, and Linda and Erik had made all the appropriate noises; embraces were exchanged, there was the excited chatter about plans and when and where. But later in my sister's bedroom while Marcus, Erik, and the kids tried out a new computer game Marcus was testing, Linda and I had the real conversation. I knew it was coming, of course, I'd seen her shoulders tense, noticed the brittle quality to her smile, the worried eyes.

"When it's right, you know," I said with a shrug. "Right?"

That's when she started to cry, just tear a little, really. But still, it was enough to cause disappointment, and not a little anxiety, to wash over me.

"I thought you liked him," I said, sinking onto the bed beside her.

"Izzy," she said, raising her eyes to the ceiling, then lowering them to mine. She took my hand. "He's just so . . . cold. There's something unavailable about him, something distant."

I shook my head. "You just need to get to know him better," I told her. "That's all. It's a cultural difference." But there was a hard knot in my middle.

She nodded and tried to smile. "Just take your time with the wedding. *You* get to know him a little bit more before you dive in."

I felt a lash of anger then. "You know what I think, Linda?"

"Don't," she said, lifting her hand.

"I think you don't really want me to be happy in a relationship."

"Stop it, Isabel."

I lowered my voice to a whisper. I didn't want everyone else to hear. "I think you're happier when I'm *unhappy*. That you're more comfortable when I'm alone so that you can be the one with everything—the great career, the perfect family."

"That's bullshit," she spat, "and you know it. You *know* I'm right. That's why you're so angry. Christ, Isabel, he's just like our father."

If I didn't love my sister so much, I would have slapped her. Instead, I got up and walked out of the room.

"Izzy," she called after me. I heard apology in her voice but I didn't care. I told Marcus I wasn't feeling well and we left soon thereafter.

I didn't talk to my sister for almost two weeks—which felt more like two years. Eventually, she called to borrow a pair of shoes and things went back to normal—no apologies, no discussion, no resolution, just water under the bridge. Marcus and I were married six months later in a small church up in Riverdale near my mother and stepfather's home. An intimate gathering of my family and friends followed. Marcus didn't have anyone to invite. At the time, it didn't really seem strange or sad. I don't recall thinking about it. We were happy; that was the only important thing.

5

Detective Grady Crowe stepped out onto Seventh Avenue, leaving St. Vincent's Hospital. He pulled his leather coat together and brought the zipper up beneath his chin, took the black knit cap from his pocket and slid it over his close-cropped hair.

It was rush hour. The streets were packed even downtown with people hustling back and forth, huddled against the frigid air. It was a Village crowd, hipper, more casual than what he'd see if he'd found himself in Midtown at this hour. Messenger bags slung across chests instead of briefcases gripped in tight fists, leather instead of cashmere, denim instead of gabardine.

He'd always liked the lower part of Manhattan best. He considered it more the real New York than Midtown, but less the real city than, say, Brooklyn. Shop windows glittered with Christmas decoration, horns sang in the bumper-to-bumper river of traffic on the avenue. In the air he could smell the wood of someone's fireplace burning. He always liked that smell, especially in the city. It made the streets seem less hard, less impersonal when you could imagine someone cozy at the hearth, maybe drinking a cup of tea.

He weaved his way across Twelfth Street through the stopped traffic toward the waiting unmarked Caprice. Exhaust billowed from behind, glowing red in the parking lights. His partner sat talking on her cell phone, her Bluetooth actually—a little device clipped to her ear which also had a microphone. From a distance, it made her look like nothing so much as a schizophrenic having a passionate conversation with herself. He'd told her this. She'd called him a Luddite. He kept meaning to look it up.

Inside the car, the heat was kicking. His partner, Jez, kept it at nearly eighty degrees in the winter. She was small, couldn't stand the cold. He didn't complain. He'd been raised to give women what they wanted. *You can fight,* his father told him. *You can bitch. If you're a real prick, you can overpower. But the pain over the long haul? Just not worth it, son. Surrender young and happily with fewer scars.* The old man was right about that. And with three sisters, Grady had occasion to learn early. But it was his wife who drove the lesson home—then drove off in his new Acura. Turns out lip service isn't enough; you have to *live* the surrender.

"So . . . what happened?"

Crowe pulled out into traffic, cutting off a cabdriver who leaned on his horn.

"Crowe?"

"You talking to me? I thought you were still on your *communicator.* You know—beam me up, Scotty." He tried to add some electronic sounds to the joke but it came off lame. Jez gave him a smile, anyway. She was cool like that.

"Very funny. Yeah, I'm talking to you. What'd you get?"

In the movies, female cops were always hot. But on the real job, to Grady's eyes, they were generally pretty butch—dirty mouths, pumped biceps, chopped hair. Jesamyn Breslow was the exception, though he wouldn't say she was *hot* exactly. She was cute. Definitely on the femme side comparatively speaking. But in spite of that button nose and blond bob, she was tough in a very real way, minus the self-conscious bravado of most cops, male or female. She knew kung fu. Really.

He relayed the story the victim had told him about her husband not coming home, about the phone call, and the people posing as FBI agents. It gelled with what they'd found, the vests discarded at the scene with the white letters stenciled on. It was a rush job. Someone who hadn't already been distraught and overwhelmed might have noticed right away that the letters were sloppy, unprofessional.

"She thinks she'd be able to identify some of the people if she saw them again, but beyond that she doesn't know anything about what happened, or why," he said, reaching for the coffee in the cup holder. It was as bitter and stone cold as his ex-wife. He drank it, anyway.

"You sure? You know you're a sucker for a pretty face." They'd seen her picture on Marcus Raine's desk. Jez had recognized her, was actually carrying a paperback of one of her novels in her bag. Isabel Connelly, her maiden name, on the jacket. Not Isabel Raine, her legal, married name.

"I'm sure," he said. "She was a mess."

Isabel Raine looked like a doll someone had dropped by the side of the road—bashed up, broken, and abandoned. He'd had the urge to dust her off, tuck her into a little bed somewhere.

"Where are we going?" she asked.

"She gave us permission to look around her apartment. Said she'd call the doorman to let us in."

"No lawyer?"

"Not yet. She's focused on finding her husband. She thinks that's the major problem, that he's missing and something's happened to him."

"Maybe she really doesn't know anything."

He gave her a quick glance, raised his eyebrows at her. "I've still got my wits about me. Not all your partners fall in love with the victim and go off the deep end." He was referring to Mateo Stenopolis, her partner when she was with Missing Persons. Stenopolis had fallen in love with a missing girl and pretty much laid waste to his life and his career trying to find her—nearly getting himself and Breslow killed in the process.

"No," she said with a laugh. "You're no romantic, Crowe."

"Just ask my ex-wife."

He listened as Breslow called her mother, told her she'd be late picking up her son, Benjamin. He found himself thinking that it was the one small mercy in his failed marriage—no kids. He saw how Breslow struggled with her on-again, off-again husband and the child they shared. You're bound forever by that life you created. As it was, there was nothing to bind him to his ex, nothing at all. They split what little money there was and that was that. He'd wanted kids, a lot of them. But she hadn't—maybe one, eventually. She was concerned about her career, didn't want to be a stay-at-home mom like her mother, not on a cop's salary. His mom had raised four on far less than he made, had never even had a job. She'd gone straight from her parents' home to her husband's. Bringing this up didn't make things better.

"Those were different times, Grady," she'd countered. "Besides, you think your mother's happy? I've never heard your parents exchange one kind word—hell, I've never even seen them kiss each other."

She was always talking about "happy" like it was a lottery she was waiting to win. As far as Grady was concerned, happiness was just where you decided to lay your eyes. You see three people dead in a downtown office, their faces contorted in such a way that you understand they died in agony, you feel bad. You go home and find the woman you love and your kids waiting for you, you feel happy. That simple.

"Obsessing about your ex again?" asked his partner, examining her cuticles.

"How could you tell?"

"You make this kind of tiny chewing motion with your jaw, like you're biting on your tongue a little. You do that whenever you're working some kind of problem in your head."

"You don't know everything," he said.

"No. I don't. But a year sitting here and I'm getting to know *you.* My advice: If you can't let it go, get help. It's turning you into a sour pain in the ass. You talk about it constantly and you think about it more. Move on, Crowe."

"Thanks, Dr. Phil." He knew she was right. He was a dog with a bone; he just couldn't stop worrying it, looking for that last bit of marrow.

Apparently satisfied that she'd made her point, she went back to business. "I put the information we had on Marcus Raine—date of birth, Social Security number—into NCIC and Vi-CAP. I'm waiting to see what comes back."

"The wife seems convinced that he's a victim in this. She's seriously rattled by that phone call, thinks it was him screaming."

"What do we believe?" she asked, really just thinking aloud.

"Could go either way. We need to dig deeper."

THEY PULLED UP to Isabel Raine's building and parked in the half-circle drive. The doorman was expecting them, gave them a key and told them to take the elevator to the ninth floor. Crowe was a little surprised by the lack of questions, but the doorman was as stoic and grim-faced as a gargoyle, his silver hair slicked back so perfectly it looked shellacked. He apparently had his orders from Isabel Raine and wasn't interested in anything further. Crowe could see he was an old-school New York City doorman, served the tenants of the building, kept his mouth shut except for niceties, and collected his big Christmas tips.

"When was the last time you saw Marcus Raine?" Crowe asked him, after writing down his name, telephone number, and address. Charlie Shane lived up in Inwood, the northernmost neighborhood in Manhattan, almost the Bronx.

"Yesterday morning, just after nine," Shane answered immediately. "He was heading off to work, I assumed. His departure was only notable because it was later than usual. Generally, he's gone by seven. Mrs. Raine works from home and comes and goes during the day unpredictably." Something about the way he leaned on that last word told Grady that, in Shane's world, unpredictability was not a good thing.

Crowe was about to ask about Shane's schedule but the doorman anticipated the question. "I work Monday through Saturday, from six A.M. to six P.M., sometimes later. I've worked in this building for twenty-five years."

Grady looked at his watch. "Working late tonight?" he asked. It was going on seven o'clock.

"The night-shift doorman, Timothy Teaford, hasn't arrived," said Shane. "I can't leave until he does."

"He call?"

"No."

"Unusual behavior?"

"Actually, yes."

"Can I get the name and address of this guy?"

"There are two other part-time doormen who take the evening shifts and rotate the Sunday shifts. But naturally, they don't have the same relationship with the tenants and the building that I do."

"Of course not," Crowe said gravely. "I'll still need their names and contact information."

"Of course, sir."

Crowe saw Breslow looking around at the lobby that opened into a courtyard with a tall stone fountain turned off for the winter. She had the class not to gawk or comment, but he could tell she was impressed. He'd seen plenty of lobbies like this one—the high ceilings, the marble floors, the large pieces of art, the plush furniture. He was Bay Ridge born and raised, working class to the bone, but had attended Regis High School in Manhattan. Regis had competitive admissions, tuition free to those who got in, so the socioeconomic structure was more diverse than at other area prep schools. But plenty of his friends and classmates were the children of the very wealthy, were now the very wealthy themselves—doctors, lawyers, writers, newscasters. He could be living like they were. But Grady had always wanted to be a cop like his father.

After Regis, he attended New York University, though he'd been accepted at Princeton, Georgetown, and Cornell. He just didn't understand spending all that money. Even with the partial scholarships he'd been offered at those schools, the tuition seemed staggering. His parents would have helped, but it would have left nothing for his sisters. NYU gave him a free ride. He joined the NYPD as soon as he graduated.

He had the sense that his family was disappointed. They'd expected something more. His father was the least pleased of all. "All that hard work you put in," he lamented. "You could have gone to public, skipped college altogether, if all you wanted out of your life was to chase skells." Like most blue-collar guys, his father had a strict and simple formula for determining success: income minus effort. Police work was hard and dangerous and you'd never get rich as an honest cop. It was bad math. You ended up giving more than you got. But the Jesuits didn't measure success that way; neither did Grady.

Because of his education, because of a year doing the most dangerous work on a South Bronx buy-and-bust detail, and because of one flashy arrest, he got his gold shield fast. Five years on the job and he was a homicide detective. Too fast for some of the guys with more years on. Because of this, Grady wasn't as popular as his old man had been. "Fuck them," his dad advised. "They're crabs in a barrel, people like that."

After Shane gave them the names and contact information of the other doormen, Grady and Breslow took the elevator up to the ninth floor and walked down the long hallway over plush carpet.

"I think we're in the wrong line of work," Jez said, running a finger along the wall.

"No doubt about it," Grady answered, just to be sociable. He appreciated nice things—good clothes, upscale restaurants—but he was unimpressed by opulence. He knocked heavily on the door, modulated his voice to be deeper than it normally was.

"NYPD. Open up, please." He knocked again hard for emphasis.

They waited a full thirty seconds, knocked one more time, then

Grady unlocked the door and pushed it open. He could see from where they stood that a vase lay shattered in the entrance hallway.

They moved to either side of the door, drew their weapons, and stepped carefully inside. They went through the apartment, room by room, checking closets, making sure the place was empty. When they were sure it was, they holstered their weapons. Jesamyn called for uniforms and a crime-scene team.

The stunning duplex with its hardwood floors and high ceilings, gleaming gourmet kitchen, second-floor master bedroom suite, had been trashed. Furniture was slashed, drapes shredded, shelves dumped, pictures shattered. Grady could see that two computer CPUs—one in the upstairs office off the bedroom and the other at a desk in the kitchen downstairs—were gone, monitors left with cords cut, just like at Razor Tech. A file cabinet hidden inside a closet stood completely empty, drawers gaping like mouths. In the master bathroom, someone had dumped a bottle of red nail polish over a framed black-and-white photo of Isabel Raine walking on the beach with a big dog and two kids. The polish was not quite dry.

Back downstairs, Grady surveyed the living room. Somehow the damage inflicted seemed angry, frenetic. A row of family photos had been swept from a shelf and stomped upon, cushions had been slashed, bleeding white stuffing. A chinz couch had been scribbled on with indelible marker. It seemed a lot more personal than the damage done in the office space.

As Grady stepped further into the room, he heard glass crunching beneath his feet. He looked down to see a ruined photograph of Isabel and Marcus Raine. She had her arms wrapped around his neck, her head thrown back in laughter, while Marcus stared directly at the camera, his eyes serious, his smile just a slight turning up of the corners of his mouth. The frame had been stomped on, the glass directly over Isabel Raine's face was smashed. But Marcus Raine's face, somehow, was untouched.

Jesamyn came to stand beside him. "Wow," she said, looking around the wreckage. "Someone's *angry.*"

He gazed at Isabel's smashed image. "Very," he said. "Very angry."

"So how'd they get in?"

They looked at each other.

"One of the doormen," said Breslow, answering her own question, as they moved quickly from the apartment. Grady paused to lock the door behind him as Jez moved down the hall to call the elevator.

"The six P.M. to six A.M. guy hadn't shown up yet when we arrived," said Crowe as the doors shut and the elevator moved down the shaft. "That polish in the bathroom was still wet. They were here during Shane's shift."

"Twelve-hour shifts?" mused Breslow. "Is that legal?"

"I don't know," said Crowe. "I guess that's the job. You do it or you don't."

"Who signs on for twelve hours of catering to rich people, letting in their maids, accepting packages, dry cleaning?"

"The doorman gig; it's like a *thing,* you know. An identity. A history of service."

"Service to the rich? No thanks."

Crowe didn't think their job was that different. Protect and serve. Not just the rich, no, but the rich always wound up getting the best service—the fastest response time, the most respect—didn't they? Even from the cops. If your brother plays golf with the senator, then people care when your daughter gets raped or your wife mugged. In the projects, girls are raped, people robbed every day. It doesn't make the news. Sometimes the uniforms don't even show. When they do, their disdain, their apathy is apparent. Not always, but often enough. He worked the South Bronx for years; he knew how those guys felt about the perps, and the vics, too. Attitudes were very different in Midtown North, where the rich lived and worked.

Charlie Shane was gone when they arrived back in the lobby. His replacement was a skinny, disshelved-looking guy with a five o'clock shadow and an untended shrub of dirty-blond hair.

Crowe pulled out his notebook and flipped through a couple of pages to find the guy's name. He wrote down everything in his notebook—details, thoughts, observations, questions. He figured it would come in handy one day when he wrote his novel. Until then it kept him sharp; writing down what people told him helped his recall. What he couldn't recall was always there.

"Timothy Teaford?" he said as they approached.

"Yeah," he said. He seemed even younger up close, and sleepier. Crowe noticed a tattoo snaking out of his cuff, looked like one of those tribal bands that were so popular these days. Crowe identified himself, explained the situation as Breslow made some more calls.

"That's messed up," Teaford said. "They're nice people. Good tippers."

"Late for work today?"

"I've been sick," he said. "Missed my shift last night. Flu."

Crowe felt Breslow shifting backward slightly. She was totally germphobic. "You don't have kids," she'd said when he first teased her about this. "Benjy gets a cold? That can trash two weeks—sleepless nights, ear infection if it doesn't go away, trips to the doctor. A flu? Forget about it."

"Can anyone confirm you were home last night?"

He shrugged. "My girlfriend brought me Taco Bell and we watched a movie. She spent the night."

"So who covered your shift here?"

"I don't know," he said. "I called in. I don't know who he got to cover."

"Who's 'he'?"

"Charlie Shane. He's the supervisor."

Grady looked back through his notes. Shane didn't mention Teaford missing his shift, only that he'd been late this evening.

"Where is he now? Still in the building?"

"Actually, the weird thing is, he wasn't here when I showed up. No one was. The door was locked and the desk was empty. One of the residents had to let me in."

"Unusual behavior for him?"

"Uh, *yeah,*" said Teaford. "I swear that guy would put a cot in the office and live here if they'd let him." He issued the sentence not with mockery but with a kind of youthful wonder, as if job dedication was something he just didn't understand, something from another era, like dinosaurs. "Honestly, I can't imagine him leaving the desk until someone showed up."

"Did he leave a note?" Breslow asked. She'd ended her call with Dispatch and was poised to dial again.

Teaford shook his head. He really was a mess—his uniform wrinkled, some kind of old washed-in stain on his collar. Crowe could see a little yellow crust in his eye. But there was something sweet about him, something innocent and appealing.

"You got a way to reach him?" Crowe asked.

Teaford leaned down, squinted, and read a number that Crowe could see was taped on the desk. Jez dialed and waited. "Voice mail," she said after a minute.

"Mr. Shane, this is NYPD Detective Jesamyn Breslow. You need to call us or return to the building immediately." She left her number.

"All the time I been here, I never got voice mail on that number. He *always* answers," Teaford said with a concerned frown. "You think he's okay?"

Crowe wasn't as worried about Shane's well-being as he was about not having had an instinct about the guy, about one of them not staying down here while the other went up. Not that it would have been smart, or even protocol, for one of them to enter the apartment alone, especially considering what they found.

"I called for uniformed officers to go wait at Shane's apartment in the unlikely event that he just went home," said Jez. She was all action, no dwelling on mistakes or wasting time second-guessing. She just worked in the present tense. He'd read somewhere that this quality, the ability to operate in the framework of how things are, not how you wish they were or think they should be, was the factor that separated those who survived extreme circumstances from those who didn't. He might have brooded for ten more minutes before doing what she'd already done.

She was at the elevator, clicking her pen vigorously on the palm of her hand, a very annoying nervous habit she had, as he finished getting Teaford's girlfriend's name, address, and phone number and telling him to stay put. Teaford looked scared when Crowe glanced back at him, but he didn't look guilty, not to Crowe. But what did he know? He'd already made one mistake in judgment; it wasn't so far-fetched that he'd make another.

"Stop fuming, Crowe," Jez told him. "We couldn't have known." She'd stepped into the elevator and was holding the door.

"It's our job to know."

"That's where you're wrong. It's our job to *find out*."

He looked back at the doorman, who was now talking on his cell phone. "I'll wait down here until the uniforms arrive."

"Suit yourself." She released the doors.

"Don't touch anything until the techs get here," he said. He saw her roll her eyes as the doors shut.

A minute later, he heard the approach of cruisers—this wasn't an emergency call, but cops liked to turn on lights and sirens to get around fast, to have some fun in an otherwise slow precinct. He remembered the adrenaline rush of the car speeding through the city streets, especially at night. It was the coolest feeling in the world, as if everything else gave way while you raced into the fray. Sometimes they'd turn down their radios so they couldn't hear when a chase had been called off, when they'd been ordered to let the perp—car thief, armed robber, whatever kind of scumbag—get away instead of risk civilian lives on the street with a car chase. They wanted to catch the skell they were pursuing; the adrenaline and testosterone racing through their systems demanded release, satisfaction. This was why so many car chases ended with the perp getting the crap kicked out of him. This was why the chases got called off.

His father frowned on this type of behavior. “The heroes are the guys that come home every night to their families,” he used to say, “who protect themselves and their partners so that they can live to be the men their wives and children need.”

Crowe heard the wisdom of this, but when you were doing eighty on Broadway, and the sirens were wailing, and some guy was bleeding out in a liquor store, shot by the punk trying to get away with it, you just forgot.

6

I woke up the next morning in my sister's guest room. I wasn't alone. Emily and the family dog, Brown, had both climbed into the queen-size bed and made themselves at home. Brown was on my feet, and Emily had spooned her narrow body up against me. I was glad for the company. Otherwise, the despair that swept over me in the moments after I opened my eyes might have washed me away entirely.

I had the dark thought that I wished that blow to the temple *had* killed me. It would have been easier than swimming the ocean of grief and fear and wonder that surely lay ahead. I squeezed Emily closer to me, drew in the scent of her shampoo.

The pain medication I took after the detective left the night before had successfully erased the questions he'd asked and their implications for the remainder of the evening. Now the physical pain had returned, and with it, his words. My agitation grew and, finally, I slipped from the bed. Emily didn't stir but Brown lifted his sad Labrador eyes. He issued a grunt to let me know I'd disturbed him and then moved into the space I'd occupied before closing his eyes again. He was Emily's dog; where she went, Brown followed.

I took off the pink flannel pajamas I was wearing—Linda's "mommy pajamas"—unflatteringly baggy, ultra soft from a thousand washes, with some kind of indeterminate washed-in stain on the sleeve. I didn't remember putting them on. I climbed into my clothes from yesterday, which were lying on the chair by the window, and quietly left the room. It was my plan to leave without waking anyone; otherwise, I knew they'd try to stop me and probably succeed. I needed to leave, get back to my own apartment, start trying to understand what was happening. But Erik was already up, drinking coffee at the bar that separated the kitchen from the living room.

Their home was a spacious loft, with high ceilings and tall windows. The morning sun, bright and warm, entered unabated by blinds. The room, decorated with simple, low furniture in bone and brown tones, large-format oils painted by my sister—a talented painter as well as a gifted photographer—on the walls, eclectic pieces of sculpture from their various travels, was once as clean and elegant as the interior of a museum. But they'd been invaded, their evolved sense of style sacked and pillaged by the smaller members of the family.

Trevor's T-shirt was draped over the chaise. A tall pile of Emily's books threatened to topple from the suede couch (which also sported a grape-juice stain that had never been successfully removed). There was a small stuffed chair shaped like a hippo and a video game system attached to the large flat screen, an unfinished game of Monopoly on the cocktail table. Brown's doggy bed was covered with his hair. The stainless-steel refrigerator, visible from where I stood, was covered with drawings, magnets, pictures, and stickers.

I didn't say anything to Erik, just moved over to my bag, which slouched by the door, checked to see if my keys and wallet were in there. It was then that I noticed my ring was gone. I stared at my naked hand, the indentation on my finger. How could I not have noticed it before? I looked up at my brother-in-law, who was watching me from the stool where he perched.

"Did you take it off at the hospital?"

He didn't ask what I meant. "No," he said gently. "It was gone when we first got to you. I'm sorry, Iz. Your sister realized right away. We just thought—why say anything until you noticed. Insult to injury."

I saw her face again, the woman at Marc's office—that pitying, disdainful expression. *That bitch took my ring.*

Erik had come over to me while he was talking. I let him put his arm around my shoulders and lead me over to the couch. As I sat down heavily, Emily's pile of books softly tumbled to the floor. We let them lie. In the corner of the room a massive Christmas tree was a riot of ornaments and multicolored lights. Its manic twinkling was too much for my tired eyes.

"I don't think it's a good idea for you to leave," he said. I noticed purple circles under his eyes, an unfamiliar stiffness to his mouth.

"I have to go home, Erik," I said. "I have to . . ." I let the sentence trail.

"What?"

"I don't know," I snapped. I wanted to rage but I managed to keep my voice low. I didn't want to wake my sister; I didn't want to look into her worried face. "Search the apartment? Look for clues? Find out what the hell happened to my husband?"

He nodded his understanding. "The police are working on that. You need to take care of yourself right now." He tapped his temple, reminding me of the wound on my head. "Let *us* take care of you."

I stood suddenly and moved back toward the door. He didn't try to stop me; it wasn't his style. He was the kind of guy who said his piece and then backed off, let people make their own decisions. He sank into the place where I had sat a moment earlier.

"There's something, Izzy," he said as I was lifting my bag and reaching for the lock. He rubbed his eyes and released a breath. "I've been debating whether or not to tell you."

I felt a thump of dread in my center. "What?"

He kept his head down for a second and then looked up, not at me but at a point above me. Something about his expression caused me to return to him, to sit kitty-corner from him in the chair. He'd been a brother to me since he fell in love with Linda. I loved him for that, for the father he was, and for the husband he was to my sister.

"I gave Marcus money. A lot of it."

He was fair like Marcus, but with a boyish sweetness to him, a bright, open look to his face, where Marcus might seem stern. Marcus's body was hard, no fat, sinewy. Erik's body, while lean and toned, had a softness to it. His embrace was a comfort in a way that Marcus's wasn't. You could sink into Erik; he enfolded you. Marcus's body held its boundaries, almost pushed you away. I noticed these things about my husband and my sister's husband. Was I comparing them? Only in the way of the observer, defining things by their differences, seeking the telling details.

"I don't understand," I said. But I was starting to, slowly.

He cleared his throat and I noticed that his hands were shaking a little. "About a month ago, he came to me and said he needed investors. He had a new game in development and when it was finished it was going to revolutionize gaming, take things to a whole new level of realism."

I shook my head slightly. I had no idea what he was talking about. Marcus had never mentioned anything like that to me.

"He showed me," he said, pointing over to the flat screen mounted on the wall. "The graphics, they were . . . *amazing.* There's no other word for it." He kept his eyes on the screen as if he was still seeing the images there. "He said people in on the ground floor stood to double their investment, at least. He wanted Linda and me to benefit from that. I had no reason to doubt him, you know? He was family. His business was already a big success."

"How much did you give him, Erik?" I said, reaching for his hand.

"A half a million," he said, pulling his hand back and resting his head on it.

He knocked the wind out of me; I released a big rush of air. I thought about a recent conversation I'd had with my sister—about private-school tuition for Emily and Trevor, about building maintenance, taxes, health insurance, life insurance, car insurance, even the parking space for their car—how their cost of living was so high it was painful, even though by most standards they were wealthy people. She said it was crushing her. That was the word she used: *crushing.*

"You guys don't have that kind of money, do you?" I asked. "Just five hundred K lying around?"

"Uh, no," he said. "We don't." He swept his arm to indicate the space around us. "We do okay, but it's not like that. I borrowed against the loft."

My sister was *not* a financial risk taker. She'd paid off the loft years earlier, after her first major gallery show, and the property had steadily been growing in value ever since. My sister was more successful than most, but an artist's income was unpredictable year to year. That loft was her security blanket, her "lifeboat," she called it. It had appreciated wildly over the last decade and was worth a fortune. If everything went to hell financially, they could sell it and live off the money for a good long time. She *needed* that kind of security to be happy, to feel like a good mom. She needed to know that she'd always be able to provide for Trevor and Emily. I knew all the reasons why this was so critical to her mental well-being—and so did Erik.

"Linda would never agree to that," I said.

The color had drained from his face and he'd pressed his mouth into a thin line. Then I understood.

"She doesn't know?" I said.

"You know how Linda is," he said, hanging his head. "She doesn't like to talk about money."

"You did this without *talking* to her?"

He lifted a hand. "It was supposed to be short term, Izzy," he said. He stood up and walked over to one of the tall windows. I glanced uneasily at the door to their bedroom, imagining that I saw Linda there, her hair tousled, her eyes bleary with sleep. *What are you guys talking about?* But the door was firmly closed. He went on, talking so softly that I could barely hear him.

"In two months, Marc said, they'd make the sale, the biggest in the history of Razor Tech. They'd had early interest from two of the big game companies; he expected a bidding war. I'd have my principal investment back plus five hundred thousand more, at least. I'd pay off the loan on the loft and put the rest in the bank. Then we'd have that; she'd have the security she needs. She'd never have to worry again. That's what I was thinking."

"But you couldn't get credit like that without her signature, Erik, could you?"

He'd given up a successful career in information technology after Trevor was born so that Linda could work and the kids wouldn't be cared for by strangers. He'd managed her career, everything from sales to publicity to Web site design and maintenance, taken care of the accounting, helped with the kids. It always seemed like the perfect arrangement, one that made them both very happy. Everything was joint; there were no separate accounts, separate incomes.

"She signed," he said, resting the heels of his hands on the windowsill. The window looked out onto another building of artists' lofts, where many residents shared my sister's aversion to blinds. "She just didn't read what she was signing."

"Oh, Erik." Crushed. I knew my sister; she was going to buckle under the weight of this.

"If it had been *anyone* else, I never would have even considered it," Erik said urgently, turning back to me. He must have seen the look on my face, wanted me to understand. "But Marc's a genius, you know? And he's *family*."

His reverent tone reminded me of a peculiar energy I'd always picked up on between my husband and brother-in-law. Linda had laughingly claimed that Erik had a *boy crush* on Marcus, like Marc was the cool kid at school and Erik just wanted to hang around him. I'd noticed it, too. I'd also observed that Marcus seemed to realize it as well, and how he appeared to enjoy it. But I figured it was harmless—at least they got along. They were buddies, met for drinks after work, took the kids to the country so that Linda and I could spend the day at Bliss, our favorite spa.

"I wasn't trying to deceive her, Izzy. Understand that. I was trying to surprise her."

I didn't know what to say. So I didn't say anything, just stared across the street.

"He was supposed to pay me back yesterday, Izzy. I was supposed to meet him for lunch and he was going to give me a check. But he never showed."

I watched a woman in a loft across the street move through a series of yoga poses, her impossibly thin body limber and strong. Another young woman chased a naked toddler across an apartment on another floor, both of them laughing. It wasn't that I hadn't heard him. I was just waiting for the words to sink in. Their implication echoed all the things Detective Crowe had said and not said the night before.

"He wouldn't cheat you, Erik," I said, my voice sounding weak. "He wouldn't. Something's happened."

Erik nodded, seemed unable to find words. I didn't like the expression on his face. Something dark. Something desperate.

"Did you tell the police?" I asked.

He nodded. "They know; I'm sorry. It felt like a betrayal but it could be . . . relevant."

I wish I could say I was numb from the shock but I wasn't. I felt as if I was standing in the middle of a city that was being bombed from above. I didn't know where to run as everything solid around me crumbled to dust. My body was flooded with adrenaline, in full fight-or-flight response.

Erik rested his hands on my shoulders. "I'm sorry, Izzy. This is not your problem. You have too much to deal with right now. I just didn't want you to find out from the police."

"It is my problem. Of course it's my *problem,* Erik."

"No," he said, closing his eyes and shaking his head. "No."

"Does she know yet?" I asked him.

He released a heavy breath. "Not yet. I need to figure out how to tell her. I . . ." He just kept shaking his head, his eyes opening and drifting over to the closed door of their bedroom where she lay sleeping. He never finished the sentence.

"Don't tell her," I said, leaving him. I grabbed my bag and unlocked the door. "Give me a little time."

"Wait, Izzy," he said, following. "What are you going to do?"

"I don't know," I said. "Something that's not just sitting around here watching all our lives go to hell."

ON THE STREET it felt good to be moving. I walked off the curb and lifted my arm at the sea of traffic that was flowing up Lafayette. An old woman in a dramatic, hot-pink pashmina wrap and long coat walking three white standard poodles stared at me. I remembered the large bandage on my head, lifted a hand to touch it as I slid inside the cab that pulled over.

"Hospital?" the driver wanted to know. I couldn't tell if he was being a smart-ass or not.

"Eighty-sixth between Broadway and Amsterdam," I told him. I wanted to go home, to examine the place that housed my life with Marcus, to tear it apart if necessary, piece by piece, in an effort to find out what had happened to my husband. There was no place for fear or grief in my mind; I was nothing but my hunger to understand what was happening to my life. In the days to come, this single-minded focus, this terrible drive would be responsible for some very bad decisions and horrific outcomes. Of course, I had no way of knowing that as my cab raced uptown; I was just doing what I knew how to do.

7

From three stories above, Linda Book watched her sister hail a cab. She knocked on the window, then struggled to open it, but the damn thing was stuck. It was no use, anyway. Linda could just see the black of Isabel's hair, the white of the bandage on her head as she disappeared and closed the door behind her. She watched the cab speed off, thinking, She's going home, no doubt. Trying to figure it all out. Trying to fix what was broken, to make it right again. Linda released an exasperated breath at her sister's stubborn streak, which was all the more annoying because it was a trait they shared.

She leaned her head against the window for a moment, considered her options: Call her? Chase after her? Leave her be? She decided to leave her to it. Izzy was an unstoppable force. And Linda had children to take care of, to dress and get off to school. More than that, Linda knew that Isabel *had* to do this; there was no other choice for her. It was the curse of the writer, a feral hunger to understand and by understanding to control.

When Linda was just starting out as a photographer, she'd done a series she called "City Faces." She'd walked around the city for weeks, just snapping pictures of people—some candid, some with permission—and wound up with a group of portraits that earned her an agent and her first major gallery show in SoHo. She'd asked her sister to write something for the brochure and they went through the photos together.

"Oh my God, Linda," Izzy said. "Look at her. This is beautiful." It was a black-and-white shot of an old woman she'd met at a bus stop. Her face was a road map of deep lines, her hair a brittle and unapologetic white, but her eyes were as wide and sharp as a child's.

"Who was she? What was her story?" Izzy wanted to know.

Linda had been confused, even a little put off by the question.

"Who knows?" she said. "I didn't talk to her. I just took her picture."

For Linda, it wasn't about the story behind the woman. It was about the beauty of that one moment, about capturing it and making it her own. It was about the universe that existed in a single frame. But that wasn't enough for Isabel. She needed to know about the significant events that led the woman to sit at the bus stop at that precise moment, what she was thinking that put the expression on her face. And if she didn't know, she'd have to make something up to satisfy herself.

They'd laughed about it, how different they were, how unalike were their individual arts and processes. In the end, Isabel wrote: "My face is what I give to the world. Look closely and you'll see what the world has given to me." Of course, it was perfect. Isabel was always pitch perfect whenever she put word to paper.

In Linda's memory, they seemed very young that afternoon, so excited by Linda's upcoming show, the publication of Izzy's first novel right around the corner. They thought, as they always had really, that the world belonged to them. They'd never been called upon to think of themselves any other way. Even the grim tragedy that marked their late childhood hadn't changed that idea very much.

Linda walked away from the window and stared at her reflection in the mirror above the dresser. Wretched. She'd never been happy with her body (too small at the chest, too wide at the hips) but she'd always liked her face. She'd always been satisfied with her easy prettiness, good skin, well-formed features, shining blue eyes. Recently, though, deeper lines had started to make their debut around her eyes and mouth. Lack of sleep and too much stress were causing her to look haggard and worn out. Even her silky blond hair seemed drier, was losing some of that estrogenic glow. She put her hands to either side of her face and pulled the skin taut to simulate a bad face-lift and made herself laugh.

She'd never thought of herself as vain, but she supposed there were things she'd taken for granted about her looks. And now that those things were fading, she realized that she was very vain indeed. She noticed things about Izzy—her slim middle, the youthful fullness of her face, the smooth skin around her eyes—and it seemed to Linda that there was suddenly a big difference in the way they looked. They'd always been opposites in their coloring, Linda favoring their mother, Isabel their father. But they'd been equal in the timbre and volume of their beauty. Their father's favorite proud refrain: "The Connelly sisters are lovely *and* smart." There wasn't a brighter one or a prettier one. Linda and Isabel had never felt the urge to compete with each other in those arenas.

Linda would not have believed that two kids and five years could make such a difference in her appearance. But then again, she'd never even *thought* about her age until recently. Lately, she'd realized that the softness at her belly would *not* be dissolved by exercise or no-carb torture. There was a sinking to her face that would not be improved without surgery or injections. But she'd always imagined herself as having too much character to succumb to surgical beauty treatments. She couldn't see herself as one of those vain, awful women who cared more about the lines on their foreheads than about their children, who thought that looking young (not that they looked younger, exactly, just *altered*) meant a reprieve from the disappointment gnawing at the edges of their lives. How much energy that must take, to fight that losing battle. She was an artist; she'd age with character and grace.

Not that any of it mattered, not really. It was just one in a legion of dark little thoughts, mental gremlins, that could nip and gnaw at her sense of well-being if they were allowed.

Of course, there were bigger problems than her fading youth. How selfish was she to be thinking about such stupid things when Isabel's life was falling apart? Linda broke away from her reflection, slipped back into bed, and pulled the heavy mass of blankets and comforter around her. She wanted to avoid the day for just a few more minutes, avoid her missing brother-in-law and the fact that her injured sister had just raced into the fray. Normally, she'd be frantic. But for some reason, she just felt drained by the whole matter, as though she'd awakened covered by a blanket of snow. A kind of emotional hypothermia had set in, stiffened her joints, robbed her of energy.

When she received the call yesterday and raced to the hospital, saw her sister pale and unmoving on the stretcher—that awful gash on her head—it felt as though she was living a terrible memory, as if it had all happened before. As afraid and shocked as she'd been before Izzy opened her eyes and started to speak, it was as though she'd been expecting some awful event relating to her sister's husband all along.

There was something wrong with Marcus Raine; she'd known it from the day she'd first lain eyes upon him. He was worse through the lens, all hard angles and an odd shadow to his eyes. As a photographer, she knew to wait for that millisecond when the face revealed itself, a flicker of the eyes, an involuntary shifting of the muscles in the jaw or forehead. This was the second when pretty people were beautiful, or beautiful people ugly, or cheerful people suddenly haunted. A face is an organic entity; it can't hold a protective posture forever. It must surface for air. She saw him clearly and early.

She'd tried to talk to Isabel but her sister wasn't hearing it. Linda realized that she'd have to accept Marcus and hope she was wrong about him, or lose her sister. That's what happened when the biological family rejects a spouse; a continental drift. If the marriage is successful, the incompatible units slowly move away from one another. Visits become less frequent until there is only the occasional phone call, the obligatory Sunday afternoon get-together, the infrequent, awkward dinner where so much goes unsaid. Linda could see how it would happen, had seen it before with her friends. Isabel was *that* in love with him. And so Linda, with an almost superhuman effort, bit her tongue and they all moved forward together. The irony was that, five years later, Linda was just starting to let her guard down about Marcus. Erik had always liked him, was beginning to convince her that she'd been mistaken. She was moving beyond just tolerance, even starting to *like* him a little. She should have known. The lens doesn't lie.

She heard the high, light tone of her son's voice and the low rumble of her husband's. Then she heard the television go on. A minute later she smelled toaster waffles. The day was beginning without her. She felt a wave of gratitude that she had most of her Christmas shopping done. She'd wrapped all the gifts and driven them up to her mother's in Riverdale last week. That's where they'd spend Christmas Eve and open gifts on Christmas morning. Soon Brown was barking to go out and, through the wall, she heard Emily yelling at him to be quiet.

She'd gone into the guest room to check on her sister last night and found Emily and Brown piled around Izzy. She marveled at the two of them, her daughter and her sister, how alike they were, how much she loved them, how the same fierce urge to protect them was a fire in her center. Tough talk, bad attitudes, strong opinions, steely expressions—all of it just hard armor to protect fatally delicate centers.

She heard her phone vibrate in the drawer by her bed and she quickly reached for it. The screen read: *1 Text Message.* She flipped the phone open.

Can I see you today? I'm desperate. She felt a powerful wash of excitement and fear.

She answered: *Family emergency. I don't know. I'll try.*

At a light knock on the door, she slid the phone under the covers, closed her eyes.

"Mom?" said Emily, poking her face in. "I can't find my black leggings."

"Okay," she said, fake groggy. "Coming."

"Izzy's gone," said Emily. Her face was still but her eyes were bright with worry.

"Izzy will be okay," Linda said, sitting up and opening her arms. Emily came to her quickly and let herself be embraced. "We'll take care of her and she'll be fine."

"But what about Marcus?"

She released a sigh and considered lying, offering some platitude. But Emily was too old and too smart for that. Lies would just make her more afraid. She took her daughter's face in her hands. Emily looked so much like Izzy that Linda felt as though she were speaking to both of them.

"The truth is, Em, we just don't know what's happening right now. The police are helping us and we're going to figure everything out. Whatever happens, we'll get through it together. That's what a family does."

Emily leaned against her, wrapped her arms around Linda's middle.

"I think you and your brother should go to school today," Linda said, rising. They moved together toward the door. "We'll come get you if anything happens."

Emily nodded uncertainly but seemed okay with it. Sending them to school would make things seem normal, which they needed. Trevor was going to bitch a blue streak; she knew he was already banking on a sick day. People generally considered her son to be the sweeter of the two children. But he was less malleable, less cooperative than his sister, more prone to defiance and tantrum.

"Your pants are folded on top of the dryer," Linda said, patting Emily on her bottom. "Go get ready."

She heard her phone buzz again under the covers, but Emily seemed not to notice as she loped from the room. "I want jelly on mine, Dad!" she called, exiting and shutting the door behind her. Brown started barking again.

Guilt, the river that runs through motherhood, threatened to rise over its banks. The day and all the misery it promised loomed like a thunderhead. She smelled the scent of coffee and figured there was no way out but through.

THE DAY MY father killed himself dawned blue and cold. I heard the hard wind rattling the windows and saw the bright sky and high cirrus clouds from my window as I woke. I looked across the room and saw my sister lying on the bed across from me. She stared up at the ceiling, her arms folded behind her head.

"I had a bad dream," she said, knowing somehow that I was awake. She looked pale, small in her bed like the child she was.

"About what?"

"I don't know. Something terrible."

"Dreams can't hurt you," I said, only because that's what she always told me. And she only told me that because that's what Mom told her. She was fifteen. I was ten. But there had been no dream, I'd learn later. She'd seen him. Linda had been the one to find my father as he lay slumped in the toolshed far behind our house, the wall sprayed with his blood, the gun lying on the floor. Somehow she was the only one to hear the blast.

It woke her from a deep sleep and she drifted out the back door to find him. He was always out there building things with wood—birdhouses, dollhouses, and tiny pieces of furniture, picture frames, curio cabinets. Everyone loved my father's work. He was always making gifts for friends and neighbors, never accepting money. My mother complained about how he wasted his time with building trinkets when the lawn needed tending and the fence repair, that his hands were splintered and calloused, rough to the touch.

Linda pushed open the door and saw him there. A cigarette still burned in the ashtray. She was surprised, had never seen him smoke. She said it was as if the rest of the scene just didn't register. All she could think about was that cigarette and how she just couldn't imagine him putting it to his lips, drawing the smoke into his lungs. She wasn't sure how long she stood there.

I often imagine her in the doorway, one hand resting on the frame, the other on the doorknob. The bright full moon making her white nightgown translucent, the slim form of her body visible beneath it. She might have shivered in the cold, wrapped her arms around herself.

"Daddy, what's wrong?"

I know he never meant for Linda or me to find him that way. We were forbidden from bothering him when he was in there. He would have expected our mother to come out raging in the morning about how he'd stayed out there all night again, and didn't he remember he had a wife?

A fog fell over our lives. And it never lifted, not really. The contrast between our life before that day and after was so stark that it seemed like two different lives. Suicide marks you in a way that no other tragedy does—especially the suicide of a parent. And maybe the worst part about the suffering that follows is that no one ever discusses it. People feel angry when they think about suicide, the coward's way out. As if all there is to life is the bravery to soldier on. There's blame for the deceased who chose to throw away something to which other people desperately cling, and even for the family he left behind. *Didn't someone know how unhappy he was?* And, of course, you have all those thoughts yourself, even and maybe especially as a child. *The Connelly sisters are lovely* and *smart,* my father always used to say. Just not lovely or smart *enough,* right, Daddy?

People step away from the topic, avert their eyes from you. I don't remember being taunted at school. The other children just seemed repelled by me, kept distance between us. As a child, this has the effect of adding shame to the powerful brew of grief, rage, and sadness. There are no platitudes to offer those grieving a suicide. No one says, "He's in a better place now" or "The Lord works in mysterious ways." He wasn't taken by accident or illness. He didn't allow himself to be part of God's plan. In the ultimate act of rebellion or surrender or just irreverence, he left.

I remembered a particular feeling I had in the year after my father's death. It was a strange lightness, a drifting feeling. Zero gravity. I understood that everything that once seemed solid and immovable might just float away. And that this was a truth of life, not an illusion in the grieving mind of a child. Everything that is hard and heavy in your world is made of billions of molecules in constant motion offering the illusion of permanence. But it all tends toward breaking down and falling away. Some things just go more quickly, more surprisingly, than others.

I had that feeling again standing in the apartment I shared with my husband. The doorman had tried to stop me, to warn me that something was terribly amiss. A uniformed police officer held me up at the elevator for a few minutes, arguing, blocking my passage with his body. And then Detective Crowe came to the door of my apartment. It was odd to see him there, *inside,* while I awaited entry in the corridor. *Infuriating* was a better word. I moved toward him quickly. But he lifted a hand, gave me a look that stopped me in my tracks—some combination of warning and compassion.

"You don't want to be here, Mrs. Raine," he said gently as I approached, the uniformed officer at my heels. "Not right now."

"I *need* to be here right now, Detective."

Something passed between us, a tacit understanding, and he moved away from the door frame, allowed me to enter the shambles of my life with a sweep of his hand.

8

He awoke with a start, breathing hard. The room was dark. But he could see by the sliver of light shining in between the edge of the blinds and the window frame that it was daylight. How long had he slept? Too long.

She shifted beside him.

"Relax," she said. "It's over. By tonight you'll be gone."

He didn't answer her. It wasn't over. The money had been transferred, the evidence destroyed, arrangements for his departure had been made. But it wasn't close to being over. In the comfortable life he'd made, he'd forgotten what it was like to be afraid.

He looked over at Sara's long, lean form, feeling the powerful arousal the sight of her body always awakened in him. But he didn't reach for her. Instead he moved away, took his phone from the pocket of his pants, which lay in a heap on the floor, and moved quietly into the bathroom.

Her apartment was a hovel, filthy. She lived like a man, without a thought toward design or cleanliness. It was just a place she came to sleep, nothing but a bedroom, a kitchen, a bathroom, all featuring a grime and neglect particular to their functions.

He opened the keyboard on his phone, started tapping with his thumbs:

I don't want you to think I didn't love you because I did. Remember that I made you happy for a while, that we were great friends and excellent lovers. And then forget me. Mourn me like I'm dead. Don't try to find me or to answer the questions you'll have. I can't protect you—or your family—if you do.

It was a foolish thing to do, close to suicidal, and he was surprised at himself for even considering it. It would be far better for her to suspect that he was dead. But he knew her, knew the lengths she would go to prove herself right or to prove him wrong. The things she would risk, just to answer the most inane question. She'd walk the most dangerous neighborhoods in the city, just to authenticate her writing. She'd go alone, just to feel the fear, to find the words to describe it. He realized that she wouldn't be able to live with the ambiguity of his disappearance. And if she couldn't, he couldn't help her, wouldn't be able to save her from herself.

"Do you ever lose control, Marcus? Have you ever just blown your stack?" Isabel wanted to know during a recent argument. "Don't you want to know what it would be like to just let it rip?"

"No," he told her with a smile. "It's not fuel-efficient. An engine runs best warm, not hot."

"And too cold, it seizes. It cracks."

But he wasn't as cold as she thought. It was just that her engine ran so white hot that everything else seemed frigid. Her temper, her passion, the heat of her desires, opinions, drives, that's what drew him to her. She thawed him. His time with her had changed him in ways he hadn't anticipated. He'd stayed with her far longer than he should have.

If he'd done what he set out to do and moved on, he wouldn't be in the position he was in now, with more blood on his hands, forced to make changes in a hurry, enlist the help of people he'd hoped not to associate with again. He felt a simmer of regret and anger in his belly. He tamped it down; he'd need to ice over again, freeze like a still lake in winter, the summer of his time with Isabel just a memory.

His finger hovered a moment over the *Send* button, and then he pressed it. He felt a rush of emotion as he did so, sadness mingled with fear. Then he removed the battery and SIM card from the phone, flushed them down the toilet, and tossed the shell in the trash.

"What are you doing?" she called. "Come back to bed."

He looked at himself in the mirror over the sink. Two days without shaving and already the stubble on this face was nearly as thick as his goatee. He had dark half moons under his eyes, a drawn, gray look to him. Not forty-eight hours ago, he was making love to his wife in their beautiful home. He had a successful business. Because of mistakes he'd made, betrayals he'd invited, it was all gone. He would go back to being what he was before he knew Isabel. Nothing. He barely took comfort in the great wealth he had amassed in his time with her, some of it earned, some of it stolen. It didn't bring him the satisfaction he'd imagined. In fact, he'd never felt more hollow, lower.

Sara called his name and he hated her. He didn't blame her. Without her, he'd be dead right now. He would never have been able to accomplish what he had in the last forty-eight hours without her help. Everything he had worked for would have been lost. But he still hated what she represented.

They'd known each other since childhood. Her body was the first place in his grim adolescence where he'd found comfort in another. But the world had treated them differently, and they had taken different paths. He tried to escape the place they came from, to take more from life than they had been offered. She, like Ivan, succumbed.

What she was now, he didn't quite know. She was vague about the details of her life since he'd left her in the Czech Republic to come to school in the U.S. He just knew that she was much changed. The vulnerability she'd had when he knew her was gone, replaced with a raw power—sexual and otherwise. He had needed her various skills, and she had helped, never asking for anything except his affection. The one thing he couldn't give her.

She pushed the door open.

"You don't have to do this," she said, moving behind him, wrapping her arms around his body. "I can take care of Camilla."

"No. It's my job to finish."

He didn't look at her or respond to her touch, and after a moment he felt her stiffen, then she left the bathroom.

"You're weak when it comes to women," she said, closing the door.

She was right about that. When he thought about Camilla and what she had done, how she'd wept when she confessed to him, he didn't feel the kind of anger that he should have. He knew what he had to do. But he had no desire to do it.

She was waiting for him now, thinking he was about to make good on years of promises he'd never intended to keep. She was dead wrong.

When he left the bathroom, he saw that Sara had returned to bed. She was staring at him in the dim light. The sheet was pulled up to just below her perfect breasts. He felt heat in his groin, that magnetic pull from her body to his drawing him near. She didn't smile; she rarely smiled. But she pulled him to her, wrapped her long legs around him. Her kiss was salty, urgent. Not sweet and yielding like Isabel's. He was deep inside her, then, fast and hard. As he made love to her, he watched her face for that vulnerability to return when she was unguarded, had surrendered to pleasure. But it never did.

Linda dialed Isabel, first at the apartment, then on her cell. Both calls went to voice mail but Linda didn't bother to leave a message at either number. She knew when her sister was avoiding her; Izzy would call when she was ready and not before. So Linda sat, phone in her hand, debating about whether to call her mother, even though her sister had expressly asked her not to do so. *Not until we're sure what's happening. There's no need for her to worry. It'll just add more tension.*

Linda didn't really want to call their mother, but still the temptation was strong, almost as though some dark motherly force compelled her to dial the number. She knew Margie was away, some spa trip with her friends, but she'd be reachable on her cell phone. A younger Linda would have called and then been angry at herself and her mother for doing the dance they always did. At some point, after becoming a mother herself, she realized that if you want to change the dance, all you have to do is sit down. So she rested the phone on the counter and walked away from it, went to the kitchen and poured herself another cup of coffee. Brown watched her from the couch, where he had no business being.

"Off the couch, Brown." He stepped off resentfully and flopped on the floor, issuing a deep sigh.

Linda and her mother had never really gotten along, not that they didn't love each other. And it wasn't that there was anything wrong with Margie particularly; she had been an intelligent and caring mother, if not a particularly loving or affectionate one. Margie rarely raised her voice, had never struck the girls, was always there when she was needed—cupcakes for school, chaperone for field trips, help with homework. But the chemistry between Margie and her eldest daughter just wasn't there. If they'd met on the street, they wouldn't have chosen each other as friends. Linda's mother claimed this was true from the womb. Though Linda was the good baby, the easy one, Margie asserted that Linda just never seemed to *like* her very much. How this could be true, Linda didn't know. It seemed a ridiculous assertion, typically vain and narcissistic. Of course, none of that—whether they liked each other or not—really mattered, because Margie was her mother. And that relationship wasn't designed for friendship necessarily; it didn't need to be that to be successful. Even though they both had ugly memories of each other after the death of Linda's father, they loved and accepted each other now; that was enough most of the time.

Erik had taken the kids to school and she was alone with Brown in the apartment. When the door closed and all their voices—usually raised, laughing or yelling or horsing around, but today quiet, muted, somber—faded with the closing of the elevator door, she released the breath she'd been holding. She always felt like that when they left, like her energy could expand and she could think. She wasn't wife and mother, monitoring needs, cleaning faces, packing lunches, answering questions, reprimanding, instructing, nagging, kissing, hugging. She was just herself, free to pour a cup of coffee, maybe even go to the bathroom without someone calling after her. This was the space where she was most creative—in the aftermath. When she knew the kids were cared for and off to start their day, she could finally see the world with the clear vision she needed to do her work.

It wasn't that motherhood made her less creative; it was just that it created a maze that she must navigate to get to that still, center space within her. And the twists and turns were guarded by hobgoblins—guilt and worry and sometimes just exhaustion—which could take her down and smother her. But somehow the gauntlet she had to run to find that energetic well made the time she spent there so much richer. It focused her attention, forced her to maximize every moment. She knew she was a better artist for the emotional wealth of her life, that she was richer for the depth and breadth of her love for her children. But a better life didn't mean an easier one.

But she wouldn't be working today. Today she needed to take care of Izzy, help her through whatever was happening. And what if Marcus was gone for good? Well, she shouldn't even think like that.

With the thought of her brother-in-law, she remembered Izzy's description of the call she'd received, and started to feel a little flutter in her belly. Maybe it wasn't such a good idea to leave her sister to it. What if the threat to her safety hadn't passed? She decided to shower and go after her sister, whether Izzy wanted her around or not. She glanced at her cell phone, which rested on the bar. No messages. She was relieved and disappointed in equal measure. She didn't have time for that particular mess.

She took her coffee into the bathroom and placed it on the marble countertop, avoiding her reflection in the mirror. She ran the water scalding hot so the bathroom filled with steam, was about to strip her pajamas and step in when the buzzer from the street door rang and Brown started barking.

Linda walked over to the intercom, expecting to see Erik and the kids on the small black-and-white screen, having forgotten homework or cell phone or lunch box, too lazy to come back up. But it wasn't her family. She drew in a deep breath at the sight of the man who stood there, snapped up the phone from its cradle.

"What are you doing here?" she hissed.

"I'm sorry," he said, peering up at the lens. "I watched them get on the train."

She raced through calculations in her mind—twenty minutes to school, fifteen to get them settled and dropped off, a stop at the bank and the grocery store. Erik would be another hour and a half at least. He'd asked that she be there when he returned, had something he needed to discuss. She told him she needed to focus on Isabel and could it wait? No, he said. It couldn't.

"You have to leave. Right now," she said. Even in her anger, in her fear, there was a snaking pleasure, a guilty desire. She shot Brown a look and he stopped barking and walked away, went back to the couch. She didn't bother reprimanding him.

"Please, Linda. I need to see you."

She thought about having him up, making love to him hard and fast in the shower. She thought about releasing all her tension with an earthquake of an orgasm. But no, she wasn't that low, that stupid.

"I'll meet you," she said. "There's a coffee shop on the corner. Go there. Ten minutes."

"Let me up," he said, moving close to the lens. She could feel her whole body go hot.

"No," she said. "You're crazy."

"I told you. I'm desperate."

She leaned her head against the wall, fought the awful waves of temptation. The thought of him walking through the door, those hands roaming her body, his desperation like a rocket through her, made her weak and ashamed. How could she be having an affair, her of all people? The good girl, the woman with the perfect marriage, the perfect life. It was disgusting. She hated herself. But she couldn't give him up.

"I'll be there in ten minutes."

"Linda."

"Go."

He groaned and disappeared from the screen.

"Shit, shit, shit," she said, moving toward the shower. She tied her hair up so that it wouldn't get wet, showered, and dressed quickly. She grabbed her coat and her bag and headed out the door. She'd stop and see him quickly, then go straight to Izzy's. Erik would have to wait.

"Be a good boy," she called to the dog who was fast asleep.

9

It felt oddly right that the apartment I shared with Marcus was in tatters. As I walked through the detritus of our life together—an oil painting we bought in Paris slashed and knocked to the floor, a crystal vase we'd received as a wedding gift in big jagged pieces, our bedding cut with scissors—I wasn't outraged in the way one would expect. I recognized the poetry of it. We'd built a life, collected memories, had things to show for that journey. As I walked through the rooms crowded by my memories, somehow it seemed appropriate in this moment that those things should be in pieces. The air hummed with malice. It didn't even seem like the place where I'd lived for the last five years of my life.

Detective Crowe was my shadow. He was kind enough to offer his silence as he followed me from room to room, but I could feel his energy—anxious, agitated by the million questions buzzing around his brain. Grit and bits of glass crunched beneath my feet as I made my way, lifting a photo of my sister, touching a spot of red nail polish someone had poured on the bathroom countertop. It had taken on the shape of a heart.

Finally, in the small office off our bedroom where I did most of my writing, I sank into the chair in front of my desk and stared at the large blank monitor. It was huge, like a wall. When I wrote, my words were giant, swimming in a bright white sea. It helped me to see them so large, as though they had more meaning, the power to keep my attention, my focus if it threatened to wander. The dark screen seemed like a hole I could fall into.

I had all my files backed up and stored at Jack's office; I wasn't worried about lost work. That was the least of my worries, and it would be hours yet before I started thinking about personal files, journals, calendars, account numbers, e-mail correspondence. Just two days before I had been sitting in this chair, Googling myself on the Internet, answering fan e-mail, visiting the Web sites of other authors—doing everything but what I should have been doing, working on my pages. I was annoyed at myself then, frustrated by my lack of focus and productivity. Today it seemed like a state of bliss. I'd have paid any sum to be back there.

"Mrs. Raine, did your husband have a history of violence or mental illness?"

I swiveled around to see that a petite woman had followed us into the room, stood behind and to the left of Detective Crowe.

"My partner, Detective Jesamyn Breslow," he said with a nod.

"No," I answered her, surprised by the question. "You think my husband did this?"

She cocked her head at me. There was a pixyish look to her, the features of her face small and perfect—a lovely upturned nose and perfect valentine of a mouth, almond-shaped eyes. She was bright, electric, as if she might glow with the force of her own coiled energy if we turned off the lights. She had short, clean fingernails, wore her hair in a neat bob. Her clothes were good quality but I could see a shine to her black blazer from too many trips to the dry cleaner. Her microfiber wedges were a bit worn at the toe. The two cops seemed striking opposites: She was a saver, he was a spender. He was cool, slow, dark; she was white hot, action first, regrets later. And yet she seemed more centered, more mature.

"There's so much rage evidenced here," she said. "The way personal things have been destroyed, photographs defaced."

"The kind of rage only a husband could manage for his wife?" I asked. Detective Breslow shrugged. I saw her eyes dart; she was thinking of something in her own life, went internal for a minute.

"Or vice versa," Detective Crowe chimed in. I remembered his true confessions from the night before, the wife who left him, his bitterness.

"There is no one cooler than Marcus," I found myself saying. My tone was harsh, even hostile. They both noticed it, exchanged a look. "He rarely raises his voice. Anger makes him silent—colder, harder. He'd never do anything like this. He wouldn't have it in him. A waste of energy, not fuel-efficient."

I said too much, realized it too late. Looking at both of them standing there, it dawned on me that I'd made a mistake giving them permission to access and search my apartment. I'd only been thinking of Marcus as a victim, someone who needed help. I had nothing to hide. It never occurred to me that *he* might.

Isabel, he'd say, drawing out my name into a gentle, paternal reprimand. *Very foolish. These people aren't here to help you. They're here to help themselves.*

"Mrs. Raine," said Detective Breslow. Her tone was tactful, respectful, but just ever so slightly condescending. "If you know anything about what's going on here, now would be the time to tell us."

"My brother-in-law gave him money," I said. "A lot of money they don't have."

Detective Crowe nodded. "Did you know anything about that? I mean before he disappeared."

Disappear: to get lost without warning or explanation, to become invisible, cease to exist. It's a common word; you'd use it for anything. *My sunglasses disappeared.* The hope of a sudden reappearance is connoted in that word. The way Detective Crowe used it, it sounded final, like a verdict.

"Erik just told me. My sister doesn't even know." I wasn't really talking to them; I was thinking aloud, still in that stunned place where my inner world and outer world were confused with each other.

"Mrs. Raine, have you checked *your* bank accounts?"

The question sliced me, its edge so sharp it didn't hurt at first. Then I felt the slow, radiating throb of dread. I moved closer to the monitor, hands poised over the keyboard, but then I stopped myself. The computer, of course, was gone. The dark screen was connected to nothing. I turned back to him.

"I have been with Marcus for six years, married for five," I said. "What you're implying with all your questions. It's just not possible."

"What do you think I'm implying?" Detective Crowe asked. He'd taken that stance again, the spreading of the legs, the folding of the arms. Detective Breslow lowered her eyes, then turned and left the room. They had a routine, roles they played. I could see that already.

"I'm asking the questions I need to ask," he went on when I didn't answer him. "If your answers are painting a disturbing picture, you need to think about that, Mrs. Raine."

I looked away from him again and this time caught sight of my reflection in the monitor. I saw a woman who'd been badly beaten and looked the part. Behind me loomed Detective Crowe, a deep, worried frown etched on his face, as if he couldn't quite figure me out. I wasn't acting like he thought a woman in my position should act. He wanted me to be a victim, I think, weeping and afraid. He didn't know me very well.

"I don't know what you want from me—my husband is missing. My home—my head—in *pieces.*" Outside I heard the wail of a distant siren, the thunder of a garbage truck. "If you think I have something to do with all of this, you need to arrest me and let me call a lawyer. Otherwise, you have to give me a minute to think."

"Okay," he said, lifting a palm, his frown softening. "I hear you. But hear me. We often know more than we think we do. Something like this happens and it seems to come out of nowhere. But it never does. When something is not right in our life, we know, even if we choose not to see it."

There was the lightest strain of piano music coming from the apartment above me. It seemed ghostly, almost eerie. Chopin. Marcus always hated Chopin—"Anemic, unsatisfying, depressing as hell," he would say.

"Philosopher cop," I said now.

That shade of a smile again, the lightest upturning of the corners of his mouth, as though everything he saw secretly amused him. But no, it wasn't awful like that. I think he was just someone who saw the humor, the divine joke of it all. He'd rather laugh than cry. Anyway, he was right.

My mother remarried more quickly than was seemly. "He's not even cold in the ground," I heard her sister whisper at the small wedding in our backyard. It was less than a year after my father's death that my mother dressed in tasteful champagne-colored chiffon and married a man my sister and I had met only twice. There was a tiered cake with flowers, tea sandwiches, some kind of punch. Frowning faces broke into tight smiles when my mother and her groom approached. My sister was as grim and silent as she had been at my father's funeral. My mother was, as ever, lovely with her strawberry-blond hair and alabaster skin; she was appropriate, not giddy, I wouldn't say happy. She looked relieved more than anything. And I stood on the edges of it all, watching faces, absorbing swatches of conversations, listening to the nuances of tone.

Over a roast chicken, she'd told us a few months earlier.

"I'll be marrying Fred. He's a good man. He'll provide for us, give us some stability." She said it as if he was someone we knew, as if it was news we should have been expecting. We'd met him once when he came to pick her up for an evening. And once he'd had dinner at our house.

Margie's such a sensible woman. She always knows what to do. That's what my father always said about her.

The news landed like a fist on the table, something inside me rattled hard. Neither Linda nor I said a word at first. We both stared at my mother and I remember her looking back and forth at each of our faces, almost defiant. My eyes drifted down to her lean, veined hands and saw that the wedding ring she'd always worn was gone. There was no mark on her finger. I wondered when she'd stopped wearing it. She cleared her throat in the silence, took a small bite of mashed potatoes, a swallow of water. My sister's face was the same stoic mask it had been since the morning she found my father. I'd yet to see her shed a tear.

"I really have no choice, girls," she went on when we said nothing. She smoothed out the napkin on her lap. "Your father has left us with nothing, and I'm afraid I'm without skills or experience. With what I could earn, we wouldn't be able to keep this house. And I think we've lost enough."

My sister pushed food around her plate and I remember the fork suddenly seemed very heavy in my hand. There was no sound but the clinking of silverware and the ticking of the large grandfather clock my father had loved. I looked over at the chair where he would have sat. He was the clown, my mother the straight man. He'd be cracking jokes, she reprimanding him with a smile, and sometimes a blush. He'd ask us about our days and really listen to our answers. My mother liked us to be dressed at dinner; there was no lounging in jeans, or eating in front of the television. We sat and ate together "like a nice family." To say I missed my father would be like saying I was thirsty when all the water in the world had drained, leaving rivers and oceans dry, beds cracking in the heat of the sun. My mother saw me looking at his chair; something passed quicksilver across the features of her face, a flash of something angry or sad.

"There were a lot of things I didn't know about your father," she said then. "Someday when you're older, you'll better understand."

"What things?" I said, finding my voice. The words sounded surprisingly sharp, loud and startling, like a hard and sudden rap on the door. How did I know I wasn't supposed to talk, to ask ugly questions? No one had ever said as much to me. But my question was an uninvited guest in the room, greeted with stiff politeness, clearly unwelcome.

My mother closed her lavender-shadowed lids, then opened them slowly. It was something she did to show us she was summoning her patience. *She gave me the lids,* our father would say.

"It's not important now, Isabel."

"I want to know what you're talking about," I said firmly. "What didn't you know?"

She shook her head, released a long breath, as if she regretted starting the conversation and now lacked the will to go on. Looking back, I realize she was very young to be a widow with two daughters, just two years older than I was the day Marcus disappeared. She'd married at nineteen, been pregnant by twenty. She was thirty-five when my father killed himself.

"I'm sorry, girls. I shouldn't have said that," she said, sounding weak and tired. "Really, the only thing you need to know is that he loved you both. Very, very much. You were everything to him."

She reached for our hands. I let her take mine. Linda snatched her hand away.

"Did you even love him?" my sister asked. All the color had drained from her face. My mother looked down at the table, tapped her outstretched hand on the wood, seemed to consider her answer.

"Marriage is not just about love. Only little girls believe that." She didn't say it unkindly. Her voice was thick, unlike her.

"He killed himself because he knew you didn't love him anymore," my sister said simply with a prim shake of her head. There was a frayed edge to her voice; her hands quavered. I felt anxiety building in my chest; it was expanding, threatening to bust me open wide.

"That's not true, Linda," my mother whispered, tears springing to her eyes. "It's just not true."

"Yes, it is," she said, strangely bright, her eyes wide. "And *everybody* knows it."

My mother dropped her head to her arm and started to sob right there in front of us. My mother, who was a study in self-control—never speaking too loudly, never laughing too hard. Her makeup was always done; her clothes were always perfect. To see her sink like a rag doll and weep was shocking. I put my hand on her back and felt her heaving, touched the silk of her hair. I remember how golden it looked against the green cotton of her shirt. She was so real in that moment, so soft and full of life, so overcome by grief. It was terrifying and at the same time exhilarating. She was solid, was tied to the world by her pain. She couldn't just drift away and be gone like him.

"You silly, selfish bitch," Linda said. Rising from the table, she looked down at our mother, who released a deep sob at her words. Linda's features glowed with a dark victory, a grimace of disgust and condescension pulled at her mouth. She was a sliver of a girl, thin and narrow as a pencil, but that night she was a titan in her rage and her sadness. Just months before, she'd loved Duran Duran and set the VCR to tape episodes of *The Young and the Restless* while we were at school. She'd slept with the same blanket she'd had since she was a baby. She'd giggled at all my stupid jokes and stories. That girl was gone, just her brittle shell remained. Then she left us there. I listened to her walk up the stairs, her pace measured and unhurried, and slam the door to our bedroom hard.

I sat rubbing my mother's back. "It's okay, Mom. Don't worry." It was all I could think to say.

"I *did* love him, Isabel," my mother whispered. "I truly did. It just wasn't enough for him."

And, even at ten, when I didn't understand the power of things like love and money and secrets between husbands and wives, I knew it was true. My father was a ghost who walked among us. He was a sweet, kind man, who always had a smile, who always said the right thing, who always

Sedro-Woolley Public Library

gave the most extravagant gifts, who never failed to hug or stroke. But even as a child I sensed that he held the largest part of himself inside, that he was too far away to ever touch. He was like a bright-red helium balloon always just about to loft away—until he did.

But I wasn't like my mother, turning away from signs, closing shadowed eyes against the things I didn't want to see or know. I couldn't be that. I'm the seer. The observer. Life is a liquid that sinks into my skin; I metabolize all the ingredients. I ask the questions, hear the answers, extrapolate meaning from the rhythm and nuance of language and tone. In our arguments, it used to come down to words. Marcus, not a native speaker, would throw up his hands, walk away, so angry that I could get hung up on the semantics, the connotations of the words he used, ignoring, he claimed, his true meaning, the argument itself. But words are all we have, their essence the only passage into our centers, the only way we can make people *feel* what we *feel.*

"You use language like a weapon, like a sword, Isabel," he said one time. "Am I your opponent? Will you cut me because I can't wield it as well as you?"

"And you use it like a blunt-force instrument—imprecise, clumsy, banging, banging, banging to get your point across. You'd use a jackhammer for needlework."

"What about the affair you mentioned?" Detective Crowe charging into my reverie, bringing me back to present tense. I don't know how much time had passed since he last spoke.

"What about it?"

I heard him sigh, as though I was being obtuse in order to exasperate him. "How did you find out about it? Did you know her name, where she lived?"

"I just knew," I told him. "I felt it. Then there was a text message. I asked him to end it; he said he would. I never knew anything about her."

He tugged at the cuff of his shirt, straightening the line that was exposed beyond his jacket, frowning.

"You don't seem like the type not to ask questions."

Maybe I was more like my mother than I wanted to admit, about some things, anyway. But it was different. I didn't want to know anything about Marc's lover at the time, didn't want any fodder for my imagination to spin. Without it, I could just cast her as a bit player, someone who glided across the stage barely noticed. Any detail might have started me weaving her into something bigger, more important than I wanted her to be.

"He met her in Philadelphia. That's all I know."

"And even that might have been a lie."

I shrugged, gave an assenting nod.

"That's what really got me, you know? About my wife? I think I could have gotten over the cheating part. It was all the lying, all the sneaking around that really irked me. You can almost understand infidelity, right? The whole lust thing—it's there. But it's the logistics that make it really ugly, unforgivable. You thought she was spending time with her mother, but she was with her boyfriend. It turns your stomach."

I didn't answer because I knew what he was doing. He was trying to make me angry, relate to me and get me talking, commiserating. I'd watched enough television to know this. I'd start talking and some "clue" would pop out of my mouth, or I'd say something I hadn't intended to, give away something that I knew. Maybe even admit that I'd killed my husband, dumped his body in the East River, killed his colleagues and trashed his business and the home we shared.

"But you forgave him, huh? Stayed with him?"

"Yes." Was it really true? Had I ever forgiven him?

"Why?" He almost spat the question. What he really wanted to ask was "How?"

I regarded him. Another natty outfit—brown wool slacks, with a dark brown leather belt and shoes, cream button-down, dark coat, black hair gelled back, the debut of purposeful stubble. His intelligence, his competence, was a thin veneer over a deep immaturity. He was a boy, a child, though it looked as though forty was right around the corner. He still believed in fairy tales.

"Because I love him, Detective."

"And love forgives." He sounded sarcastic, bitter.

"Love *accepts,* moves forward. Maybe forgiveness comes in time."

The answer seemed to startle the smugness off his face; the inside points of his eyebrows turned up quickly and then returned to their place in the arch. Sadness.

He recovered quickly. "What do you think they were looking for here, Mrs. Raine? At first glance, what's missing other than the computers and the files in that cabinet?"

He exhausted me with all his questions, his attitude, and the way he kept saying my name. All the drive and energy I'd had in the cab had drained from me. I felt as if I'd been filled up with sand. "I don't know."

I looked at my naked hand. He caught the glance. "Where's your wedding ring?"

"It's gone," I answered. "My brother-in-law said it was gone when they came to the hospital."

It meant something; we both knew that. Neither of us knew what. He wrote it down in his book. He asked a few questions about the ring, scribbled my answers. There wasn't much to tell—a two-carat cushion-cut ruby in a platinum setting. It was the only material possession in the world that held any value for me.

The phone in my pocket vibrated and I withdrew it and looked at the screen. I flipped it open to read the text message there, then snapped it shut.

"Who was that?" asked Detective Crowe. A little rude, I thought, and none of his business.

"My sister's worried," I told him. He nodded as if he knew all about worried sisters. I felt my chest start to swell, my shoulders tense.

"You're looking a little pale again," he said after a beat.

I stood and moved toward the door. "You know what? You were right. I shouldn't be here. I don't *want* to be here. I have to leave."

He blocked my passage with his body, which I did not like. I took a step back.

"We have a lot to talk about," he said, mellow but firm. "Since you insisted on being here, we might as well do it now."

"I know. But I'd rather do it someplace else," I said. "You said yourself I shouldn't be here, and you were right. Anyway, you must have enough to keep you busy here for a while—fingerprints, DNA, whatever."

"That's for the techs, the forensics teams. They've come and gone. While they analyze what they've found, all I have to do is ask questions. Hopefully the right ones lead to answers that help me to understand why three people are dead, your home and office have been trashed, and your husband, *Marcus Raine*, the point at which all of this connects, is missing."

He leaned on the name heavily, oddly.

"Why did you say his name like that?" I asked.

He raised a finger in the air. "Now, *that's* a good question."

His doppelgänger had returned, the shadow my addled brain was creating behind him. I felt some kind of dizzying combination of anger, dread, and dislike for the man who was crowding me in my very small office with his thick body. I took another step back and was against the wall.

"Marcus Raine, born in the Czech Republic in 1968, emigrated to the U.S. in 1990, attended Columbia University on scholarship and obtained a bachelor's and then a master's in computer science from that institution. Lived in the U.S. first on a student, then a work visa, before he became a U.S. citizen in 1997."

"That's right." With the exception of the last piece of information, I'd told him as much last night. He wasn't wowing me with his detective skills.

"Worked for a start-up called Red Gravity, made a small fortune when the company went public in 1998."

I nodded. It wasn't enough money to retire forever. But it was more money than Marcus ever thought he'd make in his lifetime—or so it had seemed at the time.

"He did well enough to set up his own company shortly after we were married," I said.

He offered a mirthless smile. "Well, no. That's the thing."

I didn't appreciate the know-it-all, smarter-than-you swagger to his bearing; it caused me to flush with the shame of a liar or a fool. I tried to push past him again. The room was suddenly too hot. He waited a second before yielding to me. I didn't go far, just to my bed, where I sat heavily, though the sheets and comforter had been shredded. It looked as though someone very strong had sunk a knife deep into the mattress and then cut ugly swaths through the material. *There's so much rage evidenced here.* Was it possible that Marcus and I had made love here just the morning before last?

"Marcus Raine," he said, following me and pulling a folded piece of paper from his jacket pocket, "disappeared in early 1999."

He handed me the paper, a printout from the *Times* online. When he did, I noticed that the skin on his knuckles was split, his hand swollen and looking sore. I almost asked about it but figured I had my own problems.

With a vein throbbing in my throat, I read a small news item about a young man, a successful software engineer, and his sudden disappearance. It told of how his parents were killed and he was raised by his aunt in a town just outside of Prague during communism, how he came to the U.S. and made good, realized every immigrant's dream of America. And just as the rags-to-riches tale came to its happy ending—he'd met a girl and fallen in love, had asked her to marry him—Marcus Raine disappeared. Didn't come to work one day. When his girlfriend reported him missing, police gained entry into his apartment. There was no sign of a struggle. Some items—keys, wallet, a watch he wore every day—were missing. The article confirmed what I had learned about missing men: No one waged much of an effort to find them. No one heard from him again. His whereabouts were still unknown.

I looked up at the detective. I don't know what he expected to see on my face, but I could tell by the way his eyes went soft that he felt sorry for me suddenly.

"Someone else with the same name," I said weakly.

"And the same life story," he said. "Possible. But how likely?"

I found myself looking at his shoes. I could tell they were expensive. From the leather and stitching, I'd say Italian. He couldn't afford shoes like that; I figured he was in debt, maybe a lot of debt. My brain switched off like this when I didn't want to deal with what was in front of me.

"Isabel."

I looked up at him. He held out a photograph, and I took it from him.

"Do you know this man?" asked Detective Crowe.

For a second, I thought I was looking at a picture of my husband. But no, this man was narrower at the shoulders, the features of his face weaker, eyes hazel, not haunting blue. Really, as I looked closely, he was nothing like Marc except for his coloring, his nearly shaved head and blond goatee.

"That's Marcus Raine, born June 9, 1968, disappeared January 2, 1999."

Same name, same life story, same birthday as my husband—but not my husband.

I guessed the photograph was taken on the observation deck of the Empire State Building; the city lay tiny and spread out behind him. This strange man with my husband's name had his arm draped around a pretty blonde. They both wore stiff tourist smiles.

"Do you know him, Isabel?"

Was there something vaguely familiar about him? It seemed as if I could have seen him before, somewhere, though I couldn't have said when or where. I'd never met anyone from Marc's life before me, not family, friends, or even colleagues.

"There's a resemblance, wouldn't you say?" said Crowe.

"I don't know," I said, not wanting to give Detective Crowe anything. "Maybe."

"What about the girl, Camilla Novak?"

The girl in the photo had that kind of hard-featured, lean beauty that seemed to characterize Czech women. I remembered noticing in Prague how gorgeous they all were in the way of gems or metals, stunning but not inviting. She had that same aura to her—*Look, don't touch.* I didn't recognize her, but something about her name rang familiar. Had I seen it or heard it somewhere? I couldn't remember.

"No. I don't know either of them."

I had a thought that caused me to get up quickly. Too quickly; I almost sank to my knees but Detective Crowe steadied me with a hand to my elbow.

"Take it easy," he said, leading me back to the bed. "What is it?"

"There was a small photo album, really a canvas-bound book with old photographs, letters, and recipes from his mother. He kept it in the back of his closet."

"I'll get it. Where is it?"

I pointed to the closet, battling a terrible nausea and dizziness. When he opened the door, I saw that all Marc's designer clothes remained untouched, arranged by color, meticulously maintained. Suits and collared shirts were hung, sweaters and knits were folded. It was an oasis of order in the chaos. It felt like an insult. But, of course, the album and all the personal items within were gone. Detective Crowe turned to show me his palms.

"There's nothing here."

I felt a rush of sadness and fear. That album, with its worn edges and yellowed pages coming loose from their binding, was the only piece of the past Marcus had, he claimed—a couple of grainy black-and-white pictures of himself as a child, a picture of the parents I'd never meet, recipes in a woman's pretty handwriting. There were letters in Czech from his aunt. I used to look at these things when he wasn't home, when we were fighting. It comforted me to know that he was a boy once, fragile, vulnerable, that there were reasons he seemed so closed off now. Was it a fabrication? I wondered now. Were those pictures of someone else?

"Seems Marcus Raine was a bit of a loner—no family, no friends really, other than the girl," said Detective Crowe. "One of those guys, I guess. Even his former colleagues at Red Gravity said he kept to himself, didn't party after work or go to lunch with anyone. He worked hard but didn't socialize. According to the notes in the file."

"What are you getting at, Detective Crowe?" I asked.

"Before I answer you, let me ask you a question." He went on without waiting for a response from me. "Last night you told me that you didn't know anything about his business, didn't have much to do with it at all."

"That's right."

"Then why is everything in your name? Why was your Social Security number used to establish the EIN?" Another bomb dropping, another structure crumbling like powder.

"It wasn't."

"But it was."

We held each other's eyes, both of us disbelieving, both of us watchful. I saw Detective Breslow come stand in the doorway to my bedroom. I think she'd been standing just outside the whole time. I broke Crowe's gaze to look at her.

"We think he used your information to avoid using his own, Mrs. Raine," said Detective Breslow.

A thin, dark film started to stain the lens of my memory. Our meeting, our passionate courtship, how quickly we married. How he waited until we returned from our honeymoon—three weeks in Italy—before he devoted himself full-time to starting up Razor Technologies. So many new beginnings; it was thrilling. When he told me that he hoped I'd be part of the business, a partner, I was touched that he wanted to share that with me. I signed a flurry of documents without really looking twice.

He insisted we change accountants, use someone who knew about his industry. I fired a man I'd worked with most of my career and let Marcus take over everything with the help of a firm with which I wasn't familiar. I signed papers quarterly and at year end for both the company and my own earnings.

When was the last time I'd looked at any of it, really perused it? Numbers frightened me, literally shut me down. I was happy someone else took it all over. My accountant left multiple messages: "Isabel, you must return my call. We need to talk about this new firm you've hired." I'm ashamed to say I ignored the voice mails, never gave him the courtesy of answering.

Dread was coming on like a bad flu. I thought of Linda. She'd done the same with Erik, put her signature where her husband asked. Two smart women who knew better, who should have learned early, the hard way, not to surrender our power, our financial security to any man. Detective Crowe was still talking.

"It's easy enough to walk around with someone else's name and résumé, especially if he had all the documents, the driver's license, the green card," Breslow went on. "They look alike enough that he—whoever he is or was—could just become Marcus Raine, especially if neither of them had any real ties."

Breslow cut in. "The afternoon of January 2, 1999, Marcus Raine, or someone posing as him with all the necessary documentation, cashed out his accounts," she said, handing me another photograph.

A man in a blue baseball cap, jeans, and a sweatshirt stood at a bank teller's window. His face was partially obscured by the brim. It could have been Marcus, true. But it could have been anyone with his build and coloring.

"This is *crazy,*" I said, finally finding my voice and some reserve of physical strength. I stood and faced both detectives. "You can't just slip into someone's identity, become that person, use his history as your own. Eventually someone would have discovered he wasn't who he said he was."

"Maybe someone *did* discover it," said Crowe. "Maybe that's what this is all about. He needed to disappear again. Everything that might have been used to identify him is"—he swept his arm—"all gone."

"His fingerprints are all over the place—here, at the office," I said. "DNA—everywhere."

"That only helps us to identify him if he's in one of the systems already," Breslow said patiently, as if she'd responded to this statement a hundred times before. "And we won't know *that* until the fingerprints and DNA we found here are processed and put through IAFIS and CODIS, the national databases that store this type of data. It could take a while—maybe a week for a priority case, between processing and getting the information to the FBI, waiting for them to respond. And if he hasn't been arrested and processed for anything else in the U.S., or if his DNA doesn't show up on another unsolved-case file, we'll have nothing."

I sank back down on the bed. I felt him slipping away, this man I loved and lived with for five years. I remembered him stepping into that elevator, calling, "I love you, Izzy," as it took him away. I thought that's what he said; I assumed it was. But maybe that's not what I heard at all. I relived that horrible screaming again, feeling a cold finger trace the back of my neck, raising the hair there.

"No," I said. "No. This is not right. You're making some kind of mistake here." It wasn't possible, was it? That the man I married was someone else entirely than I believed him to be?

Detective Crowe was leaning against the wall, staring at me hard. "He needed your Social Security number to start his business. The name Marcus Raine doesn't appear anywhere on the corporation documents. He's not even an employee of the company. Everything's in your name. Yours and Rick Marino's."

I didn't even know what to say. I just sat there mute, reeling.

"Do you know what Social he used to apply for your marriage license?" asked Breslow. Her tone was gentle, empathetic. I glanced over at her and saw compassion on her face; she was a woman who'd been lied to, knew how it felt. It hadn't made her bitter, like it had with Crowe. It had made her smarter.

Our files were all gone; they knew that. "I have no idea."

She handed me three more pieces of paper. A copy of Marcus Raine's green card with his picture, a copy of his Social Security card, and a copy of our marriage license.

"That's Marcus Raine," she said. She came to stand beside me, pointed a finger at the stranger's picture. Then she tapped the copy of the Social Security card, then the marriage license. The numbers were the same.

Crowe picked up a picture of Marc from my desk. "This is not the same man."

We were all quiet, my mind racing through options, possibilities, ways this might all be a mistake.

"So you're saying that he stole another man's identity, used his Social Security number to marry me, then used my name and Social to establish a corporation for Razor Technologies."

I couldn't believe I was still speaking. I was shredded like the mattress I was sitting on, little pieces of me drifting into the air and floating away.

Breslow nodded. "It looks that way to us at the moment."

"Then what happened to this man?" I asked, holding up the copy of the green card.

"That's another very good question," said Crowe.

I thought I should rail in defense of my husband, the real Marcus Raine, rant about what a terrible mistake they were making, threaten to sue, do something other than sit there and stare at the wall. But I couldn't.

"So, *Mrs.* Raine, any thoughts on who you might have married?"

I had the oddest sensation, sitting in my ruined bedroom faced with two detectives who knew more about my husband than I did. It was as if my train had reached its final destination, except when I stepped out onto the platform, I was in a place I hadn't intended to visit and couldn't name, but one that was vaguely familiar just the same.

My phone vibrated in my pocket again. I flipped it open and read the text message there, feeling the bottom drop out of my stomach. I tried to keep my expression neutral but my cheeks warmed.

"Your sister again?" Crowe asked. I couldn't tell if there was suspicion in his tone. I nodded but couldn't find my voice, shoved the phone back in my pocket, walked over to the window.

"Mrs. Raine," said Detective Breslow, "I strongly suggest you check your bank accounts." Her tone implied that she already knew what I'd find.

SHE LET HIM take her against the heavy porcelain sink in the unisex bathroom. She clung to his wide back in what she knew he thought was passion. Really she was just afraid that their weight was going to pull the sink, cold and painful beneath her buttocks with each deep thrust, from the wall. She felt his passion, his desperation. And even if she didn't share it necessarily, it felt so good to be wanted like this. Wanted by someone who hadn't watched her give birth, who didn't shave while she peed, who hadn't seen her sick in bed with the flu. With him, she was a mistress, still a mystery, something not quite possessed.

"I love you," he whispered, his voice tight, his eyes closed in pleasure. "I'm sorry, I do."

She'd asked him not to say it. She didn't feel obliged to answer. She found herself watching his face, thinking, No, I don't love you. And as she succumbed to an earthquake of an orgasm, she buried her face in his shoulder to keep herself from crying out, *I don't love you. I love my husband.* Strange as it was to be thinking this as he shuddered and moaned with pleasure. "Oh, God." He let his weight press against her. She felt his chest heaving and she clung to him.

She was someone else with Ben, not a mother, not a wife, not someone defined by her relationships with other people. She was an artist, an unencumbered heroine in a story that took place in her imagination.

"Are you okay?" he asked, pulling up his pants and glancing at the door they'd locked behind them. She always hated these moments when the pleasure had passed and they hastily pulled on their clothes. The groping and ripping off of garments was always exciting. The aftermath was just *cheap*. A grimy HAPPY HOLIDAYS sign hanging on the back of the door just made it worse.

She turned away from him, lifting her panties over her hips and letting her skirt fall. She looked at herself in the mirror. She didn't look so bad after all, did she? Maybe it was the lighting.

"You can't do this," she said lamely. "Turn up at my apartment like that. We both have families."

"I know," he said, looking ashamed and miserable. "I know."

She didn't feel guilty yet. That would come later when he was gone, when the kids came home, or when she was laughing with her husband.

Now she just felt sated, or rather as if something that pained her had been salved.

"I have to go," she said, moving to him, resting against him.

"What's going on?" He put a gentle hand on her arm, looked at her with concern. "A family emergency, you said."

She hated when he did this, acted like their relationship was real, not some asinine mistake they were both making. He always wanted to chat and cuddle, or talk about his feelings like some teenage girl. Didn't he understand? She just wanted to *forget* about herself for five minutes. When they first started seeing each other, what thrilled her the most was that her worries about the kids, money, her career, disappeared during these little romps. If the relationship evolved, all those worries would just carry over into this new place. The euphoria, the blessed escape of it would disappear; it would become just another thing to worry about. And that she couldn't manage.

She told him quickly about Marcus and her sister, tried not to be curt or dismissive. Someone knocked on the restroom door; it was the only one in the back of the small coffee shop. Outside, she heard the clinking of silverware, the mutter of conversation. The aroma of bacon and maple syrup made her remember she'd skipped breakfast.

"I'll be just a minute," she called. There was no answer.

"What do you think happened to him?" he asked.

"I don't know," she said, pulling her phone from her pocket and glancing at it, looking for messages.

"I'll see what I can find out," he offered. "I know the crime-beat reporter pretty well."

She'd met Ben at a gallery opening for her work. He was an art critic who'd been less than kind to her in an earlier review. *Common, maudlin,* were the words that stuck in her mind. But still, she found herself drawn to him. He was a tall, powerful man with close-cropped dark hair and a neat goatee, a small silver hoop in each ear. From the nastiness of his written comments and his striking appearance, she expected him to be verbose, loud or overbearing. Instead she found him soft-spoken, carrying an aura of vulnerability. She found herself watching his face, for that moment when he thought no one was looking, when the muscles shifted and relaxed, revealing the true man. It never came. He was guarded, always.

"Seems like it's always the people who do the least with their lives who have the nastiest things to say about those who do the most," she'd said to him the night of their meeting, having had a bit too much to drink. The circle of people standing around them went silent, but she could feel Erik smiling beside her. He liked it when she got feisty.

Ben gave her a slow nod, took a sip of wine. "I'm sure it must seem that way. But how do you feel about all those critics who have nice things to say? Do you hold them in such disdain?"

She had to laugh. It came out deep and throaty and she saw his eyes shine at the sound of it.

"Of course not," she answered. "*Those* critics are obviously brilliant." And everyone joined in their laughter, relieved that the tension had dissipated.

"I love your work, Linda," he said, and she saw a flash of arrogance. The way he talked to her in that group, the way he said her name as if they were old friends—it gave her a strange charge. "I hold you to a very high standard. That's why I'm so disappointed when your work doesn't meet your abilities. Which, admittedly, isn't often."

He raised a glass to her and the others in their group did the same. She could have been gracious here, but she wasn't.

"So, are you a failed photographer, like so many critics? Do you have stacks of photographs somewhere that no magazine would buy, no agent would represent?"

Linda felt Erik give her a little warning squeeze on her lower back; they both knew wine changed her personality a bit, made her more aggressive, prone to saying things she never would sober. She held Ben's eyes, enjoying the slow smile that spread across his face.

"No," he said. "Even as a child my only ambition was to stand in judgment of artistic achievement."

The group let out a roar of laughter that caused everyone else in the gallery to look at them.

Linda and Ben were fucking within the week.

"That would be great," she said, moving into him, wrapping her arms around his middle. He was much bigger than Erik, broader through the shoulders, fuller in the middle. She liked this about him, his size. It made her feel safe, even though there was nothing safe about him or anything they did.

"I'll text you," he said into her hair.

She broke away from him and unlocked the door, peered out and didn't see anyone waiting in the slim hallway leading back to the restaurant dining area. She cast him a backward glance and saw a sad look of longing on his face that made her heart catch.

"I'm sorry," she said, though she didn't know why.

"Me, too," he said.

The difference between them was that he wasn't happy in his marriage. Love had left his relationship long ago. He told her that he stayed with his wife because of their two daughters, ages six and eight. She'd seen pictures of them, both sweet faced, one dark, one light, just like her and Isabel. The sight of them made her feel such acute shame that she had to force herself not to look away when he trotted out whatever new photographs he had with him. She couldn't imagine bringing pictures of her kids to these meetings, couldn't understand why he did that.

Linda didn't know which of them was guiltier in this affair, though she was fairly certain she was doing the most harm. Here she was, someone blessed with love and success and still unsatisfied. As she walked through the restaurant, no one noticed her—none of the diners, not the waitress at the busy counter or the cook over the grill. She loved the anonymity of New York City. You were always alone; no one cared what you did, what you wore, with whom you were sleeping. Everyone was so wrapped up in the dream of their own lives and what they wanted to be that they never saw you at all.

She called her sister again from the cab heading uptown. No answer.

10

I did as Detective Breslow suggested, starting checking my accounts. At the accountant's office, there was no answer and no voice mail, though business hours were well under way. Not a good sign. With our computers gone, my normal way of checking accounts and credit cards was out of the question. So Detective Crowe and I walked down to the ATM on Broadway. It didn't take long to confirm their suspicions; all our accounts had been reduced to a hundred dollars. I stared at the glowing numbers on the small screen and felt a burning in my chest, as if bile was coming up from my empty stomach. Four accounts—a checking, a savings, and two money markets—all empty except for a hundred dollars each, the minimum required to keep the accounts opened.

"I don't believe this," I said.

"I'm sorry," said Detective Crowe, scribbling in his little book.

"Hey, are you done?" Some guy waiting impatiently behind us, shifting from foot to foot, gripping a cell phone in his hand. "You're holding up the line."

We moved from the queue and I ducked into a doorway, just so that I could lean against something, get out of the sidewalk crowd. People hurried past; the traffic on Broadway was a river of noise.

"How much are we talking about here?"

"Those are just the liquid accounts," I said. The concrete beneath my feet felt like sand, shifting and unstable. "I don't know, maybe around seventy thousand between the four of them?"

He nodded, not offering judgment, just writing, always writing in that stupid little book. I wanted to say something, but inside I was in a free fall, wondering about everything it had taken me so long to earn and grow. I wondered about the investment accounts—the IRAs, the pensions, the stocks. Of course, they would all be gone, too. The weight of it was starting to hit me; everything was gone. A hollow space was opening in my middle and I thought of my mother again.

MARGIE HAS THESE perfect long fingers, always bejeweled unapologetically with all manner of chunky gems.

"An old woman should wear jewels, big ones," she says. "She's earned them and they distract from her fading looks. I may not be young anymore, but at least I'm rich. And that's something."

That's Margie.

Except for the night she told us that she planned to marry Fred, I have never seen her lose herself—not in happiness, not in grief. She would smile but never indulge in a belly laugh. She would frown but never yell. As a younger woman, it was hard for me to imagine her as a girl buffeted by the same passions, desires, and ambitions that rocketed me through my education and career. I couldn't imagine her lost in passion or crushed by disappointment. She seemed as stoic and steady as a stone column. This was a comfort in some ways, because she was always a place to moor in rough weather.

Years after I left home, after I'd graduated NYU and made my first real money, my mother told me about the months after my father's death, about the staggering debt of which she'd been ignorant, the gambling addiction that drained him of everything he owned, including his will to live. It only took a week for her to discover that our home was about to go into foreclosure, our vehicles about to be repossessed, that everything she thought she owned, down to the new range, belonged to a bank that hadn't been paid in months.

In the throes of grief for her husband, she was forced to face the reality that during their marriage he had lied about everything, spent all their money and beyond, and then abandoned us to live with his deceptions and mistakes. We were weeks from being homeless.

"I felt as though I'd swallowed drain cleaner," she told me. "Everything inside me *burned.* I'll never forget those nights, how I worried. How angry I was at your father, at myself for being so ignorant and weak. I had nowhere to turn. No one in our family had the kind of money I needed in order to save us. But then, of course, there was Fred."

He'd loved her for years, she said, respectfully, from a distance. They'd met at church, where my mother had always gone alone on Sunday mornings. He was a wealthy man, came from money, inherited several very successful grocery stores, then made a fortune selling out to one of the big chains, made wise investments. He paid off all the debt my father left behind, the mortgage on our house.

"I don't know what would have happened to us if it weren't for Fred."

"But did you love him, Mom?"

A pause, a sip of coffee where a monolithic emerald glinted in the sunlight. We watched Fred from the window as he filled a birdhouse with seed in their expansive backyard. Their Riverdale home was palatial; I've never heard them fight.

"I learned to love him. He's a good man," she said finally. "Anyway, it's overrated, romantic love. Maybe it doesn't even exist."

I remember them holding hands while Fred drove us all in the Mercedes to the city for lunch and museums, plays. He was always kind to us. But he was not my father. For years I neither loved him nor disliked him. We did, however, form a friendship over time, a kind of mutual tenderness and respect that was somehow forged by our love for Margie.

"Why are you telling me this now?" Sitting there with her, I suddenly, vividly remembered that night when she told us she planned to marry Fred. These were the things she wouldn't share then.

"Because you're a grown woman, just starting out in your life. I want you to know things no one ever taught me."

She got up and walked to the coffeepot on the counter, warmed her cup and carried the pot back to the table and refilled my mug, too. She was still beautiful; the years hadn't robbed her of that, though she claimed they had. She complained about her neck, the skin under her eyes. But she was too afraid to go under the knife for vanity. Her words. "It's like asking God to punish you for your silliness and then laying yourself out on a table for His ease." She was more regal, more powerful than I remembered her when I was growing up.

"Money is power, Isabel," she said, looking at something above and beyond me. "It's freedom. It's choice. No, it won't buy you happiness. But it will buy you everything else. Unhappiness is a lot easier to bare when you have money."

"Mom," I said. She held up a hand.

"In my love for your father, I turned everything over to him. I never wrote a check in all the years of our marriage. I didn't even know how much money he made. It seems foolish now, but I suppose I was a foolish girl who went from my father's house to my husband's house. I never learned to take care of myself."

"You took care of us. Not everyone can do that."

She nodded. "I knew how to do those things—bake cookies and bandage knees, listen to worries and sew up dolls. But this is something more important. Something I have to tell you because I couldn't show you."

"Don't worry, Mom. I have my own money," I said. She reached for my hand and gripped it hard.

"That's good. But hear this. When you find the right man and fall in love, Izzy, give yourself heart and soul, if you must. But don't *ever* give him your money."

She was watching me urgently, the same way she had when she told me never to get in a stranger's car or never to get behind the wheel if I'd been drinking, the dire consequences of those actions having already played out in her mind. I found myself growing annoyed, uncomfortable. I wasn't the same kind of woman she was; I didn't need a man to take care of me.

"Okay, Mom, okay," I said, drawing my hand back from hers. "I get it."

STANDING ON THE street with Detective Crowe, I felt the first dawning of a terrible anger. Around me, lampposts were wrapped with green garland, people were carrying festive bags packed with gifts, and an electronics store was blaring "Jingle Bells" from outdoor speakers. I barely registered any of it. The depth and breadth of my husband's betrayal was opening a chasm to reveal a dark abyss. I found myself ticking back through the years of our marriage and realized that there *had* been signs for me to see, places where I might have asked questions but didn't. I had to ask myself now: Had I written the story of my marriage to Marcus, unwilling, unable to see the man I'd cast in the vital role of husband? I found myself backing away from the detective, panic fluttering in my chest like a cage of birds.

"Where are you going, Isabel?" he asked, his voice wary, a warning.

"I have to get out of here," I said, lifting my arm to the traffic. A yellow cab pulled over immediately.

The detective didn't move to stop me, though he looked as if he wanted to. I saw his arm lift and then drop back to his side. He seemed still, careful, trying not to frighten a butterfly he wanted to net.

"Stay in touch with me," he warned. "Don't make me think I have to worry about your role in this."

I turned and grabbed the door handle and got into the cab quickly. I saw the detective shaking his head—in confusion, in disapproval, I couldn't be sure—as the taxi pulled into traffic. He put a hand to his jaw, his eyes still locked on the disappearing vehicle.

"Where to?" asked the cabbie. I could see only the back of his bald head; in his picture on the dash he looked like the Crusher.

"I'm not sure yet. Just drive north."

Only now, alone, in the quiet of the cab, did I allow myself to look again at the text message on my phone. The second one was not from Linda, but from Marcus.

> I don't want you to think I didn't love you because I did. Remember that I made you happy for a while, that we were great friends and excellent lovers. And then forget me. Grieve me like I'm dead. Move on. Don't try to find me or to answer the questions you'll have. I can't protect you—or your family—if you do.

My hand started to shake. I knew it was pointless to text him back or try to call. I also knew that was the last communication I'd receive from him. I stared at the words on the screen, still disbelieving that this was happening, still waiting to wake up.

I flashed on scenes, a woman who knew him in a Paris nightclub, who called him by another name and touched him lightly on the cheek before he pushed her hand away and said there had been some mistake. The voice mail from just a couple of weeks ago: *Marcus, my friend, it's Ivan. Just in from Czech. There's so much to talk about.* His tone, light and friendly, still managed to sound ominous. He left a number to call. Marcus seemed to go stiff as I relayed the message, then claimed he had no idea who it might have been. "Erase it," he said. "Wrong number." When I pressed him about it, he said, "Who knows? Someone from Czech, looking for a job, wanting something for nothing, thinking I owed something to a fellow countryman. No thanks." I let it go, even though I was sure there was more to it. If he didn't want to talk about it, there must have been a good reason.

There was something else, too. Something recent and strange that I had ignored. I kept receiving bizarre e-mails in the mailbox on my Web site. Normally, I received multiple messages a day from fans, detractors, booksellers inviting me for events, conference invitations, and the like. Every now and again, I'd get an e-mail from someone who wanted me to write his story or from someone with a "brilliant idea" for my next novel. And sometimes the mail was just from crazy people, with threats, rantings about mistakes they thought I'd made, inappropriate requests for pictures, and blatant come-ons.

Over the last few weeks, I'd received two or three messages from someone claiming to have information about my husband. "You're in danger," I remember one e-mail reading. "Your husband is not who you think he is." I'd had so much strange e-mail over the years that I just pressed *Delete,* without giving it so much as a second thought. Now I racked my brain for the name of the sender, for more of what had been included in the text of the messages. But I'd barely glanced at them; deleted them and forgotten them.

Then, suddenly, I knew where to go. Somewhere safe, somewhere where I could use a computer, get on the Internet and figure out what to do next, try to find those e-mails, which might still linger in my trash folder. The thought gave me a new energy, a feeling of purpose and strength. One thing I wasn't going to do? Move on. If Marcus thought I was just going to crawl under the covers and grieve him, I was as much a stranger to him as he was to me.

Grady watched the cab disappear into a stream of other taxies up Broadway. He'd considered physically restraining Isabel Raine. But instead he let her go. Had to. No legal reason to hold her. If he put his hands on her, he was opening himself up to seven kinds of trouble. Trouble he didn't need. So he let her have her flight response and hoped she came back to him when he called. Or on her own when she realized how badly she needed help from the police.

She was beautiful, in a Manhattan kind of way. That is to say edgy, with nice style and pretty skin. But she wasn't his type. Not that he'd been asked, but a woman like Isabel Raine was not for him—too much angst, too much intellect—like his ex. He wanted someone who didn't think about being happy. He just wanted someone who *was* happy, who went with the current of life and love, not someone bent on swimming upstream all the time.

"Where'd she go?" Breslow at his elbow.

"She freaked. Her accounts are close to empty."

She nodded as though it was news she expected. "What's she going to do?"

"My guess?" he said, still looking up Broadway in the direction of the cab that had sped Isabel away. "Something stupid." Out of the corner of his eye, he saw Jez nod her agreement.

"Let's find Camilla Novak," Breslow said after a moment. "I think we have to go back to that point to figure out what's happening here."

Grady shrugged. He didn't have any better ideas. But he stood rooted in place; there was something else nagging at him. He couldn't quite get a hold on it, though.

"*Today,* Crowe," said Breslow impatiently. "I've got to pick up Benjy at three in Riverdale."

"The doorman," said Crowe.

"Who? Shane?"

"Yeah."

"Never showed up at his apartment today."

"Let's get a warrant and search his place first."

"I don't think we'll get a warrant just because the guy didn't turn up at home after work."

"He had opportunity to let the intruders in, he left his post before the next guy showed, and he withheld information. Let's try."

She raised her eyebrows at him and gave a quick nod, took her phone from her coat. She always made these kinds of calls, had more finesse, more relationships and less of a temper. Things just always seemed to go easier when Jez handled them. Crowe found he could rub a certain kind of person the wrong way. He had no idea why.

His ex had called the night before last. He knew it was her when he heard the phone ring, though she hadn't called him in months. He'd just finished working out on the weight bench he kept in the basement of the Bay Ridge row house they'd shared.

"Keep it, Grady," she'd said of the house when they were splitting up assets. "I hate Brooklyn. And I hate this house." They'd inherited the house from his grandparents and hadn't been able to afford to change much. So they walked over the same linoleum floors his father had as a child, endured the same pink-tiled bathrooms, and climbed the same creaky steps. But he loved that house, and it was theirs free and clear—paid off long ago, taxes insanely low. *So we sell it. Buy something that's ours.* He wouldn't, couldn't sell the house where his father had grown up, where he had, too, essentially. Their first and angriest arguments were about that house.

He was breathless, his shirt damp with sweat, when he heard the phone ringing. Something about the way it traveled through the house, how he heard the ringing through thc floorboards, made his palms tingle. He took the stairs two at a time and got to the phone, an avocado-green wall unit, by the third ring.

"Crowe," he answered.

Just silence on the line. But it was her silence. He'd know the sound of her anywhere.

"Clara. Don't hang up."

A round release of air, as though she was trying to cloud cold glass with her breath. When she spoke, her voice was taut. "How did you know it was me?"

"Every time the phone rings, I think it's you. I just happened to be right tonight."

"Stop it."

"I miss you. Clara," he said, and it sounded like a plea, "I could die from how much. I keep thinking about the last time."

He heard the sharp intake of breath that he knew meant she was going to cry, and he felt close to tears himself, a thickness in his throat.

"Come back to me." It wasn't the first time he'd begged.

"I have to go. I shouldn't have called you."

"Wait," he said quickly. She hung up and he leaned his head against the wall. "Wait," he said again into dead air. He drew his fist back and punched the wall hard. The plaster buckled in a near-perfect circle and he brought his hand back fast to his chest. The pain started dull, slow, then radiated up his arm, his knuckles split and bleeding.

"Fuck," he whispered, though he wanted to scream. The pain felt good. He'd rather have physical pain than the raw gnawing he'd had in his chest since Clara left. Unfortunately, now he had both.

"I've been meaning to ask what happened to your hand," said Jez as they sped up the Henry Hudson, the dirty river glinting to their left, the city rising to their right. The warrant issued through some magic on Jez's part, they were headed to Charlie Shane's Inwood address.

"Bar fight."

"Yeah, right."

"What?"

"Let's just say I see you more as a lover than a fighter."

"Nice," he answered, slightly offended. They were partners after all; supposed to have each other's back. Did she really think he couldn't hold his own in a brawl? He stopped short of asking.

"Seriously."

"Hurt it working out. Punching bag."

She nodded, looked skeptical, but didn't say anything else. She had that motherly way about her, always with a tissue in her purse and a nose for bullshit. She always had snacks, too—peanut-butter crackers or granola bars.

"I know it's not easy," she said finally, looking out the window and not at him, almost as if she was thinking aloud. He didn't bother pretending that he didn't know what she was talking about. They took the rest of the ride in silence.

11

Fred was standing in the doorway when I reached the front step of the house. He wore an expression of concern as he watched the taxi depart. In his gray cardigan sweater and pressed navy slacks, he was solid, comforting, stronger than his seventy-five years.

"Isabel Blue," he said.

He'd called me this since we first became friends, a few years after he married my mother. The timing of this coincided with my sister leaving for college. When she moved into the city to go to Columbia University, she took a lot of her anger with her. I'd always adored and worshipped my older sister and I grieved her departure from the house, but even I had to admit that the dynamics in our home shifted for the better without her.

Like sand over ice, her absence allowed us to find firmer footing with each other. We were able to welcome my father's memory home—hanging old photographs, my mother and I talking openly, fondly, about him and the good things we remembered. Linda had hated for anyone to mention him, had sunk into despair on his birthday, Father's Day. For Linda, sadness had always been best expressed through anger. And her outbursts were frequent and passionate. With therapy and Erik, that had changed in her adult life. But out of loyalty to her—and not a little fear of her temper—I had kept my distance from Fred for the early years of his marriage to our mother.

Fred always weathered the storms of Linda's unhappiness with patient stoicism, as though he believed on some level that he deserved her anger. Maybe he did. I don't know. With the fog of her unhappiness dissipated, Fred and I saw each other for the first time over the kitchen table. I was dressed for school, feeling sad, missing my sister. He said, "Isabel Blue."

I looked at him and he offered me a warm smile. "It's not so bad, Isabel. She's just a train ride away."

I didn't have words for it then, the sad hollow inside me, the recognition that everything changes, that people die or they just leave you, and that you're expected to move along in the current of your life as though nothing has happened. It seemed terribly unfair to me at thirteen years old. Why did people even bother with anything if it was all just going to fade away or be wrested from you?

"My barn having burned to the ground, I can now see the moon." Fred was fond of haiku.

What a weirdo with his stupid sayings and those long, slow walks. How could she have married him? My sister's nasty comments lingered in my head. But that morning I suddenly saw someone different. Now that she was gone, not always whispering something in my ear, I saw someone kind, much like my father, but someone present, mindful—*not* like my father. Even when my father was smiling, laughing, joking, I could sometimes see it behind his eyes—anxiety, unhappiness—flickering like a firefly in a jar.

"What does that mean?" I asked. I liked the rhythm of the words. I liked the way each word fell to the ground with its particular weight but how the meaning seemed to hover somewhere just above me.

"Think about it."

I did. I thought about it a lot.

"YOUR MOTHER'S NOT here, dear," Fred said, stepping aside and sweeping me into the house with a strong arm around my shoulder. I saw him looking at the bandage on my head, but he didn't mention it, as though he thought that might be rude. "She's off for some pampering with her girlfriends at Canyon Ranch."

"I know," I said, letting him take my wrap, avoiding eye contact.

He laid it over the settee in the triple-height grand foyer. The entry was bathed in a sunny wash from the skylights above. The sunlight caught on the million tiny crystals in the chandelier and cast rainbow flecks around us on the floor.

If my mother had been home, there'd be noise—a television, music, the sound of her chatting on the phone. The sound would bounce off the high ceilings, the marble floors, seem to come from everywhere and nowhere. She couldn't stand a quiet house, or a dark one. There must always be sound and light. Today it seemed to echo with her absence with Fred's thoughtful, quiet energy.

"What's happened to you, Isabel?" he asked finally, turning me gently to face him with hands on my shoulders. "Who did this to you?"

"I—" I started, trying to think of a lie. But then I didn't have the energy. "I don't exactly know."

"Let's sit you down somewhere," he said, again moving me along with that strong arm. I felt myself rest against him, the weight of it all just too much suddenly. He brought me to the large plush couch in front of the fireplace, which was lit but dwindling to embers. I sank into the soft chenille, the cushions seeming to fold around me like an embrace. I told Fred what happened to me, withholding nothing, from Marcus not coming home two nights ago through my visit to the ATM.

"I need to use the computer, figure out how much he's taken from me. I need to try to do some research into this other missing Marcus Raine."

Fred sat on the hassock in front of me. He'd paced and frowned during my surprisingly calm and distanced telling of events, then came to sit there and put a hand on my arm.

"What you need is rest, Isabel." His tone was gentle but firm. "I'm going to call our lawyer and some people we know in the police department, and they're going to handle this mess. You are going to take a bath and get into bed."

"Fred, I can't do that—" I started to say. But the couch was so soft and the room was so warm. He lifted my feet from the floor and placed them on the hassock where he'd sat a moment before. I sank deeper into the cushions. The room around me started to get blurry and I thought of how that ER doctor had told me I needed to rest or suffer the consequences. I wondered if this sudden fading of will and awareness was what he meant. I felt the weight of a blanket on top of me.

"Don't worry, Isabel. We'll figure this all out."

"I just need to use the computer," I said, but it didn't sound like my voice, the words thick in my mouth.

"I'll bring you the laptop," he said. "We're wireless now, after Trevor and Emily complained during their last visit." I thought he might be humoring me but I suddenly lacked the strength to say so. The gray air darkened and swallowed me.

WHEN A HARD, loud crack, like a thick branch snapping, brought me back, I felt myself swim up through layers of deep sleep before I broke into the bright light of the room. The sound still echoed in my head, though now there was only silence. I listened to the quiet noises of the house—the ticking of the clock, the hum of heat through the vents—my whole body tense and tingling, my breathing heavy.

Like a honeycomb, all the rooms downstairs in Fred and Margie's house connected by small hallways and pocket doors, creating a kind of circle of adjacent rooms around the foyer—the parlor led to the dining area, which flowed into the kitchen. Another exit from the kitchen led to a short, narrow passage that drifted into a massive library and study with a second-floor landing. That room reconnected to the foyer.

The sliding doors that led from the parlor to the foyer were closed, but the doors that connected it to the large dining room were open. I heard a soft click, like the sound of a lock turning.

I almost called out Fred's name but something stopped me. Instead I slipped from the couch and let the blanket that covered me fall to the floor. I walked quietly over plush carpet toward the dining room in time to see three bulky shadows drift across the far wall. I felt a deep thump of dread in my chest, and suddenly the air around me, time itself, seemed thick and toxic with the energy of my own fear.

I scanned the room quickly for anything I might use to defend myself, and my eyes came to rest on the wrought-iron fire poker on the hearth. I grabbed it too quickly, sending the stand and the other tools toppling loudly to the stone. In the aftermath of sound, even the house seemed to hold its breath. There was a deafening stillness where my mind raced through various options, none of them particularly appealing.

I DIDN'T GROW up in this house. Fred and my mother moved here shortly after I left home to go to NYU. Until then we'd stayed in the other house, a large, rambling, rundown old place, because my mother felt we'd lost too much to leave the only home we'd ever known. The studio where my father died was torn down and replaced with a garden my mother tended with care. "She spends more time out there than she ever did with him," my sister observed bitterly. It was true, of course. And seeing her out there, on her knees in the dirt, pulling weeds and planting new bulbs in the spring, was not a comfort to us as the gardening must have been to her.

My sister and I could have left that house easily, every room, every creaking floorboard, every water stain akin to some memory of my father. Maybe it was my mother who wasn't ready to leave it behind. Fred contented himself with laborious repairs and renovations that he could have easily hired out. Over time, he managed to update the plumbing and electricity, replace the roof, strip and stain old floors. There was painting and wallpapering, new carpets. By the time Margie and Fred left, the old house was fully renovated and sold to a young couple starting a family who wanted to leave the city. Fred told me later that it was therapy for him to restore that old house. There were a lot of things my father left behind that he couldn't heal, places in the other man's wake where he wasn't wanted. But that house responded to his ministration, let him patch and repair its broken places. Like my mother's memorial garden, it didn't chafe with the attention, didn't struggle, rebuff, or withdraw.

This house, this new house built to my mother's specifications, was familiar but not native. I didn't know which boards creaked. It didn't have the hidden passages, old dumbwaiters, and storage cubbies. In this house, I couldn't hide. I'd have to fight.

Luckily, terror is a shot of adrenaline to the heart. I've never been more awake or more alert as I moved carefully toward the dining room. But as I turned the corner, poker raised like a baseball bat, I found the room was empty. I paused at the entryway and listened, wondering for a moment if I was being paranoid, imagined the things I'd heard.

I moved quickly around the circle of rooms, wondering if I'd come upon a serene Fred sitting in his study. He'd be surprised to see me wielding a fire poker. But all the rooms were empty until I came to the foyer.

It took a second for the scene to register. Fred, that kind and good man, who'd cared for us all with patience and respect, lay still and white on the marble floor, an impossible amount of blood pooling from beneath his head. His arms and legs were slightly akimbo, as though he was preparing to make a snow angel. I dropped to my knees beside him, let the poker clatter to rest on the floor.

I didn't have time to weep or scream. Those bulky shadows rose on the wall in front of me. I wasn't alone. I spun around to see three men move into the foyer from the study. I realized that they must have been following me around the circle of rooms. I reached for the poker, but one of them kicked it away from me.

In spite of his tremendous size—six foot four at least, and well over 250 pounds—there was something sickly and almost fragile about this man, something unwell around the eyes. He was pale to the point of being gray. He held a ridiculously large gun, which he raised slowly, almost reluctantly, in my direction. I held very still, tried to take in all the details.

The other men, similarly armed, were slighter but just as menacing, shared his same unhealthy pallor. The two smaller men looked like brothers, each with sandy-blond hair and something weak about the set of their jaws. I tried to say something but the horror of my situation had made my mouth dry, filled my throat with gauze. I found myself inching backward, like a crab, on feet and hands. Every instinct in my body made me want to be away from these men.

The large man raised his free hand. "Just stay still," he said with a smile. "Please don't move."

I recognized his voice instantly from the voice mail I'd heard. Ivan. But I was smart enough not to say so. I looked at each pair of eyes, searching for something I could relate to. But there was no fear, no remorse there. None of them even glanced in Fred's direction, as if they were accustomed to being in the presence of violence and spilled blood.

"Just tell us where he is. And," Ivan said, shrugging and pointing to the door, "we leave."

I had completely lost my ability to communicate; this scenario was so far out of my frame of reference, something that I might have imagined and written. But nothing in my life had prepared me for this type of event. I looked over at Fred, then back at Ivan. He gave me an almost friendly smile but there was something terrible about it, something dark.

"He's not dead," he said lightly. He pointed to Fred and then to his own square brow. "The head. It bleeds a lot, you know?"

To illustrate, he walked over to Fred and gave him a soft kick in the ribs. I was elated to hear my stepfather groan in pain, see his eyelids flutter. I moved over to him quickly, felt his blood soak through my skirt. I put a hand on his forehead; it was cool and clammy. I looked up at the three men.

"If you're looking for Marcus," I said, finally finding my voice, "I have no idea where he is."

Ivan regarded me carefully, seemed to size me up and consider my words. I became conscious of time passing quickly. My cell phone was in the pocket of my skirt. I wondered if I could press 911 and send without him noticing. Fred needed help fast.

"He betrayed me, stole from me," Ivan said, angry, almost petulant. "He tried to kill me."

He lifted his shirt with his free hand to show me a swath of bandages around his chest, too much blood—garish red against the white—seeping through the gauze. I saw sweat emerge on his gray forehead. Was he the one I'd heard screaming? One of his colleagues lit a cigarette and leaned against the wall. The smell filled my sinuses. I shifted my hand into my pocket. But Ivan shook his head at me. I removed it slowly.

"He betrayed me, too," I said finally. We could have been discussing anything—the crumbling economy, bad weather, gravity, forces out of our control that can change our lives. I felt a sudden wash of rage.

"Look at me!" I yelled suddenly, startling all of them. Both of the smaller men raised their guns. The smoker let his cigarette drop to the floor. I pointed to my own head. "Someone did this to me. A tall woman, a blonde, from Czech like you. She destroyed Marcus's office, probably my home, too. They took everything from me. If I knew where he was, do you think I'd be *here*?"

Ivan considered me. I noticed a deep scar on his face, that his hands were callused. I was still yelling, trying to make him understand.

"Hush, hush," he said, as though he was talking to a weeping child. And I realized I *was* weeping, big rivers of tears streaming down my face. I wiped at them with my sleeve. "Don't yell."

I saw it then, the way he didn't like me yelling, was uncomfortable with my tears. He was a bit on the slow side, not quite disabled but someone with a very low IQ. There was something babyish about him, too, and something skittish. A child used to being brutalized, one who'd developed a flinch. Suddenly there was a strangely familiar expression on his face, something around his red-rimmed eyes, the corners of his mouth. I thought of Marcus's photo album. Had he been in there? Had I seen him before?

"She was tall. Nearly as tall as you, with blond hair and green eyes," I said more softly. "She knew Marcus," I continued when he didn't say anything.

He nodded slowly, a deep frown furrowing his brow, his expression going dark.

"Do you know who I'm talking about?"

He nodded again, but this time to his two friends. He said something in Czech that I didn't understand. The two men both looked at me for a second and I wondered if I'd made a terrible mistake. They got what they wanted from me and now they'd have no use for me or Fred. I'd lost my gamble. I closed my eyes.

When I opened them again, the two smaller men had moved toward the door and were exiting. I heard their footfalls on the landing. They were bold, these men. Coming and going in broad daylight, not hiding themselves or their vehicle. Were they careless or apathetic? Aware that the property was removed from the street, not visible to the neighbors? They must have been watching the apartment, followed me up here from the city. I'd been too oblivious, too naive to notice.

A second later, with my heart a turbine engine in my chest, I heard a car hum to life outside. Ivan raised his gun at me, but this time I didn't look away. I didn't want to make it easier for him to kill me; I wanted him to see my eyes.

"Who is he?" I asked. "What's his name?"

Fred shifted and moaned beside me. Ivan offered that same weird smile again, this time accompanied by a low chuckle.

"Tell me," I said, holding his gaze. "I need to know. If you're going to kill me, I want to know my husband's name before I die."

Something strange passed between us. Two people who might as well be living on different planets, our experiences and ideas, our intellects were so opposite. In that moment, we were unified by rage and betrayal. He lowered his gun.

"His name is Kristof Ragan." The smile dropped from his face. "He is my brother."

He raised a finger to his lips then and made a shushing noise. Then he took that same finger and drew it slowly across his neck, whispering something in Czech that I didn't understand. On the other hand, I don't suppose I needed an interpreter.

Then he turned and left, more quickly and gracefully than I would have imagined possible of a man his size. I was already dialing 911 when I heard the car move down the drive.

BY THE TIME Linda returned to the loft, she was frazzled and drained. After a long, slow trip uptown to Isabel's apartment, she learned that she'd missed her sister by minutes, according to the cop in the hallway. She was shocked to look over his shoulder and see Izzy's apartment trashed, but she wasn't allowed inside. The detectives working the case had also left, following up a lead. She left feeling frustrated and filled with a sick anxiety. She'd inherited her mother's proclivity for worry. Fight it as she might, she'd never quite been able to overcome it.

She had a tension headache brewing when she closed the door and saw Erik waiting on the couch. Something about the look on her husband's face ratcheted the pain up a notch. Dread and guilt duked it out in her chest as she moved closer to him.

"What?" she said by way of greeting, more testily than she'd intended.

"We need to talk, Linda." She felt a jangle of alarm as she flashed on her assignation in the bathroom at the Java Stop. So tawdry. So foolish. Did she *want* to ruin her life and marriage? Erik could have easily seen her coming or going. Maybe someone in the building had heard Ben pleading at the intercom, mentioned it to Erik.

"Sure," she said, laying her bag by the door. She moved over to the couch and curled herself up in a ball there. In spite of the tension, she still found herself glancing about at the perpetual mess that was their home. If it was cluttered, at least it was clean—but only because of the weekly cleaning woman. How long had Trevor's soccer jersey been hanging off that chaise? Wasn't it anybody else's responsibility but hers to pick up after the kids? Weren't they old enough to pick up their own stuff?

"Don't worry about the mess, Linda. I'll take care of it in a minute."

"I didn't say anything."

He released a breath through his nose. He was perched on a stool, a half-full glass of water in his hand. She found she couldn't look at him directly, couldn't hold those earnest, loving eyes. She didn't deserve that gaze. She looked down at her fingernails. Her nails were a mess; she needed a manicure.

"I've made a terrible mistake," he said. He shifted off the stool and came over to her, sat heavily beside her on the couch. "I've done something really stupid, possibly unforgivable, Linda."

Relief mingled with concern and she raised her eyes to his face. She saw him then, maybe for the first time in days. Their busy life was a perpetual swing dance between kids and home, her work and his, meals and pickups and drop-offs from various activities—kung fu for Emma, violin lessons for Trevor. Sometimes they just fell into a heap on the couch after the kids went to bed and watched an hour of television, or read in bed until one fell asleep and the other turned off the light. She thought some days he noticed the dishes in the sink before he noticed what she was wearing or that she'd changed her perfume. Sometimes she thought they'd see each other more if they worked apart, each of them going to an office and returning home at the end of the day.

She regarded his sandy stubble and ocean-blue eyes, the lean lines of his high cheekbones, his aquiline nose. That face had tamed her heart. He had sunshine at his core, a breezy summer day at the beach.

"What are you so mad about?" he'd asked early in their relationship. A swank gallery in SoHo; he was fifteen minutes late. It wasn't even her show. But she raged at him on the street in the rain. "Because I *know* you're not this angry about my being fifteen minutes late."

She felt as if he'd thrown a bucket of cold water on her. Embarrassed, sobered, she caught sight of her reflection in the gallery's picture window. She didn't recognize her own expression, her own posture. A few people were watching; one strikingly thin woman smirked, a small plastic cup of wine in her hand. Why he didn't walk away right then, she never could figure out.

"You're too young, too beautiful, too good to let yourself be this way," he whispered, taking her hands. She knew then that he really *saw* her, that he might have been the first and only person who ever had, other than her sister. The face she wore for everyone else, the demure and polite smile, the unfailingly kind demeanor, the proper girl who did everything right . . . he didn't even notice it. When he looked at her he saw straight to the heart of her.

Within a month, she was seeing a shrink, trying to figure out why indeed she was so angry. And then she had to claw her way out of the quicksand of her own inner life before coming to shore. In a cozy office on the Upper West Side, a motherly psychologist with a comforting wave of gray hair and a soft bosom asked her, over time, questions she almost couldn't stand to hear.

"Do you really blame your mother for moving on, for doing what she thought she had to save herself and her girls? Do you really hate Fred for loving your mother? Isn't it just that you're angry with your father for abandoning you, for being absent emotionally before that? Isn't it just safer to be angry at living people because there's no way to resolve the anger you have toward your father? Do you really think he loved your sister more than he did you?"

These were the hard things she had to face and answer. But she never would have thought to confront them at all if not for Erik. And where would she be then? She reached for him, touched his face and let her hand drift down to his shoulder.

"How could *anything* you've done be unforgivable?" she asked. He lowered his head at this, put his chin all the way to his chest.

"Linda."

"I forgive you," she said. "Whatever it is."

She slid into him and wrapped him tight in her arms. She held on to him, her buoy against the great tides of regret and shame, guilt for the things she'd done, how she'd betrayed him. *I'm so sorry,* she said to his heart. *I'll never see him again.*

"Linda," he said again, pulling away from her. She looked at his face and didn't like what she saw there. Despair. A dark flower of dread started to bloom in her center.

"Erik," she said, releasing a breath with his name. "What is it?"

It had seemed like only seconds after the 911 call, as I begged and pleaded with Fred to open his eyes, that police and paramedics were at the scene. The next thing I knew, Fred was lifted into the back of an ambulance, I climbed in after him, and we raced toward the hospital. More police were waiting when we arrived and Fred was wheeled away.

I stared after him, wondering if my carelessness had ended his life. I didn't feel anything but a kind of numbness. A voice in my head kept telling me, *This is not happening. Wake up.*

A cop started asking me questions: What happened? How was it that I was already injured? Could I describe the men who did this to my stepfather? I asked for Detective Crowe. He was called. I was escorted to a waiting area.

I waited, pacing. Fatigue was replaced by nervous energy. I couldn't stop moving, couldn't keep my mind from racing back over the story of my marriage, looking for the chinks, the flaws in the plot. And there they were, the clues, the foreshadowing that the hero was really a villain, waiting behind the curtain with his dagger drawn.

But no. Life's not so simple. People are many things, each of them true. Marcus was my husband. He was right: We were great friends and excellent lovers. That was true once, even if it didn't matter much now.

I came back to the present when a doctor pushed into the room, told me that a bullet had grazed Fred's head, leaving a valley over his ear but never penetrating his skull. He'd lost a lot of blood but he'd walk away from the injury. A lucky man. Then, suddenly, Detective Crowe was there with his little black notebook and expensive pen, taking a statement from me that I now barely remember giving. I wondered how he'd gotten there so fast, and he told me they'd been in Inwood, searching the apartment of Charlie Shane, my doorman, another familiar figure in my life who, it seemed, was not what he appeared. They'd found nothing useful. But Charlie had disappeared.

I vaguely recall offering Detective Crowe a recount of the events at Fred and Margie's house. Was it skepticism that I saw on his face as I recounted the scene?

"Isabel." There was that friendly use of my name again. "Are you leaving something out?" His pen hovered.

"Of course not," I answered, indignant.

I felt the weight of his gaze. "Don't be foolish," he said quietly, moving a little closer to me.

"I don't know what you mean."

He let an awkward minute pass, during which I looked at my cuticles in the horrid white fluorescent light. I watched nurses with their swift, quiet steps, listened to the incessant electronic rippling of a telephone that no one answered.

"You know what's starting to bother me?" he asked finally.

"What's that?"

"You seem to be having all these run-ins with unsavory types—FBI impersonators and European thugs—and yet you always emerge unscathed. Meanwhile, the bodies of the injured and dead litter the scene." Poetry again, from the gentleman cop.

I fixated on the word choice a moment, as I'm prone to do, analyzed it for its appropriateness. *Unscathed*: without suffering any injury or harm.

"I wouldn't exactly say I've 'emerged unscathed,' Detective. Quite the opposite." I pointed to my head but I was thinking of the deeper injuries, my riven life, the derailed narrative of my marriage.

"Relatively speaking," he said with an assenting lift of his shoulders. "What I meant was, there was really no reason I can see for any of these people to leave you breathing. We're not talking about people operating with conscience. We're talking about murderers and thieves. So I find myself asking: Why are you still alive?"

It was a good question and one I'd certainly asked myself, even posed to my sister.

"Any theories?" I asked, only half a smart-ass.

"One theory might be that you have a greater involvement in this than we initially suspected. That rather than a victim, you might be an accomplice, hiding in plain sight, playing the role of the injured wife."

I shook my head. "No."

"Because to me, you don't seem like the type for this sort of thing. This woman you see on the talk shows—her husband has another family in Kalamazoo, or her suitor took off with her life savings—that's not you. You're sharp, aren't you? Together."

"Maybe not sharp enough to be immune to subterfuge, but definitely too sharp to be a part of anything like this. People dead around me, my stepfather very nearly killed, all my money gone, my sister's money? No. No." Just the recounting of it all filled me with that dangerous cocktail of rage and fear. I realized suddenly that both of my fists were clenched hard, nails digging ruthlessly into my palms. I released them with difficulty.

"Then just tell me what you're holding back."

"Nothing," I said, trying to look as earnest as possible. "I swear."

Lies are a contagion, a virus that replicates itself. Marc's deception was the germ that had infected me. I was sick with it, fevered with a compulsion to understand how he'd managed to deceive me and why, so I was coughing up lies of my own. The detective was right. I was withholding information. The text message from Marcus, the name given to me by Ivan, his alleged brother—those things belonged to me. It felt like all I had left. If I let him have these things, I'd have lost ownership of them as well.

"I don't believe you," he said simply.

"I want a lawyer."

He raised a hand, gave me a warning look. "If you go down that road, it puts us on opposite teams."

Oh, spare me. Did he really think he could manipulate me out of my rights?

"Our conversation ended thirty seconds ago," I said.

The detective pressed his mouth into a thin, tight line and I saw his nostrils flare just slightly. Would he blush or pale with his frustration? I wondered. Then his cheeks fired up, a lovely rosey blush on the white of his skin. Marcus always used to go gray when he was angry. It didn't seem healthy. Red is the color of emotion brought forth, a brilliant rush of flame that burns hot and incinerates itself. Gray is the color of ire that's eating you up inside, hollowing you out.

Detective Crowe opened his mouth and then clamped it shut again. We had a brief staring contest, which I won. He lowered his eyes, turned and left the waiting room, the electricity of everything he had wanted to say trailing behind him. He'd have slammed the door, I'm sure, but the hydraulic hinge only allowed it to close with an unsatisfying hiss.

He wasn't gone long—I was still staring at the door—when Linda and Erik burst through. I'd called Linda upon arriving at the hospital, quite by instinct. I barely remembered the conversation. Her arrival caused some odd combination of anxiety and relief. Trevor and Emily followed behind, holding hands, looking like bush babies with wide eyes and nervous smiles. The sight of this made me sad. If they weren't fighting, they were scared. I had to take responsibility for everything. I'd let Marcus into our lives, and he'd damaged us all.

"Have you seen Fred since he arrived? What happened?" Linda asked, rushing to me, grabbing me hard with both arms. Then, "How could you just race off like that? And why haven't you answered my calls? I've been really *worried* about you."

I let myself sink into her strong embrace, into the soft cashmere of her coat, didn't even bother answering her questions. Over her shoulder, I looked at Erik, who gave me a sad nod. Suddenly I could feel the undercurrent of tension between them and I knew he'd told Linda everything.

"Fred's okay," I said into her shoulder. "He's going to be fine."

I recounted the events at the house, leaving out the details I'd kept from Detective Crowe. I didn't want them to know anything that could get them in trouble later.

"You need a lawyer," Erik said, pulling his cell phone from his coat.

"Call Fred and Margie's guy," Linda said to him, her tone polite but clipped. "I left messages for Mom—one on her cell phone and a message at the hotel desk. They said they'd find her and tell her there was an emergency. I know she'll come right home." She shot me an apologetic look. "With Fred being hurt, I had to call her."

I nodded my understanding. "I called, too, of course."

Emily and Trevor hadn't said a word, something I wouldn't have thought possible just two days ago. I knelt down and opened my arms and they both came to me. I held on to them, felt their arms wrap around my body.

"It's okay," I whispered, even though this was a lie, that disease again.

"Mom is really mad at Daddy," Emily whispered. Out of the corner of my eye I saw Linda bow her head. Erik turned toward the window and looked out at the parking lot. He seemed to be scrolling through the phone book on his cell; I could hear the soft musical beeping as he scanned contacts.

"It's okay," I repeated. "Everything is going to be fine."

I pulled back, looked at their sad little faces, gave them each a kiss, then reluctantly moved away.

"I'm going to check on Fred," I said to Linda.

"I'll come with you." I didn't want her to, but I could hardly refuse. I grabbed my bag off the chair and Erik's voice followed us out.

"This is Erik Book, Fred and Margie Thompson's son-in-law. Is John Brace in?"

In the hall Linda grabbed my hand and held on tight as we walked.

"You already know," she said. Not a question.

"Yes," I said, squeezing her hand. "It's going to be okay." This was fast becoming my stock response as everything fell apart around us. But I found I couldn't look at her long, or give her the comfort of my gaze. Her blue, blue eyes seemed to glow in the pale landscape of her face. The purple smudges under her eyes, the strain around her mouth hurt me too much. She didn't have to say anything else; I knew every emotion rocketing through her. I could feel it through her skin. And she knew she didn't have to say anything. We'd talk later, dissect and analyze, figure and resolve.

But for the moment we moved down the hall toward the room Fred now occupied, not saying a word. Before we got to his door, I stopped and took both her hands.

"Forgive him, Linda. As awful as it is, he did it for you."

"I forgive him," she said, not looking at me. "I just don't know if I can live with it. I feel like Mom. He did all this, risked our whole future, and I didn't even know. There are other things, too. My fault. I don't know if we're strong enough to survive everything that's wrong."

"Don't say that." The thought of their marriage falling apart because of a mistake I had made filled me with a terrible anxiety. "Please. Let me fix this."

"This is not for you to fix, Iz," she said, putting a gentle hand on my face. "Don't you get that? You didn't do anything wrong. You loved him."

"You warned me. This is my fault."

"Even I didn't imagine this, honey. *This* is not what I meant. I just thought he was a jerk, that he couldn't love you the way you deserved."

"You were right," I said. I let her take me in her arms, rested my head on her shoulder. "Don't leave him, Linda. Your marriage, your family. It's real, it's solid. It can survive anything. It's only money."

She squeezed me hard but didn't answer. "Let's go see about Fred," she said after a moment, pulling away from me and taking my hand. She didn't want to talk anymore; I let her off the hook and led her to Fred's room.

We stopped at the entrance to the dim space, watched Fred's still, narrow form, listening to the reassuring tones of his heart monitor. I was buffeted by twin tides of regret and anger. But when he saw us huddling in the doorway, he smiled. That was Fred. He could always manage a smile. Or maybe it was the pain medication.

"You look just like when you were girls," he said. A dreamy, loopy quality to his words made me wish for a little dose of whatever they'd given him. Linda moved to the bed and took his hand. The births of Emily and Trevor had brought them closer. Fred was a wonderful grandfather, the only one her children knew. He showered them with love, and I think in recent years she was finally able to see the man we all saw. She'd take care of him until Margie got back; I knew that. The good girl.

"I'm sorry, Fred," I said from the doorway. "I'd never have come to you if I knew . . ." I let the sentence trail.

He shook his head slowly. "I'm glad you did. I just wish I could have protected you, Isabel. I keep forgetting I'm an old man."

I went to his bedside and leaned down to gently kiss his forehead. He pointed to his bandage. "Maybe we could get everyone else to wear one just so we don't look so silly."

We both smiled and Linda leaned in to kiss him on the cheek when her phone rang. She answered it quickly.

"Mom," she said. "Everything's okay."

With Linda talking and Fred looking at her expectantly, neither of them noticed as I slipped from the room. I backed into the hallway and then walked toward the elevator bank, just missing the closing doors of one car. I pressed the button hard a couple of times, but the digital screen above it told me the car was floors away and I might be waiting awhile. I decided on the stairs.

"Where are you going, Izzy?"

I turned to see Trevor looking slim and stylish in faded jeans and a retro rock-and-roll Ramones T, Vans on his feet. His curls were wild; a worried smile flashed his face, then turned into a frown.

"I'm going to get some air," I lied.

He shook his head just slightly, and in that moment he looked so much like his mother—the same knowing aura, the same curious narrowing of the eyes. I saw him taking in details—the wrap on my shoulders, the bag strapped around my body.

"You're going to find him, aren't you?"

I considered lying again. But instead I nodded, lifted a finger to my mouth, and started backing toward the door.

"Do you have a gun?"

"No," I said, startled by his boyish question, which seemed at the same time frighteningly practical. New York City kids are just a little too savvy for their own good. "Of course not."

He shrugged. "You might need one."

I might at that. "Don't tell them you saw me leave."

"Maybe I should. Maybe this is a bad idea." He was one of the best players on his chess team. He could see that I was outmatched and about to make a stupid move that might cost me the game. Suddenly this little kid who I'd watch enter the world, who I'd rocked and carried, fed and changed, seemed smarter, more worldly than I was.

"Don't," was all I could manage. "Not for the next fifteen minutes."

"Izzy?" I heard him say as I turned and moved quickly through the door and flew down the stairs as fast as I could. I knew him. He was a good egg, wanted things orderly, still thought the world was black and white, just like his mother. He'd tell—but he'd hesitate, just because he was a boy, because he liked the idea of being in on a secret. With luck, I'd be gone before anyone tried to come after me.

A HUNDRED YEARS ago Marcus and I were in Paris. For our first anniversary, he'd surprised me on a Thursday with tickets to leave the next day. We joked that we'd probably saved about a thousand dollars in pre-trip shopping—but I made up for it once we arrived.

"He did what?!" my sister shrieked when I called her. Her delight rang over the line and I knew he'd climbed a rung in her estimation, which filled me with childish pleasure. "That's *soooo* romantic. Oh, I love Paris!"

"Dude, you're making me look bad," Erik complained when we were all on speakerphone together.

"Yeah, *really* bad," said Linda. But I could hear the smile in her voice. They'd had their share of romantic trips and enviable moments. And now they had kids, as Linda liked to say. *Romance is a pizza delivery and a bottle of wine after Emily and Trevor go to bed.*

We stayed in a small, intimate hotel near Jardins des Tuilleries on the tranquil rue Saint-Hyacinthe and passed our days shopping, eating, drinking, fairly skipping through the streets of that magnificent city. I spent my mornings writing in a small café, ensconced at a tiny table in the corner, the competing aromas of fresh bread, coffee grinds, and cigarette smoke mingling in the air with lively conversation and the clinking of cups and silverware, while Marcus slept until nearly noon.

In the evenings, we dined slowly, lingering for hours over beautiful meals, then visiting nightclubs, dancing and drinking, returning to the hotel to make love. I don't remember even the tiniest disagreement on that trip, but maybe that's revisionist history. Maybe we argued over what sights to see, or whether we could afford more than one Hermès scarf, or where to go for dinner—all the normal negotiations of living a life together, that might blow up into something bigger. But I don't remember anything like that.

On the other hand, there are some things that come back to me now, moments I hadn't given much thought to then. He said he'd never been to Paris, that my surprise was secretly a gift for himself, too. But he seemed strangely at ease on its streets, as if he knew his way around.

"Are you sure you haven't been here before?" I asked, my nose in our guidebook. He navigated the Metro with ease, quickly found exactly the café or shop or museum we were searching for, while I might as well have been on the moon.

"Maybe in another life," he answered. There was something solemn to his tone that caused me to look up from my reading. But he was smiling when our eyes met. He pointed to his temple. "Smart. You married a very smart man."

The truth was Marcus always seemed to know where we were or how to get to any destination. He had a mind for navigation, an uncanny internal GPS. I might wander lost and confused, even in my own city, turned around after a ride on the subway, unsure of east and west. Not Marcus. Not ever. It was annoying, how he was always right, but I found myself relying on it. A man like Marcus was the reason other men didn't ask for directions.

Our last night in Paris, we were returning to the hotel, both of us a bit glum that the trip was coming to a close.

"One more," Marcus said, grabbing my hand.

A narrow stairwell led down beneath the sidewalk. An electric strain of music seemed to waft up from the darkness. It was late. We had an early flight.

"Why not?" he said when I hesitated. "This time tomorrow we'll be home."

The damp stone staircase ended at a heavy wooden door. When he pulled it open, sound and smoke came out in a wave that pushed us back, then washed us in. Soon we were one with a throbbing mass of bodies that seemed to pulse in unison with the dance beat. We made our way to the bar, where Marcus shouted something at the pierced and scantily clad young woman who leaned in to take our drink order.

I normally don't like crowds, overwhelmed as I become by details, energies, expressions on faces. But I felt oddly centered, able to coolly observe my environment. I could tell it was a local haunt; it lacked that Parisian self-awareness of its place in the dreams of the rest of the world. There was something gritty and slapdash about it, as though you could come back tomorrow and it might be gone. The chic, lithe Parisians I'd been staring at in envy for days in high-end shops and restaurants were replaced by an alternative set, tattoo covered and glinting with metal in odd places, nipples and tongues, eyebrows. I watched an androgynous couple make out near the door, a woman moving slowly to some internal beat, her eyes pressed closed. On a small stage, three men with identically styled dark hair and black garb were surrounded by electronic instruments and computers; they seemed to be the origin of the sound, though they were as grim and stone-faced as undertakers. I turned to comment to Marcus, but he was gone. I peered through the crowd and saw the back of his head as he moved toward the bathrooms. He must have yelled to me and I didn't hear him over the din. There was a fresh drink on the tall table beside me which I assumed he'd left for me—something bitter and heavily alcoholic. When nearly twenty minutes passed, my drink gone, my interest in the scene around me dwindling, I headed in the direction I'd seen him disappear.

When I saw him, he was standing with a woman—she was emaciated and pale, with features too sharp, too angular for her to be quite pretty. She was talking to him heatedly, and he was looking around, clearly uncomfortable. Just as I approached them, she reached out and touched his face. I saw him grab her hand and push it gently away. She looked so injured, so confused, that I felt my heart clench for her.

He turned away and almost ran right into me.

"What's going on?" I asked. It was quieter away from the stage but I still had to yell.

"Some crazy woman thinks she knows me. I can't convince her otherwise," he said, grabbing my arm. "Let's go."

"Kristof, please!" she yelled after us. "Please."

He didn't turn back to her, just hurried me toward the door. I felt some kind of primal tug to look at her again. She was yelling something I couldn't make out.

"You don't know her?" I asked him when we were outside. I felt oddly shaken, a slight tremble in my hands.

He was already walking away, came back and grabbed my hand. "No," he said with a scowl. "Of course not."

"The way she touched you—" I said, and found I couldn't finish. From where I stood, I would have thought them lovers. Her touch was so intimate—her eyes so desperate. I stood rooted, not willing to follow him. I kept an eye on the door, wondering if she'd come out after us. I saw his eyes drift there, too.

"Isabel, she was *high*," he said, tugging at me, his hand still in mine. I resisted, made him move back closer to me. "She called me by another name. You heard it yourself. She was clearly unwell or at least impaired."

I found myself studying his face. His expression was earnest, even amused. His eyes were wide, brow lifted. He matched my gaze and then finally dropped his eyes to the sidewalk.

"Okay, you caught me," he said, lifting his hands. "I have a girlfriend here in Paris. This whole trip was just a ruse so that I could rendezvous with her this last night—while you stood a few yards away."

He gave me that magic smile then and the lightest drizzle started to fall. It all just washed away as he pulled me close.

"You're not the jealous type, Iz."

I bristled. It wasn't about me being jealous or not. It was about a woman who wore an expression I recognized on some cellular level. Loss, betrayal, a touch of anger. I knew that face; I'd worn it for different reasons. But I didn't say anything else. I let him drop his arm around my shoulder and steer me toward the hotel. I stole one last look behind us, sure I'd see her standing there grim and lonely in the rain. But the stairwell was dark and empty; I didn't hear the music that had drawn us there anymore, either.

I WENT BACK to Linda and Erik's. I had a key and knew that the apartment was empty; maybe not the best idea in the world but I was desperate. I needed space to think, a change of clothes, and some time on a computer. I also needed to figure out how to get some money. I'd stopped at the ATM and cleared out the rest of my cash, a hundred from each account. Now I had five hundred dollars, the money from the accounts plus what I'd already had in my wallet. I knew it wouldn't last long. I still had my credit cards but I knew I couldn't use them without creating a trail that was easily followed—that is, if he hadn't maxed those out as well.

I took a shower in Linda's bathroom, the only uncluttered space in the house. Her sanctuary with its stone walls and steam shower. The kids weren't even allowed to enter. Sometimes I think she'd force Erik to use the kids' bathroom if she could. I tried not to wet the bandage but failed and wound up peeling it off painfully.

After my shower, I looked at myself in the long mirrored wall over the marble sink and was shocked at how horrible the cut on my head looked, reaching from the middle of my brow to my temple—like something out of a horror film. My hair had been hideously shaved back a bit, which was bad enough. And the wound itself was too red, some dark yellow puss leaking out between the black stitching. I didn't think the leakage was healthy, but I didn't have time to worry about it. I found some gauze and medical tape in the first-aid kit under the sink and bandaged myself up again, nearly nauseated by how much the wound hurt to the touch. I recalled then that I was supposed to be taking antibiotics. Were they in my bag? I couldn't remember. Brown watched me mournfully, hands on his paws. He emitted a low whine from the doorway, as if he was concerned about me.

"It's okay, Brown," I said. "Don't worry."

I padded into the kitchen with him at my heels, put some food in his bowl and changed his water, gave him a doggie treat. He seemed to feel better about things after this.

After choosing a pair of jeans and a black wool sweater from Linda's closet, a matching pink bra and panties from her underwear drawer, I dressed and went into Trevor's room, where I knew the computer was on 24/7, no log-in required.

I tried my accountant's office again and just got an endless ringing, no voice mail ever picking up. I called directory assistance, tucking Trevor's cordless phone between my shoulder and ear while simultaneously searching for the firm on Google. Maybe I had the wrong number.

"No listing for a Benjamin and Heller, Inc., in Manhattan or the five boroughs, ma'am." And nothing online.

I realized I'd never visited their offices or even made a call to Arthur, the man who came to our house at tax time, who called me with the occasional question about my expenses, requesting this receipt or that canceled check. I let Marc handle it all. I just signed the quarterly tax reports and year-end returns without so much as a glance.

The computer screen swam before my tired eyes as I rechecked my bank accounts, since I knew those log-ins and passwords by heart. Nothing had changed except my recent withdrawals, when I'd basically cleaned myself out.

Then I checked our American Express bill, looking for Marc's last charges, knowing he was too smart to be using his cards now. I was just grasping at what little information was available to me. All the usual charges—the smoothie shop at the gym, take-out places we liked, the grocery store, our local bar. I started scrolling back through the last few months.

Linda did this all the time, I knew. She checked the Amex bill daily, since they used it like cash, tracked all their expenses that way.

"Poor Erik can't even buy a cup of coffee at Starbucks without my knowing about it," she joked. The joke was on her, though, wasn't it? She was so busy looking at the little things that the big ones completely eluded her. Not that I was one to judge.

I hadn't looked at my credit-card statements in months, charged what I wanted, took out cash from the accounts I was told to and never once thought about what I was spending. I'd only checked a couple of months ago because my card had been declined.

"You're using an expired card, Isabel," said Marcus when I'd called him. Funny how I'd not thought to contact Amex or my accountant. "I left the new one on the kitchen counter about three weeks ago."

I sifted through a pile of mail and found it with a little note: "Tear up your old card and use this one. Love you, M."

Still I'd been sufficiently annoyed to think I should start taking more interest in our finances. But I'd quickly lost interest after a couple of days of checking things out.

At Trevor's desk I found myself scanning Marc's charges, his small-business card sharing an interface with our personal cards.

I sifted through a few months of charges before I started to see a pattern emerge. On or around the fifteenth of every month, there was a large charge on Marc's business card, nearly two thousand dollars spent at a vendor listed on the statement as Services Unlimited, Inc. It really could have been any kind of legitimate business service, cleaning or document shredding or some kind of software licensing maybe. But it was the only thing that I could see that brought up any questions—even his charges on our personal card at Cornucopia (my favorite florist), dinner at the Mandarin Oriental, an obscene sum at La Perla, all coincided with gifts and evenings out that I remembered well.

I searched the Internet for Services Unlimited and found a Web site offering temporary "reception services." Uniquely beautiful women in scanty business attire leaned over provocatively to take dictation or reach for files, listened attentively with pens in their mouths at a board meeting. I would have laughed under other circumstances at the raunchy silliness of it, but instead my insides clenched as I scrolled through page after page of leggy, pouty girls offering their "business skills." Services Unlimited was an escort service, legal, ostensibly not offering sex, just arm candy. They took credit cards like any legitimate business. I tried to imagine Marcus with the type of woman I saw on page after page; I just couldn't. I tried to imagine him paying for sex. He was too arrogant; it didn't seem possible. But what did I know about Marcus? About anything? I'd only in the last few hours learned his real name.

I grabbed a worn Transformers notebook and a purple-inked pen from the shelf above Trevor's computer. I was about to write down the number emblazoned across the top of the screen, a 718 exchange, meaning one of the outer boroughs, when I saw her, the woman from Marcus's office. She was listed simply as "S." Her description read: *Six feet of pure stamina and efficiency.*

I unconsciously lifted a finger to the cut on my head and startled myself with the pain—of the physical wound and the memory of the text message. *I can still feel you inside me.*

I tried to force the pieces together—the text message, the woman who'd attacked me carrying a gun, impersonating an FBI agent, now vamping on this Web site, the monthly charge on my husband's credit card. This was beyond my experience, beyond my ability to weave a narrative from disconnected facts. I was still staring at her, all kinds of dark imaginings parading through my thoughts, when my phone started ringing. I checked the screen. *Jack calling.* My agent.

"Hey," he said when I picked up. "Good news. A nice check arrived. On signing from the UK sale."

She seemed to be challenging me, standing with her legs spread apart, clutching a phone, lips parted. I wanted to leap through the screen and strangle her, all my rage at the situation directed at her. *Who are you? Who are you to my husband?*

"Iz?"

"Yeah, I'm here."

"What's wrong?"

"Nothing. I'm fine." When would all this hit the news? I wondered. Soon, I would think. Authors are rarely celebrities, but something like this could make me one. It would be just the kind of hook the media needed to sell the story: BESTSELLING AUTHOR'S HUSBAND TURNED VILLIAN—TRUTH STRANGER THAN FICTION.

"I need that money, Jack."

"Okay," he said, drawing out the word. "I'll wire it tomorrow."

"No. I need it today. In cash."

There was a pause where I heard him tapping on his keyboard—multitasking, which I hated. Then: "Very funny."

"Jack, pay attention," I said. "I'm not kidding."

Another pause, but the tapping stopped abruptly. "What's going on?"

Jack and I had been friends since NYU. We met in a creative writing class. But he never had the patience—or the talent—for the actual writing, he realized. He just wanted the sale. After graduation he went straight to work at a literary agency, where a few years later he represented and sold my first novel. Eventually he started his own agency. We were allies, friends, and colleagues.

And once, just weeks before I met Marcus, we'd traveled together to a conference, where we'd gotten loaded at a local bar and wound up sleeping together. It might have always been there, this attraction, just beneath the surface, but the friendship and business relationship were so good that we'd just ignored the other, more volatile, aspect of our affection. I talked to him almost as often as I did my sister or my husband, but neither of us had ever again addressed the night we spent together. In the wee hours after our lovemaking, I'd dressed hastily and left his hotel room while he slumbered heavily. I wasn't even certain if he remembered what happened that night.

Now I told him everything about the recent events of my life. Everything beginning with the night Marc didn't return home, ending with the Web site open in front of me.

"Holy *Christ,*" he whispered into the phone when I was done. "Isabel, is this for real?"

"Yeah," I said. "Unfortunately, it is."

"You're hurt. Are you okay? Really okay?"

"I think so. How do I know? How is one supposed to handle a situation like this?"

"I think you're *not,* Iz. I think you're supposed to get into a bed somewhere and let the professionals handle it. Cops, lawyers—that's what these people *do.*"

If we were in the room together, he'd put a hand on my shoulder or usher me to a chair somewhere. I imagined him running a big hand through his thick, dark hair. I wished I was looking into the warmth of his dark eyes, noticing he needed a shave, feeling relaxed and calmed by his presence. Instead I stared at the harsh beauty of the woman still on my screen and felt something akin to indigestion, some acidic brew of anger and fear.

"I can't do that. I've already given too much power away. He stole from me. He hurt my family. He's not going to stroll off, with the police always just behind chasing warrants and following leads. No."

Jack issued the exasperated sigh that I've heard often in our relationship, a kind of tired blowing out of his lips. He regarded me as generally pig-headed and stubborn and had said so many times—during contract negotiations, with editorial matters, regarding women he'd dated whom I found wanting, or where to have lunch.

"So now what?" His voice had raised an octave in concern. "You're on the run from the police? This is not good. We need to rethink this."

"I'm not 'on the run.' I didn't do anything. I'm just trying to figure out what's happened here, to fix all the damage. So, are you going to give me my money or what?"

"Am I aiding and abetting you right now?"

"I didn't do anything," I repeated.

"But if asked by the police, I'm supposed to say you haven't contacted me and I don't know where you are?"

"I haven't. You called me," I said. "And you don't know where I am."

There was silence on the line. "Okay. I'll get you some cash."

"I'll find you later." I was about to end the call but I heard his voice and put the phone back to my ear.

"I wish I could say I was surprised that this guy turned out to be a disaster," he was saying. "I never liked him."

"*This guy?* He's my husband of five years."

"I know. I never liked him," he said, sounding grave. "Seriously."

"You never said so."

"You never asked."

"Still."

"I was trying to be supportive. I could see that . . . you loved him."

There was a strange pitch to his voice, something I hadn't heard before. And in that moment I realized: He did remember.

"Jack."

"Just please be careful."

After I'd finished with Jack, I wrote down the number on the screen. But rather than dialing, I searched the online reverse directory and got an address in Queens. I wrote that down as well. It took all the strength I had to stop looking at my dirty-hot assailant. But I felt a clock ticking, knowing that the longer I was here, the more likely whoever might be looking for me—police or otherwise—would catch up.

I logged on to my Web site e-mail account and searched the trash folder, which I'd never emptied. The second of the two e-mails I'd received was still there; the first one was gone. I knew that the trash folder automatically purged after a week. I stared at the message, the cursor bar blinking blue over it. The name in the "from" field was Camilla Novak. The subject line read: *Your husband . . .*

The text in the body read:

> *Your husband is a liar and a murderer. The past is about to catch up with him. And you need to save yourself. You're in great danger. Please call me.*

She ended with her name and a phone number.

Even reading it now, I can see why I deleted it. It was so overwrought, so silly. A week ago, I would have imagined it spam, on par with all those e-mails announcing that I'd won some European lottery, or that someone who'd had a crush on me in high school was looking for me. My box was always full of this kind of garbage. They were lures, looking for the most gullible, loneliest, most paranoid fish in the pond. I deleted mercilessly. Too bad I didn't have such good judgment in the real world.

I hesitated just a moment and then dialed the number on the screen from my cell phone. It rang so long, I didn't think anyone would pick up. Then there was a very sultry female voice on the line.

"Hello?"

I found I wasn't sure what I wanted to say. I hesitated, almost hung up.

"Hello?" she said again.

Finally, I found my voice: "It's Isabel Raine."

There was only silence on the line where I heard her breathing.

"You wrote to me about my husband," I went on. "You said he was a murderer and a liar. That I was in danger." I sounded amazingly cool and distant, my voice not betraying the adrenaline pulsing through my veins.

Still silence. Then: "I made a mistake. I lied. I'm sorry."

"No. Don't. You need to tell me the truth."

"It's too late. It's too late." I heard a buzzer ring on her end. "I have to go. Don't call again."

She hung up, and I immediately called her back. My call went straight to voice mail.

"I know about your boyfriend, about the real Marcus Raine. What happened to him? You have to help me." But I was talking to air.

I quickly found a local listing for Camilla Novak online, wrote down the address and phone number, hoping it was the right person. The listing was in SoHo, not too far from where I was now. Then I Googled: "marcus raine missing nyc." I wanted more details. I needed to arm myself with information before I raced into the fray.

A list of matches filled the screen and I scrolled through old newspaper articles, which didn't offer any new information beyond what I'd already learned from Detective Crowe. The rest were inaccurate links: Another Marcus Raine was looking for a girlfriend on a dating site, someone named Marcus who lived on Raine Street was selling a mattress, an old man left his dog Marcus out in the rain (misspelled raine) and wrote a ridiculous poem about it.

I was about to move on when a listing toward the bottom of the page caught my eye: *What happened to Marcus Raine?* I clicked on the link and it brought me to a site called forgottennycrimes.com.

"On television, the haunted cop works the case until he retires—and even then he can't let it go. But in the real world, people disappear and no one ever finds out what happened to them," some copy on the makeshift page read. "Someone goes out for groceries and never comes home, is never heard from again. Everyone moves on except for those of us who are left behind, haunted by loss, anger, and unanswered questions."

Grainy images faded in and then faded out on the screen—school portraits, mug shots, vacation shots, candid and posed images.

I clicked on Marcus Raine's name and saw the same image Crowe had shown me, except that the girlfriend had been cropped out. The blurb there, about how Raine was living the American dream when he disappeared, how he'd been raised by his aunt in communist Czechoslovakia, how his parents died, how he came to the U.S. and was educated, got rich, was my husband's story exactly.

> Camilla Novak, another émigré from the Czech Republic, thought he was acting oddly in the weeks before his death. He seemed paranoid, installing several new locks on the door, refusing to answer his phone unless she called him by coded ring, phoning once, hanging up, and calling again. "He believed he was being watched. But he wouldn't say by whom or why. I was worried; mental illness ran in his family," Novak said. "But I never thought he was really in danger."

There was a phone number on the site, too. *If you have any information, call 1-21-COLD-CASE.*

On a whim, I entered the name Kristof Ragan into the search engine. But nothing useful appeared, just lists of names for schools and corporations that included "Kristof" or "Ragan." I kept looking through page after page on the screen, just hoping, becoming more desperate with each bad link. Finally, I reached the end. And that's when I lost it for the first time.

In my nephew's bedroom, surrounded by *Star Wars* and Skater Boy paraphernalia, stuffed animals and sports posters—walls, ceilings covered with it all—bunk beds the size of apartments I'd had, I put my head on his desk and wept, feeling all my rage, confusion, and grief pour out of me in one mighty rush. I could have drowned in it. Two days ago, I would have turned to my imperfect husband for his intellect and calm in such a storm. I would have reached for him and he would have lifted me from the chaos of my emotions.

"Isabel, relax," he'd say. "Clear your head."

And I'd feel that fog—the one that descends over me in time of stress or high emotion, the one that inhibits logical thought—I'd feel it start to lift.

"There is no problem that doesn't have a solution. There's always a way," he'd tell me. And I'd listen, know he was right.

I felt his loss so profoundly that I almost just crawled into Trevor's bed and pulled the covers over my head. My friend, my husband, my lover was a liar at least, quite possibly a criminal as well. But still the thought of being without him nearly crippled me. For all the fractures in our marriage, all the things that caused me pain, I truly loved him, had the most basic kind of faith in him, even if I'd never *really* trusted him again after his affair.

For some reason, I found myself thinking back to my conversation with Detective Crowe. *And love forgives?* he'd asked bitterly. *Love accepts, moves forward,* I'd answered him. But maybe, in my case, love accepts too much, wants to live so badly that it creates what it needs to survive.

Next to the computer keyboard my cell phone vibrated, started shimmying along the smooth white surface of the desk. I looked at the little screen. *Erik calling.* I hesitated, then answered it but didn't say anything.

"Don't do this, Iz," he said. "You don't have to do this. Just come back and we'll work it out together."

I didn't say anything.

"Or at least go to the lawyer's office. You know where he is, right? John Brace and Son, on Park Avenue. He'll know what to do. That detective said if we can't get you to come back, he's going to consider you a person of interest in all of this. A *suspect,* Iz. Let's not have this get any worse than it already is."

I pressed the *End* button on my phone and set it back down. It started buzzing again a second later. *Linda calling.* I let it shimmy itself off the desk and fall to the floor. Eventually it stopped ringing.

As I got up and walked away from it, it started buzzing again. That little phone, the fat silver weight of it, smooth and warm like a worry stone, had always been a source of comfort to me. Seemed like it was always in my hand, all the people in my life just one push button away. All those voices—my sister, my mother, my husband—at least as loud as my own, often louder. I left them all there calling after me.

I took an old coat from my sister's closet and I was about to leave when I had a thought. I ran to the room Erik used as an office and went into their file cabinet, which I knew they left unlocked. It was easy to find their passports—and mine among them. Linda and I had traveled with the kids last summer, an impromptu trip to Mexico. In the melee of traveling with two kids, our passports got confused. I had Linda's at my apartment, or did. She had mine. I grabbed it with a wash of relief and euphoria. I thought that sometimes fate smiled on you, even when she had been slapping you around in every other way like the abusive, narcissistic bitch she is.

* * *

Grady Crowe hated hospitals—not that anyone liked them especially. But he didn't dislike them for the same reasons as other people. He hadn't watched anyone die in a hospital; he didn't feel uncomfortable around sick people. It didn't remind him of his own mortality.

He just didn't like the lighting, the stale decor, or the smell of an institutional kitchen. These things offended his aesthetic sensibilities, made him anxious and uncomfortable. And it annoyed him that people suffering from disease weren't treated to a more pleasant environment. Wouldn't it help them to feel better if they didn't have to look at gray Formica and dirty white walls, if they didn't have to look at themselves beneath the ugly glare of fluorescent lighting? And if their last days had to be spent here, shouldn't a little more attention be paid to detail? Should the last thing they see be peeling wallpaper or a metal bed rail? Then again, maybe not everyone was as affected by these things as he was.

His phone rang.

"She's moving," Jez said on the other end. He heard a siren wailing in the background and she sounded a bit breathless.

"Are you on foot?" he asked.

"I am now. She took a cab to her sister's apartment. I've been sitting here, waiting. She just left on foot, moving fast. I thought she'd hail another cab but she didn't."

"Where's the vehicle?"

"Parked illegally across the street from the Books' building."

"Where's she going?"

"I don't know," she said, drawing out the words as if she was talking to a toddler. "That's why I'm following her."

"Keep me posted," he said, glancing up at Linda Book, then over to the two kids who both seemed pretty bored or unhappy or both. He'd been asking them questions in the family waiting area, getting nowhere.

"Where are you going?" Jez asked.

"I don't know yet."

"Then you keep me posted, too."

In the first smart move he'd made in twenty-four hours, he had left Jez outside the hospital while he went inside. He couldn't hold Isabel Raine; he knew he had no legal reason to do so. But one of them could stay on her, see where she went. Maybe she'd lead them to her husband. Maybe they'd see someone following her, like the alleged thugs who'd nearly killed her stepfather.

Isabel Raine was a runner. Not that he thought she was guilty necessarily, but she had an idea of herself that made her a flight risk. She was angry, she was arrogant, and she'd been betrayed. And she was looking for answers, thought she was better qualified than anyone to find them. She didn't disappoint him, took the first opportunity she had to bolt. But, he'd noted, she'd waited until she knew her stepfather was okay, knew that he had family nearby, before she left. To him it said that she was a good girl at her core, if not a rule follower. Her staying when she could have more easily left was what they called in the business a telling detail. Not in the police business, in the writing business. The little quirk that spoke volumes about character.

He'd read this in one of the myriad books he'd read about fiction writing. It had stayed with him. He thought it was something that made sense in real life, too, in police work. The two professions weren't really so different. You had to have the belly of fire, that drive to know and solve and speculate, to follow your hunches and go where incident and evidence impelled you. You had to have a terrible curiosity about character, about what made people do the awful, wonderful, terrifying, brilliant things they do.

He looked up at Linda Book, who was watching him.

"She went to your apartment."

Linda nodded, as if this didn't surprise her. "She has a key."

She stood by the window, leaned against the sill and looked out, her arms wrapped tight around her body. He noticed that the skin on her hands was creamy white, her nails short, sensible squares. She wore a honker of a diamond, cushion cut, a carat and a half at least. She clenched and unclenched this hand unconsciously, squeezing the thick cashmere of her coat. He could tell it was cashmere, had always been good about identifying fine fabrics by sight or touch.

The way the light came in from the window, the golden light of afternoon, it caught the highlights of her hair. In the line of her nose and something about her brow, he saw Isabel Raine. It was easy to see they were sisters, though they had opposite coloring. Isabel Raine looked like she'd been dipped in milk. Linda Book was gilded by sunlight. They were both beautiful, but Linda Book was softer, more real somehow. It was the mother factor. There was a look to a certain type of mom, a compassionate knowledge of the human condition that can only come from changing diapers and soothing tantrums, bandaging knees and assuaging fears.

"Where will she go, Ms. Book?"

"Wherever she thinks the answers are," she said, looking out the window again. He felt a wash of frustration. Stubborn stoicism must run in the family.

"You're not helping her," he said. "You're not protecting her."

"I've never been able to do either of those things, Detective. Never. Not unless she wants me to." He watched her eyes drift over to her daughter, a tiny dark-haired girl who slumped in an uncomfortable chair, pretending to be asleep. "If I knew where she was going, I'd tell you."

His phone rang again. He saw it was Jez, so he answered quickly.

"I lost her," she said, yelling over street noise.

"What? How?" he said sharply, causing both Linda and the girl to look at him.

"I got caught in the crowd pushing out of the train and she snaked in. The doors closed and she was gone."

"What train?"

"The uptown N/R."

"Fuck *me.*"

Linda Book shot him an annoyed look, shook her head. The girl smiled, a small, amused turning up of the corner of her mouth. And in that second she was identical to her aunt. Detective Crowe was really starting to dislike this family of stubborn, too-smart women with bad attitudes.

"What are you going to do?" he asked her, sounding a little petulant even to himself.

"What *can* I do, Crowe?"

"See if you can catch her at the next station." He heard her release an exasperated breath.

"Okay." She said it as if he was an idiot and it would never work but she'd try it anyway. He ended the call. If he'd been alone, he'd have kicked something, issued a string of expletives to blow off steam. But he managed to keep his composure.

"I have an idea." It was the girl, looking at him as if he might be interested in her thoughts.

"Really," he said, sarcastic and annoyed. He saw anger, anger rather than intimidation, flash on her small face. He hated to admit it, but it cowed him a bit. He kept his eyes on her. She turned to her mother, as if he no longer deserved to be spoken to.

"Make Daddy go home and check the computer," she said. "You can use the spyware you installed to see what sites she visited and try to figure out where she went that way."

"What spyware?" asked Linda, widening her eyes and lifting her brow in a bad imitation of innocence.

"Yeah, right," said Emily. "Like we don't *know,* Mom."

"Hey, that's a good idea, kid," he said, surprised.

Emily Book gave him a nasty smirk. "Duh."

Five minutes later Erik Book was on his way downtown. Linda Book looked uneasy, rubbed her temples with the spread thumb and index finger of one hand, as though she was wondering if she was helping or hurting her sister.

WHEN THEY WERE girls, before their father died—because after that neither of them were ever girls again—everyone thought of Izzy as the difficult one. If Izzy had been first, Margie famously told everyone, there wouldn't have been two. She was the one with colic, the bad sleeper, the finicky eater, the one who never napped. It had been said so many times that it became a kind of family legacy.

But Linda knew the truth. Izzy was wild, yes, where Linda was obedient. Izzy was outspoken where Linda was quiet. Izzy was honest where Linda was tactful. All these things added up to make Linda seem like the angel and Izzy the rebel. But as for who was the good girl, and who was the bad, Linda knew the truth.

She watched Emily now and saw the same pure soul she knew existed in her sister. In Trevor she saw the same conviction that good would always triumph over evil, a belief fueled by the mythologies of his comics and the legends of *Star Wars,* that there was a clear right and wrong in every situation. He sulked over by the doorway, battling his conscience and the nagging feeling she knew he had that following the rules in this case might not have been that right thing. He looked confused. She wanted to tell him that he was only going to get more confused as time went on, that things would never be as clear as they were right now. She'd been like him once, so righteous and sure. Poor Fred could attest to her punishing standards. She wanted to tell her son that it was all just shades of gray. But that was a lesson for another day.

"You did good, Trev," she said to comfort him. "Izzy needs our help right now, even if she doesn't know it."

Her son nodded uncertainly, wrapped his arms tightly around his thin middle. Emily gave Trevor a dirty look.

"Tattletale," she hissed. "What a *baby*."

"Shut up," he said, his voice rising high and breaking. "It was *your* idea to check the spyware."

"Emily, give me a break," Linda said.

"What?" she said. "He *is*."

They started yelling, speaking over each other unintelligibly. They always did this, reacted to stress by fighting with each other. The sound of it was maddening.

"That's enough," Linda said, raising her voice. They both stopped and stared at her, mouths in wide, surprised *O*'s. Emily returned to her seat and flopped herself down dramatically. Trevor went back to his corner to sulk.

"I need some quiet," she said more softly. "Please. I have to think."

She wanted to be angry with her sister for bolting again. But she couldn't, the same way you couldn't be mad at a cat for scratching furniture or a dog for chewing up your shoes. Isabel was just being Isabel.

There was an experiment Linda had read about, where people were asked to deliver electric shocks to a person seated in another room out of sight. The experiment revealed that most people would keep delivering the shocks, no matter how loud and tortured the screams from the other room became, as long as someone in authority told them to do it. Linda knew that she'd be one of those people. She'd be racked with guilt and self-doubt, but she'd keep pressing that button until someone told her it was time to stop.

Izzy would be the one who stood up and protested, who bucked authority. She'd beat the crap out of the person delivering orders and then race to rescue the injured. And in some circles, this would make her a bad seed, an undesirable.

Until her affair with Ben, Linda had never broken a rule in her life. And she'd been brutally judgmental of people who in her opinion had. She tortured Margie and Fred for years, because to her it seemed that Margie should have kept her vows to her husband, even in death. And, of course, her father had been the ultimate rule breaker. He'd defied the strictest rules of all: *Don't go. Don't leave me. Love me forever, Daddy.* And how she'd hated him for it. It took years of therapy for her to come to this realization.

Even in her art she never took risks, followed the rules of convention, the typical ideas about what comprised a beautiful image. And how she'd been praised for it, lauded and paid ridiculous sums for art and journalistic photographs that she secretly believed were common, maudlin—as Ben had reviewed her—or appealing to a base and silly chicken soup sentimentality.

Reflexively, she dialed Izzy's number and was surprised when her own husband answered.

"Hey," he said. Even in that one word, she heard all his shame and despair. She ignored it, could not deal with his emotions or what he'd done to their life. In her mind, financial infidelity was a more egregious betrayal than a sexual one. She honestly didn't know what the future held for them, but for the time being, she couldn't think about it. She'd forgiven him before he'd even confessed; she'd meant it, too. But that didn't mean she didn't hate him at the moment.

"You found her," she said, feeling the flood of relief. She felt both Emily's and Trevor's eyes on her.

"Uh, no. She left her phone. I found it on the floor of Trevor's room."

"Oh, God." She shook her head at the kids, and both of them seemed to slump in disappointment. Izzy had dropped the line that connected them, gone off the grid. This terrified Linda more than anything else.

"I'll find her. I promise," he said. She could hear how badly he wanted to do that, to be the hero here. "She Googled someone named Camilla Novak. Do you know who that is?"

She searched the memory banks of her rattled brain. "No," she said finally.

"There's an address in SoHo, not far from here."

Linda rummaged through her bag and found a capless Bic pen and a receipt from the coffee shop where she'd fucked Ben just hours before. It reminded her that they both had a lot to regret.

"Give it to me," she said, her tone harder, less yielding than she intended. She just couldn't help her anger, couldn't keep from expressing it. She scribbled down the address, wondering aloud to Erik why Izzy had taken the uptown N/R.

"I don't know. But she also looked up someone named Kristof Ragan. Ring any bells?"

"No."

She wrote the name down. "Anything else?"

"She went to some site called Services Unlimited. It looks like an escort service masked as temp services. Weird."

"Why would she go to a site like that?"

"No idea."

"Anything else?"

"Just American Express. She was probably trying to track charges."

"Is that it?"

"That's it. Hey, are you going to give that to the detective?"

"Well, yeah."

"Okay," he said, then he paused and issued a sharp breath. "Just give me a head start. If I can get to her first, maybe I can convince her to turn herself in to the lawyer. We don't want her taken into custody, right? She's been through enough."

The detective returned to the room then with sodas for the kids and a coffee for her. She thought he wore too much cologne; it made her sinuses ache.

"Okay," she said. "Give me a call back when you find something."

She ended the call and stuffed the paper in her bag. She looked at the detective, offered him a grateful smile for the coffee he handed her. "He's checking the computer now. He's going to call right back."

The detective nodded. "Okay," he said, handing her a card. "Call me on my cell if he finds anything."

"Where are you going?

"I have a lead I want to follow up."

They stared at each other and in that moment it was hard to keep what she knew from him, an authority figure. He'd been open with her, told her everything he'd learned about Izzy's husband. She felt guilty, nervous for keeping things from him, even if it was only to give Erik a head start so that he might talk some sense into her crazy sister. She was glad when he moved toward the door.

"Let me ask you something," he said. He paused with the knob in his hand and turned back to look at her. "Did you ever suspect that your brother-in-law wasn't who he said he was? Was there ever anything that gave you pause, something that's coming back to you now?"

She'd thought about it since he'd told her everything, about the missing man, the stolen identity. But other than the nebulous feeling she'd had that she didn't care for him or trust him and didn't think he was good enough for Izzy, no, there was nothing, no clue that might help them now. She told him as much.

"Just think about it. Let me know if anything comes to mind. No matter how small or inconsequential it might seem."

Then: "Does the name Camilla Novak mean anything to you?"

She couldn't hold his eyes, dropped her gaze to the floor. "No," she said. "Uh-uh."

He let a beat pass. Then: "You sure?"

She nodded and forced herself to meet his eyes with a wide, earnest gaze. "Why? Who is she?"

"Someone who might have information. We'll see. Call me," he said, and then left the room.

"Did you just lie?" Emily asked, incredulous. Linda considered lying again but didn't have the heart, not with both of them staring at her like that.

"Shh," Linda said, moving over and sitting next to her daughter, dropping an arm around her shoulders. Her little girl felt so thin, so fragile.

"You lied to the police?" Trevor said, his voice high with anguish, looking like he did the day she had to break it to him about Santa.

"I'm just giving Dad a head start," she whispered, glancing over at the door. She moved over to him and put both her hands on his thin shoulders. "We want to find Isabel before the police do."

"I thought you said I did the right thing."

"God, stop whining for once," said Emily.

"You *did,*" said Linda. "You did do the right thing. But this is the right thing, too. In a different way."

It was nothing but shades of gray, she wanted to tell him, none of it black and white. But instead she opened her free arm to him and he came and sat on her lap; he wasn't too big for that. Emily rested her head on Linda's shoulder and she took her brother's hand and squeezed. They could be so mean to each other, scream and whine to beat the band, but Linda knew they shared the same ferocious love that she and Izzy did. And now, with foundations shifting, and life as they knew it crashing around them—in ways they weren't yet aware—they'd have this. They'd always have this.

12

He felt an acute annoyance as she bled out, died slowly. Her eyelids fluttered quickly, butterfly wings of panic and resistance. There was a hopeless rattle to her breath. He looked away when he saw her hand start to twitch, her eyes go blank. His annoyance resided at first in the back of his throat, then became an ache just above his brow line.

A slow unraveling occurs when one thread separates from the fabric; it can't help but catch on something. One tiny pull, then another, and eventually the whole garment comes apart. He'd broken the first rule he'd set for himself: Leave at the first sign of trouble; cut your losses, take what you can, and change that garment before you're left half naked in the cold. It was attachment and arrogance that brought him to this place. Sara's earlier admonition rang in his ears.

He moved over to the couch and sat, put his chin on one fist, watched her. There was a time when he thought he could love her. But when she'd given herself to him so easily and served her purpose, his passion for her cooled quickly.

HE'D MET MARCUS Raine at Red Gravity, where they were both programmers. Though they'd been raised in the same country, just miles apart, Marcus Raine didn't want to be friends—not with his fellow countryman, not with anyone. Their colleagues laughed about Raine behind his back, joked that he just powered down at the end of the day, sat slumped at his desk until morning. He was there when everyone arrived, there when they left in the evenings. He seemed to have five sets of nearly identical outfits—black pants and Rockport shoes, button-down shirts in some shade of brown or gray. The receptionist took notes—brown on Monday, charcoal on Tuesday, slate on Wednesday, chocolate on Thursday, gunmetal on Friday. He didn't often acknowledge the weather, wore the same three-quarter-length lightweight black jacket, rain or shine, summer or winter. Sometimes he wore a stocking cap when it was very, very cold. Sometimes, in the blistering heat, he didn't wear the jacket at all.

He didn't join in the laughter. He was only slightly more sociable than Marcus Raine. But even this was design, part of his invisibility. Friendly enough not to stand apart but never intimate, never revealing. As a result, he was fairly certain that none of his Red Gravity colleagues would even remember his name. Sometimes he forgot it, too, would go days without thinking of himself even with the name his mother had given him. Now, after so many years, the name Kristof Ragan seemed to belong to someone else, someone who'd lived a meaningless life and been forgotten.

Beneath their jokes about Marcus Raine was a current of resentment. Marcus had been hired early, before any of them. He'd been paid a very low salary and given a large number of company shares to make up for it. When the company went public, Raine became a very rich man. The company rewarded his loyalty and hard work by raising his salary on top of it. Rumor had it—and in a small company there were always rumors—he made nearly as much as the CEO. But he didn't begrudge Marcus Raine his success; it didn't make him angry or jealous. It made him curious. What was it like to be Marcus Raine?

Isabel got a certain look on her face when she was working—and she didn't have to be sitting at her computer to be working. It was a faraway glaze to her eyes, a kind of thoughtful cock to her head. He could almost see synapses firing in her brain as it struggled to *know*. It was a place she went to imagine, to understand, to be something that she wasn't so that she could write it. He found it fascinating but not foreign. He had the same drives, the same desires for very different reasons. He'd had them all his life.

It was Camilla, Raine's girlfriend, who impelled him to action. Raine, apparently, had forgotten his lunch. He brought the same lunch every day. Some type of meat on whole wheat bread and an apple. He drank water from the cooler, in a cup he kept in his desk and washed in the break-room sink when he was done. He was so precise, like an old clock, so predictable and self-contained. He never could have imagined Raine with a woman like Camilla. She breezed into the office, wearing a flouncy, printed dress, extraordinarily lean, delicately muscular, outstanding legs ending in dangerously high heels—red. She had an electrifying energy, white-blond hair, a voice that sounded like a singing bird to him.

"Can I just leave this for Marcus Raine?" she asked, holding up a brown bag.

"Oh, I'll call him," the receptionist said with unmasked enthusiasm. She wanted to see him interact with his girlfriend. "Can I give him your name?"

She hesitated, looked around. "Camilla," she said finally.

The reception desk stood directly in front of the door; behind that was the field of cubicles where everyone sat. One by one, people found a reason to look over the walls, like prairie dogs popping quick, curious heads up from their holes. From where he sat, he had an unobstructed view as Marcus Raine strode up to the front and took the bag from her hand. He watched Camilla's face brighten at the sight of him. Her smile widened—no, deepened—as Raine wound a strong arm around her waist and kissed her. He whispered something to her in Czech and she laughed, a tinkling, musical sound like ice in a glass.

Suddenly Marcus Raine didn't seem so laughable. He watched the faces of their colleagues, mocking smiles dropping in surprise, resentment waxing like a moon, cold and hard.

HE HADN'T THOUGHT about the way he met Camilla in a long time, about the desire he'd had from the first moment he saw her. It was different from the desire he'd had for Isabel, which was cooler, more intellectual. His love for Isabel connected him to the higher parts of himself, the better man inside. His hunger for Camilla had been primal, a raptor ripping meat from a carcass on the jungle floor.

He saw her again later in the week. This time it was no accident. He worked at his station until he saw the top of Raine's head float by his cube. He quickly gathered his things and ran down the stairs while the old elevator slowly carried Raine toward the street. He arrived on the ground floor just in time to see the other man exit through the glass doors onto Canal Street. It was summer, still light at nearly eight P.M.

The humidity in the air raised an instant sheen of sweat on his brow. From a distance, he followed Raine through the chaos of the busy street, beside the garish electronics shops, just gaping holes in buildings, loud with booming speakers, and stands loaded with knockoff bags, the air smelling of exhaust and crispy duck.

Camilla, resplendent in shades of blue, a simple blouse and flowing skirt, flippy sandals on her feet, was waiting for Raine by the subway station. She was like a breeze of clean air in the filth of the city around her. Raine kissed her quickly and together they descended below the street.

He rode between two cars and watched the couple through the thick, dirty window that separated them. They were oblivious, totally wrapped up in each other, one of Raine's arms around her shoulder, the other holding her delicate hand. She looked up at him with that wide-open smile. Raine seemed like a different person, animated, laughing, relaxed, not like the gargoyle he usually was, staring joylessly at his screen, skulking over his sandwich in the break room, grunting his replies to questions, issuing terse one-line e-mails. To look into Camilla's face, you'd imagine he was the most charming, charismatic bastard who ever walked the face of the earth.

When they exited uptown, he followed them again, watched as they entered a beautiful prewar building on the Upper West Side. A doorman in a navy blue uniform pulled the door open for them, and they disappeared. Left behind on the street, a terrible current of covetousness rushed through him. It literally caused him to feel nauseous when he thought of the hovel he lived in out in Williamsburg, shared with his disgusting slob of a brother. Even earning the kind of money that would make him a king at home, he lived like a pauper in this whore of a city, where everything he'd ever wanted was right in front him but always out of reach.

He'd learned quickly that the only certain way to succeed in this country was as a thief. The wealthy Americans of everyone's dreams hadn't worked their way to the top, hadn't gone from rags to riches through hard work and good morals, as they would have everyone believe. The wealthiest had either gotten lucky—like Marcus Raine—or gone crooked, stolen and cheated and killed to earn their riches. They were pirates. This didn't make him angry. It made him hungry. It made him creative.

Ivan, unlike Marcus, had had no interest in getting an education and a job, had already aligned himself with an unsavory element. Almost as soon as they arrived, Ivan connected with two brothers who ran with the Albanian mob. Their crimes were petty—ATM heists, transporting Albanian girls who thought they were going to be models and wound up addicted to meth, wrapping their lithe bodies around poles in filthy strip bars. But Ivan was making more money—much more—even though he had a limited intelligence, wasn't much more than a child in some ways. Ivan was always the one who treated at clubs and dinners out.

On the long ride home to Brooklyn, he'd thought about why he'd come to this country, what he'd hoped to accomplish here. He didn't want to be a paycheck player, someone who lived by another man's rules. He hadn't imagined himself a slave to a company, asking permission to take time off for sickness, his only free hours squeezed in between grueling work days and the two weeks a year he was allotted for holiday. Suddenly, it seemed to him that Ivan, whom he'd always regarded as slow and essentially lazy, had been right all along.

When he got back to their apartment, Ivan was lying on the couch surrounded by a field of fast-food wrappers. He'd unapologetically unbuttoned his pants to allow his belly to expand and was staring blankly at the television set. Ivan breathed heavily, evenly, like someone sleeping though he was obviously awake. He lifted a hand in greeting.

"Ivan," he said, closing the door loudly behind him and placing his laptop bag on the floor near his brother's feet. The place was a hovel—a couch they'd rescued from the curb, an old table with two plastic chairs, futons for beds. Sheets acted as curtains. The place hadn't been cleaned since the last time he'd lost his patience with the filth, about a month earlier. But he didn't care about that at the moment. "I've been thinking."

"What have you been thinking?" Ivan asked apathetically. The massive Sony television and surrounding equipment—a PlayStation, audio system and speakers, DVD player—filled the far wall. Ivan might not shower for days, but he took his audiovisual very seriously. Where all the equipment had come from a few weeks earlier, whether bought or stolen, he didn't know and didn't care to know.

He told his brother about Marcus Raine, about the ideas he'd had. Ivan had a good laugh. "All these years I've been saying that you work too hard for too little. What finally changes your mind? Just one pretty girl?"

He couldn't say what had changed his mind. At the time, he thought it was Camilla, the force of his desire for her. But, no. It was as if he'd lost the will to keep swimming against the current of his life. He'd just stopped kicking, stopped stroking, and let the flow take him. Ivan had a good laugh, patted him on the back, and congratulated him on seeing things as they were. And then they got to work. It seemed like so long ago. It was. A lifetime. He was a different man with a different name then.

Camilla was beautiful even in death. He stood over her still body and remembered how warm her skin had been, how wet she always was for him. He imagined that she'd sensed his evil and, instead of repelling her, it excited her. He'd been wrong about that, though. When she saw him, really understood what he was, she'd turned against him.

He crouched down and pushed back the collar of her white shirt and saw the lace of her bra over the swell of her perfect breast. French and Italian women were always lauded for their sensual beauty. But Czech women, with their fine, hard features and their slim, long bodies, went unmentioned. Maybe it was their apparent lack of warmth, the unyielding quality of their aura—like Prague itself. Compared to Prague, Paris paled. But Prague was a side trip, somewhere Americans might spend a few days on their European tour. No one dreamed of Prague the way they did Paris. Paris glittered and danced for her audience, had already lifted her skirts and offered her treasures to the world. Prague still stood in the wings, holding herself aloof, offering nothing but coy glimpses of her perfection.

"I should have killed you long ago," he whispered.

Then the buzzer rang, the sound startling him so badly, he felt as if he'd been jolted by an electric shock. He froze in his crouch by the body, and felt every breath he took until the buzzer rang again. Then there was silence and he waited. He heard a few buzzers ringing in other apartments. Whoever was down there was hoping someone would just open the door, maybe expecting a delivery or a maid. And then he heard the sound of the door unlocking, opening quickly and then slamming, the sound carrying up the stairwell. And then it was quiet. It was quiet for so long, he started to relax.

When the knob started to turn, he remembered too late that he hadn't locked it behind him.

13

As soon as I exited my sister's apartment, I saw her. She sat in an unmarked Caprice across the street, trying to hide behind a newspaper. But I recognized Jesamyn Breslow by the blond crown of her head, saw a flash of her face as she flipped the page of the newspaper. That's why it had been so easy for me to get away. They wanted me to, thinking I might lead them to my husband.

I wanted to walk over and pound on her window, rage at her for following me when they should be doing some police work of their own. Tell her that I didn't know any more than they did and was following the pathetic leads they unwittingly gave me. But instead I headed to the N/R station on Prince Street. I heard the car door slam and knew she had gotten out and was following me on foot. I walked fast, eventually ducking into the station.

A quick glance showed that she was still behind me. She was trying to hang back, still hiding behind that newspaper. I managed to lose her by squeezing onto a crowded uptown train. I took it one stop to Astor Place and then took the next train back downtown. I walked to Camilla Novak's building on West Broadway and Broome Street. I'd always loved SoHo, something so grand and yet terminally hip about it, somehow swank and grunge at the same time—the galleries and upscale shops with huge picture windows representing outrageous rents, narrow residential buildings, tony cafés, only the very coolest bars and restaurants.

Once known as the Cast Iron District, SoHo boasted huge historic buildings with gigantic windows and upper floors that were wide-open loft spaces, appealing to artists because of the square footage, natural light, and cheap rents. They moved into the spaces illegally in the 1970s, ignoring the city zoning at the time, but the depressed city was too embroiled in its other messes—rampant crime, a shattered economy—to care.

Most people didn't realize that more than 250 buildings were made with cast iron. Architects found cast iron to be cheap, could be fashioned into the most intricate design patterns, and was easily repaired. It was also the strength and pliability of this metal that allowed for the carving of magnificent frames and the tall windows so beloved by artists. Unfortunately, when exposed to heat, cast iron buckled. Steel brought a rapid end to the use of cast iron. I know all of this because of Jack, the original New York City geek.

When I came to the address I'd written down, I rang the buzzer hard, a few times. *Novak, 4A* was scrawled on her mailbox; otherwise, I wouldn't have known what buzzer to push. I realized that this was the reason they (the ubiquitous *they* with all their cautionary tales) told you not to put your last name beside the buzzer at the street door.

But there wasn't any answer. I didn't have any reason to believe that she'd been here when I talked to her; I might have reached her on her cell phone. And if she had been here, maybe she'd left afraid that I'd do exactly what I'd done, look her up on the Web and show up at her door. She'd wanted to talk to me once. Why had she changed her mind?

I rang the buzzer again. When there was still no answer, I started ringing other buzzers in the building, hoping someone would just let me in. I had no clear idea what I would do if I had gained admittance. I was just operating on a kind of autopilot, moving forward on instinct with little planning and no visibility beyond the present tense.

I was about to give up when a voice carried over the intercom.

"Who is it?"

"It's Camilla," I lied. "I forgot my keys."

"Again?" crackled an elderly voice. "I'm not letting you in next time."

I heard the door unlock and I pushed my way into the foyer. Black and white tile beneath my feet, cool concrete walls, milky light washing in from a window on the first landing. Now what, genius? I thought, pushing through the second door.

I peered up the staircase. I could hear the sound of a cat mewing, the frenzy of a game show on someone's television. Somewhere in the building a baby was crying. As I started up the stairs, I patted my bag for my cell phone, on reflex wanting to call my sister. But it was gone, I remembered. I'd left it behind. I felt suddenly as if I was alone in the dark without a flashlight. In the woods, feeling my way.

On the fourth floor, I paused, then walked slowly in the grainy light filtering in from a frosted, double-paned window at the end of the hallway. 4A was the first door on the right. I looked at it; someone had painted it recently, a glossy black compared to the dull gray of the others on the floor. What would I do? Knock? Listen at the door? I almost turned around and left, almost took Erik's advice and headed uptown to the lawyer's office. Instead I put my hand on the knob and, against all better judgment, turned it and found the door unlocked. This, I knew, was not a good thing.

The rules dictated a hasty retreat, a return to the fold. Like my nephew, I could suddenly see five moves ahead and know that I was out of my depth. And yet I kept moving, pushing the door, heading inside the apartment like a lemming to the precipice.

Inside, the lighting was dim, all the shades drawn. I heard the ringing of a cellular phone, light and musical. It stopped. Then, a second later, it started ringing again. I stayed rooted in the door frame, my hand still on the knob. Finally, I stepped through onto the hardwood floor.

"Hello?" I said. "Camilla?"

The phone had stopped ringing, and muffled street noise was the only sound I heard. The apartment was tidy, with simple inexpensive furnishing—a matching beige overstuffed couch and chair, a low coffee table, an older television on a stand by the window. A large Oriental rug on the floor, some cheaply framed posters, a gray throw blanket over a footstool. The phone started ringing again. I could see it came from a handbag, which lay on the couch next to a coat.

I moved toward the sound. That's when I saw her lying on the floor, legs folded demurely to one side, blood spilling an angry red on the floor, on her clothes, sprayed on the white wall. Her impossibly white throat bore a deep gash so dark, so hideous, it almost seemed fake. She was dressed in white jeans, a tight white blouse, now marred with gore.

There was a thick thud within my center, a tingling at the wound in my head that spread across the top of my skull and traveled down my spine. I tried to take in the details of the scene, to process what was before me. But the whole room was shifting and tilting. I was only aware of a terrible nausea, a desire to get away. Then I saw movement out of the corner of my eye.

"Isabel. Don't turn around."

But of course I did. And there he was. My lover, my friend, the stranger with whom I'd shared my life. I found myself reaching for him but he backed away. The lines that connected us, that would have drawn us together the day before, were sundered. He was on the water and I was onshore. He had drifted, not far but too far to reach. He was in view but gone for good.

"Why are you doing this?" I asked him. I glanced down and saw the gun in his hand. There was blood on his hands, on his shirt.

Even these things failed to shock me into fear. I could have—should have—been screaming, begging, weeping. But instead I found myself floating above it all, observing . . . the body on the floor, my husband's hands wet with blood. He was so familiar, the surface so well known. But his depths were pure mystery, uncharted, now undiscoverable. All I could think to say was, "Why have you done this?"

When the words were in the air, my middle clenched with nausea. I looked down at Camilla Novak, her stillness, and saw the finality of it all. A door had closed. None of us would ever walk though it again. Our life, my life, was gone. Still, there was no rage rushing to the surface, no tears, no urge to yell. The girl on the floor was dead. But I was undead, moving around stiff and unnatural, my soul sucked from me.

"There's no answer for that," he said quietly. "Not one you'll understand."

His voice sounded different, gravelly and cold, seemed to echo from those unknowable depths. I didn't know anything about my husband, if asked, couldn't extrapolate on one certain detail to understand all the evil he had done.

I don't know how long we stood like that, two strangers who recognized each other from another life. When he started to move toward the door, I made to follow. But he lifted the gun and I froze. I looked at his face, a cool and distant star. He'd use that gun, without hesitation. He'd kill me where I stood and walk away. The knowledge cut too deep for pain.

"Isabel. Don't come after me." I was used to this tone. Paternal. Uncompromising. "Start over. Forget. You'll be fine."

I think I smiled at him. Then, beneath the thin mantle of numbness, a rage filled me, replacing any love I'd ever had for him. It was a transformation that took place in minutes—no, seconds.

"If you think you'll walk away from this, you're wrong. I'll find you or die trying."

I saw something on his face—anger, fear, pity, I couldn't tell. He opened his mouth to speak but then changed his mind. I didn't try to stop him as he moved toward the door again. I closed my eyes instead, willing him away. When I opened them, he was gone.

part two

dead reckoning

Character gives us qualities, but it is in actions—what we do—that we are happy or the reverse. . . . All human happiness and misery take the form of action.

—ARISTOTLE

Writing a novel is like driving a car at night. You can only see as far as your headlights, but you can make the whole trip that way.

—E. L. DOCTOROW

14

"You mean there aren't ever any new days?" Trevor asked. He was young, really young. Anyway, too young for an existential crisis. "Just the same days repeating over and over again forever?"

There was something like horror on his face, as if he couldn't believe life could be *that* mundane, with so few surprises. I'd been charged with watching him for the afternoon while Linda took a meeting with her agent and Erik was with Em on some father-daughter trip. Trevor and I had planned for a walk to the chess shop off Washington Square Park, then some kind of high-caloric snack his parents would never allow between lunch and dinner. Maybe he was five or thereabouts.

At the chess shop, we'd lingered for nearly an hour, inspecting chess pieces of all shapes and sizes and incarnations—dragons and wizards, Alice in Wonderland characters, medieval courts, Smurfs. There were elaborate boards of marble and glass, soapstone and metal, plastic. In the end, he chose a simple wooden set with hand-carved pieces. Our Trev, the purist. He had his prize in a bag and we were sitting on a bench in the park, near the speed-chess players, with the leaves changing colors and NYU students moving about with dense backpacks, some kids doing skateboard jumps, and a homeless man aggressively jangling a cup of change.

"But how do you know? You don't know what will happen in forever," he said, always practical. "No one does."

I shrugged, feeling the full weight of my failure to explain this matter. "It's just the way it is, kiddo."

It made a kind of hopeful sense that we might wake up one day and it wouldn't be Tuesday or Saturday, but *Purple*day or *Marshmallow*day. And on this day, things would be different; maybe gravity would be just slightly altered so everything would seem lighter, or the sun would have a slightly pinkish tint to it and everyone would look a little prettier.

"These markers of the passage of time are constructed by the human mind," I told Trevor. He couldn't have really understood me. But he seemed to, gazing at me thoughtfully. "The days are always the same because people made it that way. To keep order."

He seemed to ponder this for a second, picking at a loose thread on his jeans.

"That's stupid," he said finally, bereft.

And I was suddenly mad at myself that I hadn't allowed him the hope that one day in his life wouldn't be exactly the day he expected it to be. I could have conceded that he was right, that, in fact, I did not know what would happen in forever. I backpedaled.

"Every day is different, Trevor, you know. Surprises and magic can happen anytime."

He nodded quickly, as though at the advanced age of five he already knew this.

"But it will always happen on a Wednesday," he said heavily. "Or a Monday."

I'd always thought of Emily as the poet, but maybe Trevor had a little bit of the tortured artist in him, always striving to make the world match his vision, always wishing for stardust where there was only ash.

"Come on, Trev, let's go get a shake and fries," I said.

He brightened then, as though the conversation that left me grieving had never occurred. That's the gift of childhood, the ability to be distracted from the big things by the little things.

* * *

FUNNY, HOW YOU find yourself thinking of the most inane things in the worst moments in your life. I could have run after Marcus but I didn't. Instead I stood rooted, for I don't know how long, stunned by the woman on the floor, by my encounter with my husband. It was impossible to reconcile my life as it was in this minute with the life I'd had just a few days ago.

I knelt down beside the woman I recognized as Camilla Novak from the photo Detective Crowe had shown me and put my hand on her shoulder. I'd just talked to her; it seemed impossible that she'd be dead. In spite of all the blood, I wondered stupidly if she might be breathing, like Fred had been. At first glance, I'd thought he was gone, since he'd been so pale, had lost so much blood. But no, her body was already unnaturally rigid, still.

I touched her for another reason, something less noble than hoping to save her life. I just wanted to see what that white, white skin felt like. I didn't feel any revulsion in that moment.

Her flesh was like clay earth. Under my hand, I could feel the warmth draining. What leaves us? When the heart stops pumping blood through our veins, when the lungs stop filling and releasing, a door opens and something exits, leaving behind the bare stage. The curtain is open but the lights come down. What is it? It's more than the failure of the machine to operate, isn't it?

"Most people would flee from a dead body, get as far away as possible," Crowe would later say. "Only in the movies do civilians lean in close to see if someone lying in a pool of blood—with her throat cut, no less—might still be alive. People literally swoon, faint, vomit at the sight of so much gore."

"I'm not most people."

"I'm getting that."

But that was much later.

"Oh my God."

I turned, startled from my thoughts, to see Erik standing in the doorway. He looked stricken, as if he might pass out. He turned away, took a step back toward the hallway.

"Shut the door," I said sharply. "Lock it."

"We have to get out of here, Isabel," he said, glancing behind him. "Right now we're going to that lawyer. *What* are you doing?"

"Christ, Erik," I hissed. "Get in here and shut the door."

He hesitated, seemed reluctant to leave the safety of the doorway, and then obeyed.

"Who did this, Izzy? Did you—"

"Did *I*?" I stared at him, incredulous. He looked so horrified, so much like Trevor, his eyes wide, this earnest line to his mouth.

He lifted his palms. "Then who?"

I looked back at Camilla Novak—her long, thin limbs, the exposed lace of her bra. On the coffee table there was a half-full cup of tea, the press of her lipstick on the rim. Her jacket and purse lay on the sofa. She was on her way somewhere when Marcus came to her door. She'd let him in. He might have been able to trick her from the street door. But she would have kept her apartment door shut until she saw him. She knew him; she opened her door and let him in. Then he killed her.

"Marcus was here," I said.

"You saw him? *Here?*"

I nodded, thinking of that look on Marc's face. It wasn't malice really, or anger. It was a look I recognized, a superior kind of patience. Who was he?

"He killed her?"

"She was the only connection to the real Marcus Raine," I said, so calmly. No emotion. I didn't even sound like myself. I got up and walked over to Camilla Novak's bag on the couch.

"What are you doing?"

It was a cheap knockoff, flimsy, fraying at the seams. I started rifling through its contents. A hot-pink cell phone, a purple sequined wallet, two tubes of lip gloss, mascara, tweezers. Then something else that gave me a little jolt of surprise.

"You're getting prints all over everything," Erik said. He stuffed his own fingers under arms folded tightly across his chest. Television had turned us all into crime-scene experts.

"Do you know what she said to me about him, the night we told you we were engaged?"

"Who? What are you talking about?"

"Linda," I said, annoyed that he wasn't following my crazed train of thought. "What she said about Marcus?"

He shook his head, looked at me as if he couldn't imagine what relevance this had, why I would be thinking about this now. His eyes fell on Camilla's body and stayed there, as though once he'd allowed himself to look, he couldn't look away.

"She said he was just like our father."

He brought his gaze back to me quickly, looked surprised. We never, and I mean never, talked about my father, so raw and angry were the wounds his parting left in us.

"What do you think she meant by that?"

He rolled his eyes, started shifting from foot to foot—boyish, anxious. "Izzy. Let's go. We'll talk about this in the cab."

"I mean," I said, all the unexpressed anger I'd had for her in that moment rising like a tide I couldn't quell, "my father was a kind, loving man. He was warm, affectionate. He had a jovial way about him, a light."

"I don't know what she meant. I didn't know your father."

"She must have told you."

"Isabel," he said, walking over to me quickly, putting firm hands on my shoulders. "Listen. To. Me. We have to get out of here *right now* or call the police and tell them what's happened. A woman is dead. Marcus was here. He's a wanted man. He's done terrible things. We're letting him get away."

"Oh, he's not getting away. I promise you that. He does have a head start, true."

"Iz." He narrowed his eyes, gripped my shoulders a little harder. I could tell by the half-worried, half-angry look on his face that he thought I was in shock, losing it a little. He couldn't have been more wrong. I'd never seen things more clearly. Or so it seemed at the time—with a head injury and a dead body at my feet, and my husband a murderous criminal on the run from the law.

"Just tell me what you think and then you can call the police."

"Oh my God." He bowed his head and released an exasperated breath. "Okay. She meant that the facade was different than the underpinnings. That Marcus presented one face, but that, like your father, there was a dark inner life. She felt his coldness. She said that your father was cold, too, in a way. Even though he seemed very sweet, very loving, that there was something about him that was afraid to truly connect, that was terrified of the intimacy of real love. He had a powerful need to isolate, that he was damaged in ways no one realized until his suicide."

I found myself nodding slowly, a great sadness swelling inside me. She saw him, both of them, with her photographer's eye. My writer's brain saw other men, men I had created and explained.

I moved into Erik and let him hold me for a second.

"I'm sorry, Erik," I said into his shoulder. Behind his back, I took Camilla's little surprise from her cheap bag, which I still held in my hand. It felt cool and light, a game of play-pretend, a fantasy.

"This is not your fault," he said. "Let's call the lawyer and the police."

"It is my fault. And really, I'm the only one who can fix this. Otherwise, it's all gone—the money, my marriage, our family as it was. He steals everything and gets away with it."

"Honey," he said sadly, "it's gone either way. We'll start again."

"No."

I moved away from him and he saw the gun in my hand, sighed and rolled his eyes at the sight of it, as though it were a toy, as though I was throwing a childish tantrum.

"You tell them I pulled a gun on you," I said, sounding a little shaky, a little nuts. "That you found me here and I wouldn't go with you."

He shook his head, gave me a disbelieving smile. "Oh, come on, Izzy."

"I love you. You're a great husband and a great dad."

He knew I'd never hurt him, and I knew he knew it. But we played out the scene; he saw something in my face and backed away from the door, put his hands up in a gesture of mock surrender.

"I wasn't enough to keep him with us. None of us were."

He blinked, somehow knowing I wasn't talking about Marc. "This is not about your father, Izzy. This is not the same."

I put Camilla's bag over my shoulder.

"What am I supposed to tell them, Iz? The police? Linda and the kids?"

"The truth. Just tell them the truth. I pulled a gun on you and now I'm going after my husband."

"The police are starting to think you're guilty, that you had something to do with all of this. How am I going to convince them otherwise if you run off like this?"

"They're right. I'm guilty, like any wife who is guilty for ignoring all the signs, all her instincts."

"You're not yourself, girl. Don't do this."

But I left him there and he didn't come after me. And I left the building and ran up the street, then ducked into the subway. I wasn't flying blind. I knew where to go, maybe where I should have been all along.

15

She never thought of that night anymore. It lived inside her like a room she never entered in a big, drafty old house. She might walk down the dark hallway, might even rest her hand on the knob, but she never opened the door. She heeded Blue Beard's warning, thought Pandora was a fool. There are some memories better abandoned. Common wisdom demanded examination of the past, probing of childhood pain and trauma. Then—acceptance, release, and ultimately forgiveness. But Linda wondered if this was always the best course. Maybe this was a philosophy that just had people picking at scabs, creating scars on flesh that might have healed better if left alone.

She didn't want to go back there to that night when she awoke with a start, and the room she shared with Isabel was washed in a moonlight so bright that for a moment she thought it was morning. But then through her window she saw the pale blue face of the moon low and bloated in the sky. She slipped from bed, not worried about waking Izzy, who slept soundly like Margie, had to be vigorously roused in the morning. She was a buried ball under the covers, her breathing so deep, so steady, it almost seemed fake. Linda moved over to the window and looked out onto the backyard. The rusting old swing set they hadn't touched in ages sagged dangerously, its frame crooked in the moonlight. The grand old oak towered, its leaves whispering just a bit in the very slight breeze. Off near the edge of the property, just before a stand of trees, her father's work shed stood wide and solid, looking righteous, though it was as rickety as the swing set.

A good wind, her mother said, *and that thing will be in splinters.*

You wish, her father countered.

She saw that one of the doors was ajar. Eagerly, she pulled on jeans under her nightgown, slipped her feet into a pair of Keds, walked quickly down the hall.

The day belonged to Isabel. But at night, when Margie and Izzy were off in their deep, dreamless sleep, Linda was Daddy's girl. Linda shared a minor case of insomnia with her father, where sometimes the night called them both, didn't offer any sleep at all.

"We're the moonwalkers, my girl. Just you and me, alone with the stars."

She crossed the yard, the dewy grass soaking through the canvas of her sneakers. She heard a rustling and banging behind her, on the side of the house. Raccoons in the garbage. Margie was going to have a fit. Linda would tell her father and they'd have a laugh. It was another thing they shared, a mischievous pleasure in the things that got her mother's "panties in a knot." She couldn't have said why at the time. But when the cool and measured Margie cursed and blustered over scattered garbage, or the same fuse that always blew, or the cabinet door that kept coming off its hinge, Linda and her father exchanged a secret smile.

"Was that the only way you could connect with your father, over a shared disdain for your mother?" Erik had asked her once. Linda felt ashamed, chastised.

"*Disdain* isn't the right word." She sounded like Isabel.

"Then what?"

"I don't know. It was almost a relief when she lost her cool. Like, wow, she's human after all—not some robot, always programmed for appropriateness. I think we liked it because—sometimes we wanted to see those frayed edges that everybody else has."

"Hmm," said Erik. "I don't see her that way, not stiff and robotic like that. I find her kind of warm, funny."

"That's because she's not your mother."

"Touché."

At the door, she'd knocked lightly. "Dad? Daddy?"

She thought she might find him dozing, sitting upright on his work stool, with his elbow on the table, chin resting on fist, eyes closed. Or he might be so focused on his work that he wouldn't hear her come in. But then he'd look at her and smile.

"Hello, Moonbeam," he'd say. "Have a seat."

And she'd have him to herself. The day belonged to Izzy. His eyes always drifted to Isabel first; he always laughed at her jokes loudest, was quicker to take her hand or stroke her hair. Not that he didn't do those things with Linda, too. But it always felt like sloppy seconds, even if—and maybe because—he didn't mean it to be.

She pushed the door and it swung wide and slow with a mournful creeking. Her sinuses began to tingle with some foreign smell that wafted out—something metallic, something sweet. The scene revealed itself in snapshots: a cigarette still burning in an ashtray, a nearly empty bottle of liquor and a toppled glass, a frozen, mocking smile, a dark swath down the white of his shirt, a pistol on the ground. Everything existed in a separate frame, nothing coalesced. It was too dark to see the gore. He'd put the gun beneath his chin, an inefficient way to end your life, better at the temple where there's no margin for error.

At the time, she'd fixated on the cigarette. She'd never seen her father smoke; it seemed like an insult, a dirty secret he'd kept. She was angry about it. But years later what she'd remember, what she'd dream about, was that smile. She'd never seen that look on him in life, that derisive grin, that "Fuck you, world" expression. But maybe it had been there all along, waiting for the veil to fall away.

There was a red wash of terror, mingling with rage that felt like a cramp; feelings she barely understood then as adrenaline rocketed through her frame. She wasn't much older than Emily was now, and younger in many ways, less sophisticated, more sheltered. Nothing had ever prepared her for the sight before her; it was so utterly incomprehensible that it was nearly invisible. They'd find her vomit beside the door in the morning; that's how they'd know she'd seen him first. She remembered a wash of numbness, a kind of internal powering down.

A dream, she told herself. *I'll close the door and go back to bed. In the morning, I'll have forgotten this.*

She told herself this with absolute conviction. In that walk from the shed, through the back door to the house, where she stepped out of her wet sneakers and wiped her feet dry on the mat, up the stairs and back into her own bed, she could believe that the power of her will might bend reality. She lay in a deep state of shock, mercifully blank until the sun rose and her sister stirred. She told her sister about her dream.

"Dreams can't hurt you," Isabel said.

Then Margie's screaming, a horrible keening wail, cut through the silence of morning, ending the world as they all knew it.

Why should she want to think about that? What good did it do? But there it was, as her children slept in the hospital bed next to Fred's, wrapped around each other like a couple of monkeys. Trevor snored lightly. Every now and then Emily would issue a low moan or a deep sigh. Fred looked so still and pale that a couple of times she'd gotten up and leaned over him to detect his shallow breathing.

Margie would be on a plane by now, on her way home. Linda had promised to wait at the hospital until her mother arrived. The kids didn't want to leave her to go to Erik's mother, so she'd made them as comfortable as she could. She was a little surprised when they drifted off quickly, clinging to each other.

Linda sat in an uncomfortable chair, staring at the ugly orange glow from the row of parking lot lampposts. It was a starless night, the moon nowhere to be seen. Another night when there would be no sleep. She would sit vigil, bear witness to whatever came next alone. Hours had passed since last she'd heard from Erik. She knew his phone was dead because her calls went straight to voice mail; the charge had been low when he left the hospital hours earlier. He had Isabel's phone but that, too, went straight to the recorded message, her sister's light, airy "Leave a message. I'll call you back." A sick dread had settled into her chest. Worry gnawed on her innards. *Where were they?*

The fresh rush of anxiety caused her to step out into the hallway and dial Ben. She didn't worry about disturbing him or arousing the suspicions of his wife. She knew if he wasn't able to take the call, he wouldn't. But he answered on the first ring.

"Hey," he said. His voice was soft, warm, and just the sound of it brought tears to her eyes. Was it just this morning that they'd been together, romping in a public restroom? Was it today that she promised herself she'd never see him again?

"Hey," she whispered, looking around. The hallway was empty. Somewhere a radio played "Silent Night" very softly. "Are you alone?"

"Yeah," he said, but didn't elaborate. "Everything okay?"

"Not really," she said, leaning against the wall. "Not at all."

"Tell me."

She glanced at the clock on the wall over the empty nurses' station. It was late, nearly ten.

"Where's your family?" she asked. Once, she'd been talking to him, flirting with him, talking sexy, and they were interrupted when his daughter asked him for some milk.

"Daddy, milk in cup?" she'd said sweetly. She was so little, maybe two, just starting to put words together in her own way.

She'd hated herself in that moment, felt so dirty and foolish. She didn't want a repeat. He didn't say anything for a second, and she thought they'd lost the connection. Then she heard him breathing, remembered how his breath felt on her neck that morning.

"They're home," he said. Then: "I'm not."

"Where are you?"

"I left," he said, solemn, final.

She remembered how he looked this morning. So sad and lost.

"Ben."

"I know, Linda. You don't have to say it."

"I can't—" she started. "I don't feel—"

"I know," he said. Was there an edge to his voice? Something angry? When he spoke again it was gone. "But that's not the point. I can. And I do feel for you enough to leave my marriage and my kids. And that's not fair to anyone, is it?"

She put her head in her free hand. Why was everyone always going on about what was *fair*? What about life or marriage or having kids was fair? When did happiness become the goddamn Holy Grail? Didn't you sometimes have to put up with a little bit of unhappiness for the sake of other people—like your kids, for instance? Who never, by the way, asked you to bring them into the world to put up with your issues?

"When did you do this?" she asked. She found herself disappointed in him, somehow less attracted to him for his having left his family.

"Yesterday."

She understood it now, his arrival at her doorstep, the desperate lovemaking. "Why didn't you tell me this morning?"

"You were so worried, so distracted. I didn't want to add to your problems."

"I'm sorry, Ben." She wasn't sure what she was apologizing for, or if it was an apology at all. Maybe it was more an expression of her sorrow at the situation they'd put themselves in.

"You love him, don't you?" he said, issuing a dry cough as though the words caused him physical pain. "Your husband."

Erik had wept today when he told her what he had done. She'd never seen him that way. She'd sat close to him and held him, rubbed the back of his neck like she did for the kids when they were upset—even though she could have righteously been screaming at him, even hitting him. She was so angry with him, so frightened about the future now. His actions had stripped them of something vital to her sense of well-being, their financial security. He'd deceived her, gone behind her back and gambled with their future. Just like her father had done to her mother. It sickened her to think that her whole life had been spent trying not to be like Margie and yet here she was. But as angry as she was at her husband, as stung as she was by what he'd done, she realized that she could never stop loving him, any more than she could stop loving Em or Trevor, or Isabel. It was that kind of love.

"I do, Ben," she said. "You know that. I've always been honest with you."

In the heavy silence that followed, she could feel how her words hurt him. Her cheeks started to burn—from shame or anger, she couldn't say.

"I should go," she said. "I shouldn't have called at all."

"You needed to talk," he said quickly. "I'm sorry."

"It's all right. Take care of yourself." Did she sound cold? She knew she did. She couldn't help it.

"Linda, wait—" She heard his voice, but she pretended she didn't, and pressed *End*, anyway. A second later, the phone, ringer off, started vibrating in her hand. It was him, calling her back. She pressed the button on the side of the phone that sent the call to voice mail and shoved it in her pocket. She slipped back into the darkened room and walked over to the window.

Trevor, Emily, and Fred all slept peacefully, their breathing a chorus of whispers—a high note, a low note, the rumble of a snore from Fred. A freezing rain started to fall, the icy flakes scratching at the window. Worry started up again, a restless anxiety that they were out there, Erik and Isabel, unreachable. She was momentarily distracted by the frame of the window, how the rain made crystalline images on the glass, how the orange glow she thought was ugly before looked golden now as it reflected off the rain. The rectangle of light from the door behind her was luminescent on the window, looked like a doorway to another place and time. She judged the light too low for the effect she'd want but itched for her camera just the same. Then she saw something that made every nerve ending in her body freeze solid like the ice on the glass.

A black Mercedes idled beneath one of the lampposts, its exhaust pluming up from behind, a filthy gray breath in the cold. She knew the car well, the dent and scratch on the driver's side door, the custom rims he couldn't really afford. She'd wept and laughed and made love and confessed in that car.

She saw the shadow of him in the driver's seat; saw a bouncing orange point of light, the burning ember of a cigarette. It was Ben.

Was he out there watching her, waiting for her? Had he *followed* them here? She had been here for hours—had he been here all that time?

The phone started to vibrate in her pocket. She took it out to look at the screen.

Ben calling.

16

The cackling was really starting to grate on him. It sounded desperate and yet somehow cruel at the same time. He had observed women like this—wondering if it was a purely urban America phenomenon—older, the wrong side of forty, emaciated, their faces hardened masks, as if permanently set against the straining of vigorous exercise. Their small breasts looked flat and hard, their nails were square and deeply lacquered. They were often rude, crass, wearing their slim bodies like some passport for poor behavior. But despite all the deprivation, the starvation, the overexertion, they were still unattractive to the point of being repellent, with nasty sneers and cutting comments. They were still lonely, unhappy, unsatisfied—and hence bitter and mean.

Grady Crowe thought that American women had been sold a concept that failed them miserably. Spend every free moment of your time fretting about your body, the media urged, exercise, buy diet books, primp, preen, pluck, wax, and a man will find you attractive and love you forever. Don't ever for one second worry about being loving or lovable, about kindness or finding fulfillment on some spiritual level. Just try to take up as little space as possible, be as small as possible, or you will be reviled and ridiculed by every industry posed to make a dime off of you—the fitness and publishing industries, even the medical industry. They'll steal your money and your self-esteem. You'll give it all and still be unhappy. In spite of all evidence to the contrary, they bought these ideas, believed whole-heartedly, built lives and lifestyles around them.

The cackling continued; Grady couldn't hear himself think. He stared at Camilla Novak's body and wanted to feel the scene, wanted to take in all the details, but he couldn't. Erik Book sat head in hands on the sofa, trying to call out on his cell phone and finally giving up. He looked miserable. Grady wondered what it would be like to have five hundred grand to lose; he couldn't muster too much sympathy for the loss of funds. But he wondered if the guy knew his wife was cheating on him. He could see it in her, something restless, something deeply unsatisfied.

He recognized it in hindsight in Clara, the way she had stopped looking at him in the same way. How she almost imperceptibly didn't want to be held, how she slipped her hand from his grasp when they were out. He thought it was just the normal cooling of their years together. Yet another error in judgment. Like the one that caused them to go to Charlie Shane's dump of a studio rather than to seek out Camilla Novak as Jez suggested. If they'd come here, maybe she'd still be alive. Shouldn't he have better instincts than this? Lately it was just one mistake after another.

He took Camilla's hand in his, feeling its weight, the delicacy of her bones through his gloves. He peered at a faint blue mark, a club stamp. He could just barely make it out: *The Topaz Room.* Never heard of it. He pulled out his cell phone and opened the Web browser, entered the name into the search engine. There was a listing up in Queens. He bookmarked it and shoved the phone back into his pocket.

More cackling, louder, more grating. He walked over to the CSI team; they all turned to look at him.

"There's a dead woman here, show a little respect." The cackler twisted her dried-up face at him.

"She can't hear us, Detective," she said nastily.

"But I can. So how about you keep your voice down?"

It wasn't uncommon for a crime scene to be a place where people laughed and made jokes, disrespecting the victim with nasty remarks. It was the general understanding that this was how cops coped with the horror of it all. But Grady didn't like it, especially in a nice girl's apartment. It was one thing in the Bronx, where a bunch of perps had shot one another up. But a girl like Camilla, living alone in the city, working, like any of his sisters. She deserved more respect. He'd make sure she got it.

"I can't think," he said to Jez.

"Let's go out in the hall for a second."

He followed her out and she leaned against the gray wall. She fished a pack of Chiclets out of her purse, shook some into his hand, and popped a few in her mouth. She used to smoke a bit, not all the time. Just when she was really stressed. Now she chewed gum.

"She was kind of our only lead," said Jez after a minute of chewing.

"There's still Charlie Shane."

"Shane, who is missing, whose apartment yielded nothing."

Grady leaned against the wall, so they were shoulder to shoulder. Well—shoulder to arm; he was a full head taller than his partner. He wondered if he should acknowledge that she had been right, that because they did what he'd suggested, they were screwed. He just couldn't. It lodged in his throat.

"Okay, so according to Book," he said instead. "He came here looking for Isabel to convince her to turn herself in. He found her here with the body. She told him that Marcus Raine had killed Camilla, that she'd just seen him."

"How'd Book get in?"

"He said the street door was ajar. He walked right in, came up the stairs."

Jez took a few thoughtful chews, pulled a pen from her pocket and started that tapping thing she did. "But Book didn't pass Raine on the way out," she said, tap, tap, tapping the pen on her thigh. "And the only other exits—on the roof and in the back—are fire doors that would have set off alarms."

Grady started picking at the scab on his knuckles. It wasn't quite ready to be removed, stung a bit; a little drop of blood sprang from the wound. "So he heard Book on the stairs and hid until he'd passed."

"Or Raine was never here." Jez hadn't looked at him, but she fished a small packet of tissues from her other pocket and held it out to him.

He took one and dabbed gingerly at his hand. The pattern of blood on the tissue brought to his mind blooming poppies in driven snow. "I don't see Isabel Raine as a killer."

Jez lifted and dropped her shoulders quickly, started tapping again. "Anyone can become a killer if the motivations are there."

Grady knew her theory on this, but he disagreed. He thought it required a special kind of ego-sickness to take a life, a core belief that your needs, your survival took precedence over all others. Unless it was a question of self-defense or to protect another, he believed you had to be at least a borderline sociopath to kill another person. Even if someone is overcome with rage, it takes amazing arrogance to kill. He didn't see that in Isabel. He saw arrogance, but not that particular brand.

"Camilla Novak was the last link to the original crime," Jez said. "Without her we don't have any live leads. Only the cold-case file. Someone knew that."

"There might be something in her apartment," said Grady. "We don't know."

"We won't find anything there," she said quickly. He knew she was thinking of the Raines' apartment and the office where every scrap of important paper and data had been removed. "If there was anything, one of the Raines took it."

"One of the Raines? You really think she could be a part of this."

Jez snapped the gum in her mouth, looked up and down the hallway. "Where would Marcus Raine hide? If he heard Book coming?"

Grady glanced around. A typical downtown building with old tile floors and high ceilings, gray walls, hard stone stairs. "He could have gone up a flight," he said. "Come back down when Book entered the apartment."

Jez tilted her head to the side, walked over to the banister and gazed up the stairwell. She gave a reluctant nod.

"After Book came inside, Isabel Raine left," Grady said, "claiming she'd find her husband and make things right for her sister's family."

"And he just let her go?"

"What was he going to do? Physically restrain her?"

"It wouldn't have been a bad idea. She'd look less guilty if she stuck around. Did she take anything with her?"

"Erik Book says no." Grady was skeptical. He felt that Book was holding back, wanting to protect his sister-in-law—or maybe his own interests. At the moment, people who looked like victims yesterday weren't looking as innocent today.

"But where's Novak's purse? Coat's on the couch, like she was getting ready to leave," Jez asked.

Grady shook his head slowly. "No purse, no cell phone, no keys, no wallet in the residence."

"Someone took her bag."

"Seems so," he said. "Did you see the stamp on her hand?"

"She's a hot, single woman living in New York City. Of course she has a club stamp on her hand."

"Yeah, but the club's in Queens."

Jez wrinkled her nose. "Queens? That's weird. No self-respecting Manhattanite goes to Queens to party."

More laughter wafted out the apartment door, and Grady felt a fresh wave of annoyance and frustration. He tried to tamp it down, didn't want to lose his temper. He was already getting a reputation.

"I really don't like that woman," Grady said.

"You don't like anyone," Jez replied with a patient smile.

"I like you."

"I guess that makes me one of the lucky few who meets with your approval. Do you ever think you might be a little too judgmental?"

"I'm a cop."

"My point exactly. You're supposed to have an investigative mind, not a mind like a steel trap."

"More insults from my partner."

She pulled a face of mock sympathy. "Think of it as tough love."

He gave a little chuckle, thought about making a comment about his ex, but Jez's earlier admonitions still rang in his head.

"Women don't usually cut each other's throats," he said after a beat. "That's an intimate act. And one that takes tremendous strength. You need to immobilize the person with one arm, draw the knife across her throat with the other." He mimed the action.

"Or it's an act of trust," Jez said. She leaned in quickly, close to him, brought the tip of her index finger to his throat and drew it quickly across. She moved back to the wall. "You wouldn't let a stranger near enough to cut your throat, unless you were overpowered. Camilla Novak let her killer in, let him get very close to her."

He remembered something Isabel Raine had told him at the hospital. "Isabel Raine said that her husband had had an affair. She said it was a couple of years ago, that she never knew with whom."

"Maybe it was Camilla Novak."

"Which gives both husband and wife possible motive here."

"And provides another connection to the missing Marcus Raine."

"So, what now? Our best leads missing and dead."

"We need to find out where all that money went. We follow it. It's easy enough for people to disappear, but money always leaves a trail."

"Already on it," Jez said. "Warrant issued, records subpoenaed. We should have everything first thing tomorrow."

"And what about cell phone records, for both of them?"

Jez rolled her eyes at him. "What am I, a rookie? And by the way, you could do some of this stuff every once in while, instead of walking around looking tortured and complaining that you can't think, trying to *feel* the scene." She waggled her fingers at him. "You're like a character cop, an idea of yourself."

"Any more insults for me today? Let's just get them all out of the way now."

"Not insults, Crowe. Just observations. Don't be so sensitive." She gave him a sly smile, knew that she was getting to him and enjoying the hell out of it. "I'm just trying to get you to keep your feet on the ground."

"You don't give me a chance," he said, sounding a little peevish even to his own ears. "You're all over this stuff. Anyway, you're better at getting things like that done. People listen to you."

"Hmm," she said, moving back toward the apartment.

"Let's get a photo of Marcus Raine the second and make a visit to Red Gravity, see if anyone there recognizes him."

"If it survived the dot bomb. A lot of those little tech companies didn't make it."

"Worth a shot."

"Another thing that'll have to wait till morning."

Grady looked at his watch; it was close to ten P.M. The morning seemed a long way off. He didn't think they could wait around on banking and cell phone records, offices that might or might not still exist.

"What till then?" he asked.

She turned back to him. "We go door-to-door and let everyone tell us they didn't see or hear anything. Then I say we take Erik Book in and talk to him a little more. I don't think he's telling us everything."

"And when he lawyers up—if he hasn't already—how 'bout we do a little clubbing?"

"You read my mind."

* * *

I WAS FEARLESS once. I remember this. I remember being so sure of myself, of my opinions, passions, and goals. I remember raging and debating in my classes at NYU—politics, literature, history. Everything seemed clear. Everyone with a different opinion was simply wrong. There wasn't one event that changed this, not that I remember.

But as I grew older, that passionate certainty faded. I became more reserved, more reticent. My righteousness was less assured. I avoided the kind of heated political debates that I once enjoyed. Existential, religious, moral arguments made me uncomfortable. There were so many opinions, so many convinced of their own righteousness. A slow dawning that the world was impossibly complicated, that differences were too often irreconcilable, made me less inclined to do battle.

I saw this mellowing in Linda, too. After our father's suicide, she was so angry. And she stayed angry—angry at him, at our mother, at Fred, at anyone who crossed her or disrespected her. She was always embroiled in some argument with this one or that, fought with clerks in various shops, waitresses, massage therapists, over any little issue. Once I had to drag her, screaming over her shoulder, from a gay sing-along bar in the Village after she fought with a drag queen over I can't even remember what. I was pretty sure it was about to come to blows.

But when Erik came into her life, something in her shifted and settled. "He removed the thorn from her paw," Fred said in his usual quiet way. Emily's arrival calmed her still more. By the time Trevor came on the scene, she seemed as serene as a monk. I'd arrive at the loft and find the place in chaos—dishes in the sink, the floor a gauntlet of baby gyms, cloth blocks, and teddy bears—and Linda peacefully lying on the living room carpet, holding up a set of keys in the light for Trevor, or reading to Emily from a towering stack of books.

"I just don't have the energy, Isabel," I remember her telling me one afternoon. I was at the loft, and she mentioned a bad review she'd received. The reviewer had called her work "common" and "maudlin." No one likes a bad review. But Linda could be expected to go off the deep end, sulking for days, making complaining phone calls to editors, writing nasty "reviews" of her reviews and sending them to the critic. But that afternoon, she just seemed to shrug it off.

"I can't afford my own temper tantrums anymore. You owe them something, you know. These kids, you bring them into the world. They didn't ask for it; you did it for all your own reasons, good or bad. The least you can do is not be a bitch all the time, someone who's always in a rage, or complaining, or depressive."

I saw the simple wisdom in this.

"I mean, look at them," she said, pointing to Trevor, who toddled about in his diaper, putting random large, colorful objects in his mouth. "We were *all* that. Every rude jackass on the street or maniac killer or corrupt politician was walking around in someone's living room with a wet diaper, chewing on rubber keys or something. When you understand that, it's so much easier to be forgiving than it is to be angry all the time."

I wondered but didn't say, When you lose that youthful assurance, that arrogance, what else goes with it? Your passion, your drive, that hunger to create? When motherhood seemed to demand so much time, energy, love—when an uninterrupted night's sleep was something to celebrate—wouldn't the artist be sacrificed?

But no. It was harder for her to work, certainly. I watched her struggle for time, for the mental space she needed to *see*. There was so much conflict in the artist mother; Linda was eloquent in her angst.

"I never knew that loving them, being a mother would occupy such a huge space in my heart. That there wouldn't be much room for anything else." But ultimately her work had more depth, more beauty than anything she'd ever done before Trevor and Emily.

I was comforted by this when I realized I was pregnant—something about which I'd been deeply ambivalent. I'd missed my period. The drugstore test confirmed my fears. I spent a full week buffeted by joy and abject terror, angst and excitement before I told Marcus.

The look on his face when I delivered the news was a low point in our marriage. A cool, half smile. *Was I joking?* Then, when he realized that I wasn't, a strange blankness, a total withdrawal from me, from the scene. He crossed his arms across his chest and walked over to the window.

"It's not a good idea, Isabel. It's not . . ." He let the sentence trail with a bemused shake of his head.

"It's not an *idea,* Marcus. It's a *person.*"

"You don't understand," he said. More than any other moment, this was the moment that should have sent the alarms jangling. But, of course, I couldn't have seen anything then through the veil of my anger and disappointment.

Now, as I sat on a rocking subway car hurtling uptown, I realized he wanted to tell me then. He wanted to confess. That was the pleading I saw on his face when he turned to look at me.

"Listen . . . ," he began. I lifted a hand, terrified of the words that were coming.

"Don't. Don't say something you won't be able to take back."

I thought he was going to tell me to end the pregnancy. And I couldn't have those words written between us, alive and gnawing at our marriage like rats in the attic. You'd try to kill them, but they'd always be up there scampering, scratching, crawling in through any hole they found. But maybe he wasn't going to say that at all; maybe he was going to tell me everything I was finding out now, the hard way.

I am a person lulled to calm by moving vehicles. The subway, even with all its filth and myriad threats, is no different. My memories and the present moment mingled in a semi-dream state. I wasn't sleeping—I was way too wired for that; it was more a kind of restless doze. Though I was aware of the rumble of the train, the stops as they came and went, I was back there in our kitchen. I could smell the marinara that simmered on the stove, hear the music from the stereo in the living room, feel the cold granite of the countertop beneath my hands.

"Don't make me hate you," I said.

He looked at me quickly, startled as though I'd slapped him. I wanted to. I wanted to pummel him, scream at him. And I might have if I didn't suspect he'd just stand there, stoic, accepting my blows.

"What do you think it means to be a parent?" he asked. There was a musing quality to his tone, as if he wasn't quite looking for an answer. I answered, anyway.

"I think it means you stop living only for yourself," I said. "I think it means you experience a different kind of love."

It sounded lame, defensive, even to my own ears. He gave me a long look.

"But what if it doesn't mean any of that?" Something in his eyes made me shiver. "What then?"

"What are you *talking* about?" I asked.

"You know as well as I that not everyone *loves* their children."

I felt a wave of nausea, the debut of a tension headache. "What is that supposed to mean?"

He shook his head, pressed his lips into a tight line. I have such clarity on this moment now, but *then* I was mystified, despairing. All I could think was, He doesn't want our child. He doesn't think he could love a baby.

I knew he'd be nervous, afraid. I expected him to be as ambivalent as I had been. But in my center I believed that, like me, under the current of all that surface intellectual confusion there would be a deep well of love and desire for a child. His frigid withdrawal, the draining of color from his face, the physical retreat—I see it now as the beginning of an end that was still too far off to perceive.

"Linda and Erik are happy," I said.

"Really. You think so?"

"You don't?"

"Is that what this about? Wanting what your sister has?"

"No," I snapped. "Of course not. This conversation is not about what I want or don't want. It's about what *is*. I'm *pregnant*."

"So you wouldn't have chosen this?"

"That's irrelevant."

He gave me a smirk, a quick nod of his head. "That's what I thought."

I felt a rush of guilt, for not wanting this enough, for having it anyway, for now trying to convince Marcus it was a good thing. It wasn't supposed to be like this. I remembered Linda and Erik's euphoria when they learned she was pregnant. They hadn't planned Emily—or Trevor, either. But they were truly happy each time. I thought it would happen that way for us.

The light outside was growing dim and we hadn't turned on the lights inside yet, so we were sitting in near darkness.

"Isabel," he said, coming nearer to me.

I wrapped my arms reflexively around my middle. How fast you start thinking of that person inside you, how early you act to protect. I moved away from him, sat in a chair at the table.

"I think I understand your position well enough, Marcus," I said, looking down at the floor. It was dusty, needed cleaning. "Let's end this discussion before the damage can't be undone."

"There are *so many* things you don't understand." I didn't like the sentence; it seemed hollow, clichéd. But I wasn't in the mood to edit him.

"Then *tell* me." I looked up at him, but he was staring out the window again, not connecting with me, not engaging in any way.

"I don't remember my parents," he said softly. "I don't remember what it was like to be someone's child."

He wasn't reaching out for reassurance with those words. He was closing a door. I sensed this, didn't even bother saying any of the things that sprung to mind. After a few beats, he moved over to the switch and turned on the light. I squinted at the sudden change. He seemed about to say something else, but instead took the jacket that lay over one of the chairs.

"I'm going to take a walk. I need some air," he said.

I lifted my palms. "Fine," I said, feeling a valley of despair open within me. Of all the reactions I imagined, this was the worst-case scenario. Even anger would have been better than abandonment.

He left then and didn't come back until much later. I didn't call my sister. There were so many things I couldn't tell her about Marcus; she was always so quick to judge him even without things like this. I thought about calling Jack, but it felt like some kind of betrayal. I just watched TV for a while, hoping Marcus would come back quickly. But it was hours, after midnight when I heard his key in the door. I was in bed with the lights off. I heard him come up the stairs, push softly into our room.

"Isabel," he whispered from the doorway.

I didn't answer, pretending to be asleep. I didn't want to talk anymore. I was so tired. I was relieved when I heard him go back downstairs and turn on the television. I made a point to leave early for the gym in the morning before he awoke and stayed away until after he'd gone for the day.

That night, he came home early from work with a gigantic teddy bear. He apologized and we pretended that everything was okay, normal. I wanted so badly to believe that he'd come around, I almost convinced myself. I tried not to notice that his smiles were forced, that his attentiveness just didn't seem sincere.

Then, of course, a few weeks later there was the miscarriage. Soon after, the affair. And yet on the night before he disappeared we made love and shared croissants in the morning. Tragedy, betrayal mingling with the mundane of everyday life, a love that manages temporary amnesia masquerading as forgiveness to survive—is that the stuff of enduring marriages? Maybe just mine.

All these buried memories exposed to the light by his disappearance. I had fooled myself, thinking I was the one who saw more than others. I saw what I wanted to see, edited and rewrote the rest. I got off the train at East Eighty-sixth Street and emerged on Fifth Avenue. I was directly across town from my own apartment, separated by the expanse of Central Park. With a dead woman's purse over my shoulder, weighted down by the first gun I'd ever touched, I felt so far away from my life that I might as well have been on the moon.

I passed the inverted ziggurat of the Guggenheim, its white expanse as vast and peaceful as a moonscape. I felt a twinge of longing to be meandering its downward spiral carefree and overwarm, gazing at the Surrealists, the Impressionists, the post-Impressionists, the early Moderns. Artists gone but art remaining, peaceful and still, even if the creator's spirit was anything but.

The neighborhood was quiet at night, the proximity of Central Park making it seem an airier neighborhood than other parts of the city. I would have felt perfectly safe on any other night. But that night I found myself looking over my shoulder at the sound of approaching footsteps, gazing at others on the street with suspicion. I dug my hand inside that strange tacky purse and rested it on the gun, feeling quite able to use it if necessary.

As I walked, all the events of the last—was it only twenty-four hours?—played in my mind: that horrible screaming on the phone, Fred's blood pooling on the marble floor, the lovely Camilla, her throat cut. I had the cold realization that I was, as Trevor suspected, terribly out of my league. I thought about my sister, how worried she must be, how furious she'd be when she learned I pulled a gun on Erik. She'd know then how desperate and stupid all of this had made me. I had a moment of clarity, my footfalls sounding loud on the concrete in the quiet night; I should call Detective Crowe and tell him everything I'd learned, then call that lawyer, get in a cab and turn myself in. I should take all the good advice and help that had been offered and stop being an ass—for the sake of my family, if for not for myself. I stopped in my tracks and took Camilla's phone from my right pocket, Detective Crowe's card from my left. I could have dialed, ended it right then and there.

I thought of S, her mean, dead eyes and perfect body. Again, the rise of bile in my throat. Pure rage had a taste and texture that I was starting to recognize. I tucked the phone and the card away. I couldn't let anyone else write the end to this story. I had to do it myself.

Don't try to find me or to answer the questions you'll have. I can't protect you—or your family—if you do.

I could hear the sound of his voice in my head, as clearly as if he were beside me.

Protect me from whom? From your other self, this shadow that was living with me, sleeping in my bed for five years? Detective Breslow asked me if he'd had a history of mental illness. Maybe he did. How could I know? The man I saw in Camilla Novak's apartment was my husband, the man I knew. Not some deranged madman who'd finally gone off the edge, not someone unrecognizable in insanity. It was him, perhaps merely, finally, unveiled.

I KEPT WALKING, turning left onto Eighty-eighth Street and moving past stately town houses until I reached the one I knew well. As I rang the bell, I thought, not for the first time: How in the world does he afford to live here? A three-story town home on the Upper East Side of Manhattan? The Gold Coast. Unaffordable to any but the super-rich. Even the merely rich were just riffraff in this rarefied world. I'd been crass enough to ask once before.

"You made me rich," he said. I laughed. Without Marcus's income, I certainly wouldn't have been living in an Upper West Side duplex. I'd still be in my apartment in the East Village.

"I haven't even made *myself* this rich."

"You do all right."

"Seriously."

I didn't recall the answer now. It's true that when he'd moved in that it was a skeleton of what it would become, with exposed rafters and wires, sagging staircases, water stains on the ceilings. He'd spent years restoring it, doing most of the work himself. Five years after closing, it was a showplace. Every time I came to see him, he was in the middle of some element of the restoration. It always reminded me of Fred, how he spent years fixing everything that was broken in our old house.

"They say a man who feels the need to build a house believes that he hasn't accomplished enough with his life," Jack told me. He was laying a hardwood floor in the upstairs hallway. I was sitting in the threshold to the bedroom, my feet up on the door frame and a beer in my hand—very helpful. I'd been married a year; Marcus was away on business. Or so I believed at the time. Who knows where he really was?

"Is that how you feel?" I asked him.

He brought the hammer down hard a couple of times, the sound echoing through still mostly empty rooms.

"I don't know," he said finally. I remembered our night together then. It came back in a vivid flash and I felt heat rise to my cheeks. I remembered his breath in my ear, *I've always loved you, Isabel.* What had I said to him in return? I didn't remember.

"What about that woman you were seeing? An editor, right?"

"She thought I needed too much revision."

My chuckle turned into a belly laugh and then we were both doubled over, tearing and clutching our middles.

Jack answered the door as quickly as if he'd been standing right behind it. He looked worried to the point of frantic.

"Christ," he said by way of greeting, throwing his hands up in relief. "It's almost eleven. I've been freaking out. Your sister's been calling and calling."

"What did you tell her?" I asked, stepping inside.

"That I hadn't heard from you. She knew I was lying."

He grabbed me by the arms and looked me up and down.

"You look awful," he went on. "That bandage is bleeding through."

I put my hand to it and realized it was wet. He dragged me down the narrow hallway to the large bathroom past the gourmet kitchen—all granite and stainless steel as if it lived in a showroom, gleamingly clean as is only possible for a man who eats takeout seven nights a week. I'd watched delivery men carry the granite in, helped Jack unwrap the appliances.

In the bathroom mirror, I saw what he saw and I almost wept. *Awful* wasn't the word—wrecked, defeated, that same pasty-ill look that Ivan had. I remembered the wound on his chest, how his bandage was bleeding through, too. I felt a bizarre camaraderie for the big, unstable man.

"This is infected," Jack said with a grimace as he removed the bandage. "Stay here."

I sank to the floor as soon as he left, sitting on the plush bath mat and leaning against the wood vanity. I heard him pound up the stairs and then come back down a minute later. He knelt on the floor beside me. I cringed when I saw the peroxide in his hand, the mass of cotton balls, gauze, and antibiotic ointment. He dabbed some of the peroxide on a cotton ball. He was in his element—he was a caretaker, the fix-it guy.

What about Jack? My sister's favorite question, asked after every dating snafu and failed relationship. *He's such a good guy. He cares about you. It's obvious.*

It's obvious we're friends. There's nothing else but that.

That's enough for a start. It's not all lightning bolts and shooting stars.

You sound like Mom.

"Isabel," Jack said, poised with a dripping ball of cotton, the scent of antiseptic heavy in the air. "This is *really* going to hurt."

"Good," I said. "I like consistency."

He gave me a look that was somehow amused and compassionate and then ruthlessly went to work on my injury while I tried to be stoic, but couldn't stop a flood of tears welling from a deep place within me.

Jack just kept saying, over and over, "I'm sorry, Iz. I'm so sorry."

* * *

"What are you doing here, Ben?"

Her breath came out in big clouds. She pulled her coat tightly around her.

"Get in the car," he said softly, not meeting her eyes. "It's cold."

"Ben. I'm not getting in your car. My children are sleeping inside that building." She turned around and pointed to the large white structure. She had an uncomfortable fluttering in her chest thinking of them sleeping a few stories up next to Fred's hospital bed. Either of them could wake, walk over to the window, and see her standing in the parking lot, talking to a strange man in his car. There would be lots of questions she couldn't answer.

He'd seen her exit the building; she could tell by the way he straightened his posture and checked his reflection in the rearview mirror. Did he think she'd be happy to see him here? Was he that delusional?

"Just for a minute. Please, Linda."

She could smell the heavy, sharp odor of too many cigarettes smoked in close quarters. He looked tired, edgy, was listening to the blues. She wasn't familiar with the song. A sad-voiced woman wailed about her lost man—her voice eerie, tinny, floating up to Linda's ears.

"No, Ben. What are you doing here? Did you *follow* me?"

He nodded, looking sheepish but not ashamed. Almost as if he thought she might find it funny or charming. She didn't.

"So that means you were sitting outside my building how long?"

"Since the coffee shop."

She saw her own reflection in the back passenger-seat window, her expression, angry, incredulous.

"That's not okay. That's—that is—" She paused to compose herself. "That's weird, Ben."

She expected him to cow, to say he was sorry, to then drive off. Tomorrow she'd tell him that they couldn't see each other any longer. Her family was in crisis and she needed to focus on them, refocus on her marriage. He'd see that it was the right thing. Maybe he'd go back to his family. But instead his face went still, the line of his mouth looked angry. He released a bitter laugh.

"I trashed my whole life for you, Linda. The least you can do is *get* in the fucking car."

His words cut through the space between them, changing everything they were to each other. His tone was such a departure from anything she'd ever heard coming from his mouth that she looked at him hard for a second, hoping in a final moment of denial that he might be joking. He wasn't.

"I never asked you to do that," she said gently. She didn't want to hurt or anger him any further than he obviously was already. She could feel his tension and it unnerved her. But she wanted, needed him to go away. "In fact, quite the opposite."

"You didn't *have* to ask!" he yelled, startling her. Then he closed his eyes, took a deep breath. When he spoke again, he almost whispered. "In your heart, you know it's what you want. I know that. I know *you.* That's love, right? Knowing what the other person wants and giving it to them without their having to ask?"

He wasn't looking at her. That was the weird thing. He was staring straight ahead as if she wasn't even there. She felt the first cold finger of fear in her abdomen as he started an odd, rhythmic gripping and releasing of the wheel.

"Come on, Ben," she said, forcing a coaxing gentleness into her voice. "Get some rest. We'll talk about this tomorrow."

He turned his head quickly and she saw the depth of his fatigue, a frightening glimmer in his eyes. She took an involuntary step back, afraid he was going to get out of the car. *How had this happened? How did they get from where they were to this place?*

"I can't," he said. "I can't sleep at all. I need you with me."

She wrapped her arms tighter around herself, her whole body

shivering with cold and fear. There was something really wrong. She'd never even seen a shade of this in him. But, she realized, they didn't really know each other well. Sex is not intimacy. Not really. Though he seemed to think it was.

She forced a smile to soothe him, moved closer to the car and rested her hand on his arm. He seemed to relax a bit, seemed more like himself. Then: "I think she was glad, you know, relieved that the charade was over. Erik will be, too. He might be as unhappy as you are."

She kept the smile on her face, even though his words almost made her knees buckle. She nodded. "You might be right. I'll talk to him. I'll call you tomorrow."

He smiled then, too, and put his hand on hers. "I'm going to make you really happy, Linda. You'll see."

"I know," she said. "Just get some rest now. Okay?"

"Okay," he said. "Okay."

"Promise?"

"Yeah."

She backed away from him, then turned and started walking back toward the hospital. Everything in her wanted to run. Her heart was an engine in her chest.

"Linda." The tone in his voice—cold, dead—stopped her. But she didn't turn around.

"You tell him," he said flatly. "Or I'm going to."

She started walking more quickly and heard him call after her one more time. This time she didn't stop until she was under the bright lights inside. She ducked quickly into the bathroom and held on to the sink until the quaking in her body subsided. Then she ran to the nearest stall and vomited—bile, water, coffee. She sank to the floor and rested her head against the mental divider.

The phone in her pocket was ringing then. She didn't recognize the number but she answered it.

"Hey, it's me."

She'd never been so happy to hear her husband's voice. He was so good. So safe. She knew his failings were nothing compared to her own.

"Hey," she said, trying to sound normal, "what's going on? I've been calling and calling."

"My phone died."

"Where are you?"

In a whisper he told her about Camilla Novak and Isabel's flight.

"She did *what*?"

"I didn't tell the police. She didn't mean it. She was just trying to give me a real reason for letting her go. It's not like she would have shot me."

"Oh my God." What was it with everyone coming apart at the seams? Were they all stretched that thin? Just a little adversity and everyone broke in two? "Where are you now?"

"The police brought me in for questioning. They're treating me—I don't know. They seem suspicious, like they think I'm holding back."

"Are you?"

"Just about the gun. And the fact that she took Camilla Novak's purse."

"What? Why?"

"Um, I don't know. She wasn't very . . . communicative. She's, you know, on a mission. She thinks she can fix everything."

She issued a sigh that turned into a sob. It surprised her, the sheer force of it. She couldn't have held it back if she wanted.

"Linda. I need you with me, okay?" His request echoed Ben's demands, making her sob harder.

"Are you still at the hospital?" He didn't wait for her to answer. "Take the kids to my mother's. She's expecting you. Then come to the precinct." He gave her the address.

"I'll have to leave Fred here alone," she said. "I promised Mom I'd wait for her."

"She'll understand."

She nodded, forgetting that he couldn't see her.

"Linda," he went on, "we're going to be okay."

"I've made mistakes, too. Big ones," she managed, wiping at her eyes, trying to catch her breath. She wanted to confess so badly, tell him everything right then. But there could hardly be a worse time.

"Just come here," he said. He sounded strong, in control. He was always exactly what she needed him to be. "And call that lawyer."

"Okay," she said, standing up, pulling herself together. "I'm coming."

She didn't know if Ben was still idling in the parking lot, and if he was, how she'd get herself and the kids out without him seeing her. But she would.

She quickly splashed some water on her face and exited the bathroom. In the wide empty foyer, she saw a frail, worried-looking woman gazing about, confused. She wore a trim navy blue coat and was toting a suitcase on wheels. It was a split second before Linda realized it was her mother; she seemed so out of place in the context of the mess of her life somehow.

"Mom."

"Oh, Linda," Margie said with relief. "What in the world is going on?"

Margie seemed to take in the all the details of her daughter's being, her tousled hair, the shadow of mascara under her eyes, the coffee stain on her coat—all the things Linda had just been focusing on in the mirror. Margie's brow sunk into a deep frown.

"What," she repeated, "in the world is going on?"

17

What surprised me the most about marriage was how quickly it settled, became not mundane, necessarily, but normal. After the euphoria of finding love, the magic of courtship, the thrill of engagement, the busy fun of planning a wedding, there's the lovely honeymoon and then all the little pleasures of setting up house, putting away the extravagant gifts, adjusting to life as married people; we, not I, us, not me. Everything shines, everything is new and fresh. And then—it's not as if it goes bad or sour, nothing like that. It's just that it becomes normal in a way I didn't expect. I guess it shouldn't have surprised me. Linda was a very canny tour guide.

"When you've really chosen well, when you really love your spouse, it's not as if the fire dies precisely," she told me one time. "It just goes from being an inferno to a pilot light. If you're not vigilant, you won't notice it until it's gone out completely."

"You and Erik still have romance," I said.

"Yes, but we work at it. The main part of our life is our children and our work. I never go to dinner or the movies without some barely conscious worry of Trevor and Emily at the back of my mind. Sometimes when we make love, I'm wondering if he remembered to paid the electric bill."

"Linda!"

A quick shrug, a flutter of the eyelids (so like Margie). "That's married with children. It's not as bad as it sounds from the outside." She smiled the smile of the older, wiser sister. "You'll see."

Not me, I thought. Never us.

And it never was quite that way with Marcus and me—not sexually. Though we fell into that domestic rhythm of work, dishes, laundry, bills, he always excited me; I never thought about the electric bill when we made love. But then again, we never had children, leaving us free from that special kind of fatigue I saw in Linda and Erik after months, going on years, of spotty sleep and an endless monitoring of needs.

And then, of course, I never really knew Marcus. I was always sleeping with a stranger, maybe subconsciously never comfortable enough, never intimate enough to allow my mind to wander. Maybe it is the unknowing that excites passion within me, the desire to understand that keeps me interested. Maybe that's why, even when things were bad—his apathy about the pregnancy and miscarriage, his affair—I stayed. Curiosity. *Who are you?*

Jack was talking, pacing the room like a preacher giving a sermon, hands waving, voice raised. I wasn't listening; I was sinking into a deep well of self-pity. I felt a barren place inside me, a place where no life could grow, where no love could last.

He'd fed me a tuna melt and made me take my antibiotics and was now lecturing me on my stupidity, threatening to call the police, or physically drag me to the lawyer himself. Jack was prone to ranting. Something to do with being born and raised in Manhattan, this loud-mouthed, totally self-assured dissertation on whatever.

"This is not some novel you're writing, Isabel," he concluded. "This is your life."

"What's the difference?"

He stopped moving and fixed me with his gaze. I don't know how to describe Jack; he's so familiar, it's almost as if I can't always see him.

His dark hair was a careful mess, his darker eyes always kind, always in on the divine joke of it all. There's an interesting shape to his nose, broken during a fistfight in high school and never healed quite right. He was fit, beefy, muscular in the way of someone who spends just enough time at the gym, soft in the way of someone who can't quite give up the foods that bring pleasure.

"You're telling me you don't know the difference between fact and fiction." His eyes rested accusingly on the cut he'd just bandaged, as if this might be the culprit responsible for my mental instability.

"Not at the moment."

"Are you just being existential, tortured? Or have you officially walked over the edge?"

The edge: the outside limit of an object, area, or surface; a place or part farthest away from the center of something. Which edge did he worry I'd stepped off—the edge of sanity, reality, reason?

"Neither. If I were writing this, right now I'd be wondering what my heroine should do next. I'd be exploring the field of possibilities. Which is precisely what I intend to do."

"In the real world there are consequences for mistakes, Isabel."

"In fiction, too."

"Fine," he snapped, frustrated with me. "But no edits, no rewrites. In the real world? Consequences are a stone wall." He smacked fist against palm for emphasis.

I turned away from him and stared at a huge engineer's sketch of the Brooklyn Bridge that was framed and hung on the wall—precise lines and exact measurements, tiny hand-scrawled notes about cable lengths and river span. I'd always envied engineers their exacting spirits, their certainty of tools and craft, their faith that the world would be as it was measured. My world seemed so liquid by comparison, everything shifting and changing so often as to be incalculable.

Jack had a point. A good one, which drained what little was left of my energy. I returned to the place of doubt I'd visited on the street. I thought of Detective Crowe and his number in my pocket. Everyone I cared about and respected wanted me to turn myself in to the lawyer. Why was I being so stubborn? What did I think I was going to do?

"Your phone's ringing," I said, lying back and examining the high white ceiling, the ornate molding, the sleek track lighting—a lovely blend of original and modern features. He really had done a stellar job with the place. I noticed a hairline crack in the ceiling, some insect corpses behind the glass in the lamps. We both listened to the faint chirping of the phone.

He shook his head. "Must be yours. Mine's right there." He pointed his chin toward the slim black device on the granite countertop.

"It's not mine. I tossed my phone."

We both looked over at Camilla's purse. It lay where I'd dropped it with my own on Jack's leather couch. We looked back at each other. I dove for it. He dove for me.

"Don't answer that," he said, grabbing my arm.

"Why not?" I pulled away from him and reached for the bag. I rummaged through the contents, until I found it still ringing and vibrating at the bottom. It was hot pink, scratched and battered. The screen blinked, *Blocked number.* I flipped it open and turned to Jack, triumphant. He looked stricken, as though he'd just watched me walk over a ledge. Overreacting, as usual. I didn't say anything, just listened.

"Camilla?" A man's voice.

I thought about it a second. "Hi," I said, after a beat. I tried to imitate her voice from what I'd heard in our brief conversation earlier. My voice just came out sounding strangled, strange. Jack was shaking his head, inching closer to me. I wondered if he was going to try to wrest the phone away from me. Then instead he blew out a breath and walked over to the refrigerator, pulled the door open angrily. It was completely empty except for a bottle of Gray Goose, a bottle of seltzer, and a bowl of limes.

"You're late," said the voice on the line.

His tone was gruff, accent thick. I didn't say anything. I wasn't trying to be crafty. I just didn't know how to best lead the conversation. I issued a cough, just to fill the silence that followed. Jack mouthed, *Hang up the phone.* He made a wide circle with his index finger at his temple. *This is crazy!*

"Well?" said the voice on the other line. The sound of traffic was loud behind him. A siren wailed nearby.

"I'm having some problems." I lowered my voice to a whisper, counting on him not being able to hear me well.

There was a pause and I thought he'd caught on, that he'd hang up.

"But you're coming?" he said finally.

I decided on silence again.

"I'll wait—but not much longer. By the Children's Gate, yes?"

"Yes."

"Do you have the files?" he asked then. "Am I wasting my time?"

I decided to end the call rather than respond. The voice on the line, harsh and unyielding though it was, had a desperate edge. Camilla had something he wanted; he was waiting, though she must have been very, very late. I thought of her lying there, bleeding out, of her cooling flesh.

Jack was drinking from a lead crystal lowball, ice chinking, eyes on me.

"What do you think you're doing?" he said. I realized I was still standing, staring at the phone in my hand.

"Do you have my money?" I asked, snapping back into the present.

The phone call had given me a little juice. The lethargy that was settling into my bones dissipated. I took Camilla's purse and emptied the contents out onto the low coffee table.

"He said something about files," I said.

Jack sat down across from me. I could see the curiosity on his face, though he wore a deep scowl. He was an agent, a broker of story—he loved a good one more than anyone else I knew.

A cheap lipstick, a bottle of glitter nail polish, a half-smoked pack of cigarettes. Or half-unsmoked, if you're an optimist.

"That depends," he said, reaching for the tube of lipstick. He opened it and rolled the bottom until the little pink tip of makeup emerged. Then he recapped and tossed it back on the table.

Her tacky sequined wallet was overstuffed with singles and receipts—a nail salon, Taco Bell, a bookstore. A small black makeup bag containing more cosmetics—lip liner, mascara, a small black compact of blush.

"You have it or you don't, Jack."

A small plastic photo book, grimy in the way of something that's been in your purse forever, well-thumbed. I flipped through the images, feeling a weight settle on me. Camilla smiled with an older woman, clearly a relative, probably her mother. Another young woman with Camilla's eyes and nose, but darker, less pretty somehow, held a sleeping, wrinkled baby wrapped in a pink blanket. A little girl in pigtails and a blue corduroy jumper smiled, revealing an adorable gap in her teeth. There was a photo of a man I recognized as the missing Marcus Raine. He sat on a bed, holding a guitar, but looked directly at the camera with a smile. A man in love.

The rest of the contents—a bag of M&Ms, a cigarette lighter, a little notebook covered with hearts—littered the table. The detritus of a life. All the stuff she collected and bought and carried with her, things that were important to her. All now in the possession of a woman she'd never met, who'd stood over her dead body, touched her dead flesh, then took off with her belongings. If someone had told her that when she bought her M&Ms, what would she have thought?

I remembered the gun, took it from my pocket and put it on the table.

"Hey—whoa. What you doing with that?"

It was a small .38 revolver. I only knew this because a cop I'd interviewed once showed me a similar one. It was a gun cops often used as an off-duty piece, smaller, less conspicuous. It was light and perfect for a woman's hand. My nephew would be pleased. *You might need one,* he'd warned, prescient.

"It was in her bag," I said. "Are you going to answer me? Did you get my money?"

"So wherever she was going, she was going armed?" I could see it in his face: curiosity breaking and entering, making off with common sense.

He reached out and picked up what I'd thought at first glance was a small silver cigarette lighter. In Jack's hand, I realized that it was a thumb drive, a tiny device that stored computer files. I reached for it quickly and he snatched it back.

"I heard the whole conversation," he said. "I know what you're thinking."

He probably did know what I was thinking. It didn't take a genius to figure it out. He held the thumb drive up in the air.

"But what's your agenda, your goal for this meeting?" he asked. "How will you recognize who you're supposed to meet, and what will you do once you're there?"

I hadn't really thought that far ahead. He should know this about me. He seemed to read it all on my face. He rolled his eyes, leaned back in his chair.

"Let's look at that drive. See what's on it," I said.

"We don't have time," he said, standing up. "And maybe it's better if we don't know." He walked over to the closet and took out a distressed brown leather jacket and shrugged it on, pulled a stocking cap over his hair.

"It's never better not to know. Trust me." I held out my palm.

He ignored me. "Do you even know what the Children's Gate is?"

I gave him a look. Mr. I Know Everything About New York City. It was a hobby of his; he was always explaining, correcting, pointing out items of interest. Sometimes it was cool; more often after our many years of friendship it was annoying.

"There are twenty gates to Central Park," I said. "That one's on Seventy-sixth and Fifth."

He raised his eyebrows in mock surprise, gave a deferential nod. "A-plus," he said, zipping up his jacket. "We're close. Let's go and get this over with."

How easily he slipped into the plot, became accomplice and co-writer.

"We have time to look at the drive," I said. "If he waited this long, he'll wait awhile longer."

He paused another moment and I thought he was going to put up more argument. But instead he moved quickly to his office down the hall. By the time I caught up with him, he was already sitting at his computer with the drive in his USB port. It was a simple room, not yet finished. Just a shining glass desk and ergonomic black chair. Atop the glass sat an impossibly thin black laptop, a spindly halogen lamp. The walls were floor-to-ceiling shelves filled with books. He was the only one in the world with more copies of my novels than I had. They lined his shelves—U.S. copies, foreign editions, trade paperbacks, mass market editions. All my stories, my imaginings bound, translated into languages I wouldn't understand, my millions of words offered in neat packages. I saw my name in myriad typefaces and colors: Isabel Connelly. Not Isabel Raine. No, I was never that in print. The place where I was most real, most alive, most myself—on the page—I was never Isabel Raine. I felt a strange gratitude for that now.

"Pictures," he was saying.

I came to stand behind him, feeling a bit wobbly, and steadied myself on his shoulder. Without looking at me, he stood and gave me the chair, keeping his eyes on the screen, his hand on the keyboard, flipping through what looked like fifty or sixty black-and-white photographs.

Four men stood in a loose group at the edge of a dock, hands in pockets, hunched against the cold. Three of them wore long black coats. The water behind them was gray and choppy. The fourth appeared to be dressed only in a suit. His shoulders were hiked up in tension, arms wrapped around his middle obviously for warmth. In the next frame one of the coated men had a big hand on the arm of the suited man. In the next a gun appeared. Each frame—grainy, moody—was separated from the last by a matter of seconds. I could almost hear the rapid shutter clicks. The next frame zoomed in and with a start I recognized two faces—Marcus and Ivan. Ivan, the man with the gun. Marcus with his arm locked in another man's grasp.

"Is that Marcus?" asked Jack, incredulous.

But I'd lost my voice. In my head I heard the screaming, that horrible keening, and all the hairs on my arms and neck started to rise. As Jack flipped through the frames, faster now, we watched as Marcus laid his hand across the hand on his arm and moved into a quick, hard, practiced twist that dropped the other man to his knees and left him on the ground, his mouth open in a scream. The camera caught a muzzle flash from Ivan's gun, but in the next frame the gun was in Marcus's hand. Each successive frame saw another man on the ground until it was just Marcus and Ivan surrounded by bleeding corpses. Two frames showed them standing there, Marcus holding the gun, Ivan with his hands up in supplication. In the next frame Ivan was on the ground. Marcus started rolling bodies into the river, the dock splattered with blood. Then it was just Marcus and Ivan again, the big man lying on his side writhing, his face a mask of pain, arms around his center, Marcus standing over him, the gun aimed at his brother's head. He lowered the gun. The camera caught him walking away, Ivan's mouth open in a scream of pain or rage or both.

"Izzy," said Jack, after a moment of us both staring at the screen. "Are you okay?"

I leaned forward and continued scrolling to watch Marcus walk, unhurried, up the dock and disappear between two large warehouses. He was wearing the suit he'd been wearing when he left me.

"He killed three people," Jack said, his voice dropping to an amazed whisper. "Left the other one to die."

I felt myself separating from a rising tide of emotion—grief, horror, fear. I rafted it like a white-water current, otherwise I would have drowned.

"Where would you say that is?" I asked. He leaned in close and I could smell the scent of Ivory soap on his skin, mingling with the vodka on his breath. He put a finger on the screen. I saw the Verrazano-Narrows Bridge in the distance.

"Brooklyn," he said. "Somewhere between Bensonhurst and Coney Island."

"You were right," I said, even though I didn't mean it. "We would have been better off not seeing that."

"Always listen to your agent," he said. He was trying to lighten things up a bit, but he just sounded sad and a little afraid.

I backed up the thumb drive on his computer, ejected and pocketed the small device. He stood by and watched me do it, folded his arms across his chest. I walked to the door and turned around to look at him.

"This is the point where I say you don't have to come with me, that I don't want you to. I want you to stay here and be safe, call the police if I don't come back or call."

He released a long, slow breath, held my eyes.

"I was hoping that this was the point where you realized you're not writing this. That the tragedy and danger are real, that you're grief-stricken and injured, that you need to lie down and let me take care of you."

I smiled at the temptation. "If *I* did that, I wouldn't be who I am."

He nodded. "And if I let you go alone, I wouldn't be who I am."

He helped me on with my coat. I gathered Camilla's things and put them in her bag, slipped the thumb drive in there, too, and slung it over my shoulder. I left my own bag behind, not wanting anything to happen to my last bit of cash, my passport and credit cards. I kept her gun in the pocket with Detective Crowe's card. I put her cell phone in the other, noticing that the charge was low.

"Do you have my cash?"

"Not on my person. But I have it in the house, yes. We'll talk about that later."

I nodded, took the revolver out of my pocket one last time and did what I hadn't yet done, looked to see if it was loaded. It was.

"Do you even know how to use a gun?" Jack asked.

"I do."

He looked at me quizzically, skeptical.

"Research," I said.

He opened the door for me and we walked out into the night.

"WHY DON'T YOU give it up, Crowe? Seriously, buddy. We're going on two years here."

Grady Crowe was sitting alone in the car outside the precinct. He'd dropped Jez off at the door, told her he'd park and be right up to deal with Erik Book. Book, as they suspected, had already contacted his lawyer and was refusing to say anything until he arrived. They'd had him ride in the back of a radio car with two uniformed officers, not cuffed, but not necessarily free to go, either. And Crowe suspected that Book was unsettled enough that he might turn on the charm and get a word or two out of him the nice way. Book seemed like a reasonable guy in over his head, maybe making mistakes out of fear, a desire to protect. He'd give him the "Look, you're not a suspect, don't need a lawyer, we just want to help" speech.

There were fewer parking spots on the street in front of the precinct than there were police vehicles, so he found a space in the back of the lot across First. With a few seconds alone in the car, he did what he'd been wanting to do all day: He called Clara's cell.

She was still thinking about him. Her late-night call told him that. Maybe she wasn't as happy with Keane as she thought she'd be. Big surprise there. He had a lofting feeling of hope in his center until Sean Keane, the man currently fucking Grady's wife, answered her phone.

Grady stared ahead, his view a chain-link fence, a patch of overgrown grass and weeds, and the tall redbrick wall of the building adjacent to the lot. To his right was the outdoor basketball court where he and Keane used to shoot hoops after a rough shift to blow off steam. Around the corner was the bar where they'd grab a beer and a burger. They'd bitch about their wives. When they were friends, more than once he'd thought, with a twinge of envy, that Keane was a *really* good-looking guy. Lean and muscular, sandy-blond hair and strong jaw, jewel-green eyes with girlish lashes. All the girls in the precinct brushed the hair out of their eyes, smiled too much, laughed too loudly when he was around. Stupid. If they knew what a dog he was, those smiles wouldn't last long.

Little did Grady know that Sean would one day be making Clara smile and so much more. He saw them talking at the Christmas party. He noticed the way she tilted her head and twirled a strand of her hair. They'd fought about it, actually.

You shouldn't be flirting at my fucking Christmas party. It's unbecoming.

Yeah? Maybe if you stayed with me, acted like my goddamn husband, I'd be flirting with you.

But that was a long time ago. "I would, *buddy*," he said, mocking Keane's use of the word. "I would let it go. Except your fiancée keeps calling me."

There was a silence on the other end of the line and Grady felt a rush of satisfaction. "All the shiny and new rubbing off? Underneath just the same old thing?"

Sean didn't give him the benefit of a reaction, but Grady heard his voice tighten when the other man spoke again.

"Give it up, Crowe. The wedding's in a week."

"Yeah. And a year from now, you're going to find yourself on another bar stool bitching about Clara the way you bitched about Angie." He let a beat pass. "Hey, how's that boy of yours? Missing his daddy?"

The line went dead and Grady enjoyed a moment of self-righteous glee. He was the injured party, the one who'd kept his vows—he liked lording that over them. It comforted him. Clara and Sean hurt a lot of people to be together; he hoped they lost a little sleep over it.

But after a moment, the rush of pleasure passed and he felt lower than he had before, which was pretty low. Now Clara would be upset with him for betraying her to Sean. If she called again, it would be in anger and disappointment. She'd phoned him in a vulnerable moment and he used it to hurt her. He wished he could take it back, what he'd said. He wished he'd protected her instead of offering her up to get his licks in with Keane.

One of Clara's more memorable cuts came back to him: *You're not even adult enough to be someone's husband. What kind of father would you be?*

"Shit." He almost hit the dash, but his fist still ached from the last miserable phone call. "Shit."

By the time he'd cooled down and was entering the precinct, Jez was exiting.

"Don't bother," she said. "The lawyer is already here. What took you so long, anyway?"

"I was looking for parking," he said lamely.

She seemed skeptical but stopped short of giving him a hard time again. Instead she patted him on the back to get him moving.

"Well, let's roll," she said. "When's the last time you went dancing?"

"So long ago, I don't even remember what it feels like."

She gave a little grunt. "Join the club."

18

I had this nervous tick of using my thumbnail to tug at the back of my wedding ring. Of course, every time I tried to do this, I was reminded that the ring was gone.

I never had a traditional wedding band, always hated the idea of that for some reason—as though it was some kind of bond to the normal, the common idea of marriage. The ring Marcus gave me at our engagement, a ruby set in a platinum band, was the only jewelry I wore. I loved its glinting red fire, the simple beauty of a single gem, something pure mined from the earth. Not flashy but stately. Not for show, for real. Of course, it was all flash, all show, none of it real. And the ring, like everything else, was gone.

"It's all I have from my mother, from my past. I don't know how she came to have this. But my aunt gave it to me when I left for the states. I had it set for you. It's yours."

I wanted to know more about the gem, about his mother. But his memories, he said, were fuzzy. He remembered a smiling face framed in curls, a wafting scent of lemon verbena. That was all. Of his father, there was nothing at all. It was terribly unsatisfying for a fiction writer, to be deprived of the texture and details of my husband's history. I imagined that the ruby had been given to his mother by a man she loved, maybe not Marcus's father, maybe a gypsy from Romania, and that she'd kept it hidden, maybe sewn inside a coat. She never looked at it, but took great comfort in thinking of its flame, that passionate blood red. It reminded her of love. I imagined that somewhere she was pleased to know the ruby was out in the light, on the hand of a woman her son loved and married. I kept these fantasies to myself. He didn't like to talk about the past, grew stiff and cold. I used to think it was because it caused him too much pain, but more likely it was because it was too much effort to keep all the lies straight.

"What are you thinking about?" Jack walked on my left, the park yawning to the right.

"My ring. It's gone. Someone took it."

"I'm sorry. I noticed. I thought maybe you took it off." There were running footfalls behind us and both of us startled, turned only to be passed quickly by a rail-thin young woman wearing headphones and breathing too hard. We started walking again.

"How could this have happened?" I asked.

He didn't answer, just gave a slow shake of his head. We were moving fast, both of us nervous, unsure what we were heading into, or why, or what we were going to do when we got there.

"You didn't like him. Neither did Linda. Okay. But this? Did you imagine this?"

"Linda didn't like him?" He seemed pleased.

"Jack," I snapped. "Answer me."

"No. Not this. Of course not. Who could imagine this?" He took a few long strides so that he was in front of me, then turned around, stopping me. The Children's Gate was just two blocks away now. He held out a hand.

"Give me the gun," he said, sounding practical, assured. He was the man, he should be holding the gun. That simple.

"No," I said, pushing past him. He grabbed my arm and didn't let go even when I struggled.

"Jack," I said, feeling anger, too much anger, rise in my chest, a kind of free fall in my belly. "Let go of me."

I tried to wrest my arm from him, but he held fast.

"I mean it," I said. "Let go."

"Calm down, Isabel," he said gently. "Look. It's me."

I looked at his face and my anger burned out. Just the eye contact calmed me, and I was aware of how rigid my body was, stiff at the shoulders, arm muscles tensed.

"We need a plan, a course of action."

"Impossible."

"Why?"

"We have no frame of reference. Nothing like this has ever happened to either one of us."

We were moving again, Jack still holding tight to my arm as though he thought I might try to bolt. "We need to decide what to say at least," he said reasonably.

And then it was too late. We both saw him, standing against the low stone wall. Just the look of him, furtive, anxious, told me that he was the one waiting for Camilla Novak. I was sure of it.

Jack and I separated. He kept so close behind me, I could feel him at my back. I look back at this moment now and think how foolish we were. New Yorkers think we own the world, that our proximity to reported crime—even if we are as pampered and sheltered as children in a nursery—makes us savvy and street smart. We believe our own international reputation as tough, rude, no-nonsense. We think we can grab a gun and confront some nameless thug on the street.

I walked right up to the stranger, who raised his eyes from the concrete to look at me. He was short, balding. His face was pockmarked and ruddy from the cold. His eyes had a kind of lazy menance, a dim nastiness.

"Camilla Novak is dead," I said simply. My hand was on the gun in my pocket. "Now I have what you want."

He looked at me blankly, pushed himself off the wall. His eyes darted toward Jack, back at the bulge in my pocket. He was making a threat assessment.

"I have some questions," I went on arrogantly. "If you answer them, I'll give you the files."

Clumsy? Yes. Short-sighted? Sure. Of all the scenarios that had played out in my mind—a struggle, some kind of slick conversation in which I got what I wanted, even though I had no idea what that was, my actually firing the weapon, him cowering in fear, him attacking me—what happened next was a surprise. There was a beat, a pause between us where I felt Jack stiffen, start to pull me back.

"Who is Kristof Ragan?" I said, even though my heart was pumping fast now, adrenaline racing through me, causing a shaking in the hand gripping the gun. "Where can I find him?"

He released a little laugh. "You make mistake. No English."

I had a moment of self-doubt when I felt very, very silly. But no. It was the same voice I'd heard on the phone, the same gruffness, the same thick accent.

"Really?" I said. I pulled Camilla's phone out of my pocket and found the number on the call log, hit send. The ringing coming from his pants—some indecipherable pop tune—seemed to startle him; he glanced annoyed at his own pocket. Then he pushed past us like a linebacker, snatching the bag from my shoulder, knocking me to the hard concrete and body-checking Jack against the wall. He broke into an impossibly fast sprint into the park. Jack and I exchanged a shocked look. I scrambled to my feet and gave chase.

"Are you crazy?" he yelled after me.

"He's got the bag!" I called, as if this justified risking my life. And in the moment it seemed to.

I broke away and ran down the concrete trail past the ornate lampposts and benches, but by the time I reached a fork in the trail, he was nowhere to be seen. Jack came up behind me. In his hands were the pieces of Camilla's cell phone, which I must have dropped when I fell to the ground. The despair that swept over me might have brought me to my knees if my attention wasn't diverted by two sharp reports cracking the night. Then Jack was on me, pulling me behind a large rock formation off the paved trail. Two more shots rang out, and a car alarm answered, filling the air with its mournful, incessant wail.

We huddled speechless until we saw the stranger stumble into view. He took a few staggering steps and then fell hard onto his belly with a low, terrible moan. Stupidly, I left the cover of the rock and kneeled beside him, touched his shoulder. He was talking, mumbling in a language I recognized but didn't understand. I leaned in close to him, barely aware of Jack behind me, pulling at my arm. He was saying something like, "Isabel, there's someone coming. Someone shot this guy; they're coming after us."

But I didn't hear him then, because I was listening to the whispering of a dying man.

"Who is Kristof Ragan?" I asked him. "Where is he? Please."

There was no reason for me to think he might know the answer to this question. And it was blindly selfish, some might even call it depraved indifference, to make demands of this person who lay bleeding on the cold concrete of Central Park. But every ounce of my drive lived in this question. And this stranger was the only one I had to ask. In all his final mutterings, which ceased in a horrifying gurgle, I only heard one word I thought I understood. Whether it was the answer to my question or not, I wouldn't know until later.

He said, "Praha."

Prague.

That magical city with its bloodred rooftops and towering castle, its muscular bone buildings and dark hidden squares. It captured me the first time I walked its cobblestone streets and marveled at its magnificent architecture. How I dreamed of Franz Kafka in the cafés he haunted. How I reveled in the predawn hush, the only quiet moment on Charles Bridge, that cascade of stone with its towering, tortured saints moaning through the ages. How I loved it even more the second time with my husband-to-be. I felt it became mine somehow when I married Marcus, someplace that would become a part of our lives, of the history of the children I hoped to bring into the world. The next time I visited Prague its secrets would try to swallow me, devour me whole. But I didn't know that yet.

It made sense to me then. He would return home, of course. How long had it been since I'd seen him in Camilla's apartment? Two, maybe three hours. He could be on a plane already, couldn't he? There'd be a stop in London, maybe Paris. But then he'd go back to the place that made him.

When I looked up again from the man whose name I never knew, I saw her standing about a hundred feet away—the woman I knew only as S. She wore a strange expression as she stared directly at me. I heard Detective Breslow's words again. *There's so much rage evidenced here.* She hated me. She envied me. I saw it there in the features of her perfect face. Why? Because he'd loved me once? She had it all now, didn't she? My husband, my money, even my ring?

She looked like any slim New Yorker taking a run in the park too late at night, except that she had Camilla's bag strapped over her shoulder and across her chest. She wore black leggings, a short white jacket with black racing stripes down the sleeves. Another man—I might have recognized him as one of the faux FBI agents who took apart Marcus's office, but I couldn't be sure—was behind her. He was dark and thick-bodied, but he hid in shadows and I couldn't clearly see the character of his face.

I rose and Jack moved in front of me. He didn't know who they were; the weapons they must have been carrying weren't apparent. But he knew their malice instinctively, acted to protect me.

I reached for the gun in my pocket and gripped it hard.

"I have a gun!" I yelled from behind Jack. I sounded pathetic and desperate.

S turned to look at her partner and they both started to laugh, filling me with childish rage. I almost took the gun out and starting firing, so unhinged was I in that moment. But they both broke into a run. As she turned, she lifted her hand in a friendly wave. And then she was gone, the shadows of the trail swallowing them both. I let them go, drained, stunned. I knew when I'd been beaten. I'd made a gamble and lost. We both stood there for I don't know how long, just staring after them. Then we heard the distant wailing of sirens.

"We should stay and wait for the police," Jack said sensibly. "Tell them what happened."

The foolish things we do in the wake of lost love. How angry we are, how desperate when it's snatched from us, as though we had some right to have and hold it forever. We don't see love as an organic thing that might fade and die like flowers in a vase. We compare it to minerals and gems, things that last unchanging through time. When love dies we see it as something precious, solid, owned, that was stolen from us. We chase it, beg for its return, revenge its loss, try to steal it back. We don't imagine that it could fade like vapor, that it was just a moment that has passed as life itself will.

I was in the grip of righteous anger.

"I need my bag and my money," I told him, holding his dark, fearful gaze.

"Iz." He turned, put his hands on my shoulders. I put my hands on top of his. The wailing of approaching sirens grew louder.

"Are you my friend?" I asked.

"Iz."

"Are you?"

"Of course."

"Then give me your keys. Tell me where the money is, and let me go."

He shook his head. "Go ahead. I dare you to pull a gun on me, too. I'm not Erik. I'll make you shoot me."

I dropped my chin to my chest. "Please, Jack. I can't let him have so much. I'll never be able to live with myself. I'll die."

I couldn't bring myself to meet his eyes. I didn't want him to see how deep was my rage and my shame, how total my desperation.

"Okay," he breathed. "Let's go."

The disease that Marcus brought into my life had infected everything and everyone connected to me, now Jack included. But he'd always been my coconspirator, the one who understood my mind best, so it was only natural that we should come together now in the writing of this story, the end unknown to both of us. We'd bandied about countless plots, argued over motivation, plausibility, fought about truth in character. Of course, he'd want to help me resolve the fiction of my life with Marcus. I might have convinced him to let me go; I knew he loved me enough to let me do what my heart dictated, no matter what. But the truth is I didn't want to face alone what lay ahead.

We joined hands and ran.

19

Linda didn't have an off-switch, not when it came to her children. She and Erik didn't take a week away, like their friends often did, leaving the kids with Izzy or one of the grandmothers. She just couldn't imagine it, boarding a vehicle that would loft into the air, separating her by hundreds or even thousands of miles from Trevor and Emily. Margie thought this was very unhealthy, that ultimately it would take a toll on the marriage, that the children would become too dependent, too needy, never self-reliant. And maybe she was right. She and Erik were in crisis. Trevor cried like a toddler when she'd left them earlier with Erik's mom; Emily sulked. But Linda thought Margie's off-switch was a bit too well-developed, that she had disconnected too easily and too often from her girls. That sometimes even when she'd been present, she'd been absent. Izzy didn't share her feelings about this, remembered things differently.

Linda remembered often feeling alone in her family, that she was no one's first thought. Her shrink thought this caused her to be overly vigilant to Trevor's and Emily's needs. It was true that since Emily was born there hadn't been a morning when she wasn't immediately upon awaking tending to one of her children. There had been no mornings of languishing in bed with her husband, no really abandoned nights out. Ever. Was this unusual? She didn't really know. Most of their friends, other artists or professionals, had chosen to have only one child. Most of them had full-time nannies or au pairs, young, live-in girls from Europe who seemed in the best cases like surrogate children (whom you'd never had to diaper and who now did the dishes and cared for the smaller child), and in the worst cases like tight-bodied interlopers gazing with barely concealed avariciousness at their wealth and husbands.

She knew her friends loved their children; she didn't judge them. But it seemed to her that only she and Erik were parenting full-time, fitting work and life around Trevor and Emily, putting personal wants and needs last or never. Which way was right? Who was better off? She honestly didn't know. She just knew she couldn't be another way.

She remembered reading somewhere that the look on your face when a child enters your field of vision is one of the single most important factors in the shaping of that child's self-esteem. Luckily, she couldn't keep the delight off her face when she looked at Trevor and Emily; their faces, the sound of their voices, their accomplishments—from walking to potty training, from academic achievement to personal blossoming—filled her with more joy and excitement than anything else she'd known in her life.

But that statement had caused her to think back to her own childhood, to remember faces, expressions. She remembered wandering eyes, hard stares into the distance, furrowed brows. Not directed at her. Just in general, the faces she saw were sad ones—and she had never been enough to brighten them.

She was thinking this as Erik emerged from wherever they'd been holding him, with Margie's lawyer, John Brace. Actually, he was the son of Brace the elder, Fred's longtime attorney, who was getting too old, too frail to come out to the police station in the middle of the night. There was something harder, not as gentlemanly, about the younger Brace. A hard-ass. His face was all sharp angles, still and pale. She examined him as he talked to Erik, low, intent. She thought, He's a wolf. Feral, lonely, merciless. Good, perfect, exactly what they needed now.

They approached her and she embraced her husband, longer, harder than was appropriate with a stranger present. But she couldn't seem to let go of him. She saw Brace turn discreetly away, give them the privacy of not staring.

"It's okay," said Erik softly, rubbing her back. "I'm okay."

Brace cleared his throat and they turned to look at him. "This is an emotional time for you. But we have a lot of ground to cover. Your financial losses. Your sister, how we get in touch with her and convince her to return to the fold. Your potential culpability in this matter. How we proceed from here to protect ourselves. Where should we do that?"

"It's late," said Erik. "Let's do it tomorrow, John."

"I don't think that's a good idea. A lot can happen between now and then. We need to be prepared."

Looking weary, anxious, Erik nodded. "Home," he said. "Let's go home."

"No," said Linda, too quickly. By the time she'd left the hospital with Trevor and Emily, and shuttled them into a waiting taxi, Ben had left. But she couldn't count on him not to be lurking around the apartment, waiting to ambush them on their return.

"Let's go to a café or something. Café Orlin is right around the corner. It's quiet, private. I'm starved."

Erik looked as if he was about to argue but then seemed to change his mind.

"Fine," he said, taking her hand. "That's fine."

Brace nodded uncertainly, took a quick glance at his watch. Then he ushered them toward the exit. Linda noticed and liked that he seemed in charge, but was still deferential. She felt safer, calmer with him there, as if there was no problem he couldn't make disappear. The elder Brace didn't have this quality, didn't seem like an enforcer, more like a trusted adviser and friend. Someone who would do his best to help, within the letter of the law, but would bow to forces bigger than himself. His face was soft at the jaw, kind and warm at the eyes.

There was no kindness or softness in the face of the younger man, just granite.

The three exited the precinct and turned left, toward First Avenue. As they proceeded down the block, Linda saw—just out of the corner of her eye—Ben, waiting in his Mercedes across the street. Her heart nearly stopped in her chest, her stomach bottomed out completely, but she kept walking, pretended not to see.

She hoped he was a coward, that he'd stay in the periphery, a looming threat that never materialized. But then she heard a car door open and slam hard. She found herself cringing, clinging close to Erik, not able to bring herself to turn around even as she heard the footfalls behind them. John and Erik, already in conversation, seemed not to notice.

"I'm going to need you to start from the beginning, Erik," John was saying. "How Marcus Raine approached you, what documentation he provided, what you signed. Then we'll work our way up to the events of this evening."

"Okay," Erik said. "I can do that."

"Can I make a suggestion? It really would be better if we went back to your place. I'm reluctant to discuss your private matters in public. And in lieu of a secretary, I'd like to record our conversation to be transcribed later."

"I agree. Linda?"

Linda barely heard them. She had the vague sense that she was being asked something that needed answering, but she couldn't hear over the rushing of blood in her ears. They were just about to turn the corner.

"Linda!" called Ben, loud, insistent. All three of them stopped moving and turned back, startled at the sound of his voice.

Ben stood there, legs spread, arms akimbo. In the dim light of the street, the bulk of his frame was dark, menacing. She could barely see his face. She found herself unable to move, to open her mouth.

Please, Ben, she wanted to say, *don't do this to him. Don't do this to me. Not now.* But she couldn't; it all lodged in her throat. Her life was a china teacup, already on its way from delicate grip to marble floor. She had no one to blame but herself. She thought of her babies, Emily and Trevor, how she'd betrayed them more than she had anyone else with her vanity and stupidity. What kind of mother was she if she could lead herself and the father of her children into a moment like this?

"Who is that?" asked Erik, his face open and earnest, even in such a moment.

Linda shook her head. She opened her mouth but still no words came.

"Don't pretend you don't know who I am!" Ben roared, moving closer.

Erik pulled Linda back, and John Brace was quick to move in front of them, hold up a hand.

"Stay back, man. What do you want?"

John Brace suddenly seemed even tougher, harder, with his shaved head and broad shoulders, deep authoritative voice. The briefcase he clutched in his hand didn't diminish this image; he looked as though he was prepared to use it as a weapon or a shield.

"She doesn't love you, Erik," Ben said, his voice cracking like an adolescent boy's. "She loves me."

Linda could see his whole body was quaking. She realized suddenly, clearly, that something was clinically wrong with him. He wasn't just desperate or upset, or lovesick. She had a cold dawning, a terrible fear for his family, those two sweet-faced girls, his pretty wife. When he moved a step closer, into the orange glow of a street lamp, he seemed deranged, eyes wild, jaw clenching and unclenching, big chest heaving.

John spread his arms out and started herding them backward. He said quietly, "He has a gun."

Then Linda saw it, too. She'd been so focused on his face, how totally unself-conscious he was, how lost in his own mind, she hadn't noticed. Then he started lifting his arm.

She broke from Erik, started running toward Ben. She felt Erik, then John's hands on her, holding her back. Heard them both yelling, following close behind as she shifted away from them. She came to stop in front of Ben, feeling small and insubstantial before him. His height and breadth, the size of his anger dwarfed her. She wanted to scream at him. Instead she put her hand on his chest and whispered, "Ben, we have children. Think about what you're doing to your girls right now. Please."

He seemed to hear, to shrink at her words. Anger left him, dropped the features of his face into a sagging sadness, left his shoulders to slump forward.

Then Erik was pulling her back and there was shouting all around them. Uniformed officers seemed to have poured out of everywhere, there were so many emerging from the doors of the precinct building and coming out of cars. A shift change.

Then so many different voices echoing on the concrete of the buildings around them. *Freeze! Drop that weapon! Drop it! Drop it! Drop it!* Coming from everywhere like the call of crows.

Erik and John pulled Linda back and she was screaming, *No, no, no!* Because she knew. She saw it in Ben's eyes and watched as it spread across his face, that smile, that "Fuck you, world" smile. She'd seen it before, it was etched in her spirit, had dictated in so many ways the course of her life. She'd looked for it in every face, beneath the flimsy veils they all wore. She'd finally found it in Ben. *No, no, no!* She saw him raise the gun beneath his chin and, without hesitating, pull the trigger. And then in a horrible explosion of light and sound, a dreadful spray of red, it all disappeared.

20

A suicide, a miscarriage, a sudden disappearance. All abbreviations, interruptions. Variations on a theme that has run through my life.

The tickets were easily purchased with Jack's credit card, and even though as we waited to board the plane I saw my picture flash briefly on one of the televisions mounted up high, no one even glanced in my direction. The sound was down for some reason. The text on the screen read: *Real-Life Mystery: The Downtown Murder of Three People Linked to Missing Husband of Bestselling Author.* The story was obviously small news at this point. It wasn't even on the screen for thirty seconds.

I was five years younger in that photo and maybe ten pounds heavier when it was taken, but I might still have been recognizable if I hadn't tied back my hair into a bun at the base of my neck, tucked it beneath a gray knit cap pulled down over the bandage on my head, and donned a pair of round wire-rimmed glasses that I needed but never wore.

But maybe it was more than that. Maybe it was the simple fact, as Marcus always claimed, that people weren't looking anymore. They've got their earbuds in. They're staring at tiny screens that fit in a palm. They're talking on the phone, eyes blank, unseeing.

Even though I knew I wasn't officially a suspect, I kept waiting for the police to arrive. Maybe my name was on some kind of a watch list of people not allowed to leave the country? I'd expected to be stopped at check-in, at security. But no, we'd glided through security checks, while a young mother was forced to empty her bags, carry a weeping toddler through one of those machines that blows air on you in sharp, quick blasts. Her little boy screamed in fright. I thought of my sister, the kids, as we walked past them.

ANOTHER THEME THAT runs though my life: airplanes. After my father's death, I spent long hours lying in the grass behind my house, staring up at the sky. I was obsessed with the idea of direction, the Catholic concept of heaven being up and hell being down. I knew suicide was a sin, punishable by eternal damnation. I tried to imagine endless suffering for my father. I couldn't. I couldn't see him punished for being too afraid, too weak, and too sad to go on. It didn't seem right—nor did the idea of his lofting up to some cloud to the sound of harp music work for me. It all seemed a bit silly, a bit earthly even to my young mind, a man-made idea, a desperate attempt to explain the unknowable.

I started noticing airplanes then. Their white, silent flight filled me with a terrible longing. I imagined the fuselage filled with passengers en route to some fabulous destination. Their lives were their own, free from tragedy and sadness. The kind of grief that held me in its grip was impossible for them. The desire to be high and far away from my life, to be someone else, anywhere else, was a physical pain, a hole in my center.

No matter where you go, there you are. Fred, of course; one of his wisdom one-liners. He'd come to join me, sat down in the wet grass beside me. I'd pointed up at the plane, told him I wished I were there. "That's the thing you can never escape, try as you might," he said. "Try as you might. Pick your poison—drugs, alcohol. You always wake up with yourself eventually."

"Not him. Not my father."

Fred went still, looked at me carefully. "Suicide is not an escape. It's an end."

"How do you know?"

He was quiet for so long, I thought he wasn't going to answer. Then: "I suppose I don't really know. But I can only imagine that an action that destroys life and hope, which leaves only anger and sadness in its wake, can't be the right course."

I didn't answer him. I didn't have the words to say that I thought his idea was incomplete, unsatisfying. That maybe it was the only course open when you finally realize you can't escape yourself and you can't live with yourself. Maybe an end *is* an escape.

"Want some ice cream?" he asked me then.

"Okay."

Maybe it was a longing like this that drove my husband. That sickening, ardent desire to be anyone, anywhere else. Maybe he chose the alternative of stepping into someone else's skin, someone else's name, someone else's life. Less final than suicide, maybe even an act of hope that someplace else is better than here.

A few hours earlier we returned to Jack's apartment and retrieved an envelope of cash from beneath his mattress. The next steps weren't as clear to him as they were to me.

"You don't even know that was an answer to your question. He was a dying man. He might not have even heard you."

The truth was, it wasn't just that. In fact, when he said the word—*Praha*—it made a deep kind of sense to me, as though I'd known it all along. Jack wouldn't buy that. After all, who was going to trust my instincts at the moment? I had to convince him.

"Marcus is not going to stay in the U.S. He can't. He has run his con and now he's going back where he came from."

"You don't know that. I thought you said he hated the Czech Republic, that he never wanted to go home."

"It's the only course open to him now."

"You don't know that," he repeated.

"He can disappear. Take back his name, Kristof Ragan, and just leave. At this point, they don't even know his real identity. He'll be swallowed. They'll never find him. What's the extradition policy between the Czech Republic and the U.S.?"

Jack looked at me blankly. "How should I know?"

The other truth was that I didn't have any ideas about where else he could be. Was it a desperate act to board a plane to Prague in search of my husband? Yes. But it didn't seem that way at the time.

Out of sheer exhaustion, not a lack of anxiety or urgency, I lay on the plush down of Jack's bed as he threw things into a large duffel bag—jeans, underwear, some old clothes of mine from a night I'd spent here after a party, a pair of sneakers I'd left after the last time we ran in Central Park together. When I closed my eyes I saw the dying stranger in Central Park. I saw my ruined home. Jack left the room for a minute and came back with a shaving kit.

"I packed you a toothbrush."

"We're not going on vacation."

"You can't travel overseas without luggage. It looks suspicious."

Jack was ever the pragmatist; I always feared his reading of my novels. "I don't get it," he'd say. "How did she get from here to there?" Or: "How did he find her in that huge crowd?" Or: "What's her motivation for doing what she did? It doesn't make sense."

He liked the linear progression, the logical course of events, motivations so obvious that they didn't brook questions. I liked the illogical leap in time and tense. Meaning that the nuts and bolts—how the window got unlocked or what vehicle was used to transport my character from this scene to that—bored and annoyed me.

It's the essence, the energy of character and action that moves me. I don't want to tell how the vase found its way to the ground. Was it dropped? Was it thrown? I just want to show the shards, glistening and sharp, on the marble floor. Because that's life. We don't always act out of logic. Things can't always be explained. Sometimes we don't know how the vase got there, just that it has shattered, irreparably.

"Let me ask you something," Jack said. He zipped up the duffel and moved it over toward the door. Then he returned to sit at the foot of the bed. "What's this about?"

"We've already had this conversation. You know what it's about."

"Is it justice you're looking for? Or revenge? When and if you find him, how exactly do you plan to dole that out?"

I didn't answer, just stared at the ceiling. He wasn't looking for an answer. This was his way. *Just put it in your pipe and smoke it,* he'd say.

"Or is it just about the why and how, Isabel? Is it just about the knowing, the understanding that you need?"

I still didn't feel compelled to answer.

"Because I'm your friend. I'm with you. I'll buy the tickets. I'll get on a plane and go with you wherever you need to go. But let's make sure it's for the right reasons."

"What makes a right reason?" I asked.

"Something that, when bad things happen and it all goes to shit, is still worth all the trouble. Something that means enough to risk everything you're risking right now."

I looked at his profile, the crooked ridge of his nose. He seemed tired to me suddenly. I looked around the room and noticed that it was another minimal space, like his office. Just the low platform bed, covered in expensive linens. The walls were white, the floor hardwood. Where was all his stuff? His magazines and dirty clothes, his photographs and unpaid bills? I remembered his dorm room from NYU—a pigsty of staggering proportions. When did he become so neat, so anti-clutter?

"My father didn't leave a note," I said. We'd never really talked about this element of my life, though of course he knew. And it had come up again and again in my fiction. He was a careful reader. He probably knew my issues relating to my father's death better than anyone, including myself. For Jack, I was an open book.

"Okay, Isabel," he said softly. "I get it."

"You don't have to come with me."

"I know that."

He moved over to the door and, with effort, I lifted myself off his bed.

"You have to do one thing before we go. Nonnegotiable," he said. "Two things, actually."

"What?"

"One: Call your sister. And two: Write down everything you didn't tell that detective and e-mail it to him. Let him know you're on his side. It might work in your favor. It might even help you get what you want—answers."

I thought about arguing, but I could tell by the look on his face that he was unmovable on these matters. Also, a small part of me still recognized a good idea when I heard one. I did what he asked. I left a message for my sister, surprised to get her voice mail. And I wrote a long note to Detective Crowe, telling him everything I had learned, including my husband's real name and mentioning the e-mail I'd had from Camilla. Then, whether it was the right action or not, for the right reasons or not, Jack and I left for the airport.

IN MY SEAT I fidgeted and squirmed, unable to relax or get comfortable. The hours stretching ahead of me seemed endless, a river I would never cross. I kept waiting for the pretty flight attendant to look at me with a frown, then go and pick up a phone somewhere and make the call. Maybe on some level I wanted this to happen. But she only smiled and brought me a glass of champagne that I downed in two swallows.

"Easy," said Jack. "That head injury has you loopy enough."

I lifted my glass and the attendant was quick to refill and I was quick to drain that as well. Jack didn't bother with any more warnings; he just leaned his head back and closed his eyes.

All I had was my husband's given name, the name of a town outside of Prague, and the vaguest idea that it was to that place Marcus might return. I thought of the last kiss we shared, the horrible scream I heard, the woman S preening on the Web site. I thought of the dying man and his last whispers. But even with all of this swimming in the dark waters of my mind, the two glasses of champagne helped me to drift into a troubled sleep. I dreamed of my father.

part three

deliverance

Imagine a tunnel of stones
Dark, insinuating, a leap of walls.
Walk through it, without blinking.

—JAMES RAGAN, "CROSSING THE CHARLES BRIDGE" FROM *The Hunger Wall*

21

They took the ride to Queens in silence, each of them lost in their thoughts. Grady kept replaying his call with Sean, hope battling despair. Maybe the call had caused trouble, and if there was trouble already, maybe that would work in his favor. Or maybe Clara would just hate him again, hate him for being such a baby; whatever weakness had impelled her to call would be cemented over with her anger.

They emerged from a slow crawl through bumper-to-bumper traffic in the Queens Midtown Tunnel, inexplicable at that hour, and were cruising down Queens Boulevard. A twelve-lane, in some areas sixteen-lane, main thoroughfare affectionately known as the Boulevard of Broken Bones because of the high rate of pedestrian deaths, it was one of the longest streets in Queens. It was modeled after the Grand Concourse in the Bronx, but to Grady it had none of that romantic aura of lost grandeur that the Concourse had, where magnificent old buildings had grayed with neglect, sagged with disappointment and sadness at the deterioration of a once-great neighborhood, modeled after the promenades of European cities. Queens Boulevard was just a thriving urban center with gigantic apartment high-rises, chains and independent businesses lining the roadway. It was New York, but somehow energetically apart, somehow its own thing, minus any of the glitz and glam of Manhattan. It was just Queens. They passed a gun shop and a liquor store, a flurry of fast-food joints, a Cuban hole-in-the-wall.

Grady pulled the Caprice into a spot across the street from a large warehouse building that bore the address he'd found on the Internet. He'd expected something garish with bright lights and lines down the block, a "gentleman's" club maybe, with cars lining the street and all the typical losers you find at such a place—the frat boys looking to party, coming off the train in packs, raucous, self-conscious; the rich guys taking a night off from their marriages, pulling up in Hummers; the pervs, quiet and badly dressed, waiting with hands in pockets.

But the block was relatively quiet; most of the businesses—a copy shop, a pet store, a men's big and tall—were all gated for the night. Every few minutes a cab would pull up—once with a group of a gorgeous young girls dressed to the hilt, the next an old man in a black wool coat, the next two young guys in business suits carrying sleek black laptop cases. They all disappeared behind a plain black door, opened from the inside by someone who stayed out of sight of the street.

"She was a working girl, wasn't she?" Jez said out of nowhere.

"What makes you say that?"

"I don't think a woman would come to this place if she wasn't in the industry—a dancer, a higher-end call girl. According to her credit report, she wasn't employed, but that SoHo apartment? A nice one-bedroom in that neighborhood? A couple grand a month, at least."

"Maybe our faux Marcus Raine was giving her money," said Grady.

She nodded. "Maybe. But why else would she come here?"

"Maybe she came here to meet someone."

"Yeah, like a john."

"Maybe," he admitted.

"Well, let's go in and take a look around, ask a few questions."

He felt the phone in his pocket vibrate. He pulled it out to see that he had an e-mail message from Isabel Connelly. He almost didn't recognize her name, he was so accustomed to thinking of her as Isabel Raine. The subject line read: "Some things you should know."

"Oh, brother," he said.

"What is it?"

He held the screen up so Jez could lean her head in, and they read Isabel's e-mail together.

WHAT GRADY FOUND interesting about people was that most of them didn't hide well. Of course, people like Kristof Ragan were different; they slipped out of the skin they were in, wrapped themselves in a cocoon, and emerged as a different creature altogether. But most people found it difficult to stray from the places that were familiar to them, the people they knew. They might be smart enough not to go back to their primary residence, but they'd hole up with friends, or sleep on their aunt's couch. They'd return to their favorite bar after a few days, thinking no one would look for them there.

He almost wasn't surprised to see Charlie Shane, the Raines' missing doorman, sticking a dollar bill in a blond strippers' G-string while she lowered her bejeweled, gravity-defying breasts to eye level. He and Jez were about to leave, had shown Camilla Novak's and Marcus Raine's picture around to blank stares and pressed lips, quick shakes of heads, some frightened shifting eyes. Meanwhile, they'd been trailed, not inconspicuously, by two ridiculously pumped, thick-necked goons.

Jez looked nervous, as if she sensed some danger he did not. She tugged on his shoulder and he leaned down so that she could yell in his ear over the music.

"We should get out of here, call for backup and get this place shut down for a few hours. We might get more cooperation."

On a T-shaped stage naked women of all shapes and sizes flaunted their goods to a hypnotic trance beat. Their mouths smiled but their eyes were empty, high or otherwise elsewhere. Some of them looked so young, too young to be here, still had that creamy fresh cast to their skin, that soft innocence about the mouth.

Grady always hated places like this. He liked a dancing naked female body as much as the next guy, but he battled an urge to run around with bathrobes, cover these girls up and take them home to their mamas. Of course, their mamas were probably in worse shape. You didn't wind up on a pole without a lot of help from your family.

Watching a redhead deftly move out of reach of a groping hand, Grady thought of Clara. How long had it been since he'd made love to her? What did Sean say, nearly two years since she'd walked out the door? A year of legal separation following that. Not counting their breakup fuck—that sad, slow final hour they shared after leaving the attorney's office. He'd convinced her to have coffee with him, and they wound up back at the new place she shared with Sean, a spacious two-bedroom in the Fifties, with a terrace and nice views, that he had no idea how they could afford. He took great pleasure in having her one last time in a bed she shared with her new boyfriend. He'd have pissed on the sheets when he was done if he could. She'd thrown him out afterward, turning from passionate, weepy, and nostalgic to angry as soon as the afterglow dimmed.

"I can't believe how I let you manipulate me. Still! Even after we're divorced."

"There's no divorce in the eyes of God. You're still my wife." He was only half kidding.

"Get out, Grady."

"Come on, Clara. You know there's still something. Don't do this."

She strode naked over to her bag, her perfect heart-shaped ass jiggling pleasantly with her stride. She fished out the papers, turned and held them up, utterly unself-conscious of her teardrop breasts and flat brown middle. "It's done. Signed, sealed, delivered."

"I'm yours." He finished the verse, trying to be funny. But the words fell flat and sad on the ground between them.

"Go."

* * *

He was about to agree with Jez that they should shut the place down, when he saw Charlie Shane, the dirty old man, pressed up against the stage. He pointed and saw Jez's face brighten as she reached to put a hand on the weapon at her hip. She wouldn't need it; she could subdue the likes of Shane with one arm. But he knew she liked the feel of it; it gave her a notion of security.

They approached Shane from behind, pushing through a throng of salivating weirdoes. They each put an arm on him and he spun from the stage. His face registered surprise and alarm, then he bent at the waist and knocked through them, causing Jez to stumble back hard into the stage. He saw her knock her head. But they both gave chase, the crowd parting. Someone started to scream at the site of the gun Crowe drew from his hip. Not that you could legally shoot a fleeing suspect in New York State. Still, it tended to stop people in their tracks.

Not Shane. He threw a terrified glance behind him, and at the sight of the gun seemed to pick up speed toward the door. Crowe reached out a hand and was just inches away from having Shane by the collar, when he felt the ground come up to meet him fast, and then he was on knees and elbows on the floor. He lost his grip on his Glock and the thing skittered away from him between the feet and ankles of the crowd gathered round. Someone had tripped him. He looked behind and saw one of the goons smiling.

He retrieved his gun and was about to get to his feet when Jez scrambled over him. He looked up at the door to see Shane exit and Jez follow. He was on his feet and out the door quickly, in time to see Jez disappear into an alleyway.

She was flying and he was already breathing hard. Luckily, he didn't have far to run. By the time he reached them, Shane was on his face in a puddle of black filth, sputtering and yelling. Jez was on his back, with his arm twisted up behind him.

"You. *Stupid.* Mother*fucker*," she was yelling, adrenaline and anger making her red and loud. She tugged on his arm and he released a girlish scream.

"Okay, easy," he said, coming up on them, pulling the cuffs from his waist. He grabbed Shane's other arm and cuffed him. He pulled Jez to her feet and kept a heavy foot on Shane's back. He pulled the cell phone from his pocket and called Dispatch for backup. They were *so* closing that shithole down for a few hours.

He saw that Jez's eye was red and the skin split and bleeding at the cheekbone. There was going to be a huge shiner; he could tell by the way the skin was already bluing beneath the red.

"He hit me," she said, incredulous. "He got a hit in on me. That out-of-shape old man."

"Okay, Kung Fu Mama. Breathe. Relax."

"I don't believe it. I turned the corner and he was waiting for me. I ran right into his fist."

"But who's on the ground now in a puddle of piss? You win."

She nodded, walked a breathless circle, hands on hips.

"I want a fucking lawyer!" screamed Shane as Grady recited his rights. "Unnecessary force!"

"Shut up, Shane," said Grady calmly, pushing hard with his shoe on Shane's back. "Really. Please shut up."

The wail of sirens was sudden and loud, seeming to come from nowhere, drowning out the sound of Shane screaming about injustice and the violation of his various rights.

By the time they let him stew in it, wet and covered in the black filth from the alley floor, he was less passionate. They seated him in an interrogation room, cuffed to the table for the better part of two hours, promising him a public defender. Meanwhile, they tended to Jez's injury, dealt with paperwork, went over and corroborated the information sent to them by Isabel Raine, checked Charlie Shane's criminal history, came up with some theories of their own. By the time they reentered the room where they'd left him, Shane seemed thoroughly broken; whatever alcohol might have been in his system had worn off. He was just a sad old man in a lot of trouble.

"Where's my lawyer?" he asked when they entered, without lifting his eyes from his hands folded in front of him.

"On his way," Grady lied. "If that's the way you want to go. I'll tell you what, though. In spite of the list of charges—obstruction of justice, fleeing custody, assaulting an officer—we're just not that interested in you. You're more or less worthless to us."

Shane didn't look up and didn't respond, but Grady could tell he was listening.

"We're interested in the man you knew as Marcus Raine."

Grady thought he saw Shane jump a little at the sound of the name but he couldn't be sure.

"Did you know there are security cameras in the lobby of your building?" Jez lied. "We know you let people in to trash the Raines' apartment. You tell us who those people are? And you'll have your face back in underage tits before the sun comes up."

Without his crisp uniform and smart cap, with a five o'clock shadow, reeking of booze and cigarettes, Shane seemed to have aged fifteen years since they saw him at the Raines' building. Grady saw that his hands were covered in angry patches of raw, red skin, that his scalp was peeling, his nose red from regular boozing. His knee was pumping like a jackhammer; he was scared. Good news for them. Grady cobbled together a little story from the information they got from Isabel Raine. Some of it was true, some of it made up, like all good fiction. He'd see where it got them.

"At this point we know quite a bit. We know that Marcus Raine was really a man named Kristof Ragan. We now believe this man killed the real Marcus Raine, stealing his money and his identity. We know about Kristof's brother, Ivan Ragan, a man with a criminal history, involved with the Albanian and Russian Mob. We suspect Ivan helped his brother in the commission of the crime. According to our research, Ivan Ragan was arrested on unrelated charges, about a week after Marcus Raine disappeared. He was recently released, serving a sentence for gun possession.

"Corresponding with his release, someone caught on that the man everyone knew as Marcus Raine was not who he said he was. So Kristof Ragan started pulling in his lines—cleaning out bank accounts, arranging for equipment to be stolen, then collecting the insurance check, taking money from his brother-in-law. Then he walked out of the life he'd made. A cleanup crew came in, trashed his office and his home, killing witnesses—four people dead so far. They destroyed or removed every possible piece of evidence. With your help."

Charlie kept his head down, still no eye contact. But Grady watched as a bead of sweat dripped from the old man's head and fell to the table between them. They'd managed to find some photographs—an Interpol photograph of Ivan Ragan and a picture of the woman Isabel Raine only knew as S from the Services Unlimited Web site.

Jez handed the shots to Grady and he laid them out on the table in front of Charlie Shane. Still he didn't glance up, didn't say a word.

"So either you were just a bit player who took a big tip to let in the cleanup crew, in which case you'll take the line we're offering here and tell us what you know. Or you know so much that you're more afraid of them than you are of us, in which case we're at an impasse and I'll have to charge you with conspiracy."

Charlie Shane looked up quickly. Grady suppressed a smile; he didn't know how much of what he'd said was true—some of it, maybe a lot of it. But he thought it sounded pretty good. He was proud of himself.

"I don't know anything," said Shane. "Mr. Raine asked me to let some friends of his in to move some files from his home to his office, and I did that. He gave me a hundred dollars to do so, and not mention it no matter who asked. How was I supposed to know there was anything criminal going on? I'm the doorman. I do what I'm asked."

"He asked you not to mention it, if asked. Gave you a hundred-dollar tip? That wasn't a clue that something unsavory was transpiring?"

Shane shrugged.

"Did you know any of the people you let in?"

"Of course not."

"Can you describe them? Would you recognize them again if you saw them?"

"Don't you have a video? You know, from those surveillance cameras in the lobby?" He gave Grady a nasty, yellow smile. Grady hadn't quite expected to fool him with his bit about the cameras; just introduce a shadow of doubt.

"That's it," said Jez. She'd been standing in the corner, silent, brooding. In spite of the ice, her eye was started to swell badly. She moved quickly to the table. Grady could see that she was pissed, wanted reason to put her hands on Charlie Shane. He thought he was going to have to intervene. But she backed away, moved toward the door. "Too much conversation. Let's get the paperwork started."

"Wait," said Shane, lifting a hand. Jez paused at the door but didn't turn around.

"Start with how you knew Camilla Novak," said Jez.

Grady placed the only picture they had of Camilla, the one he'd found on the Internet, in front of him. Shane shook his head.

"We found her dead body in her apartment today," Grady said. "She had a stamp on her hand from the Topaz Room, where we found you just a few hours ago. You were the doorman in the building of the man who more than probably killed her boyfriend and stole his identity. You knew her."

More silence. Jez turned the knob and opened the door.

"I knew her," he said quickly. "I knew her."

"Now we're getting somewhere." Jez closed the door and turned around.

"More than a few weeks ago—maybe closer to two months—I was covering Teaford's shift and I heard yelling out on the street. It was after midnight. A woman, screaming."

He released a deep breath, rubbed at his temples.

"I left my post and went out to the street and saw Miss Novak yelling at Mr. Raine."

"What was she saying?"

"She was saying, 'You love her, you love her. You weren't supposed to love her.' "

"And what was Raine doing?"

"He was trying to calm her down, speaking in low tones. She screamed, 'I betrayed him for you. I thought we were going to be together. I have blood on my hands for nothing.' Something like that." He waved a hand. "I don't remember her exact words."

His leg was still pumping and he was sweating as if he'd just spent an hour working out hard in the gym.

"Mr. Raine said, 'Be patient. It's almost through.' He tried to walk away but she followed, yelling, 'You liar, you liar. I'm going to burn it down. All of it.' She grabbed hold of his arm. But he slapped her hard and she went reeling back. He saw me standing there then. 'Call the police if she follows me,' he told me. I was stunned. 'Charlie, I know I can count on your discretion.' He left her weeping on the street."

"What did you do at that point?" asked Jez.

"I couldn't just leave her there. After he went upstairs, I brought her into the lobby, gave her some ice for her mouth, asked if I could call her a taxi."

"Where'd you get the ice?" asked Jez with a frown.

"What?" asked Shane. It must have seemed like a stupid question, apropos of nothing. But Grady knew why Jez had asked it. Lies lived in the little things, the details people threw in to make their stories sound truer.

"From a cooler I bring my meals in. I use an ice pack to keep things cold."

She nodded, satisfied. Shane stared at the wall in front of him. "She seemed very fragile to me, unwell. I felt sorry for her. We talked awhile. I asked her what it was all about, the argument. Who had she betrayed? She said that she'd betrayed herself—over and over until she didn't even remember who she was or what she wanted anymore. I told her that she wasn't so different from anyone. We all betray ourselves one way or another. She said, 'Not like this. Someone loved me, really loved me. And I betrayed him for a life I thought was in my reach.' She wouldn't tell me more."

He paused a second. "She was beautiful, you know. But she seemed like a bird or a butterfly. You couldn't catch her or touch her. Just look."

"But you touched her, didn't you?" Jez had returned to her corner; she was partially hidden in shadow. "A lot of people touched her. She was a call girl, right?"

He nodded reluctantly. "We made an arrangement."

"You kept an eye on Raine, told her anything you saw suspicious or out of the ordinary, his comings and goings? And she gave herself to you in exchange?"

He gave a weak shrug. "Herself, once. Then passes to the Topaz Room. Other girls there."

"But why would she want to know that? What was she looking for in particular?"

"She wanted to know things like how often the Raines went out, did they look happy, did he bring her flowers. She wanted to know if he stayed out late, brought any other women back to the apartment when Mrs. Raine was out of town. Things like that—jealous girlfriend things."

"And what about Raine? Did he mention the incident again?"

Shane nodded. "On the way out to work the next morning, he gave me a hundred dollars, asked that I keep what happened the night before to myself. I agreed, of course. He said he'd continue to appreciate my discretion. And he did—with money, once tickets to a play, once a nice bottle of scotch."

"So you played them both."

He bristled. "I *obliged* them both. Gave them both what they wanted."

"Like any good doorman."

"That's right, sir." But his chin dropped to his chest, shoulders lost their square.

"And this woman?" Grady tapped the photo of S.

Shane nodded. "She was one of the women I let into the apartment. There were four of them. Two women, two men. I let them in and out through the service door behind the building. They came with big empty sacks. When they left, they were all full. I didn't ask any questions or say a word to any of them. Of course, I had no idea people had been murdered, that crimes had been committed. Until you came that night, I didn't understand what I had done. I was afraid then. I ran."

"Was he one of them?" Grady asked, pointing to the photograph of Ivan Ragan.

Shane shook his head. "No. Him—I've never seen."

Isabel Raine had given them a lot of information—the photographs from the thumb drive in Camilla Novak's purse, addresses, Web sites, names. She'd even drawn a few connections. Authors didn't make bad detectives, it turned out.

"What else, Shane? What else do you have for us?"

Shane shook his head. "I am paid to be of service. And I did that for the Raines. It's not my job to ask questions or pass judgment. I just hold open the door."

Grady just stared at him for a minute. Shane was an oddity he didn't quite understand. Grady couldn't *stop* asking questions; finding the answers drove him. Analyzing, extrapolating meaning, finding connections—it was his job, his life. Maybe he had it all wrong.

"Camilla was a good girl, I think," Shane said. "She made mistakes, had problems. But she wanted to be good." He was just thinking out loud, Grady thought. Shane was tired, sinking into the depression that follows too much alcohol.

"Wanting to be good doesn't make you good," said Jez quietly, maybe a little sadly. She was looking down at her feet. Grady thought she should spring for a new pair of shoes.

"So what are we thinking here?" asked Grady. They were back at their desks on the homicide floor, facing each other. It was late, most everyone long gone for the night. They were both exhausted, but the adrenaline blast from earlier in the evening still had them edgy and wired.

Jez's desk was a study of organization—neat stacks of folders, a few photos of her son, and nothing else. Grady's was a field of clutter—papers waiting to be filed, a box of pens spilling its contents, a crumpled white bag from some meal he'd eaten there in the last week, an old mug in which coffee had solidified and was beginning to send off an odor. He dumped the cup in the trash rather than wash it, cleared a space to rest his elbows.

Jez had a printout of Isabel's e-mail in front of her and was reading rather than looking at Grady.

"Camilla Novak and Kristof Ragan, if that's really his name, conspired to kill Marcus Raine and steal his money," she said. It sounded as if she was certain. This was how they did it—came up with theories, tried to shoot them down, see if they held.

"Then how did Ragan wind up married to Isabel Connelly, running a legitmate business, leaving Camilla Novak weeping on the sidewalk outside his luxury, doorman building?"

She thought about it for a minute, tapping her pen. "He was a con. Isabel Connelly was his next mark. Somehow he convinced Novak to wait, promised her the payout would be even bigger after he'd run his con on Isabel Connelly and her family. Maybe he gave her money, continued their love affair, keeping her hope alive. But she got tired of waiting."

Grady thought about it, about the e-mail Isabel had forwarded to him. "She started e-mailing Isabel Raine—trying to burn it down, like she threatened on the street."

"He wasn't supposed to fall in love with Isabel. But he did. He fell in love with her, with the life they made," said Jez.

"He didn't want to leave her," Grady agreed.

"And his brother, Ivan Ragan?"

Grady already had a theory about this. "Okay. So Ivan and Kristof Ragan both come to the U.S. at the same time. Kristof is the good one, goes to college, gets a job at Red Gravity. There he meets Marcus Raine, decides he wants what this guy has—money, the girl. He enlists the help of his criminal brother—someone to do the dirty work, the kill, the disposal—for a share of the haul."

"But at the end of the day, Kristof doesn't want to share," added Jez. She shifted through her file and found the arrest report for Ivan Ragan, handed it to Grady. "Ivan Ragan was arrested after an anonymous tip that he had enough guns in his home for a small army."

"Kristof Ragan betrayed his brother, had him sent away."

"Why not kill him? Why take the risk that Ivan would use what he knew to get off?"

Grady shrugged. "Maybe he didn't want to kill his brother. Maybe he believed that Ivan wouldn't betray him, wouldn't suspect that his brother had been the one to turn *him* over to police."

"But Kristof had to know Ivan would get out one day, that he'd have to pay his brother off at some point."

"Maybe he thought he'd be long gone by then. He didn't expect to fall in love with Isabel. This was the one thing he didn't plan for, the thing that caused him to stay too long."

Grady looked down at the photographs of Kristof and Ivan Ragan and the other unidentified men on the dock. "Ivan found out his brother betrayed him," he said.

"Looks that way."

Jez was looking down at her own set of prints, shaking her head slightly.

"Is money really that important?" Grady asked, thinking about Kristof Ragan and how he'd deceived and manipulated, stolen and killed. Ragan betrayed his own brother, shot him and left him for dead.

She raised her eyebrows. "Money *is* important. It's very important."

"So important that you sell your ethics, your morals, betray people who love you, murder?"

"For some. But I'm not sure that's just about money."

"What's it about then?"

She looked down at her desk, tapped her fingers. "An idea, an image of what money is, what it brings to your life, how it defines your worth."

He shook his head. "It's hard to understand."

"Is it?" she asked. "Before Benjy, I never worried about money. I thought as long as I had what I needed to pay the bills, put some away for later, and have a few extras, that's all I needed. I've seen those skells—pimps and drug dealers—with all their money. It bought them everything, cars and clothes, flat screens and leather couches. But they were still scum, still dirty, still nothing."

"And now?"

"And now, there's Benjy's private school education and saving for college and the cost of health care, gas and groceries through the roof. And he goes to school with all these rich kids, and they have these sneakers that cost $200 and jeans that cost as much and more. Even the T-shirt he wanted? $150. I want him to have those things. I can't always give them."

Grady had never heard her say anything like that. He always thought of her as so sensible, pragmatic, not the type to worry about whether her kid had designer jeans or not.

"But he doesn't *need* those things," Grady said. "I never had them when I was a kid. Yeah, it sucked then. But I was better for it. And don't they wear uniforms at private school?"

"Yeah, they do," she said with a nod. "But after school and at parties, you know. Those kids are his friends. They live in homes that look like hotels. They show up in Polo and Izod. I hate sending him in less. But I have to. I won't go into debt or sacrifice his future. And it's almost Christmas. He wants a Wii, and a new bike. I can't afford to get him all the things his friends will get."

He could tell by the line of her mouth that she was sad, that these things worried her in bed at night. He wished good people didn't have to fret over money.

"But I bet none of them has a mom who knows kung fu."

"That's true," she said with a slow grin. "I *am* cool."

"And cool beats rich any day. You could kick all the other moms' asses."

"Thanks, G."

She looked down at her cuticles, snapping her right thumb and pinkie nail together. Something she did when she felt awkward or uncomfortable.

"I guess what I'm saying is that it's not so hard to understand why Kristof Ragan liked what he had with Isabel Raine—the money, the lifestyle, the image. If it hadn't been for Camilla Novak making threats, I doubt he would have fled. He'd still be running his company, maybe screwing around, but I think he liked the whole successful urban couple thing. He liked what he was with her."

It made sense to Grady. Kristof Ragan had the life he wanted. Why would he leave it for Camilla Novak? He wouldn't. He may have wanted her once; she was beautiful. But Isabel Connelly was the golden ticket—not just money. Class. Respect. With her, he had entrée into a whole other world.

"So who was the crew that trashed his office and home?" Jez said, flipping through the file, staring at the crime-scene photos. "How did he have associations like this?"

"Through his brother?"

Jez held up one of the frames Isabel Connelly had sent. Kristof Ragan surrounded by grim-faced, black-coated men on a Brooklyn pier. One of them his brother.

"I don't think his brother's allies were interested in working with him anymore, do you?"

"Maybe not," he admitted.

Anyone else would be dead, but Kristof Ragan was still alive. He flipped through the photos, watching events unfold a frame at a time.

"He was combat-trained somewhere," he said. "You don't take down four armed men like that without some training."

"The real question is: Who took these pictures? Who else was watching?" said Jez.

Somewhere a phone started ringing. Grady could hear a television set on down the hall—some kind of game, people cheering.

"And how did they get in Camilla Novak's possession? Who was she giving them to? And why?" she went on, writing down her own questions in a notebook.

"No ID yet on the shooting victim in Central Park. I just checked with the morgue."

"And who's *this* chick?" Jez held up the picture of S.

"I don't know but I'm glad she's not my girlfriend. You'd never know if she was going to make love to you or kill you while you slept."

Jez had a good laugh at that one, and he joined in until they were both doubled over, tearing. They were punchy now—overworked and overtired.

When they'd recovered, Grady e-mailed the photograph to Interpol and his contacts at the FBI, along with the photographs of the Ragan brothers on the pier, asking for an assist. They split up the paperwork. He had the banking records. Jez had the cell phone logs.

"I'm going to work this at home, catch a few hours, and take my baby to school in the morning," said Jez.

"He's ten. Not a baby."

She smiled. "You sound like my ex. He'll always be my baby. Ten, sixteen, sixty—you're always a baby to your mama."

"True," he said, thinking of his own ma.

They turned out their desk lamps and walked together to the door.

"You think Shane told us everything?" asked Jez.

"Probably not," he said, holding the door for her. "But your eye doesn't look as bad as I thought it was going to." The swelling had gone down some, and instead of blooming purple, the blue had started to fade.

"I've taken worse hits in class. You bruise less over time."

"You're so butch."

Another laugh from Jez. He liked to make her laugh; he didn't know why.

22

At night, the smaller boys cried. They tried to be quiet. But they were always heard. In the morning, those who had wept were ridiculed mercilessly, beaten if they dared to fight back. Kristof had cried; not Ivan. But no one dared to beat him, because of the size and temper of his older brother. Neither he nor Ivan joined in the humiliations of the younger children.

Sometimes, even now, he awoke in the night hearing the sound of a child's soft whimper, despair and loneliness cutting a swath through his center. Sometimes he was back there, a little boy, still weeping for his mother. Ivan had been a sweet and loyal brother, letting Kristof climb into his cot at night, waking earlier enough to shoo him out before the other boys woke. But Kristof stopped crying eventually, didn't need Ivan's comfort for long.

This morning he had awoken, hearing the sound of his brother roaring in pain, bleeding on the dock where he'd brought Kristof to die.

"You betrayed me!" he'd screamed. "You're my brother!"

The other men, he'd shot to kill. Rolled them, still alive, into the water. Ivan, he'd shot to wound, to warn. He might have survived the injury, might have time to think about things, come to his senses.

"You owe me some money, Kristof," Ivan had said in the car. It seemed like months ago—it hadn't even been a week. They had left Manhattan,

Isabel, the life he'd made, behind and were on the Brooklyn Bridge. He was still thinking about his wife, how she'd looked in the last moments he saw her on the street, getting ready for her run. Strong, determined, ready to battle the calories of the croissant she'd eaten. He almost smiled.

"Yes," he said. "I've been saving it for you, Ivan. For your release from prison."

"You're such a good brother," Ivan said grimly, looking at the road ahead. He spoke in Czech. Outside the sky was turning grayish black. Snow.

Ivan turned on the radio. He liked classical music, found a violin concerto Kristof didn't recognize, kept the volume low.

"I had a lot of time to think. To wonder who might have informed the police about the guns in our apartment, Kristof."

It was the apartment they'd shared. He'd cleared out his stuff and found another place before making the call, knowing that Ivan would never tell the police that they shared the apartment. There was no lease; his name was on nothing, not even the electric bill. Kristof felt a thump begin in his chest.

"And?"

"I was never able to figure it out."

"Where are we going, Ivan?"

His brother ignored him. "Then, just days before my release, I had a visitor."

Kristof thought it was best to stay silent. He knew who had visited Ivan.

"Camilla Novak. The girl you loved so much, the one you had to have. She said you betrayed me to the police. That you broke all your promises to her. That we did all the work—she getting you access to the apartment, his accounts and passwords, all his identification. I took care of the murder, the disposal of the body. And you? You took all the money."

Kristof smiled. "Ivan, come on. She's lying. She's angry because I don't want her any longer. You know how I am with women. Easily bored."

"Then who?"

"How should I know? I'm sorry it happened. But I can help you now. There's money, a lot of it. What's mine is yours. You're my brother."

He patted the big man on the shoulder. Ivan didn't turn to look at him. Kristof knew it was too late. Ivan was lost to the silent rage brewing within him.

"Where are we going, Ivan?"

"Some people want to talk to you."

"What people?"

"Friends of mine."

Kristof's mind was racing. How was he going to get himself out of this? Ivan had locked the doors. He was unarmed, outweighed by Ivan. He had no choice but to play it out.

"I always took care of you. I always loved you," said Ivan. He looked so sad.

"I know."

Kristof looked out the window of the passing landscape of concrete buildings, the gunmetal sky. Ivan was fast, silent. Kristof never even heard him reach for the gun and deliver a sure blow to the side of his head. The world just grayed out. Then, the next thing he knew, he was facedown on a cold, hard floor, surrounded by Ivan and his gloved, black-clad friends. It wasn't much of a party and it didn't end well.

HE THOUGHT OF this as he trekked across the uneven gray cobblestones of the ancient Karluv Most, the Charles Bridge, in Prague. The hours of unpleasantness, his ultimate escape thanks to moves he had learned from, of all people, Sara. They knew the day might come when he'd have to extract himself from a bad outcome, had planned for it. The memory of Ivan, his time in the warehouse, the last moments on the dock caused him to look over his shoulder.

The bridge was mobbed with tourists, snapping pictures of the towering saints—St. Francis Borgia, St. John the Baptist, St. Ann, St. Joseph—leaning over the edge to gaze at the swans in the gray water of the Vltava River. The bridge had stood since 1357. Now people strolled across it sipping soda and listening to iPods. He didn't resent them. In fact, he was always glad for a crowd. Easier to be invisible.

He passed the Old Town Bridge Tower, a magnificent Gothic structure reaching into the sky with a pinnacled wedge spire. Tourists sat at its base eating ice cream cones, in spite of the cold. Shops lining the street sold wooden toys and Czech glass, T-shirts and rolls of film and candy bars.

He made a left and passed a popular chain called Bohemia Bagel and was suddenly off the main drag, alone on a narrow street. To his right a courtyard behind a high, wrought-iron gate, a dark alley to his left where a woman's shoe lay in a puddle of black water. The street was quiet, as if the crowded street just a hundred feet away didn't exist at all. Prague was like that. Turn one corner and you move from the modern to the ancient, as though you've stepped through a portal to another time and place.

For now he was home. He was safe. All threats delayed or neutralized. The streets of Prague welcomed their native son, allowed him to blend into their gray mystery, took him into their sandstone arms, hid him no matter what he'd done elsewhere in the world. It didn't matter here. Prague was the mother he'd never had.

He ducked into the dark side entrance of the building where Beethoven himself composed during his stay in Prague, when the building was known as the Inn of the Golden and White Unicorn. He liked the romance of that, even if he doubted its veracity. Now it housed sleek, trendy condos with all the modern amenities. Real-estate ventures had come to Prague. He'd bought the apartment pre-construction in 2003 and now it was worth a fortune. There were legitimate ways to make money. Of course, one had to *have* money first in order to do that.

He unlocked the heavy wooden door and pushed inside. He had a futon and a large flat-screen television equipped with satellite, pulling in hundreds of channels from around the world. In one of the bedrooms, there was a simple platform bed. Then just a desk and his laptop computer. The place smelled of fresh paint and new linens.

In the kitchen, he made himself an espresso and thought of the coffee he'd shared with Isabel on their last morning together. He searched for the pain and the sadness he'd felt as he'd driven off with Ivan. But it was gone. He wondered if he'd ever felt anything at all. Or was it all part of a charade he'd played too well? What did it really mean to love someone? Did it have to last forever to have existed at all?

He took his coffee and sat on the futon, flipped on the television, scanning the menu for CNN. He didn't have to wait long for the story. After ten minutes of enduring news of the real-estate and mortgage crisis, the discovery of a Texas cult compound, the newest way to lose those extra ten pounds, before he saw Isabel's face on the screen, then his own. He turned up the volume.

"Detectives working the case have tied the recent crimes to the unsolved 1999 disappearance of Marcus Raine, a man they now believe was murdered. They say they are exploring connections from the current crimes, including the recent murder of Camilla Novak, who was also the girlfriend of the man who went missing in 1999." A picture of Camilla filled the screen.

Her image faded to an image of his face. This did not disturb him; his facial hair grew quickly and he'd more than doubled his caloric intake. Within a few days, he'd look different enough to pass anywhere unnoticed. Until then he'd stay out of sight.

"This man, whom officials say is Kristof Ragan, is a Czech immigrant who came to the U.S. on a student visa in 1990 and disappeared in violation of his visa after graduating from Hunter College in 1994 with a degree in computer science, and is the husband of bestselling author Isabel Connelly."

That disturbed him. How had they learned a portion of his true history and his given name? Of course, he wasn't using that name now, but still. Who knew the truth about him? Sara would not betray him; he knew that. The only other possibility was Ivan. He regretted his decision to spare his brother. Another weakness, another mistake made out of love—or something like it.

"Isabel Connelly is considered a person of interest. Her whereabouts are currently unknown."

"We urge Ms. Connelly to turn herself in," said a handsome detective. He was well-dressed, his shield on a chain around his neck. "Kristof Ragan is a dangerous man."

The shellacked, plastic woman who passed as a newscaster looked deeply into the lens of the camera and said, "In a case that involves murder, identity theft, and the disappearance of over a million dollars, truth, it would seem, is stranger than fiction."

In his stomach, he felt an uncomfortable mingling of anger and fear. Sara had warned him: "You let Camilla live, and look where it got you. It will be the same with this one. She'll rest no easier, I promise you."

"She will," he'd said, not actually believing it himself. "She has too much to tie her to her life—her work, her family. A threat to them will keep her in line. She can't afford to come after me."

"Hmm," Sara had said skeptically. "I saw her. I think nothing could keep her from coming after you."

"If that happens, it will be my problem."

Another error in judgment, another knot to be tied now.

Then the cell phone in his pocket rang. It was a disposable phone he'd picked up at the airport, and only one person had the number. He answered quickly, surprised.

"I didn't think you'd call," he said by way of greeting.

There was a pause, a light breathing on the line. He could almost smell the peppermint on her breath.

"I didn't think I would, either," she said finally. Her voice was sweet, with a lilting British accent that spoke volumes of her wealth and education. "What you said, about not having time to play games. I liked it. I . . . don't want to play games, either."

"Then I'll see you tonight?" He had a way of making his voice sound halting, nervous, and vulnerable when he was anything but.

"Yes," she said softly. "Yes, I'd like that very much."

23

In the East Village studio where he lived, police found evidence of Ben Jameson's powerful obsession with Linda Book. Stacks of newspaper clippings, photographs from interviews, as well as many taken while she shopped with her kids or dined with her husband or attended her yoga class—he'd been watching her. He'd kept a journal of their imagined affair.

He'd been married, had two small girls. But his wife had left him years ago; he had only limited, supervised time with his children. His wife had cited abuse, mental illness, finally left him after he put her in the hospital with a concussion and a broken nose. She loved him still but was afraid of his terrible rages, the deep well of depression where he often disappeared for weeks, months.

On medication, he was the kindest man, loving and gentle, thoughtful and romantic, she claimed. But without, he could be a monster. She'd been hopeful over the last year. He'd been stable, dutiful about his meds, had seemed almost happy. His visits with the girls were enjoyable, peaceful. But it was his fantasy about Linda Book that had been bolstering him. When he stopped his medication, the downward spiral was quick and final.

"We met at the gallery that was showing my work, at the opening party," Linda told Erik. "You remember, we had an encounter over a bad review he wrote about one of my shows. But it was fine, even funny.

He called a few days later to apologize. We met for coffee. I was networking, you know. But then he kept calling. A week later I bumped into him outside my yoga studio. He said that he'd been in the neighborhood interviewing another artist. But that was the first time I realized there might be something wrong."

"Why didn't you say anything?"

"I didn't want anyone to worry."

"How long has this been going on, Linda?"

"Six months, on and off."

"Linda."

"It's been so stressful lately. I didn't want to add anything to our plate. Maybe I thought by ignoring it, it would just go away. He was always polite, never crazy. I don't know, maybe I liked the attention."

Erik was silent, his head in his hands.

"I'm sorry."

She hated herself for her sins of omission, but she couldn't bring herself to tell the truth, to take another brick out of the foundation of their marriage. Ben was dead. His obsession with her was obvious and documented. No one even seemed to suspect that there was an actual affair. She'd never left him a voice-mail message or sent him an e-mail. She knew his cell phone records, if it came to that, would show a lot of calls to her, but only a couple from her phone. Returning his calls, she'd say. She thought they were friendly, she'd say, if not quite friends. She didn't want to be rude. He was a reviewer for a major paper, after all. She knew even the text messages she'd sent were purposely vague, innocuous.

"Did you sleep with him, Linda? Were you having an affair?"

She hadn't expected him to ask the question flat out like that. She tried to muster righteous indignation, but she couldn't. She couldn't even bring herself to answer.

"Last night on the phone you said, 'I've made mistakes, too.' Do you remember?"

She nodded. They were alone, for the first time since "the event," as she'd heard it referred to a number of times. The event of a man blowing his head off in front of their eyes. She found she couldn't remember anything but the sound of her own screaming. No one should have to see such a thing twice; her psyche seemed to know this and cut her a break. The event, from the moment she heard him call her name on the street, was now a vague black-and-red blur in her memory.

John Brace had left them, finally. Trevor and Emily were still with Erik's mom and would be for a couple of days until they figured things out. Fred was back at home being tended to by Margie, with staff, of course, to do any of the heavy lifting. And Izzy was out in the fray.

Isabel had left a message saying that she was going to make things right, and not to worry. "Linda, don't worry. I promise, I'm going to make everything all right for you and Erik again. And I swear I wouldn't have shot him." She sounded so young and sweet and silly. Isabel thought that it was about the *money*. She thought if she could get that money back, she'd fix what was broken in all of their lives, that retrieving it would begin the healing all of them needed so desperately now.

Why didn't she see that it was about betrayal? Infidelity? That it was about secrets and lies, an erosion of trust? Why didn't she know that those things cannot be fixed? You can't restore torn fabric to its original state. You can patch it, you can sew it—but there will always be a seam, a place you can touch with your finger, a place that's weaker, prone to tearing again.

"I did say that. I remember," Linda said, looking at her husband.

She was about to deny everything because she could. Because it would be better for her, for him. She could deny any wrongdoing to her grave, and never worry about proof to the contrary, but she realized, in that moment, that more lies would only weaken them further. They needed to accept the truth of each other, to see each other for all their individual flaws and weaknesses and choose to continue on just the same. Or not at all. More lies didn't mean less pain. Maybe in the moment, but not down the road. She was about to tell him this. She was about to tell him everything. But he spoke first.

"Then let's move forward from here, Linda. Can we?" He had moved from the couch where he had been sitting beside her, and now kneeled on the floor. He took her hands in both of his, pressed his chest against her knees. "If we've both made mistakes and love each other still, can we just move ahead without looking back in regret and recrimination?"

She shook her head. "But Erik, I—"

"I'm begging you," he interrupted. "Can you forgive me for what I've done?"

"Erik, yes," she said, squeezing his hands, closing her eyes. "But I need forgiveness, too."

"It's already done. Don't say another word. From right here, from this place, let's move forward and do better for each other. Without looking back even once. Can we? Can we, Linda?"

The look on his face was so wide open, so earnest. He'd known all along she'd been having an affair, hadn't he? She could see the pain and the understanding and forgiveness in the blue wells of his eyes. She could even see that it was the reason he'd done what he did. He thought that if he could give her the security she craved, she wouldn't be tempted to seek the cheap and foolish comfort she'd sought elsewhere. She bowed her head in shame.

She'd not been able to keep her father from leaving her. But she could hold her family together now; she could forgive them all, even herself.

"Yes," she said after a moment. She looked up at him. *From this place,* he'd said. He hadn't meant the actual apartment, of course. But it was here that they'd conceived their children. These rooms had been the battleground for every major argument, the place where they'd first made love, where'd they laughed so hard it hurt, where they'd wept and yelled and cooked their meals. Sure, it was hocked up to heaven at the moment, but it didn't make it any less theirs. She thought of one of

Fred's Zen adages: The journey of a thousand miles begins with just one step.

"Yes, of course we can."

She felt grief for Ben. She'd cared for him, made love to him, considered him a friend. She felt some culpability—however irrational—for his death. But she also knew that he was a very sick man. The knowledge of what he would have done to Erik, to her, to both of their children, eclipsed the feelings of affection she'd had for him. She found she couldn't muster much compassion for him, in spite of her sadness.

She remembered that closed-down, shut-off feeling from the night her father killed himself, as if some critical part of her had drifted off into space. When she could feel anything at all, it was only rage. If he'd loved her, he'd have remembered the moon was full. He'd have remembered the night belonged to her. He'd have known she'd find him. She'd always believed this in her darkest heart. But now she understood he hadn't been thinking about anything except his own unbearable psychic pain.

When she wept in her husband's arms then, she knew it was the first time she'd allowed herself to really cry for her father. She wept for him as much as she did for everything she'd almost destroyed in her life because she just couldn't let him go.

Hello, Moonbeam.

Good-bye, Daddy.

THE MOON WAS full and high in the sky when he pulled into his driveway. It wasn't until he'd exited the vehicle, a brand-new beefy, black Mustang that he'd bought to comfort himself after Clara left him with their new Acura, that he saw the silver RSX parked on the street. He stopped and checked the tags and knew it was hers. There was a light burning in the living-room window of his row house. He'd never asked her for her keys, hoping that she'd decide to use them one day to come home.

He opened the door and found her asleep on the couch, a light on, the television on CNN with the volume low. She'd taken a blanket from the upstairs linen closet and covered herself. She was curled in a tight ball, her hair fanned out on the pillow. She looked like a child when she slept, small and pale. He stood in the doorway looking at her, feeling his heart in his throat.

A couple of times he'd come home and saw a light in the window. Each time he felt his heart leap, only to be crushed when he realized he'd left the kitchen or the bedroom light on when he'd left for work.

But now she was here. She inhaled deeply, issued a soft sigh, as she shifted in sleep. He was afraid to move, afraid to dissolve the mirage. He did mental calculations. It was nearly four A.M.; if she was here, where was Sean? He didn't work midnights anymore, so it's not as if she could be out at this hour unnoticed. They must have fought after the phone call he and Grady had had earlier. She wouldn't have had anywhere else to go. Both her best girlfriends were happily married with kids; she wouldn't barge in on them, wouldn't want to lose face again, after already being divorced once. She would never go to her parents, couldn't bear the nagging and the judgment she'd surely receive from them. Her mom still sent Grady cards for Christmas and his birthday. "Be patient. She'll come back to you," she'd scrawled in the last one. He kept the card in the nightstand by his bed.

She opened her eyes and saw him, sat up slowly. He stepped into the living room from the tiny foyer, pushing the door closed behind him.

"Hey," he said. He shifted off his coat, hung it over the banister, sat on the bottom landing of the staircase, respecting her distance. He caught his reflection in the mirror hanging on the opposite wall. He looked tired, disheveled, thick in the middle from months of fast food almost every day.

"You told him I called you." She rubbed her eyes, then lifted her hands high above her head in a deep stretch.

"I'm sorry."

"No, you're not."

"Okay. No, I'm not."

The room was exactly as she'd decorated it. She'd picked out the plush cream carpet, the suede sectional, the flat-screen television and entertainment center. It was nice stuff, expensive. He was still paying for it. Even the blanket over her was a gift from their wedding. Thick chenille, her favorite. Feeling petty and mean, he wouldn't let her take it; it was a gift from his sister on the occasion of their marriage. She had no right to it, he told her.

"So. What? You had a fight?"

She narrowed her eyes at him, gave an annoyed shake of her head. "What do you think, Sherlock?"

He shrugged. "You left him?"

She folded her slim arms across her middle, looked at something on the floor, then picked at some invisible scab on her elbow. She didn't want to meet his eyes. He saw her shoulders start to shake. Then she buried her eyes in the palms of her hands. He stayed put. She didn't like to be touched when she was crying. It made her angry.

"I really am sorry, Clara," he said from his perch. "I just wanted to make him mad. I didn't mean to fuck things up for you."

"Oh," she said into her hands, issuing a mirthless laugh, "I don't need any help with that. I do just fine fucking things up on my own, Grady."

He wanted to feel her skin, bury his face in her hair. His hands wanted to roam her body, reclaim her in this room that was the home of their young marriage. He wanted to hear her breathing in the dark of their bedroom, look at the sliver of light under the bathroom door when she got up in the night. He wanted to listen to her blow-dry her hair in the morning while she sang out of tune to whatever was playing on the radio. He wanted to sit on the porch with her on Friday nights and sip wine, watch the neighborhood kids play stickball in the street like he used to a lifetime ago. Such little things he wanted, nothing fancy—not weekends in Paris and Veuve Clicquot. But there was so much distance to cross, such rough terrain between where they were now and that warm, comfortable place. He didn't even know if she wanted those things, too. He realized he'd never asked her what she wanted, that even now he had no idea what might make her happy.

"He didn't get mad about the phone call. That's the worst part. He wasn't even angry. It'd been you? You'd be screaming like a jealous little boy."

He took the hit and didn't argue. She was right. He'd have blown his stack had he been on the other end of that call.

"Then what?"

She ran her fingers through her hair. "He just asked me why I'd called. Was I missing you? Was I sure I was ready to move on?"

She blew out a breath, pushed the blanket aside and crossed her legs. She was wearing black leggings and one of his old Regis sweatshirts, soft and faded from years and years of washing. Her at-home uniform, he used to call it.

"He said he wanted to know we were both there, heart and soul, before we walked down the aisle. He didn't want to marry Angie. She was pregnant and they were young. He thought he had to do that. Maybe he did. But he never loved her enough to ride the ups and downs of a real relationship. He didn't want to make another mistake, this time marrying someone who didn't love *him* enough."

He was about to make a smart comment about what a deep guy his good friend Sean was, so wise in the ways of love, but he could tell by the look on her face that she was actually *waiting* for him to say something shitty. Suddenly he knew he had to man up now, tread carefully, or watch her walk back to Mr. Wonderful. He went for a solemn head nod. In the mirror, it looked good.

"And what did you tell him?"

"I told him why I called you, what I called to tell you."

"Why *did* you call?"

"I told him I was pregnant," she said, simply, quietly, still not looking at him. "That we made love after the divorce hearing and that three weeks later I didn't get my period."

Grady felt as if something had washed over him, some cleansing rush of air. He felt as if it would carry him away if he let it. He stood up.

"I didn't tell him that I think about you every day, wonder where you are, what you're doing, if you've found someone new. I didn't tell him that when he and I are"—she looked up at him, embarrassed—"together, I'm remembering how it used to be with you."

He was afraid for a minute that he was dreaming, that he was going to wake up crushed by disappointment. He'd dreamed scenes like this before, could barely get out of bed afterward from the weight of his sadness when he realized she was still gone.

"Clara."

"And before you ask how I know it's yours and ruin everything—Sean had a vasectomy after their second child. He intended to try to reverse it if we decided later on that we wanted children together."

She looked up at him then, her hazel eyes—green in the center, fading out to brown at the edges—locked on him. He felt paralyzed.

"I'm pregnant, Grady. I want to come home, but there have to be changes. A lot of changes—or I'll be on my own, raising this child without you. I'm not afraid to do that."

"No. No," he said, moving over to her quickly. "I know I have a lot to learn, that I have to grow up to be the man you deserve. I'm capable of that. You'll see." He hoped it was true; he would have promised her anything.

He dropped to his knees before her, put his hands on her hips. He took in the scent of her, the citrus of her shampoo mingling with her skin. She already felt softer to him, wider at the hips in a nice way. She leaned down to kiss him and he pressed his lips to hers. He felt her open to him like a flower. She was so soft, so sweet.

"I'll do anything, Clara," he said, pulling away. He pushed the hair back from her face with both hands. "I'd die for you."

He realized then that he was crying. He hadn't cried once in his adult life, not even when she'd left him.

"I need you to *live* for me, Grady." She put her hands to her belly. "For us."

"Yes," he said, putting his head in her lap. She rested her hands on his head. "Yes," he said again, but his voice was just a raspy whisper. He wasn't sure she'd heard.

24

I look back on it all now and see that my motivations were murky. Then it all seemed very clear. I remembered Ivan's sullen anger: *He betrayed me.* And I thought that was it for me, too. He'd stolen my money, he'd stolen from Linda and Erik, jeopardized Emily and Trevor's education, their future. He'd taken my love and used it for his own purposes. He'd made a fool of me; I, the seer, the one who misses nothing, never once suspected he wasn't who he claimed to be. There was a powerful drive. Sometimes I thought I was looking for justice. Sometimes I acknowledged it might be revenge I wanted. Other times I thought I just wanted to get our money back, at least something to bring to Linda and Erik, some offering. She'd warned me after all, hadn't she? *Just wait and get to know him better before you jump in. Izzy, he's so cold.*

But maybe it wasn't any of these things. I risked my life, my best friend's life, our futures, to get on a plane to follow a ghost of a man, when I wasn't even certain I was heading in the right direction. But now I think I wasn't chasing Marcus at all. I was chasing my father.

There was a light in my father's eye for me that wasn't there for anyone else. And even as a little girl I knew it. He loved Linda; they shared their unique bond. But when he looked at me, there was something—maybe it was just a chemistry—that I knew was unique to us. Linda and I never discussed it. We never talked about our father at all after his death. Her wounds stayed raw for years; some of them still bled occasionally.

Linda chased him in life; she was always at his heels, pulling at his coat. *Look at me, Daddy.* She saw his death as the ultimate abandonment, which, of course, it was. And all her adoration—which in the end meant nothing to him—turned to rage. She turned away from him forever. After his death, it was my turn to chase. *Daddy, why?*

It's the word that drives me, the question, the answer just on the next page if only I can get there. I write, letting a river of possibility flow through me, letting all the energy of all the stories in the world pass from the air onto the page. Some writers fear the enormity of the blankness before them, that empty white field. I live for it.

"Is it just about the knowing?" Jack asked me again. "Is that what this is about? Is it worth it?"

Could anything be more worth it? In every character is a universe, every shade of black and white, every potential darkness, even the potential to turn from darkness and walk into the light. I have to go there, into the shadow of unknowing. I'd rather die in the dark alley than bask a lifetime ignorant in the light.

"Well, that's just ridiculous," Jack said. "In fact, that's the stupidest thing I've ever heard. Most people run from the dark, Isabel. With good reason."

"I'm not most people."

"I know." He sounded sad, nearly pitying, when he said it.

"WHAT ARE YOU thinking about?"

We were at the end of a long day that had yielded nothing, both of us tired, drained. We sat at a thick wooden table in a dark pub, much like the one where Marcus proposed. It was dark, lit by candlelight—sconces on the wall, glass votives on the table. Huge orange flames leapt in the stone fireplace.

"You know."

"I know."

* * *

WE'D RENTED A car at Ruzyne Airport, a big, black late-model Mercedes, and drove a highway studded with brightly colored billboards and road signs neither of us could read, while I tried to navigate us into the city with a map I didn't understand. With the blind luck of fools, we managed not to get ourselves killed and arrived on the cobblestone streets of Prague. After another harrowing twenty minutes during which we nearly collided with a tram, narrowly avoided running over an old woman with a cane, and drove the wrong way up a one-way street, Jack suggested I consult our Prague guidebook to figure out what the street signs meant.

"Tourists should not drive in Prague," the guide read. "The city's complex web of one-way streets and the large number of pedestrian-only areas around the historic core of the city make driving confusing and dangerous for foreigners."

We eventually found our way to our hotel, a narrow slice of a building at the end of a long, winding street across from a park. I have never been so glad to see a valet drive off with a vehicle in my life.

The rest of the day was spent trying to find someone to help us get around, someone to help us talk to locals, since Czech, a West Slavic language, has never resonated with me. I've found its pronunciation nearly impossible and continually made an ass out of myself during my two previous visits. Finally, through some arrangement Jack made, the concierge's cousin agreed to meet us in the morning and, for one hundred U.S. dollars, spend the day with us trying to follow up the few leads I had.

"He can't come tonight?"

"No. It's not possible. I'm sorry."

"Is there anyone else?" I sounded petulant, and too American. The concierge gave me an apathetic shrug.

"That's fine," said Jack. "The morning is fine."

Jack smiled at the concierge and pressed some money into his hand, which seemed to simultaneously please and annoy the man.

"The morning is *not* fine," I whispered to Jack as he pushed me up the flight of stairs to our room.

"It'll have to be."

The room was nice, a suite, everything polished and new. Hardwood floors, brocade drapes, elaborate faux antique furniture, a large comfortable bed. The bathroom featured gleaming marble surfaces and big plush towels. I had suggested the Four Seasons. Jack said that fugitives were not accepted at five-star hotels. I am *sure* that's not true.

I sank into the bed and felt despair lash me to the mattress. A powerful fatigue weighted down my limbs, my head. The full scope of my folly was suddenly clear. The wound on my head throbbed.

"This is a mistake," I said. "He's not even here."

Jack sat beside me, put a hand on my forehead. "*We're* here. We'll try, Izzy. If he's not? We'll go home. At least you'll know you did your best. It will help you to live with all of this better; it will help you to move on."

It was then that I realized he was humoring me. He didn't believe that Marcus was here, or that we'd find him, or that I'd get anything that I needed in this mad enterprise. He had come because he knew if he didn't, I'd go alone. He'd come simply to hold my hand, then pick up the pieces and carry them all home. I made the decision right then and there to ditch him as soon as possible.

"Let's get something to eat," he said softly into the silence that followed. Somewhere there was a little girl laughing; a light strain of music came through the ceiling from the room above us. The air smelled a little too floral; too much air freshener. I let Jack pull me up off the bed and corral me toward the door.

"And don't think you're going to unload me, leave me in a bar or restaurant somewhere, or sneak out of here in the night and go it alone."

"I would never do that."

"Sure." There was something in his tone, maybe a little anger. I realized we were talking about something else.

AT THE BEER garden, we sipped from big mugs of rich golden ale. They'd served us a ridiculously large cast-iron pan filled with pork, chicken, and potatoes. It was almost exactly like every meal I'd eaten here with Marcus. I thought we'd eat all night and never make a dent. But Jack seemed to be plowing his way through, while I pushed a piece of meat around my plate. I had no appetite, though I couldn't remember the last time I'd eaten.

"Try, Iz. You know how you get when your blood sugar is low."

"And how's that?" I snapped.

He raised his eyebrows at me.

It was dark and we were both exhausted when we crossed the Charles Bridge to return to our hotel. Jack went up to the room and I stopped at the single computer monitor in the lobby to check my e-mail. There were nearly twenty messages, from booksellers and fans who had seen the news, one from my editor asking if everything was okay, another from my sister. The message box was blank but the subject line was: "Goddammit, you stubborn pain in the ass . . . COME HOME. I love you."

Then there was one from Detective Grady Crowe, subject "Things YOU should know."

> First of all, it's my duty to tell you to turn yourself in, to your lawyer or to me. You are a person of interest in this case, and being unavailable to me is not in your best interest. You are out of your depth and in big trouble.

That said, much of the information you provided has proved valuable to us.

He went on to tell me about the events at the Topaz Room, Charlie Shane's relationship to Camilla Novak, how my husband paid Shane to keep quiet about what he heard on the street and to let people into our apartment. I had been betrayed so deeply by someone I trusted completely that this small betrayal didn't even register.

Whoever Kristof Ragan is—and we don't know—he has no criminal record here or abroad. Whoever he is, he's dangerous. According to what you told Erik Book, he killed Camilla Novak. If this is true, do you think he'll hesitate to kill you when he realizes you haven't just let him walk away with your money?

We have not been able to identify the woman you know as S. Her photograph does not match those in any domestic criminal files; Interpol will take longer. But we do know that Ivan Ragan is associated with the Albanian and Russian Mob, that he was recently released from state prison for gun possession. He was arrested after an anonymous tip was phoned into police. I'd bet money that Kristof betrayed him after the Marcus Raine disappearance—probably murder—and theft went down, which is probably why he wound up on that dock about to be fitted for a pair of cement shoes.

A question: I have been going over the banking records for Razor Tech. Every quarter there was a ten-thousand-dollar donation to an orphanage in the Czech Republic. What do you know about this?

He had a name and an address of an orphanage in a town I knew to be about forty minutes outside the city. The information caused my whole body to tingle. Was he really asking me about this orphanage, or giving me a lead?

> Does this mean anything to you?
>
> Anyway, be careful, Isabel. You've got a tiger by the tail. Make sure he doesn't turn around.

The lights went off in the lobby then, making me jump, and I was alone with the glowing screen. I walked over to the front desk and saw that the clerk who'd been sitting there was gone. His computer screen was dark; he'd obviously gone home for the night. No twenty-four-hour service at this little hotel. A little sign featured a number to call for emergencies.

I went back to the computer and printed out Detective Crowe's e-mail and the attachment, a copy of the transfer order for the money being donated to the orphanage. Then I headed upstairs to Jack. It seemed he had already fallen asleep on the couch, fully clothed, with the television on, tuned to the BBC. There was an image of my face on the screen. The sound was down but there was a ticker running beneath my picture: *Person of interest wanted for questioning relating to crimes in the U.S. Notify police if spotted.* It was such a surreal moment, it almost didn't register.

One arm rested over his forehead, the other was folded over his middle. I thought about leaving Jack in that moment, my decision to ditch him coming back to me. He was a sound sleeper. I could pack a few things, leave him a note, and take off on him. He'd have to wait here or go home, not knowing where I'd gone. But the truth was I didn't want to leave him. I wasn't brave enough.

I don't know how long I stood there staring at him, suddenly remembering the night we'd shared. What had I felt that night? I tried to remember. How had it compared to what I felt for Marcus? Was it any more or less real? Instead of leaving, I found myself kneeling beside him and touching his face. I felt a familiar warmth in my center, a feeling I associated only with him.

I trusted him completely and I always had, like I trusted my sister, like I trusted myself. Meaning that I understood the way his mind worked, what moved and motivated him, what was important to him. I never felt that way about my husband, I realized. I did trust him for a time, but on some level didn't I always sense he was a stranger? Is that what kept me with him? The shadow of unknowing; the place that drew me inexorably.

Jack opened his eyes but didn't startle. We stared at each other for a minute. He raised a hand to push the hair back from my face.

"Did you see your picture on the television?" he asked.

I nodded.

"We're in trouble if someone at the hotel recognizes you," he said. I'd kept my hat and glasses on. My hair, my most distinguishable feature, had been caged beneath my cap. I was hoping that was enough.

"Why did you come?" I asked.

He held my eyes, let a beat pass. "You know why. Don't you?"

I nodded. Then: "You remember?"

He didn't ask me what I meant. "Of course. Did you think I didn't?"

"I didn't know what to think."

"You left. You were gone when I woke up."

I thought about it a second. Why had I left him there? Snuck off in the early morning before he woke? I remember thinking that he was my only successful male relationship and I had just screwed it up for good. Maybe if I left, pretended it never happened, we could remain as we had always been.

"I didn't know how you'd feel in the morning. If there'd be regrets. There's never been any awkwardness between us. I couldn't bare it."

"Isabel," he said. "You were drunk. I wasn't, not really."

"Yes you were."

"No. I was loose, maybe. Uninhibited. But I knew what I was doing. What I was saying."

I've always loved you, Isabel. The words hung between us. I looked away from him, sat on the floor. He sat up, planted his feet on the ground.

"I think I took advantage of you that night."

"No." I shook my head.

He hung his head, released a slow breath. "Anyway, you can trust me now. I know what you need here. I'll be that. You take the bed. This couch is pretty comfortable."

"Jack."

He reached out and pulled the cap off my head, then ran his hand along my cheek. I took his hand and held it, closed my eyes.

"This is the last thing we need to talk about right now," he said. "Let's fix what's broken, leave everything else be."

I didn't argue, and handed him the e-mail, which he read.

"I guess we know where we're headed tomorrow. The guide will be here at six. Let's get some rest."

SHE WAS PRETTY. Not like Isabel, whose beauty came as much from some radiance within as the quality of her features. Not like Camilla with her desperate fire. But she *was* pretty, if too thin, anemic looking even, with a straining collarbone and wrists that looked as though they could snap like twigs. Her name was Martina; he'd met her at the Four Seasons cocktail lounge. She thought it was a chance meeting. It wasn't.

There was also something else to her, a quality they all shared. Longing. Camilla longed to be lifted out of the life she was in, thought she needed money and the right man to do that for her. Isabel longed to experience "real" love, even though she claimed when they met that she'd given up on that. He wasn't sure what Martina longed for, but he could tell by the way she was looking at him that she thought she'd found it.

He understood longing. It lived in him, always had. Even when he'd satisfied every desire, when everything he had wanted was in hand during his years with Isabel, it lived in him. He understood only recently that it was a chronic condition that might be treated but never cured.

"What are you thinking?"

"I'm thinking that you have a special kind of beauty, very delicate, pure. Like an orchid."

The color rose on her cheeks and she bowed her head. "Charmer," she whispered with a smile. She let him take her hand.

Walking past the outdoor cafés where people sat even in winter, coated, beneath heat lamps, they moved through Old Town Square decorated with festive Christmas trees. The craft market, set up for the holiday, was teeming with people. A gypsy played an accordion, and some young people danced with his vested monkey.

They strolled along a narrow street, picking their way through the crowd, and moved toward the Charles Bridge. Kristof remembered how he'd charmed Isabel on this very walk, pointing out all the attractions, speaking to locals in Czech. It hadn't even been Christmas then. Now it was like a fairy tale, with a light snow falling. It couldn't have been more romantic. Martina was enchanted.

On the bridge, vendors lined up with their wares—wood carvings, watercolor paintings, marionettes. Prague had turned into a bit of a circus in recent years, mobbed with tourists. Every year since the fall of communism, the city changed, more people came. First the gray cast that had hidden the beauty of the buildings was washed away, revealing pinks and yellows, oranges, elaborately decorated facades. Heavy iron doors were finally unlocked, revealing squares and gardens no one knew were there.

During communism, no one was allowed to have any flourish or show. Now people planted flower boxes in their windows, restored what had been neglected or destroyed. It was a revival that drew the world. Tourists flocked to this jewel of Europe. But Prague wasn't the Czech Republic, and what visitors saw while following their guidebooks wasn't really Prague.

"Do the tourists bother you?" she asked.

He shook his head. "Not really."

"You're frowning."

"Ah," he said, forcing a smile. "Maybe they bother me a little."

He leaned in and gave her a light kiss on the lips. Their first. He pulled away to look at her face—she seemed surprised, pleased. He kissed her again, deeper, snaking an arm around the small of her back. Her body melted into his. He felt nothing really. No warmth, no affection for her. He only felt a physical arousal and the thrill of success, of conquest. He might have felt something different for Isabel, even for Camilla. But those moments were distant, like all the other lives he had lived.

It was then, with the blush of success on his cheek, that he saw that dark river of curls, that confident gait. For a moment, he thought he was hallucinating, that she was so much on his mind he was seeing her where she wasn't.

But no. Isabel moved past him, unseeing. Her face was pale; she looked so unhappy, so angry. He turned away quickly, pretended to guide Martina over to the stone wall. He pointed across the black and brooding water to an outdoor café.

"The best view in Prague is had at those tables," he said. He wondered if his voice betrayed the adrenaline racing through his system.

"So let's go," she said.

Nothing could keep her from coming after you. Sara's warnings echoed in his ears. *You're weak when it comes to women.*

He kept his arm around her and watched Isabel as she disappeared into the throng on the bridge. Just before she did, he realized she wasn't alone. Beside her was someone, a man he recognized, but it took him a moment to place the face. When he did, a cold rage filled him.

"Are you all right?" Martina asked, maybe sensing the change in his mood. "Marek, are you unwell?"

"I'm fine," he said. "Walk with me."

He took her hand and he followed after them.

* * *

"She's here."

He knew Martina thought it was strange that he'd cut their date short, but he had no choice. He'd made an excuse, seizing on her question about his not feeling well, and brought her back to her hotel, promising to see her tomorrow. He could tell she was hurt. He'd make it up to her.

On the way back to his apartment, he called Sara. She sighed.

"I told you."

"I need some help."

"I'll take care of it."

He felt a rush of urgency. "*I* need to take care of it, Sara."

More silence on the line. Then: "As you like it. Where is she staying?"

25

The Greek philosopher Heracleitus believed that the universe was in a constant state of flux, that the only permanent condition was change. He said, "No man ever steps in the same river twice, for it's not the same river and he's not the same man." And I believe this to be true. But I also believe that some things don't pass over us like a rushing river, they pass through us. They leave us altered from the inside out and the river becomes a stagnant pool where we languish, our development halted by an inability to climb from the muck of it.

Even from the road there was a palpable aura of despair, though there was nothing especially grim about the building, gray and squat against the green countryside. I'd read enough about postcommunist-era orphanages to be a little worried about what we'd find. But as we drew near, the building and surrounding lawns looked tidy and well kept, if barren in the winter months. Some tall trees must have, in summer, provided leafy green shade over a winding walkway, and kids who just looked like your average U.S. high-school students milled about. One girl read a book under a tree in spite of the cold temperature, another listened to headphones with her eyes closed, sitting on the steps that led up to the double-door entrance. A group of boys gathered off to the side, smoking cigarettes. They looked a little on the gaunt side, a little on the rough side, with very young eyes.

I felt all their gazes fall on us as we emerged from the Mercedes and climbed up the stairs. A youngish American couple with an obviously local guide pulling up in a Mercedes caught the attention of the place. I saw some small forms move to the windows above.

"The healthy Czech and Ukrainian infants go right away," said our guide, Ales, in his perfect English. "But these Romas will be here until their eighteenth birthday. Then—who knows? They'll deal drugs, become prostitutes."

"Romas?" asked Jack.

Ales couldn't hide his disdain, though he seemed to try to keep his tone neutral. "Gypsies. They cause a lot of problems here politically, economically."

Marcus had told me about the hatred in Czech for the Romas, the terrible crimes that were committed against them throughout history and to this day. Even the most liberal, educated Czechs cursed the Romas, considered them only thieves and criminals, addicts, cons, a terrible drain on social systems. I thought of a line from one of Emily's books, *Madeline and the Gypsies:* "For gypsies do not like to stay. They only come to go away." But the Czech government had outlawed their nomadic lifestyle and then was forced to create housing for them, fostering more resentment and hatred from the Romas and the Czechs for different reasons. "A bad situation without end," Marcus said. "Like so many bad things."

"Look how they watch you," said Ales with a sneer. "They think you are like Brad Pitt and Angelina Jolie, come to take one of them home to your mansion in America."

He was a young man, maybe just in his early twenties. He was pale, with light blond hair and hazel eyes. There was something wolfish about him, with his hunched shoulders and ranging gait. When he smiled, you could see his teeth were sharp and yellow. I didn't like him, but we were stuck with him for the time being and he *did* seem to know his way around.

"Did you hear that?" Jack whispered. "He thinks I look like Brad Pitt." He was trying to be funny but I didn't have the energy to laugh.

"I hope your car is here when we get back," said Ales, issuing a throaty laugh that morphed into a smoker's cough. He had smoked unapologetically out an open window the whole way here; both Jack and I were too polite to ask him to stop.

I glanced behind me. One of the boys had already left the group and was circling the vehicle while his buddies looked on laughing.

Inside, Ales said something softly in Czech to the young girl at the reception desk. She stood up from her perch, disappeared for a few moments, then returned and uttered a few words. He nodded and ushered us over to a few orange plastic seats.

"I told her you were a journalist doing a story on Czech orphanages. She said someone will come."

I frowned at him. Not the best tack to take, I thought. Czech orphanages were not exactly the darling of the media. I remembered a recent BBC report that they were still keeping disabled children in "cage beds." Though I have to admit that in the footage the beds actually looked more like cribs than cages. Still, it was a sensational story that captured world attention.

"Maybe we should just tell them the truth," I said.

He shook his head. "This is better. You'll see."

Minutes turned into nearly an hour and, finally, Ales left us to go chain-smoke on the stairs. Jack had been mostly quiet, tense, barely saying a word all day. We'd been roaming the Czech town I'd visited with Marcus, and other towns in the area, showing pictures and asking questions, receiving only blank stares and shaking heads. Even with the help of our guide, we were treated like interlopers, a nuisance. One woman threw us out of her store.

"She said she doesn't like Americans," Ales explained with a sneer. "She thinks you're all pigs."

"That's nice," said Jack. "Great."

Ales laughed, finding some humor that eluded us. By the time we'd arrived at the orphanage, I was demoralized and exhausted. By the looks of him, Jack wasn't feeling much better.

"I wonder what it's like to grow up in a place like this," he said when Ales left.

I looked around at the gray institutional walls, the heavy metal doors, the harsh fluorescent lights.

"Lonely," I said.

A young woman emerged from behind a closed door. Petite and pale, with blond hair pulled back dramatically from her face, she wore strangely garish red lipstick, though her outfit—narrow gray pencil skirt, white oxford button-down, and plain black pumps—was very conservative, professional.

"I'm Gabriela Pavelka, the director here. Can I help you?"

"You speak English," I said, relieved. I didn't want to have another conversation through Ales.

"Yes," she said with a nod. I could tell in the way her shoulders squared that she was proud of this fact. "Are you a journalist?"

"No," I said, looking back at Ales, who was leaning against a railing talking to a young girl with a tattoo on her face, something tribal looking around the eyes. She was smiling at him, took a cigarette he offered. "Our guide misunderstood. Is there someplace we can talk?"

"May I ask what this is about? I am not at liberty to discuss anything with the media."

"It's about a private donation."

"We can talk in my office," she said, moving toward the door that led back into the building. I glanced over at Jack who lifted a hand indicating that he'd stay where he was, then I followed the director. I assumed Jack felt the need to keep his eye on our guide and the rental car, which didn't seem like such a bad idea.

Gabriela escorted me to a small drab office. The first thing I noticed was a wedding photo—her in white lace, kissing a handsome man with a wide jaw and short-cropped brown hair. Then, a small diamond ring and thin gold band on her slender finger. On her desk: A cup of coffee gone cold. A shiny red BlackBerry. A copy of *British Vogue,* hastily stuck under stacks of files. There was another picture of her in a frame with a dark-haired child on her hip. I recognized the background as Central Park.

"You've been to New York," I said.

"Yes," she said. "I was an au pair for three years after college. This is where I learn better English."

"Your English is excellent," I told her, meaning it but also playing to her pride in the matter.

"Thank you," she said, her professional smile suddenly seeming more genuine. "You're American. From New York?"

"Yes."

She picked up the picture and gazed at it. "I miss it. I loved it there."

"Why did you come home?"

"Because too many young people are leaving the Czech Republic and not coming back. If we all leave, what happens to this country? I wanted to do something important with children, so I came here to run this orphanage." She swept a hand around her.

"It's important work."

"Yes," she said gravely, looking down at the picture for another moment, then returning it to her desk. "Now, the matter you wanted to discuss . . ."

From my bag, I extracted the copy of the transfer order Detective Crowe had attached to the e-mail, held it in my hand. I stared at it for a moment while she waited.

"Have you ever been lied to?" I asked her. I saw her eyes shoot over to her wedding picture.

"Everyone's been lied to," she said with a shrug. "That's life. People lie."

I told her what happened to me, leaving out some of the gory details. I saw her inch up in her seat as I spun the tale for her. By the time I was done, she was practically lying on her desk, she had leaned so far forward.

"I'm looking for him now," I said. "I don't know if you can help me, but this is the only connection I have."

She shook her head slowly. "It's terrible. I'm sorry. But I don't know what I can do."

"Do you know anything about the man who makes these donations?"

"I know of the donations, of course," she said. "To us, this is a lot of money, forty thousand U.S. dollars a year. The donations come anonymously. The rumor is that the man who makes them lived out his boyhood here, applied for scholarships to the U.S., and left to go to school there when he turned eighteen. That now he is very rich and successful and wants to help other orphans like himself. But this is just a rumor."

Outside the window, there was a wide expanse of flat land. In the distance, a large black bird flew a low wide circle in the air. I felt myself coming to a dead end. Yes, the money had come here. But so what?

"My husband's real name is Kristof Ragan. He has a brother named Ivan. Do you have old records?"

She was already shaking her head before I finished speaking. "Since the fall of communism, all new records are being computerized. Old records were incomplete, nonexistent, or destroyed. In recent years there's been a lot of purging."

"But there must be something. Maybe someone who has been here for many years."

"By purging, I don't just mean old records. This is a privately run orphanage now but once orphanages like this were run by the state. The practices were archaic, the officials corrupt to an extreme. We've had to distance ourselves from those old ways to better serve the children in our care."

She must have seen the despair on my face, offered a sad smile.

What had I hoped? That someone here would know him, that they'd have a current address? That they'd open up old records for me and I'd find something there? I don't know. I realized how pointless this trip had been. My husband was gone. His history was lost. Had he grown up in a place like this, in a communist orphanage, afraid and alone? Had anything he'd told me about himself been true? I had to face the fact that I might never know.

"I'm sorry," the young woman said. "I don't know how to help you. You know more about our anonymous donor than I do."

I MUST HAVE looked dejected on returning to the waiting room, because Jack rose to his feet quickly.

"What did you find out?"

"Nothing, really." I recounted the conversation for him as we exited and moved toward the car.

"Where's our guide?" I asked. We looked around. The wind had picked up and the chill in the air deepened. All the kids who had been scattered about had disappeared.

"I don't know," said Jack. "But we better find him. He has the keys to the car."

I returned to the staircase and sat on one of the low steps.

"I saw Ales talking to some young girl," I said. Jack walked a restless circle around the car.

"Do you think Marcus grew up here?" I said.

"It would explain a lot."

"I suppose it would."

The cloud cover was growing thicker, the sky taking on the silver gray cast of threatening snow. I wrapped my arms around myself against the cold. But the chill I felt came from within. Nothing would warm me.

"I have a bad feeling, Jack."

He came to stand in front of me. The wind tousled his hair and played with his coat. Behind him, I saw Ales emerge from the trees. The girl I saw earlier followed at his heels. She had dark black hair and a thick frame, wide shoulders and narrow hips. Her eyes were black and the tattoos on her face looked like a mask. She's hiding, protecting herself with that, I found myself thinking. Tattoos are armor; they keep the world from seeing what's beneath them. Her hair was mussed. There was dirt and dried grass on the back of her jacket.

"We're ready to go," Jack said to Ales as he approached. "Where did you go with her?"

Ales nodded toward the girl. "She think she knows where you can find the man you're looking for."

When I looked past the tattoos and heavy, dark eye shadow, I saw someone very young, very scared, and I wondered how many different ways a girl like this had been violated. I felt the urge to wrap my arms around her. But everything about her—her appearance, her attitude—pushed me away.

"How?" I asked, looking at her. She bowed her head, refused to return my gaze.

"She doesn't speak English," Ales said. "But she says Kristof Ragan and his brother, Ivan, are like legends here. That they lived here during communism but then went to the U.S. and are now famous and successful businessmen, rich and living in big houses. They send money back to this place. That's why they have computers and good schoolbooks here."

The girl kept her eyes to the ground. I had the strong feeling I was being played—whether by the girl or the guide, I couldn't be sure. But I was just desperate enough to play along.

"Kde?" I asked her. *Where?* She looked at me, startled. "Prosím," I said. *Please.* "Kde je Kristof Ragan?"

26

Kde je Kristof Ragan?

Then there is just this eerie quiet where all I can hear is my own scrambling over the snow, my own labored breathing. Before me a curved cobblestone street, disappearing beneath the falling snow gathering on steps and window frames. Two more shots ring out and I hear a whisper past my left ear and realize it has come that close. I turned to see him, a black tower against the white.

He is unhurried and yet still gaining as I limp, moving slowly uphill past a closed café, a leather shop, a store of children's clothing. I start pounding on doors, yelling. But the city seems to swallow all sound. No one answers or comes to their door. Up ahead, there are two black iron doors ajar, opening onto a square. I move inside and pull the doors closed behind me. I can't run anymore. I have to hide.

The wind is captive in the square, howling around the four corners. I edge along the perimeter, trying to walk where no snow has fallen so as not to leave a trail. There is an open door that leads into darkness. I reach it and enter just as I hear the creaking of the door from the street opening. I remember what I said to Jack, *I'd rather die in the dark alley than bask a lifetime ignorant in the light.* I didn't mean it.

"Isabel!" he calls. He sounds so even, so measured. He could be calling me to ask if I remembered to buy razors or did I steal his gym socks. But that's not why he's calling me. I lean against the cold stone of the wall; the space behind me echoes. I hear water dripping. I am unarmed, trapped. I close my eyes and try to harness my breathing.

"Isabel, let's talk. I'll put the gun down." I peer out the slim opening in the door and see him lay his weapon in the snow, raise his hands into the air. Every instinct in my body screams to stay still, to stay hidden, to move further into the darkness, to hide. But that one question, the one that drives me, the one that is responsible for every bad decision I've made over the last few days, forces me forward. Even with all he's told me, I still don't have the answer. I still want to know. *Why?*

I push open the door and it emits a loud groan. He turns to face me and the wind picks up, howls around the courtyard, lifts a flurry of snow. The world is gray and white and black. He looks different, somehow. He has let his hair and his beard grow and it looks darker as a result, closer to brown than the dark blond I was used to seeing. We stand there for a moment, regarding each other. He drops his hands to his side, then stuffs them in his pockets.

I wonder if I look as strange to him as he does to me. I am self-conscious of my tattered clothing, my one shoe. I fold my arms across my chest. He gives me a sad smile.

"Isabel," he says. "This has always been your problem. You're too trusting."

Before I can ask him what he means, he's pulling another gun from his coat, and all I really see before a white-hot, mind-altering pain in my center is a muzzle flash. The cold of the ground is shocking as I hit it hard and the sky is an impossibly silvery gray. There is another color in the world now. A deep red. The only thing I hear is the muted sound of his footfalls. He's walking slowly away.

"KDE JE KRISTOF Ragan?"

I hear the sound of my own voice asking that question. Before that, we were still safe. If I hadn't asked that question and the girl hadn't answered, I'd probably be on a plane home to New York right now. I feel elevated above the pain, risen high above the fire in my gut. Not far away, I think I hear the sound of gunfire. But I can't be sure what's real—it might just be the beating of my heart. I watch the snow fall in big, wet flakes, a starfield through which I'm traveling. The events of the last few hours play back for me.

THE GIRL WITH the tattoos on her face answered Ales in Czech. She spoke softly, quickly. I couldn't understand her at all.

He nodded and looked at me. "She says she can take you to a place where they'll know."

Jack gives me a look; it's a warning. "This is a bad idea."

"What does she want?" I asked.

"What does everyone want?" said Ales, lighting another cigarette. "Money. Two hundred U.S.?"

"Fine."

Jack took hold of my arm, pulled me away from them. "This is crazy. Let's go. I'm not letting you follow this girl to wherever. Think about it. They're *playing* you."

He looked at Ales, not releasing my arm. I could tell that he'd reached the end of his patience with what he considered a flight of my fancy, a desperate act he'd expected to yield nothing. Now he was afraid. Afraid that I might actually find what I'd come here to find.

"Make her tell us where he is," he said. "She can still have her money. But we're not going with you unless she tells us right now where she wants to take us."

Ales relayed Jack's words but it seemed to me that the girl understood, was looking at Jack with a sullen resentment. She uttered a curt sentence in Czech.

"There's a place where they know him. You can get what you want at this place—drugs, guns, whatever," Ales translated.

"What kind of *place*?" asked Jack. He was angry now, sounding hostile. His neck was shading red, and a vein was starting to throb next to his eye.

The girl turned, muttered something else to Ales, and then started to walk away. Ales shrugged. "She says forget it. She doesn't have to help you. She doesn't want your filthy American money."

"Good," said Jack, physically moving me toward the car. "Let's get out of here."

He stopped, still holding on to my arm, and looked over at Ales, I suppose remembered that we stupidly let our guide hold the key.

"What about you?" Jack said. "Do *you* want our filthy American money?"

Ales just looked at him with that same bitterness I saw everywhere overseas these days. He gave a slight nod.

"Then let's go."

"Wait!" I yelled after the girl. She was already halfway across the large lawn. She stopped and turned back toward us. I wrested myself from Jack and ran after her.

"Isabel!" Jack called.

"Jack. Please. Wait with the car. I'll be right back."

He put his head in his hands, leaned up against the Mercedes. I heard him talking to himself but I didn't hear what he was saying.

"You speak English," I said to her. Not a question.

"A little."

"Can you help me?"

She nodded. "I can help you find him."

I remember thinking she might have been pretty before all the tattoos, a series of black swirls around her eyes, across her nose, framing her mouth. I wondered how badly it hurt to have your face tattooed, where she'd gotten the money to have it done. She smelled of cigarettes and sex. Was it allowed at the orphanage to do this type of thing to yourself? Were there no counselors? Did no one care? There was something dead to her eyes, something flat and empty like the eyes of a cat. I didn't know whether to believe her or not. Under other circumstances I probably would not have, but desperation made me stupid.

"Okay," I said. "Let's go."

We returned to the car. Jack and I argued for fifteen minutes, while Ales and the girl looked on from a distance, smoking, smug and superior. Eventually, Jack and I were so angry at each other, there was nothing left to say. We climbed into the car, and a moment later the other two joined us. As the girl climbed in, I noticed that she clutched a small nylon bag.

"Don't you need to ask someone if you can leave?" I asked her. I glanced over at the building, expecting to see someone come out, ask us where we were taking the girl, but the whole place suddenly had an aura of desertion to it, even though I knew there were plenty of people inside. She gave an unkind little laugh.

"What is your name?" I asked the girl. But she'd gone back to not speaking English, just looked at me blankly.

"Her name is Petra," said Ales from the front seat. He was pulling from the drive onto the long, winding road we traveled to get here. The sun was sinking; it was late afternoon. And there were no other cars as far as the eye could see ahead or behind us.

"She can just leave the orphanage whenever she wants?" I asked, still fixating on this, wondering if we'd just kidnapped a child.

"She's not an orphan," said Ales finally, impatiently. "She doesn't live there."

"Then who is she?"

Petra and I sat in the backseat, with Ales and Jack up front. Jack, who had been staring out the window, not talking—sulking—turned to look at our driver.

"Then who is she?" he repeated.

Ales opened his mouth to answer, when the car seemed to lose power, to slow to a crawl, and then silently die. He deftly maneuvered it to the side of the road.

"What's wrong?" asked Jack, sitting forward. He had a hard, suspicious frown on his face.

"I don't know," said Ales. Our guide reached down and pulled a lever and I watched the hood pop open. Jack got out of the car, too, and they were both obscured by the open hood. I moved to exit as well, suddenly feeling that I didn't want Jack out of my sight. But Petra caught my arm. I looked at her; she was smiling, shaking her head. I saw the gun then.

"Jack!" I yelled, backing away from her. "Jack!"

The hood slammed down then. Only Ales stood, looking at us through the windshield. I tried scrambling for my door but the painful poke of the gun in my kidneys stopped me cold. Ales got in, started the car easily, and locked the doors.

"Where is he?" I was screaming, hysterical, in full-scale panic.

Neither Petra nor Ales said a word as Ales threw the car into reverse and then pulled back onto the road. Petra kept her dead eyes on me, the gun pressed into my flesh. Out the rear windshield, I saw Jack lying on the shoulder of the road.

"Jack! Jack!"

I nearly wept with relief when I saw one of his legs move. Then he was on his feet, running after the car, arms waving. As the Mercedes took a sharp turn in the road, he was out of sight. I barely felt the blow to the back of my head that turned the whole world black. Again.

27

I see Trevor standing in the corner of the courtyard. "Merry Christmas, Izzy."

"What are you doing here, Trev? It's not safe."

He walks over slowly. "Izzy, I told you. You needed a gun."

"I know. I know. You're a smart kid. Listen, Trevor? Tell your mom how much I love her, okay? Tell her I'm sorry."

"Tell her yourself." He says it with a smile.

But no, I'm alone in the courtyard still. I see that it's filled with junk. A stack of old tires, a splintering wooden table, a box of sodden books. There's a chair on three legs, some broken planters. A black cat leaps from nowhere onto a metal drum that sags with rust and age. The cat sits, watching me. There are voices now, I think. And the wail of sirens. I think I hear my name. But maybe it's just the wind.

Isabel . . . Isabel.

How did I get here? I wonder. Memory comes back in pieces.

WHEN I CAME to again, I was lying on a cold concrete floor. Ales and Petra were gone. But my ankles were bound, as were my wrists. I went from unconscious to hyperconscious, started immediately working at the bindings. There was very little light, just a milky gray coming in from a small sliver of a window up high on the wall. A basement. I could tell by the chill, by the mold, by the dark. I was in a kind of cage. All around me, nearly empty cages. One held a bicycle and a bookshelf. Another held a stack of suitcases and a box of books, an old treadmill. It was a storage basement, I realized. Little used from the look of things.

I had seen how gigantic doors glide open by remote in Prague buildings, and cars disappear into spaces you wouldn't have believed were there. I have seen this at embassies and luxury condos.

Trying to figure out how I got there, I imagined that my captors had driven my rented Mercedes into such a door, that I have disappeared inside the walls of this old city. Jack would not be able to find me. Panic and anger started their dance in my chest. I worked against my bindings vigorously for a few more minutes before I realized that I was not alone.

He sat in the corner of the room outside the cage, shrouded in the dark. I didn't have to see his face to know his form.

I really didn't want it to come to this, you know. I warned you to let me go. He issued a cough. The damp has always bothered him.

How could you think I would? Don't you know me at all?

I hoped, Isabel. I hoped you would.

Why did you do this to me? A mutinous sob I couldn't stop. *I loved you. Did you ever love me?*

Of course I loved you. I'd have stayed if I could.

Was anything you told me about yourself the truth?

No. Nothing.

Tell me now.

Why?

You owe me that much, don't you? I don't even know what to call you now.

Just call me Marcus. In the world we shared, that was my name. That's all that matters.

Tell me.

There's nothing to tell. His usual cool and disinterested tone. *My father died, my mother couldn't keep my brother and me; she couldn't afford us or didn't want us. What does it matter? We were taken to the orphanage you visited. We were old enough to know we'd been left. It was a painful, stark, and lonely way to grow up.*

He shifted in his seat, the only sign that his memories made him uncomfortable, that they might cause him pain.

But we managed. We survived, and communism did not. Ivan and I left for the U.S. I applied to colleges, received a scholarship, came on a student visa. Ivan came on a work visa, but the company that sponsored him was not legitimate. Ivan is a small-time criminal, always has been. Even as children, he bullied and stole—

I'm not interested in Ivan.

What do you want to know?

Start with Marcus Raine.

He paused, took a deep breath as if summoning his patience.

I wanted what he had. His money, his girlfriend. I took it.

How?

I seduced Camilla. She loved Marcus Raine—or maybe just his money, I don't know. But his plan was to return to Czech. He wanted to take the money he earned in the U.S. and start a business in Prague. He went to America, like me, to work, to get rich. But he wanted to go home and enrich the country. He didn't believe all the intelligent, young Czech people should leave for good. Go, find opportunities, make money abroad, and then return to help the Czech Republic. The last place Camilla wanted to go was back to Czech.

I knew what she wanted. I promised it to her. She got me a key to Marcus Raine's apartment, helped me get past his doorman. And I killed him—well, Ivan did. His associates helped us to dispose of him, a mortuary in Queens cremated the body. It was seamless. I took his life . . . his identification, his money. It was really that easy.

I told Camilla that we had to be apart for a while, that it would be suspicious if we moved too fast. Then I met you.

You sought me out.

Yes.

Why?

Because you understood Prague.

So you thought I'd understand you?

Maybe.

Camilla got tired of waiting?

Yes, seven years is a long time to ask someone to wait. For a while, I could convince her that the payoff would be worth it. I gave her money every month. Continued seeing her. Then she realized.

What?

That I had what I wanted. That I loved you. That I wouldn't leave you unless I had to.

So she got angry, started making scenes, sending me e-mail. Why didn't you kill her then?

I couldn't. I didn't know who she'd told. I suspected she'd gone to the authorities. I couldn't risk killing her yet.

Not until you had already disappeared, destroyed evidence, transferred the money from our accounts. Then you went back to tie up that loose end. You slit her throat.

Still risky but necessary, I thought.

My mind was racing through all the million questions I had. But I was starting to feel fuzzy, confused, fear and multiple blows to the head addling my thoughts.

That morning when you left, did you know you'd never see me again?

No. I would have been gone soon, maybe even in the next day or two. But not that morning.

What happened?

Ivan came to see me. I betrayed him after the murder of Marcus Raine, called the police and reported guns in the apartment. He went to prison. Camilla went to see him in her anger, told him what I'd done. He came to see me. Not just for money. For revenge.

You killed all those men. But you left Ivan alive. You could have killed him, too. Why didn't you?

Isabel, so many questions.

Tell me why.

The same reason I didn't kill him years earlier. Because he's my brother. I wanted him to think about what he'd done. I didn't necessarily want him to die. Why does this matter now? It's over.

It matters, how the pieces fit together. I need to know.

And that's why you risked your life to follow me.

I can't be other than who I am.

That's why I loved you, Isabel. You have always been so sure of who you are.

If you loved me, then tell me everything.

Another long sigh. Another cough. All the while, I was working the bindings. Before he started talking again, I felt my wrist come free. It was dark. He didn't see.

What else do you want to know?

Who is S?

I didn't expect him to answer, but he did. *Sara. A woman I loved a lifetime ago. My first love, I suppose. I left her in the Czech Republic. I went to college; she joined the military. Eventually, she was discharged, served some time for injuring a man who tried to rape her—as justice in Czech would have it. She sought me out in the U.S., had started her own business.*

Services Unlimited. A prostitution ring?

Among other things.

You had an affair with her. She was the one who sent that message.

He gave an assenting lift of his palms.

It's complicated, our relationship. I loved her once. But she belongs to no one now.

She trashed our office. Our home. She hated me; I saw it in her eyes in your office.

Someone like Sara doesn't hate. She's jealous, possessive, angry that I loved you too much to let her end your life for my convenience.

Did she take your mother's ring? Did you give it to her?

You're so naive. Such a little girl.

The ring never belonged to your mother.

Of course not.

Was anything you told me true? Anything?

He looked at me with unmasked pity. *Why is that so important to you? What we had was real. Now it's gone.*

Just make me understand why.

What did you just say to me? I can't be other than I am.

THE CONVERSATION IS an echo in my head, as though I am listening to it on headphones. I see the whole thing playing out on the wall across from me. There are other sounds, too, voices and sirens. Another sharp, insistent rattle. Gunfire? But it is so distant. The wind is still calling my name.

ENOUGH QUESTIONS. HE rose from his seat. He was just a shadow among other shadows in that milky light. While he spoke, I'd managed to get my hands and feet free. The bindings were careless. He'd underestimated me again.

He moved toward the door and opened the storage cage. I wondered if he'd want to cut my throat as he had Camilla's, if he liked the power and the intimacy of that. When he was near, I lunged for him and knocked him back. I heard him release a grunt as my shoulder dug into his abdomen.

I'd surprised him; whatever weapon he'd held in his hand clattered to the floor. I tried to run past him, but he caught the neck of my sweater, ripping a long gash. Nausea and dizziness were twin forces within me, threatening to take me down. He grabbed me and threw me hard against the metal of the cage. I felt my lip split as my face connected with the metal.

But I also felt the door open, and I kept moving. Out of the cage, running blind for a rectangle of light that I knew was an open door. I heard him roaring as I found a staircase and took the stairs two at a time, adrenaline giving me more strength than I had a right to, injured as I was. At the top of the stairs, another door let me out into the cold. By the light and the hush, I figured it was right before dawn. I had no idea where I was or where I was going. But I just ran. I heard him exit, a door banging, echoing off the stone all around, not far behind me.

Isabel. His voice sounded like the moaning of the saints I always imagined on the bridge. *Isabel.*

I still had so many questions. But I'd finally developed, too late, enough sense to run from the darkness and hope the light still let me return.

I moved through the narrow cobblestone streets, surrounded by the muscular, ornate buildings that rose beautiful and quiet beside me, passed closed cafés and fountains turned off for winter. Then I broke free from the maze of streets into Old Town Square and thought for a moment that I'd lost him. But then I heard running footfalls behind me. A light snow started to fall. Against a bench, I lost my battle to hold on to the light. The darkness took me, if only for a moment. I heard the question I wished I'd never asked.

Kde je Kristof Ragan?

IN SPITE OF the cold, in spite of all the red around me, I am starting to feel warm now, happy, lighter. Some distant voice within me is telling me that it's not a good thing to feel so comfortable. I hear more gunfire, voices, footfalls, closer now, then farther away. It all seems to be happening somewhere else. I think of my father, how he drifted away from us. And I think I understand the pull to nothingness. It's such a chaos all the time—within.

I am thinking how nice it would be for things just to go quiet, when I hear a very loud, bossy voice in my head. *Izzy, if you fall asleep, you'll die. Do you understand? Get up. I know it hurts, but get up. Get moving, get help. Don't give up. We need you.* My sister's voice. For once, I do as I am told.

The world comes into sharp focus and with it the fire in my gut. I am sick with the pain but I know I really don't want to die here in this place. Suddenly the thought terrifies me. Fear gives me another shot of adrenaline and I pull myself to my feet. I manage not to scream, though the pain is white lightning through me—physical and beyond somehow.

The world is tilting but I use the wall and make my way to the doors through which he left. In the snow, there's a trail of blood. I remember hearing the gunfire. Is he hurt? Has someone shot him out here in the street? But he kept moving like I plan to do now. The snow on the ground is a chaos of footsteps, slowly filling in with the falling snow. I follow the trail of his blood, leaving a trail of my own.

A quiet has fallen, or maybe I have just stopped hearing as I wind down a steep slope, past a closed café near the Little Quarter Bridge Tower. A young man passes me, gives me a strange look but keeps walking, more quickly. He doesn't look back or offer help. Smart guy.

I grip a black metal rail and follow down a steep set of narrow steps. Before me a sloping cobblestone lane—a marionette shop, its windows shuttered, a small hotel, a new condo building rise up to my left. Ahead I see the canal they call Certovka—the Devil's Stream.

There is more blood now—his and mine. I keep following until I come to the landing above the bank. It's so quiet. A family of swans drift peacefully, gray water below them, snow falling, disappearing into their white feathers. Down further I see a large wooden mill wheel, slowly turning water, impervious to drama.

Then I see him. He stands on a small boat, docked below me. He is untying the lines. I can see that he is hurt, afraid. I am about to call for him, when the world explodes with sound. There are rough hands on me, pulling me away from the edge, but I hold on to the railing. I am surrounded by police officers, all of them yelling, guns drawn. I am yelling, too, calling his name, over and over. I don't want him to die, not yet. There is too much I don't understand.

He stands for a moment, dropping the lines, and I think he might surrender. The boat starts to drift and there is still so much yelling, still hands tugging. He and I lock eyes. But there's nothing there. He is blank. Then he's raising his gun.

I find myself screaming his name again, but his body is jerking, dancing with the impact of bullets. He falls to his knees and the boat rocks but doesn't tip. I hear his gun hit the water with a heavy splash. He sinks down on his side, and I watch life leave him. That terrible stillness settles as the boat slowly drifts away in the current. I let myself be pulled back, lose my battle to stand in spite of the hands on me. And then I am on the cold, hard ground, clinging to consciousness. But the world is turning fuzzy, all the color draining. A woman is talking to me, yelling at me. But I don't understand her, wouldn't have the energy to answer her if I did.

I see him then. Jack. He is gold in my black-and-white-and-red world. But there's so much cold distance between us, I am afraid I'll never reach him now. He's running, then being held back from me. I see uniformed men push past him with a stretcher. I want to tell Jack that he was right. No second, third, and final draft. Just the words as you first wrote them, the plot as you first conceived it. You can't go back and make it better, change the ending so that it is happier, more satisfying. You have to live with it or die trying.

28

There's a universe in a moment, in a single frame. Not in every frame. Just the perfect one, where light and shadow mingle, when an expression tells a story—beginning, middle, and end—when a reflection offers meaning. The "now" frozen, everything that came before and after rendered meaningless.

Linda Book stood in the far corner of the gallery and watched them looking at her photographs—pointing, smiling, frowning, nodding "ahh." Her show, called *Assignations,* was drawing a lot of attention, more attention than her last few. She liked to think that her art had reached a new level, but probably not. Mimicking candid shots that might have been taken by a private eye, she'd captured lovers around the city—exchanging glances, embraces, passionate kisses. Some were candid. Some staged. She wouldn't say which was which. Some critics called it shameless, in view of her family's recent scandals. Others called it magnificent, sensational. *Art Forum* wrote, "Linda Book's most captivating show in years—maybe ever."

It was a week after the opening and the gallery was still packed—on a Tuesday, no less. No one recognized the photographer. Her publicity photo was far too old, airbrushed even then. She looked like a windblown goddess in her photo, untouched by grief or childbirth or disappointment, or infidelity of any kind. Only her husband, who drifted, eavesdropping on conversations, offered her a secret, knowing smile. He was the only one who knew her, here or anywhere.

To see them, the way they made love in the mornings after the kids went to school, the way they held hands again in the cab on the way here, the way he smiled at her now, one might believe that she was still that young girl untouched by life's trials, after all.

Through the large picture window, she saw Isabel and Jack walking up the sidewalk slowly. Her sister looked so small, still leaning on Jack a bit as she walked. Her injuries—internal and external—would take much more time to heal. But heal they would. She'd see to it.

She moved away from the wall and met her husband in the center of the room. They left together to walk with Jack and Isabel back to the loft—it was still theirs for now—for dinner, and to watch something on television that none of them was quite sure they wanted to watch.

The kids were staying with Margie and Fred, so that Linda and Eric could have some couple time, something they had been sorely lacking. Now that there was a wireless hub, sixty-four-inch flat screen and a Wii in the Riverdale home, Emily and Trevor no longer considered a visit with their grandparents a hardship. There was a minimum of grousing. Therefore, Linda had only a minimum of guilt. Even when Emily called to complain that Margie was making fish and wouldn't let them order pizza instead, Linda only smiled and told her daughter that fish was good for her and she'd have to bare up.

"You don't want to see the show again?" Linda teased her sister, embracing her gingerly, afraid to cause her pain. Izzy gave a weak laugh; she'd been to the show several times, had seen it even before it opened. She waited for a smart comment in return, but her sister didn't say anything. In Linda's arms, Isabel felt fragile. Linda was still waiting for the haunted look to disappear from her face. She felt as if she hadn't seen her sister even really smile in months. Not that she could be blamed.

* * *

Back at the loft, Erik ordered Chinese and then turned on the television. Izzy hadn't said much on the walk home and Linda was starting to worry that they were making a mistake.

"Are you sure this is a good idea?" Linda asked.

"I happen to think it's a terrible idea," said Jack. "It's not as if we're going to learn anything we don't already know. This is the psychological equivalent to scab picking."

Erik nodded his agreement. "He's right."

"I want to see it," Izzy said, lowering herself on the couch. "I need to."

No one else offered any arguments. Anyway, it was too late. The newsmagazine show had already begun.

A bestselling writer and her software designer husband are living the ultimate urban dream. With a beautiful home in Manhattan, skyrocketing careers, and an extravagant lifestyle, they seemed to want for little. Except that when it came to Isabel Connelly and the man everyone knew as Marcus Raine, nothing was as it seemed.

"We were called to the scene of a triple homicide in the West Village at the offices of Razor Technologies," said a well-coiffed Detective Grady Crowe. He was sharply dressed and looking very much the role of the celebrity cop. "We found the bodies of Rick Marino, Eileen Charlton, and Ronald Falco, the office trashed, every file and computer removed, and Isabel Connelly unconscious in her husband's office. We knew we were looking at something big. We didn't realize at the time that it was international in its scope and that it reached back to the unsolved case of a missing man from years earlier."

The hour wound on, detailing the disappearance and assumed murder of Marcus Raine after the betrayal of his girlfriend, Camilla Novak, how Kristof Ragan was able to steal the other man's money and identity, then use Izzy's Social Security number to establish an EIN for his new business. Some time was devoted to Kristof Ragan's childhood in an orphanage, how he nearly made good by winning a scholarship to an American university.

He was smart, charming, hardworking, could have made a legitimate success out of himself. What made him choose murder, identity theft, fraud? lamented the reporter in a voice-over, where they showed b-roll of the modern-day orphanage, where children sat at computers, played soccer, read books at round tables. They called in an expert psychologist to offer an explanation.

"It wouldn't be hard to understand the despair a child like Kristof Ragan felt, abandoned to an orphanage, possibly mistreated under communist rule," said the very proper-looking gentleman with round glasses and a red bow tie. "It might cause long-reaching damage, a self-hatred, a desire to *be* someone else. Someone like Kristof Ragan was most likely a sociopath, operating without a conscience, using people like Camilla Novak and Isabel Connelly to further his own agenda."

Linda looked at Izzy. Her sister's face registered no expression at all. But Linda was pleased to see her leaning into Jack. He had his arm around her shoulder.

"We're just friends, same as ever," Isabel had insisted just the other day. But Linda could see clearly that it was much more than that. "I'm not ready for anything else," she'd said.

"Not yet," said Linda.

"Not yet," her sister conceded.

But when Camilla Novak decided she no longer wanted to be a pawn in Kristof Ragan's game, she turned to the FBI, who launched a month-long investigation with Camilla Novak's help. But the day before a raid was scheduled on Raine's office and home, another kind of raid took place.

The footage switched to the woman Izzy knew as S being led away in handcuffs from a Queens building by Detective Grady Crowe.

"By pouring over banking and cell phone records, we saw that multiple calls were made to a cell phone registered to a Sara Benes," said Detective Breslow to the camera, looking much more polished and a bit older than she did in real life.

A former Czech intelligence officer, Benes allied herself with organized crime to run Services Unlimited, an escort service that was actually a prostitution ring. Apparently long associated with the two Ragan brothers—since childhood—and a longtime lover of Kristof Ragan, Benes was there when Ragan needed to pull up the lines on his life, assembling a team of thugs to trash Ragan's office and home, removing any and all evidence that might have allowed for prosecution. Benes faces charges of murder, conspiracy, and obstruction of justice. But she won't face her charges in the U.S. In the country illegally, she'll be deported to the Czech Republic.

Linda watched as her sister absently lifted a finger to trace the scar on her forehead.

Did Camilla Novak get cold feet and reveal her betrayal to Kristof Ragan in the hope that he would forgive her? Is that how he knew the FBI was closing in on him?

"We think so." *Special Agent Tyler Long headed the federal investigation that was destroyed by Sara Benes and her crew.*

"Camilla Novak loved Ragan. She came to us out of hurt that he had used her and kept her dangling for so many years. In the end, I think she didn't want to betray him. She would have gone with him if he'd let her."

But Kristof Ragan wasn't the forgiving sort. Beware that the following images are quite graphic. On the screen flashed the pictures Izzy had retrieved from the thumb drive, showing Kristof Ragan killing the three men and leaving his brother to die on the dock.

"When we first saw this, we thought that he must have some military training," said Detective Grady. "But the Czech government denies all knowledge of him. So we don't really know where he learned to take down four armed men, but it's not something everyone could do, is it?"

But in the end, it was Kristof Ragan who was going down. Isabel Raine couldn't endure her husband's betrayal, and when she suspected that he'd returned to the Czech Republic, she followed. Her investigation led her to the orphanage where Ragan grew up. Banking records revealed that Ragan had been making anonymous donations to the facility for years.

But Ragan, it seemed, was one step ahead of her. He arranged for her abduction and would likely have killed her if it hadn't been for the work of NYPD detectives Crowe and Breslow.

"We knew she was gone but we didn't know where, though we had our suspicions," said Detective Crowe. Linda knew her sister had promised him not to tell anyone about the e-mail he sent her, and she'd kept her promise.

"After pouring over years' worth of banking records for Razor Technologies, we learned that the company had purchased an apartment in Prague some years earlier. We contacted the local Czech authorities and they sent a team to the residence. Police arrived just as Isabel Raine was escaping from her husband. A chase ensued, ending with the shooting death of Kristof Ragan."

More graphic footage here from the camcorder of a tourist who heard commotion out his window early Christmas morning.

A grainy, wobbly, black-and-white film sequence showed Kristof Ragan running, limping, gun drawn, across a cobblestone street, near a canal. He ran down a flight of stairs and hopped onto a small boat that was docked, stuffed the gun in his pocket, and began undoing lines. Then Izzy moved into view. She stood at the rail alone for a moment before the police moved in behind her, started pulling her away. Linda watched her sister struggle and scream as Kristof Ragan raised his gun and the police started to fire.

Now, sitting on the couch, Izzy covered her eyes and started to sob, while Jack wrapped his arms around her.

"Turn this off, Erik," Jack said quietly. Erik reached for the remote and started fumbling with it.

Kristof Ragan died at the scene, his reign of deception and murder at an end on Devil's Stream in Prague.

"No," said Isabel. "I want to finish it."

Isabel Raine, known to millions as Isabel Connelly, declined to be interviewed for this segment, but we know from her agent and spokesperson,

Jack Mannes, that she is recovering from injuries inflicted upon her by her husband, and is fully cooperating with the ongoing investigation. When the investigation is complete, some portion of the funds stolen from her and her family will be returned, though much of it seems to have disappeared without a trace.

The reporter wrapped up with the same old cliché they'd been hearing for weeks about truth being stranger than fiction. Erik clicked off the television, and for a minute they all sat there looking at the blank screen, lost in their own thoughts.

When the buzzer rang, everyone jumped, then laughed at themselves a bit.

"The Chinese food," Erik said, getting up.

As they all rose to pull dishes from the cabinets, set the table, open the wine, Linda thought about how even in the shadow of the extraordinary, the ordinary still occupied them. They still slept, still cared for the children, still made love and ordered takeout.

She and Erik were both guilty of terrible betrayals of trust, and yet he still kissed her as he handed her a glass of Pinot Grigio. Isabel had been injured in every way a person could be, but she offered an ironic smile as Jack mentioned that some of her books were back on the bestseller lists because of the recent events of her life. A man Linda had an affair with and cared for had almost laid waste to her life before ending his own, but she still said things like, "This soup is too salty."

She looked around the loft that they loved. They weren't sure yet if they would have to sell it. Some of the money Kristof Ragan wire-transferred before he fled had been traced. No one would tell them how much or when they might see it. But her show was going well; she'd had some good sales. And Isabel had a new book contract. So they'd be all right. In comparison to everything that was almost lost, the money didn't seem as important as it once had. What was important was that they were all together, safe, and if not happy exactly, if still damaged and haunted and unsure of the future, then at least hopeful.

No one seemed to know what to say until Jack raised a glass and they all joined him.

"Onward and forward. No looking back."

As she sipped her wine, Linda thought they'd all endured awful, life-changing events—some, maybe all, of those events invited through their own blindness and selfish deeds. But the foliage of mundane life just grew over the past a bit every day if you let it. And maybe that was the most extraordinary event of all.

29

I am alone with my keyboard again, weaving a universe culled from my experiences and my imagination—though I struggle with the idea that nothing I can imagine would compare to the actual events of my recent life. But I write because I have to, because I cannot do anything but this. I must metabolize my experience on the blank page, put it down, order it, control it in my way. This is how I understand the world. How I answer the question: *Why?*

I write about a boy who was abandoned by his mother to an orphanage in communist Europe. I imagine his frightening early days and lonely, miserable nights. I imagine his longing for the mother who left him, for the comfort of the bed to which he was accustomed. I know about abandonment, about loss, about fear. I know about longing to be anyone, anyplace else. This boy is not known to me. But his feelings are; I can manage compassion for him even if the man he grew into almost destroyed me, put a bullet in me, tried to end my life to save his own. It is on the page that I can answer the question: Why? And the answers I find here are enough. They have to be.

I hear Jack downstairs hammering. He is at work again on the house, building shelves for a room he calls my study. I tell him that we are not living together. That I am just staying with him until I can sell the apartment I shared with my husband and figure out how to move ahead with my life. *Of course,* he says. *I know.*

Kristof Ragan was never my husband, not legally, not in any way. Just someone I loved and thought I knew. I still hear his voice, the wisdom he had and shared with me. I have happy memories of him. I do.

The other morning I met Detective Grady Crowe for coffee in the East Village at Veselka's on Second Avenue. I got there early and sat in the back watching the students, the goths and clubbers for whom it was late, not early, artist types, professionals—the typical New York City mix of people, not typical anywhere else.

He looked fresh, well and happy as he walked in, scanned the crowd, then made his way over to me.

"You look good," he said, smiling, shaking my hand. "Don't get up."

He sat across from me. We'd been through all the professional stuff, the questioning, the accusations, the reprimands. I found I actually liked him in spite of what had passed between us when he thought we were on opposite sides.

"You look happy," I said.

He held up his left hand, tapped his ring. "My wife. She came back. We're having a baby."

The information hurt more than it should, made my stomach bottom out with a powerful regret and sadness. He saw it.

"I'm sorry. I'm an insensitive jerk sometimes. A lot of the time."

"No," I said, shaking my head. "You deserve to be happy."

"So do you."

I thought of Jack. "I'm getting there."

We ordered some coffee and potato pancakes.

"So what's up? Or did you just miss me?" he asked with a smart smile. He was a handsome guy, I realized. Much better looking happy than bitter and angry—like everyone, I suppose.

"I don't know. I guess I just wondered if there's anything I don't know. Something you held back from that news show, from me?"

"Like what?"

"I don't know. I was wondering about the FBI. When they started their investigation, how Kristof found out about it. Why they didn't act sooner."

"Camilla went to the FBI about a month before Ragan disappeared. They started their investigation right away, but the feds are all about collecting evidence for their case. They take their time." He took a sip of his coffee. "They suspect that Camilla told Ragan at the last minute, giving him time to get away before their raid. She felt guilty about betraying him. Maybe she thought he would forgive her. He didn't."

"But who was Camilla meeting in the park? The man I watched die? Why was she bringing those pictures to him?"

"The man who died that night was identified as Vasco Berisha, an Albanian thug with ties to Ivan Ragan, among others."

"Why would they want those pictures? What use would they be? And if they were surveillance shots, how did they come to be in her possession?"

"They weren't technically surveillance shots. Camilla Novak took them. She was following Ragan, using information Charlie Shane gave her about his comings and goings, working for the FBI. We found them on her digital camera, too. She turned over a set to the FBI and was apparently bringing them to Berisha. My personal theory is that *after* she confessed her betrayal to Ragan, and *before* he killed her, she realized she'd misplayed her hand. She knew he wasn't going to forgive her and take her away after all. I suspect she didn't think the FBI would be able to find Kristof Ragan, but his brother's associates would. He killed some of their men; they'd want revenge. She wanted them to have it."

I shook my head.

"What?" Grady asked.

"Then Berisha couldn't have known where Kristof Ragan had gone. He was just a lackey. He was the reason I went to Prague. I thought he said, 'Praha.' Prague in Czech. But maybe he didn't say that."

"But Ragan *was* in Prague. Maybe Berisha—whatever he said—just gave you an excuse to follow your instincts. Or maybe he did know. It's possible."

"I heard what I wanted to hear."

"Maybe. You knew where he would go, but maybe you didn't trust yourself anymore. You needed something else besides your gut to follow."

I thought about that night in the park. I am sure that's what he said. But Detective Crowe was right, I didn't trust myself very much about these things.

"Do you have a contact at the FBI who might talk to me about all of this?"

"It doesn't much matter now, does it?"

It matters. How the pieces fit together. It helps me to understand what happened to me. But that's the problem with life, as opposed to fiction; sometimes the pieces don't fit. The waitress brought our order and I poured some cream in my coffee.

"I've been guilty, as you know, of not asking enough questions. Of seeing what I wanted to see and editing out the rest. I don't want to do that here."

He nodded his understanding.

"There's nothing I haven't told you. I promise. But I'll put you in touch with Agent Long. He's a good guy."

"Okay. Thanks."

He gave me a sly look. "You're not writing a book about all this, are you?"

I smiled at that but didn't answer.

We chatted a bit. He told me he'd read one of my books and liked it but mentioned that I'd gotten some procedure wrong. I asked him if I could call with questions in the future. He agreed, seemed to like the idea.

"So—*are* you going to write about what happened to you?" he asked, again not letting me off the hook.

"Probably. One way or another, it will turn up. It doesn't work the way you think it does. It's more elliptical, more organic."

He nodded, looking thoughtful, but he didn't say anything else about it.

We said our good-byes on the street, shook hands and parted. I was a half a block away when he called me back.

"Hey, something you said helped me," he said.

"What's that?"

"Remember in your apartment that time? You said, 'Love accepts. Maybe forgiveness comes in time.' That helped me."

"I'm glad."

He lifted a hand and then turned to walk away. I watched as he climbed into an unmarked Caprice where Detective Breslow waited at the wheel. I wondered briefly what was next for them.

LOVE ACCEPTS. FORGIVENESS comes in time. It makes me think of Linda and Erik. It makes me think of my father—the "why" I have never been able to answer in all my years trying. It makes me think of the man I knew as Marcus, a man I loved, one I forgave, when his first betrayal really should have set me to asking questions about him, about myself. But there's no point looking back in regret.

ON MY WAY back home from meeting the detective, I stopped at the post office box I maintained but which I hadn't visited in months. I knew it would be packed with junk and fliers and maybe one or two important items, like invitations to conferences and maybe a fan letter or two. But I figured I should check it, get back into some of my old routines, let normalcy return.

I used my key to unlock the box and pulled out the mass of paper that was crammed in there, tossing most of it into the recycle bin, as it was, indeed, the predicted junk. I retained the envelopes with handwriting on the front and stuffed them into my bag. I peered inside one more time before closing the door and saw a small brown box, all the way in the back. I reached for it and held it in my hand. There was no return address.

DOWNSTAIRS JACK IS still hammering. I open the drawer in the desk and take out the box. I've been keeping it there but haven't told anyone about it. Not even Jack. Not even Linda. I lift the lid and hold the ruby ring between my thumb and index finger.

I think I know what it means. I don't have to write it, make it up. I think it means he would have loved me if he could. That's what he wanted me to know. I feel a twinge in my abdomen, the wound that hasn't yet had time to heal. I look into the fire of the red stone and remember how he left me to die, slowly, alone, and in terrible agony in a cold, strange place. If it hadn't been for Jack getting to the police, for Detectives Breslow and Crowe figuring out where Marc was staying, I'd be dead. I remember Rick's shirt that last time I saw him: *Love Kills Slowly.*

Kristof Ragan set his sights on another woman after me. Her name was Martina Nevins. I heard it on the news, had seen her interviewed, a wealthy British heiress who'd lost her fiancé a few years earlier and had been despondent since then. She was celebrating the holidays with her family in Prague. She'd have been Kristof's next mark. She had the look about her. The fragility of loss. The vulnerability of hope.

He might have given her the ring, said to her what he said to me, "This is my heart. I'm giving it to you. I'd die for you."

Instead he sent it back to me. And I'll keep it to remember that love is what we do, not what we say. That not everyone has the strength or the ability to love another, or even himself. And that some of us have a secret heart that cannot be shared.

I close the lid on my laptop and take the ring down to Jack. I want him to see it. I want him to know what it means to me and how it has helped me to understand Kristof Ragan, my father, and myself. Because I want Jack to share his heart with me. But I think that to ask him to do that, I have to share mine first.

He turns from the tall shelves he is building—an effort I recognize as his act of hope—when he hears me come into the room. I hold the ring in my palm and show it to him. He takes it with a frown and holds it up to the light, then looks back at me. There's worry on his face.

"Where did this come from?"

I tell him.

"What are you going to do with it?

I tell him that, too. I think he understands. He puts his strong, thick arms carefully around me and leans down, brings his mouth gently, tentatively to mine. We share our first kiss since the night we spent together a lifetime ago.

There's no why to Jack, no questions to answer, no curiosity to satisfy. He is not a mystery, not a stranger. He is my dearest, most beloved friend. My sister thinks that is enough for a start. And she is, as always, so right.

Author's Notes

This book might not have been written if I hadn't had the opportunity to visit Prague for five weeks in the summer of 2007. My family and I embarked on a home exchange with a lovely Czech family and spent five weeks wandering the streets of Prague, one of the most magnificent cities I have visited. I was truly inspired by its winding cobblestone rues, its hidden squares, grand buildings, and aura of mystery. If you haven't been there, go. If you have, go again.

During my visit, I was fortunate enough to meet the acclaimed screenwriter and poet James Ragan. A Czech who returns every summer to teach at St. Charles University, James showed me his city, taking me places I never would have known to go without him, telling me about its evolution since the fall of communism. He and his lovely family embraced us and enriched our experience more than they might have guessed. His wonderful book of poetry *The Hunger Wall* continued to inspire me and feed my dreams of Prague long after we returned home.

I was also welcomed to Prague by the talented team at my Czech publisher, Euromedia Group. Denisa Novotna, the PR manager, was a smart, funny, and lovely woman who endured my many questions, while arranging a stunning lineup of media interviews. During my stay, I was on television and radio and had multiple newspaper interviews—which caused me to learn how to get around the city by taxi, subway, and on foot. There's really no better way to get acquainted with a strange place (where you can hardly speak a word of the language!) than to insist that you can get yourself around without help—and then prove it.

Through one my law enforcement connections, I had the opportunity to share a few hours with a CIA agent who has spent many years in the Czech Republic and has an intimate knowledge of Prague since the Velvet Revolution and the fall of communism. His anecdotes and information heavily influenced my imaginings. I am not at liberty to reveal his name.

I also relied on *The Prague Post* online (www.praguepost.com) and the city's tourist site www.prague.cz, as well as the BBC online (www.bbc.com) for all gaps in knowledge and experience.

All mistakes I have made, liberties I have taken, and geographic alterations committed in the name of narrative flow are my own.

Acknowledgments

With every novel it gets more difficult to acknowledge the people who contribute to my process, as my web of supporters seems to grow and expand each year. What did I do to deserve them? I don't know. But I will take this opportunity to shower them with praise.

My husband, Jeffrey Unger, and our daughter, Ocean Rae, are the glimmering center of my universe. Every day they inspire and nourish me, make me think, make me laugh, and keep me grounded in reality. In my daughter's wide blue eyes, I see the whole world. My husband holds that world together. I wouldn't be the writer I am or the person I am without them.

My stellar agent, Elaine Markson, and her wonderful assistant, Gary Johnson, are more than business associates; they are my close and dear friends. Each day they provide something invaluable to my life and to my career, even if it's just a chat on the phone about nothing in particular. They take care of me. I count on them in more ways than I can begin to list. So, this one's for you, Elaine!

Special Agent Paul Bouffard (Ret.) and his wife, Wendy Bouffard, offer so much more than their wonderful friendship and beer on tap. They give me a space to write when I need it. Paul remains my source for all things legal and illegal, continuing to field every question, no matter how bizarre or inane, with equanimity and keen interest. And Wendy gave invaluable insights during her read of this manuscript. I am truly blessed by their presence in our lives. They also have two nice cats—Freon and Fenway.

A home like Crown/Shaye Areheart Books is every writer's dream, full of intelligent, creative, passionate people who really care about books. Shaye Areheart is a truly brilliant editor and one of the most wonderful and loving people I have known. Jenny Frost has offered her continuing support and enthusiasm and seems to forever be coming up with new and wonderful ways to get more copies out into the world. I also offer my humble thanks to Philip Patrick, Jill Flaxman, Whitney Cookman, David Tran, Patricia Shaw, Jie Yang, Jacqui LeBow, Andy Augusto, Kira Walton, Patty Berg, Donna Passanante, Katie Wainwright, Annsley Rosner, Sarah Brievogel, Linda Kaplan, Karin Schulze, Kate Kennedy, and Christine Kopprasch. And, of course, I can't heap enough praise on the top-notch sales force. Every time I visit a bookseller, I hear about their tireless efforts on my behalf. Each member of the team at Crown/Shaye Areheart Books brings his or her unique talent to bear on every publication and for that I am eternally grateful.

As ever, my family and friends continue to bolster, support, cajole, comfort, and cheer me on in this crazy writing life. My parents, Joseph and Virginia Miscione—formerly Team Houston, now Team PA—are forever bragging about me, buying books, and spreading the word. They're facing books out in a whole new state! Their support is everything to me. My brother Joe Miscione and his wife, Tara Teaford Miscione, are endlessly kind, helpful, and supportive. And Tara has become one of my early and most important readers. Thanks, T! My thanks to Heather Mikesell for her eagle-eye editing and endless reading of my work. I can hardly imagine publishing anything she hasn't read first. How she must dread the e-mail subject line: "Can you just read this really quickly???" Marion Chartoff and Tara Popick, friendships that endure the test of time, continue to nourish me in more ways than I can count. I am a very lucky girl.

About the Author

Lisa Unger is the *New York Times* and *San Francisco Chronicle* bestselling author of *Black Out, Beautiful Lies,* and *Sliver of Truth.* Her novels have been published in twenty-six countries, receiving rave reviews and appearing on bestseller lists around the world.

Lisa was born in Connecticut and lived in Holland and England with her family before returning to the United States. She is a graduate of the New School for Social Research, Eugene Lang College. She now lives in Florida with her husband and daughter and is at work on her next novel.

F
UNGER